The Royals Next Door

OTHER TITLES BY KARINA HALLE

Before I Ever Met You
After All
Rocked Up
Wild Card (North Ridge #1)
Maverick (North Ridge #2)
Hot Shot (North Ridge #3)
Bad at Love
My Life in Shambles
Discretion (Dumonts #1)
Disarm (Dumonts #2)
Disavow (Dumonts #3)
Lovewrecked
One Hot Italian Summer
All the Love in the World (Anthology)

ROMANTIC SUSPENSE NOVELS

On Every Street (An Artists Trilogy Novella #0.5)
Sins and Needles (The Artists Trilogy #1)
Shooting Scars (The Artists Trilogy #2)
Bold Tricks (The Artists Trilogy #3)
Dirty Angels (Dirty Angels #1)
Dirty Deeds (Dirty Angels #2)
Dirty Promises (Dirty Angels #3)
Black Hearts (Sins Duet #1)
Dirty Souls (Sins Duet #2)

HORROR & PARANORMAL ROMANCES

Darkhouse (EIT #1)
Red Fox (EIT #2)

The Royals Next Door

KARINA HALLE

JOVE
NEW YORK

A JOVE BOOK
Published by Berkley
An imprint of Penguin Random House LLC
penguinrandomhouse.com

Library of Congress Cataloging-in-Publication Data

Names: Halle, Karina, author.
Title: The royals next door / Karina Halle.
Description: First edition. | New York: Jove, 2021.
Identifiers: LCCN 2021001293 (print) | LCCN 2021001294 (ebook) |
ISBN 9780593334195 (trade paperback) | ISBN 9780593334201 (ebook)
Subjects: GSAFD: Love stories.
Classification: LCC PR9199.4.H356239 R69 2021 (print) |
LCC PR9199.4.H356239 (ebook) | DDC 813/.6—dc23
LC record available at https://lccn.loc.gov/2021001293
LC ebook record available at https://lccn.loc.gov/2021001294

First Edition: August 2021

Printed in the United States of America
1st Printing

Book design by Ashley Tucker

For Taylor

And to my parents, Tuuli & Sven

The Royals Next Door

One

NICKY GRAVES JUST THREW UP IN MY HANDBAG.

It's my fault, really. I knew he was sick, even though he tried to muster up some eight-year-old bravado and pretend he wasn't. I know that when I was his age, if my forehead felt remotely hot, I'd be in the nurse's office all day, waiting for my mom to come and get me. Any excuse to miss school.

But Nicky loves school (and since I'm his second-grade teacher, I *should* be honored by this), so he pretended he was fine until he wasn't.

I saw it happen in slow motion too. I was reading to the class from one of their favorite series, Mercy Watson, talking about the pig's love for butter, when Nicky's face went a wicked shade of green. His hand shot up to his mouth, and before I could do anything, he was running to the trash can beside my desk. Which would have been great had I not left my purse beside the trash and had Nicky possessed a LeBron James style of pinpoint accuracy.

"I'm sorry, Miss Evans!" Nicky wails, standing beside what used to be a nice leather bag I picked up in Mexico years ago when I was on vacation with my ex, Joey. I suppose it's fitting that in the end it's just a pile of vomit, which is exactly what our relationship turned out to be. Metaphors 101.

"It's okay, Nicky," I tell him, trying to sound calm even though I can feel the class descending into panic as cries of "Ewwww!" and "Nicky puked! Sicky Nicky!" and "I'm gonna barf!" fill the room.

I practically throw the book down and run over to him, trying to hold it together myself. This is not my favorite part of the job, and I'm probably the only elementary school teacher who still gets easily grossed out. I grab an entire box of tissues and somehow manage to get Nicky cleaned up, call the nurse's office and his mother to come get him, and calm down the class.

It isn't until the bell rings that I have time to deal with the purse of puke.

I'm staring at it, wondering if I should call it a wash and just throw it all away, when there's a knock at the door. It's the first-grade teacher, Cynthia Bautista, poking her head in, sympathy all over her face. Maybe a tinge of disgust.

"You okay? I heard you had a sickie today."

I gesture to the bag, which I still haven't touched. "Well, I'm in the market for a new purse."

She walks in and eyes it, flinching. "Oh. Fuck me." Then she covers her mouth and bursts out laughing. "I'm sorry. It's not funny."

"Don't worry, if it had happened to you, I'd be laughing too." Cynthia is one of the few teachers here that I'd consider a friend. Not that I'm a hard person to get along with—people pleasing is something that's been ingrained in me since I was a child—but there aren't that many people who "get" me, especially where I live, especially in the school system. There's a very rigid set of rules and hierarchy at SSI Elementary, and I'm still treated like a newcomer, even though I've worked here and lived here long enough. They say that most people who move to Salt Spring Island only last a few years, and if you make it to five, then you're considered a "real islander." I've made it to five, and I haven't managed to get close to anyone. People seem to think I'll eventually go back out with the tide.

"I think you're going to have to throw it away," Cynthia says, her nose scrunched up. "Anything valuable in there?"

I sigh, nodding. "My wallet. Some makeup. A book. Tic Tacs."

My antianxiety medication, I finish in my head. But she doesn't need to know *that.*

Then I remember. "Oh wait. Maybe . . ." I crouch down and gingerly poke at the outside pocket where I remember sliding my bank cards this morning after getting my morning coffee at Salty Seas Coffee & Goods. My bank card and credit card seem untouched by the contents of Nicky's stomach. Unfortunately, those are the only things saved.

"Shit." I slap the cards on my desk and give Cynthia a tired look. "Feel like doing me a favor?"

"Hell no," she says, shaking her head adamantly. Cynthia is a pretty tough cookie, emigrated here from the Philippines by herself when she was twenty, went through an awful divorce, and is now raising her ten-year-old daughter by herself. "That bag and everything in it is a lost cause. You can always get another driver's license. And makeup. And books. And Tic Tacs."

She's right. I glance at the clock. It's just past three, which means there's plenty of time to get to the insurance place and get a new driver's license. Luckily our school is right in the middle of our tiny town and close to everything. "I guess I'll go do that now before I forget. Do we have a toxic waste receptacle here?" I eye the purse.

Cynthia gives me a look like I'm crazy. "You want to try to get your license now? Have you even stepped outside today?"

I shake my head. During recess and lunch hour I stayed at my desk and read my book, preparing for the podcast I'm doing tonight. I'd already read it, but I wanted to skim through it to beef up my talking points in the review.

"Why, what's happening?"

This island is small, and nothing much ever happens here. Perhaps there's some hippie protest about a cell phone tower or something.

Cynthia's eyes go wide, and she gets this excited, knowing look upon her face. "You haven't heard?"

I stare at her blankly and cross my arms. Obviously not. "*What?*"

"You know Prince Edward and MRed?"

Do I know Prince Edward and MRed, aka Monica Red, aka Monica, Duchess of Fairfax? "Cynthia, I live *on* a rock, not under a rock."

"Well apparently you live under one too. They're here! Like, today. Now. And looking for real estate. The whole island has been losing their mind over it. Paparazzi have been arriving in float planes all morning, the ferries are full of looky-loos or however you call it. The town is at a standstill."

My tired brain can hardly comprehend any of this.

You see, Prince Edward, the younger, stoic son of Queen Beatrix and her husband, Prince Albert, recently married a Grammy-winning singer named MRed, and the press has been up in arms about it. Not only is Monica Black, but she's American and she had a successful career, which may have included a lot of risqué songs, scantily clad videos, performances gone viral, etc. In other words, the UK media has been absolutely brutal to the both of them, with racism and slut-shaming at every turn. I mean, I'm by no means a royal fanatic, but I've been keeping up with it (they dominate the news everywhere), and I don't see the media ever attacking Eddie's older brother, Prince Daniel, who remains a womanizing bachelor.

At any rate, it was reported everywhere that Monica and Eddie were leaving the UK for a yearlong break for undisclosed reasons. A sabbatical of sorts. Some people thought they'd go to Seattle, to be near her parents. Others thought the ski resort town of Whistler, where the royal family spent winter vacations when Eddie and Daniel were young. Others yet thought India, where the couple often did charity work.

Never in a million years did I think they would pick this island in British Columbia, Canada, a small yet eccentric haven between Vancouver Island and the mainland.

Honestly, I still can't believe it. None of this seems right.

"Are you sure?" I ask Cynthia. "Maybe it's just an actor or something." Our island is known for being the perfect hermit's hideaway (and I can attest to that—if I didn't have to work, I think I'd rarely leave the house). There are lots of known authors who toil away in their writing studios, and ex-musicians who sometimes play the local pub, and everyone from Barbra Streisand to Raffi has had a summer home here at some point.

"No, it's Eddie and Monica," Cynthia says adamantly. "Don't believe me? Just walk to town and you'll be swallowed up by the frenzy."

She sounds breathless when she says "frenzy," and there's a feverish sheen to her eyes. Something tells me that Cynthia is absolutely loving this. Our quiet little town turned into a paparazzi-driven chaos? That sounds awful to me. I can't even handle the crowds when summer holidays hit, and that's two weeks from now.

"Okay. I guess I'll just go home and hope I don't run into any cops."

"Nah, they're all out trying to contain the madness." She says this gleefully, tapping her fingertips together like Mr. Burns from *The Simpsons*.

We say goodbye, and I pick up the puke purse and take it down to the nurse's office, where Judy is still tidying up (school nurse by day, restaurant server who never gets my order right at the Sitka Spruce Restaurant by night). She doesn't even bat an eyeball at it and says she'll dispose of it for me, like she's getting rid of a dead body. At this point, that's what it kind of feels like, and I get out of there before she changes her mind.

The school after three p.m. is probably my favorite place to be. There are usually a few students straggling about, killing time and waiting to be picked up, but today is warm, sunny, and dry (opposed to the usual cold, gloomy, and wet), so any kids who are left are outside. It's just me in the halls, enjoying being out of the house and away from any stress and responsibilities, and getting to be alone at the same time.

I take a moment to slowly walk down the hall, smiling at all the art the kids have showcased on the walls, and then I'm out the door and heading to my car in the parking lot. It's a 2000 Honda Civic hatchback that I've always called the Garbage Pail (since it's silver and dented), and I added fuzzy green seat covers for that Oscar the Grouch feel. Almost everyone on the island has an electric car, and it's definitely on my list of things to get (along with the goal of saving money), but since I essentially take care of both myself and my mother under one income, a new car seems like just another one of my dreams, along with traveling the world and falling in love with someone who deserves it.

Still, I have great affection for the Garbage Pail. I could get the dents fixed, but on this island, no one bats an eye, and it does really well on gas. Hanging from the mirror is a pair of fuzzy dice that my father won for me at an arcade when I was a teen, before he ditched out on us, and my glove compartment is stuffed with Tic Tacs, which I have a borderline addiction to, ferry receipts, and who knows what else.

I get in, and even though I'm not driving through town to get home, I already know what Cynthia means. On the sides of the main road leading into the center, cars are lined up and parked in haphazard lines. This isn't normal for a Thursday afternoon in June. It looks more like the crowds we get during our Saturday market during the peak of summer, but on steroids, and I guess instead of people perusing the organic vegetables or hemp-based clothing or homemade vegan vagina purses (yes, those are a thing and they're exactly what they sound like), these visitors have their cameras and phones all ready, hoping to catch a glimpse of the renegade royals.

I shake my head and turn off the road, glad that I don't have to deal with any of that today. I still think that maybe Cynthia's mistaken about all of this. I mean, I like living here because it's gorgeous and affordable and I can be a recluse and no one thinks anything of it, but I'm not sure why Prince Eddie and MRed would be attracted to this place. I mean, yeah, it's beautiful and secluded. But you're also kind of *stuck* here too.

My house is located at the end of a peninsula called Scott Point, one of the most affluent and tightly knit communities on the island.

Naturally, I'm like a sliver you can't get rid of along the narrow finger of the peninsula. Yes, we own the house, an adorable cedar-shingle three-bedroom that used to be the servants' quarters to the mansion next to it, but I still drive the Garbage Pail among all the shiny Range Rovers and Teslas (full disclosure: the GP used to be my mother's car until she wrecked my Kia Soul, but anyway . . . long story), and my mother and I aren't exactly overly friendly with our neighbors. We don't belong here, but we make it work.

It sure is stunning, though. The only way through is via a narrow road that cuts through the middle of the peninsula like an artery lined with evergreen arbutus trees, their peeling red bark as thin and delicate as Japanese rice paper. On either side are houses hidden by tall cedar fences, each with a witty name like Henry's Haven and Oceanside Retreat carved up on custom-made signs. Between the houses you can catch glimpses of the ocean, the sun glinting off it in such a way that shivers run down your spine. That glint at this time of day tells me that summer is in full swing, and summer is my dreaming period.

I'm already dreaming about getting a mug of tea and heading down to the dock to enjoy the sun when I suddenly have to slam on my brakes.

Instead of the usual deer or quail family crossing the road, there's a very tall, broad-shouldered tree of a man standing in the middle of the road at the top of the small hill, holding his hand out to me like he's trying out for the Supremes.

Shit. Pins and needles start to form in my lungs, my heart pounding. My anxiety has no problems jumping to the worst-case scenario, and it's always that something has happened to my mother while I was at work. There's not a moment when that exact fear isn't lurking at the back of my mind, so the fact that there's a very grim-faced stranger in a dark suit striding downhill toward me makes me think my worst nightmare is going to come true.

My window is already rolled down, so I hear him say, "Excuse me, miss?" in a very strong, raspy British accent. He's more curt than sympathetic, which makes me calm just a little.

"Yes? What's wrong?" I ask him, trying not to panic.

Now that he's up close, I can get a better look at him. His suit is navy blue with a touch of teal, looking sharp and well-tailored, with a pressed white shirt underneath and a dark gray tie. It's the kind of suit that screams money, and not the kind of money that the people on this street have, more of a worldly, next-level kind of money. The kind that class brings.

He's also way more imposing up close, built like a Douglas fir, barrel-chested and sturdy in a graceful way. My eyes trail up to his face and see that it matches the brusqueness of his voice. He's got aviator sunglasses on that reflect my own bewildered expression (and make me realize my hair is a blond rat's nest from driving with the window down), but even so, I can *feel* his eyes on me. If they're anything like the wrinkles in his forehead and the seemingly permanent line etched between his dark arched brows, then I'm definitely intimidated.

There's also something about him that's vaguely familiar, but for the life of me I can't recall why. It's like he reminds me of a famous actor or something.

"I need you to turn around," he says stiffly, making a motion for me to pivot and go.

"But I live here," I protest.

The line between his brows deepens, and his full mouth sets into a hard line. This man is no joke. He jerks his very strong, manly, bearded chin down the road. "I'm going to need you to turn around," he repeats.

I blink at him. "I'm sorry, but who even are you? I'm not turning around. I live here. And if you don't let me go home to my mother, who, by the way, suffers from DPD and BPD, she's going to end up calling the police when I don't show up. Hell, I'll call the police right now and report you."

The man stares at me, and I stare right back at my frazzled reflection, my eyes drifting briefly to notice that his ears stick out, just a little. That bit of information is enough to take the intimidation factor down a notch.

When he finally speaks, I expect him to ask me to leave again, but instead he asks, "What's DPD?"

I sigh. I didn't mean to drag my mother's mental illness into this. In fact, there are very few people around me who know exactly what she has, so the fact that I told *him*—this very commanding, rude British stranger in a suit—the truth feels wrong.

"It stands for dependent personality disorder. And before you ask about BPD, that stands for borderline personality disorder."

He raises his chin, and I'm not sure if this is an act of defiance or if he's going to ask me further questions that he can obviously go and Google later. Then he says in his low, raspy voice, "What's your address?"

I'm about to tell him, but I stop myself. "Wait a minute, you never told me who you are. Why should I tell a stranger my address? You think I want to see your face peeping through my window while I'm sleeping?"

His frown amplifies. "You think I'm a Peeping Tom?"

"I don't know. Is your name Tom?"

"It's Harrison," he says reluctantly. "Harrison Cole, PPO. And I'm afraid that unless you prove you live where you say you do, you'll have to turn around. I've been turning away cars all day, and I have no problems doing it to you."

Wow. What an asshole. I clear my throat. "Sorry, Harrison Cole? Is that a made-up name or your real name?"

He grunts in response, and if his brows furrow any deeper, I'm afraid his face might split in two.

I continue, no longer intimidated by him and his overtly manly, gruff ways. "And since you asked me what DPD stood for when you should have minded your own business, I'm going to have to ask you what a PPO is. Petty paralegal oaf? Perfectly pissy oligarch?"

"Personal protection officer," he booms. "By order of Her Majesty, the Queen of the United Kingdom."

I blink at him as things slowly come together in my brain. "Like a bodyguard? Are you . . . oh my god, are you Eddie and MRed's bodyguard?"

He doesn't say anything, and he doesn't have to. It dawns on me, one big bright lightbulb going on in my head, that the reason I thought he looked familiar isn't because he's an actor but because I have seen him in the tabloids and on the news. Usually out of sight but sometimes in the background behind Eddie and Monica. He's the one the public (or at least the voracious users of the #FairfaxFans hashtag on Twitter) has dubbed the Broody Bodyguard and Sexy Secret Agent, and I've stumbled across more than a few fanfics about him. (And by *stumbled*, I mean purposefully devoured. For my podcast . . .)

And he's standing here, in front of me, telling me to go. Which means that the royal couple have to be farther up the road!

"I'll let you go to your house if you can prove you live there," the infamous Broody Bodyguard eventually says. "Let me see your driver's license."

Oh . . . that.

Shit.

Two

I STARE AT THE SEXY SECRET AGENT FOR A MOMENT, wondering if he'll even believe my excuse. "I . . . I don't have it," I tell him.

I can feel him studying me with disbelief. "You don't have your driver's license?"

"I know, I know. I had it this morning, but a kid puked in my bag. Sicky Nicky, the kids called him. It was my fault, really."

"A kid did what?" Then he shakes his head. "Likely excuse."

He's got to be joking if he thinks that's an excuse. I'm used to the-dog-ate-my-homework excuses at work, and generally the more outlandish they are, the more they seem to be true. I mean, unless their homework was eaten by velociraptors or something.

"I'm serious," I tell him. "I was planning on going after work to get a new one, but the whole town has gone crazy because, well, *you're* in town."

"Then I'm sure you can produce your insurance papers," he says calmly, folding his hands at his crotch, my eyes following. "They should have your address on them."

I quickly look away from his crotch and open the glove compartment, a whole bunch of empty Tic Tac containers rolling out onto the floor.

"Uh," I say, rummaging through the containers and a wild, loose stack of papers, looking up over my shoulder at the PPO, who is watching me with raised brows. At least he's not frowning. "Sorry. Just a minute."

"That's a lot of Tic Tacs." A pause. "You must have very fresh breath."

Is he making . . . a joke? Does he even know what a joke is?

My hands close over the plastic covering of my insurance papers, and I breathlessly sit back in my seat, handing them to him with aplomb. "I do have fresh breath. I stress-eat them."

Probably didn't need to add the second part.

He takes the papers from me and opens the plastic, pulling out what's inside. He holds it far away from him, glancing at the papers underneath, and then turns it over to me.

"Miss, this is a letter to Santa Claus from some girl named Chamomile." He then slides another piece of paper in front of it as if he's a lawyer producing damning evidence during a trial. "This is a letter from a boy named Spruce who wants a bongo drum for Christmas."

"What?" I reach out and snatch the papers from him. There's a letter from Chamomile, from Spruce, from Jet, from Eunice. Shit. Now I know where I put all those Christmas letters I promised I'd mail last year.

"Interesting names," he comments. "I can't tell if you're a schoolteacher or the matriarch of a hippie commune."

"Most definitely the former." I lean back over the passenger side and start rifling through the glove compartment again. There are rabies shot papers from the vet for my dog, Liza, two

Sarah MacLean historical romances, a million receipts. I think for a moment that I've found the papers, but I quickly realize that what I'm holding is just the menu for our local noodle bar.

"Miss, I'm sorry, but I've dealt with a lot of people like you before," I hear him say as I frantically start ripping everything apart. "You make up any excuse but don't have the evidence to back it. I gather that you aren't a photographer or journalist and probably just a super fan, but either way, you're going to have to leave before I call the police."

I straighten up, my hair messy, my face red and vaguely sweaty. I narrow my eyes at his aviators. "What do you mean, you don't think I could be a journalist?"

He sighs, sounding tired, and does that dismissive hand wave thing again. "If you please." Then he pauses, seeing something in the distance. "Finally."

I crane my neck to look behind me. It's a cop car, the SUV of our chief of police, Bert Collins, pulling up behind me.

"Oh thank god," I say out loud, much to the surprise of Agent Grump.

Bert gets out of the SUV and strolls toward us. "Sorry I'm late," Bert says to Mr. Broody. "Got held up in town. Utter madness."

"Bert!" I cry out before the PPO can get a word in. I practically hang my upper body out the window. "Hey!"

"Hey there, Piper," he says, his mustache moving as he speaks. Bert has a mustache that would strike envy in the hearts of both Tom Selleck and Kenny Rogers, like someone stuck a densely bristled shoe-shine brush to his upper lip.

"Bert, one of the kids threw up in my handbag today and I had to throw it away and it had my wallet in it. I was going to get a temporary license after school, but the town looked crazy." I side-eye Harrison before I continue. "And this guy doesn't believe that I live here."

Bert folds his arms. "You know you can get in trouble for driving without a license." He sighs and looks to Harrison with a jovial expression. "But I can vouch for her."

"She doesn't have her insurance papers either," Harrison blurts out.

What the actual fuck? This dude is throwing me under the bus now.

Bert frowns at me in overblown disappointment, and I can't help but cringe. "Is this true? You're driving around without a license *and* without insurance papers?"

I give him a shaky smile. "I was just in the middle of looking for them when you showed up. Hold on."

I'm about to turn back to the rummage pile when Bert says, "No, it's fine. I trust you'll find them." He looks back at Harrison. "She's okay. She lives at the big property at the very end."

Harrison's frown deepens, a canyon between his brows. "But that's where . . . that's the real estate in question. We were told it was unoccupied, no renters."

"She lives in the guest cottage."

The PPO's forehead wrinkles like a shar-pei.

"It's a separate property," I point out. "Back in the day, it was the guest quarters for the main house. For the help and all that. My mom bought it five years ago when it had just been subdivided into two different properties. We share a driveway, but that's it."

I know I can't see his eyes, but I can feel the resentment in them, the fact that he's going to be sharing a driveway with me.

Oh. Wait a minute.

I'm going to be sharing a driveway with *them*.

Holy shit.

They're going to be my neighbors!

"Nothing is final," Harrison quickly says, reading my building excitement. "I don't even know if they'll want to rent it or not. They're just looking at their options."

Bert shrugs with one shoulder. "If they don't, there are plenty of other properties on the island that might suit them. Privacy, space, we have that in spades." He pauses. "That said . . . are you sure they really want to move here? I mean, no offense, but judging from how the town was today, I'm not sure our fair little island can handle it."

"I'm sure they'll take that into consideration," Harrison comments, in a way that says they most likely won't.

"So, am I free to go home now?" I ask.

"Of course," Bert says, but Harrison holds out his hand in that "stop" gesture again. My goodness, he has large hands.

"Just a minute, Miss Chamomile."

"Piper," I say imploringly. "My name is Piper. Chamomile is the name of one of my students." He's smart enough to remember my name, so it's obvious he's just doing this to be a dick.

"Because you share a driveway, I have to trust you not to go up to the property or take any pictures or tip off anyone or . . . You know what? I'll escort you to your house."

I jerk my chin back, which I'm sure is very flattering. "You will not." I look at Bert with wide eyes. "He can't escort me."

Bert's mustache twitches with sympathy. "The royals are a part of our commonwealth, and the *Royal* Canadian Mounted Police is in charge of providing their overall safety when they visit. I can escort you, Piper, if you want, but if they are calling for it, then I'm afraid I have no choice but to provide the service."

"They aren't calling for it. *He* is." I side-eye Harrison again.

His face could be made of stone. "As head of security for the Duke and Duchess of Fairfax, I make the calls, and my word is law."

Whoa. That's dramatic. I glance at Bert, thinking I'll catch a hint of a smile buried under his lip bush, but to my surprise, he's looking at Harrison in awe.

Bert finally wipes the fanboy expression off his face and looks at me. "I'm still more than happy to escort you, if you're not comfortable with this gentleman."

Oh great. Now it sounds like I'm scared.

"I'm absolutely comfortable with this . . . man." I make a weak gesture to him. "I've never had a male escort before, so why not start now?"

I flash him an overly cheery smile, and he grunts at me in response.

With a heavy exhale, he nods at Bert. "Do you mind blocking the road while I escort this woman to her house? No one is allowed through unless they have proof of address."

"No problem," Bert says, and then he goes and actually salutes the man.

Harrison nods in response, and then to my surprise he walks around the front of the car and opens the passenger door. For some reason I thought he would walk beside my car or something like that, like . . . *escort* me. Not actually get in the car with me.

I don't think I'm ready for this level of intimacy.

But he pauses, half in the car, which seems far too small for his massive frame, eyeing the disaster on the seat. I quickly start picking up all the junk with both hands and throwing it in the back seat.

Finally he sits down, his knees comically rammed against the glove compartment.

"There's a lever at the side," I tell him, "to adjust your seat."

He moves the lever back and forth until the seat slams all the way to the back.

THWACK!

For a dude who probably had to do some epic training with crazy dangerous situations, he seems completely out of sorts in the fuzzy green seat.

I try not to laugh, especially since he looks so serious as he dutifully buckles himself in. He looks down at the seats and the dice.

"Interesting décor. Did you skin Oscar the Grouch?"

"Pretty much," I tell him. "I'm sure you're used to riding around in Bentleys and whatnot."

He doesn't say anything to that, just faces straight ahead. I glance out the window, hoping for some camaraderie from Bert, but he's just as serious and gives me the nod to keep driving.

Of course, my car hates this small hill normally, so since we're at a standstill, I have to press my foot down on the gas and hold it there until the RPMs are going wild and it takes off like a shot.

Okay, it takes off like an injured baby impala. One big jerk forward, followed by pathetic hops, and maybe Harrison was right about making sure he was strapped in, because it looks like he's already succumbing to whiplash.

"Sorry," I cry out as the car finally gets going and we chug up to the top of the hill. "Not long now."

It's actually only about thirty seconds down the slight slope to the very end of the undulating peninsula, but it manages to feel like a million years with this British beast of a man trapped in my car. He's so big that his shoulder brushes against mine from time to time, and I can feel the heat off him. Doesn't help that it's warm outside and I don't have air conditioning. I also can't tell if it's him that smells like balsam and sea salt or if it's the air outside.

He remains silent and visibly uncomfortable, and I take a little too much glee in that. Serves him right for escorting me to my own damn house. I mean, do I look like the type of person who is going to go home and get her camera and climb up through the tangled salal bushes and overgrown ferns just to get a glimpse of them? Does he think I'll show up at their door, peer in through their windows, and post it all to my Instagram stories?

I'm guessing so. I totally get him needing to be protective of them, but this seems like overkill, especially since Bert seemed to vouch for my character. Though I guess he could have said a few more complimentary things just in case. So far Harrison knows I live here, but I'm pretty sure I've only given him evidence that I'm some quirky manic pixie dream girl, minus the dream part. Nightmare is more like it.

The road ends in a narrow cul-de-sac with barely enough room to turn around, the ocean on either side crashing against kelp-strewn rocks. So far the street has been quiet, so I guess Harrison has been doing a good job keeping people away, if anyone has caught on yet that this is actually where Eddie and Monica are.

The driveway that we share runs off the end of the turnaround, up another slight hill where it forks into two. I take the driveway to the left, which plunks us into my parking spot beside a tall western red cedar. From here you can see a bit of the cul-de-sac, but you can't see the mansion at all.

It's a really interesting property. Even though it takes over the very tip of the peninsula, with the ocean on nearly all sides, where they placed the servants' quarters (aka my house) is among tall cedar and arbutus trees. It's on the dark side, and you can only see glimpses of the ocean through the trees. I've talked about taking down a few to improve the view, but my mother has extreme paranoia and thinks if I do that, it means people can spy on us easier, so I've just let the trees grow and the branches continue to block the ocean. But we're lucky that there's a path that takes you to rickety steps that lead down to deepwater moorage. The dock is crooked, and one end is sometimes underwater, but when I'm craving the sun and blue sky, that's where I go.

And while there is a fence separating us from the road, there's no gate and there's also no fence between the properties. We just know where the lines are and we keep to our side, even though the mansion has been vacant for as long as we've been here. Sure, sometimes there are families or couples staying there, but we never really see or meet them, and I'm sure it's more the owner's friends coming to stay rather than an Airbnb or some other vacation rental.

That said, I still have no idea who owns the place. There were rumors in the past that it belonged to the infamous Hearst family, but I doubt that's true. Whoever they are, however, they must have some kind of connection to Eddie and Monica.

"So," I say innocently, turning to Harrison as I put the Garbage Pail in park and turn off the engine, "if they're just looking to rent and not buy, who are they renting it from?"

He doesn't even look at me. "I'm not at liberty to say."

"Are Eddie and Monica in the house right now?"

"I'm not at liberty to say."

I roll my eyes. "What *are* you at liberty to say?"

"Just that I need to make sure that you're not going to be of harm to the Fairfaxes."

I gesture to my house. It's small and quaint, with a garden out front that my mother dutifully attends to. Most of the plants have to thrive in the shade or part shade, but she's got a green thumb, and even the zinnias are doing well. "Look. That's where I live. I wasn't lying when I said this was my address, and I can definitely promise you I'm not going to harm them in any way. I'm a schoolteacher. I read romance novels. I like Tic Tacs. I have a rescue pup. My bones ache when a cold front comes in."

He eyes me. "What does that have to do with anything?"

"I'm just trying to prove that I'm human."

"I never said you were a robot. I said I need to make sure you aren't a threat. And for your information, Tic Tacs were Ted Bundy's candy of choice."

"So now you're comparing me to one of America's most famous serial killers?"

He opens the door and gets out of the car. This already seems like a classic Harrison response and I don't even know the guy.

"By the way," I tell him, getting out of the car and looking at him over the roof, "Tic Tacs aren't candy. They are mints."

"I find the fact that you stress-eat them troubling."

"And also, if Ted Bundy really ate Tic Tacs, he wouldn't have been able to sneak up on anyone. You would have heard him coming."

"Doesn't change a thing."

I throw my arms out. "Fine. Do you want to call the school principal and get a reference of character or something? I guess the chief of police wasn't good enough."

He stares at me, and even in the shadow of the trees, he still hasn't removed his sunglasses. I'm starting to think he goes to sleep in them.

It doesn't matter. I'm done here. Any excitement I should be feeling over the fact that the royals might be moving next door has been absolutely dashed due to this sexy British dick on a power trip.

Whoops. Did I say sexy? *Definitely* didn't mean that.

I grumble under my breath and start walking toward the house, noticing the light in the kitchen is on, which means my mother is probably up. I steady myself internally.

"I need to walk you to the door," Harrison says, slamming the car door hard enough to make the Garbage Pail shake, and I look over my shoulder to see him striding purposefully over to me.

I blink at him, shaking my head before I turn around and start walking to the front door, hoping my mother doesn't have to see any of this.

"You, sir, have control issues," I point out.

"It's my bloody job to have control issues," he snaps.

I pause and look at him. Whoa. Defensive much? I think this is the first display of any sort of emotion I've seen from him.

He realizes how he's come across too, because it's like he wipes his face clean and there it is, that blank but broody slate again. He clears his throat, raises his strong chin in defiance. "Control is an important factor of my job."

Yeah, that's not what you said the first time, 007.

I head for the door up the winding woodland-style path with prehistoric-looking hostas lining the sides, and stop on the front steps, ivy crawling up the sides of the overhang. "Okay, well, here I am at the door. Satisfied? Or are you going to demand to come inside too, because I know for a fact that you'll need to provide a search warrant and I can scream real loud."

He studies me for a moment, and I so know that he wants to

tell me some bullshit about inspecting my house to make sure I don't have dead bodies in my freezer, but instead he just nods. "That will be all."

He's turning to leave just as the door opens.

I freeze in place.

He freezes in place.

My mother is there, her head poking through the narrow opening as she eyes us both suspiciously. Her hair is a mess, and I cringe inwardly in embarrassment until I remember that my hair is a mess too. Like mother, like daughter.

"What are you doing? Why are you late? Who is that?" At the last question she narrows her eyes into slits, venomous daggers directed at Harrison.

I know I have to lie. My mom has paranoid delusions and distrusts authority, and if she found out the truth about Harrison, she'd start freaking out, and that's when Harrison would *really* consider us a threat.

"Mom," I say quickly, gesturing to Harrison. "This is Harrison Cole. He's, uh, our new neighbor."

I can feel his frown at my back, and I keep on smiling, hoping he'll play along. Then again, I don't think the man knows what the concept of *play* is. He probably supervised other children on the playground when he was young.

"Harrison Ford?" she asks.

"Harrison *Cole*," I tell her. Then I do a weird thing where I lean back and grab Harrison's forearm and pull him forward so he's standing next to me, and I don't let go of his arm. His very strong, muscly arm. Holy crap. Just touching him feels like it's scrambled my brain. I clear my throat and try to ignore it. "He might rent the house next door, so I thought I'd show him where we live."

To his credit, Harrison hasn't yanked himself out of my grasp, nor has he corrected me on this white lie.

My mother eyes my grasp on him, and then a strange look of realization comes over her face. I know what that look is. She thinks I'm interested in this man, like, sexually, because so far, he seems exactly like all the assholes I used to be attracted to: handsome, emotionally constipated, and very controlling.

"Okay," she finally says. "Welcome to the neighborhood, then. Do you want to come in?"

"No," I say quickly, my voice bordering on a yelp. "No, no. It's fine." Harrison opens his mouth to say something, but I blabber on through. "He has to go back; this was just a quick visit. I'm sure you'll see him again if he rents the place."

My mom shrugs, suddenly disinterested. "Okay," she says, then closes the door on the both of us.

"What was that?" Harrison says to me after a beat.

"You mean my mother? She's like that. Don't take it personally."

"No, I mean, why did you lie? Why didn't you tell her who I was?"

"It's a long story," I tell him. And none of his business, but I don't feel like antagonizing him anymore. He did his part by keeping his mouth shut, and that's good enough for me. Now if only I didn't have to see him again. Something tells me that might be a tall order. "But thanks for playing along."

"I didn't seem to have a choice," he admits gruffly.

I fold my arms and shrug. "Well, I'm afraid that despite what my mother just said, this is where we part ways. If you feel like harassing me further, feel free to leave a letter in our mailbox."

He watches me for a moment, exhaling harshly through his nose. Then he gives a stern nod. "I'll be in touch. If they do end up renting this place, we'll need to put a security gate at the start of the driveway, and I'm sure we'll need your permission for that. I'll make sure to put the forms in your mailbox."

He then turns around and walks down the path, past the Garbage Pail and the cedars until I can't see him anymore.

I let out a long, heavy sigh and straighten my shoulders before I open the door and step into the house.

Three

"SO, NEW NEIGHBOR, HUH?" MY MOTHER ASKS FROM THE kitchen while I take off my boots in the hallway.

I slide on my sheepskin slippers (step one of decompressing from work) and pad on into the kitchen, where she's sorting out packets of herbs that she dried herself and sprinkling them into a diffuser that fits over her giant teapot.

The kitchen is a total mess—mint and lavender scattered everywhere, unwashed dishes, leftover coffee grinds, oat milk spills— but it barely registers. Once upon a time, I would have lost my temper, which in turn would have made my mother lose *her* temper, so now I just let it get worse and worse and then after she goes to bed tonight, I'll clean everything so that she can destroy it again tomorrow.

I know that sounds really callous of me, but ever since my father left us, back when I was fourteen, my mother has become my dependent. Dependent personality disorder is exactly that; when you combine it with borderline personality disorder, it means that I'm really the only person she has to keep her in line. She's not a fan of doctors, she hates that she has to take medication (I'm here to make sure she does), I'm an only child, and my father has a new family out in Toronto (we're friendly and talk a couple of times a month, but he doesn't offer any help), so it all falls on me.

I'm used to it. Doesn't mean I like it, doesn't mean that while I provide care for my mother when she needs it, I'm not emotionally disconnected at the same time. I have to be, for my own sanity. It's taken me years of therapy to finally come to terms with my own issues and the coping skills I developed during my childhood and distance myself from them. Avoiding conflict, always being a mediator, being attracted to emotionally unavailable men, becoming a doormat and doing whatever people want in order to keep the peace. Through my therapists (plural, because finding the right one for you takes a lot of trial and error . . . it's like dating, but way more expensive), I learned that my coping strategies ensured my survival as a child and teenager, but as an adult, I've been learning to let them go.

Which I guess I'm doing an okay job of, because when I think back to my interactions with the pissy protection officer, people pleasing was the last thing on my mind, and I think I created more conflict than what was warranted.

(I should probably stop thinking about him; he's making my blood boil all over again.)

"Want some tea?" my mother asks, grabbing two mugs from the cupboard. She always makes me a cup regardless of what I say.

"Sure," I tell her, taking a seat at the kitchen island. "Where's Liza?"

"Napping in the sun."

Liza is my adopted pit bull, a short, gray, fat little hippo with the cutest face and laziest personality in the world. Her favorite place is the corner of the deck where one bare patch of trees lets the light in.

My mother named her after her obsession with Liza Min-
nelli, and she makes a really good companion/emotional support
animal for her. Liza was rescued when she was a year old after
being abused, and yet she's come full circle and really helped all
of us heal just as she was healing.

"Back to the neighbor," she says to me, fixing her eyes on me.
Despite the messy hair and the fact that she's in her pajamas, she
seems to be doing okay today. "When did he move in? I haven't
seen any moving trucks."

"When was the last time you left the house?"

She shrugs. "Yesterday I took Liza to the ferry terminal and
back. Didn't see anything unusual."

"Well, technically he's looking to rent the place. Nothing has
been finalized."

"Does he have a wife?"

"No," I tell her, even though now I'm thinking back to whether
Harrison had a ring on. I mean, he could have a wife, but for this
version of the story, he won't.

"You sure?" She squints at me. "I know that's your favorite
type."

I give her a stiff smile. Even though she's just being blunt and
isn't trying to be mean, it always feels like a punch to the gut
when she brings up my past mistakes, and I've made some pretty
major ones.

"He's not married," I repeat.

"But you were grabbing on to him like he and you were together. So that's something." She tilts her head, studying me. "I
don't mean to be a nag, Piper, but you were so proud of those
revelations you had during therapy with Dr. Edgar."

"I'm still proud of them. And I'm not interested in this guy."

"Harrison Cole," she says.

"Yes. I was just being nice."

Come to think of it, there really had been no reason for me to hang on to him like I had. I don't know what I was thinking or what I was doing.

"So he doesn't have a wife—does he have kids?"

"Uh, no."

She turns her back to me as she mulls that over, checking on the teapot. "No wife, no kids. How is he going to afford that place? Doesn't it belong to the Hearsts? What does he do for a job?"

"I'm not sure," I tell her, and that turns out to be the wrong answer, because I see her shoulders stiffen and she slowly turns around to look at me with wide eyes.

"You don't know what he does? Piper . . . he could be a drug dealer. A mobster. A criminal. How else would he afford that place?"

Uh-oh.

"He's probably a lawyer," I point out. "A successful one. Maybe a film producer. Perhaps he's related to royalty . . ."

She shakes her head, and I know she's not going to let go of whatever paranoid theory her brain conspires. "You can't trust lawyers either."

"How about next time I see him, I'll ask him?" I say, hoping to soothe her. "Who knows, he may not even move in."

That thought gives her pause. "I hope not. I don't like strangers."

"I know you don't. It'll be fine, I promise."

And there I go, trying to be the mediator, trying to promise things that I have no control over. It's hard to rise out of your old roles in life when you're still so tied to your parents.

After she makes me some tea, I head out to the dock and sit

there, taking in the peace and quiet and the soft summer air and the waning sunshine. A seal pops his head up in the water, his big dark eyes taking me in before he ducks under. A bald eagle soars overhead, heading for the group of nests by the marina farther down the narrow isthmus of Long Harbour.

This is the best part of living here, being one with nature, having time to de-stress and breathe in the fresh salty air and the breezes that rattle through the arbutus leaves and the smell of sunbaked moss.

If the royals end up moving next door, there's a chance that all of this could change. I'm not a huge fan of change; I like my routine, as do a lot of people on the island. Bert wasn't too far off when he said this might not be the best place for any kind of celebrity, especially a royal couple who have created headlines for two years straight and are now the hot topic of all media.

They could throw all the peace and serenity of the place into a tizzy. If they move next door, the paparazzi from the US and the UK will quickly find out, and they'll be camped out here day and night. I won't be able to sit on this dock without photographers on boats and Jet Skis flying past, disrupting the tranquility.

Most of all, someone like my mother, who can't handle any change at all, will likely have a breakdown at the intrusion, thrusting her into the public eye.

It could all get very messy, very fast.

And I'm not even allowed to talk to anyone about it. Not that I have any close friends, but even so, this is a hard thing to keep to myself.

Unless . . .

After I'm done with my tea, I head back into the house, where I whip up a quick casserole for dinner, and then I'm in my bedroom, ready for my weekly podcast.

I usually record an episode during the week and then I publish it on Fridays. Tonight is a recording day, but suddenly, reviewing historical romance is the last thing I want to do.

I'm inspired. I want to talk about the royals.

My romance podcast—*Romancing the Podcast*—is quite popular, but I run it anonymously. Any social media I have is linked to the podcast, and it has its own email address for questions or review requests from authors. Most of the time, though, I just read the books I want to read. Less pressure that way.

It's not that I'm ashamed of reading romance either; I'm pretty proud and vocal about it in my real life. But being a schoolteacher, I think we're held to different standards, and I don't want to feel censored on what I can and can't talk about. If I want to read out a graphic sex scene, I want to be able to do that without fear that the public will find out and chastise me. In the worst-case scenario, I could lose my job over it. There are a lot of uptight fuddy-duddies on this island.

But tonight, I don't want to talk about books. I want to talk about real-life romance. I want to talk about Monica and Eddie and what direction their love story could go now that they've chosen that love over the duties of being royals.

I sit down at my desk, open my laptop, and pull out my microphone.

Press record.

"Hello, my fellow romance enthusiasts, lovers of love, readers of smut, and proud bibliophiles. Welcome to another episode of *Romancing the Podcast.*" I take in a deep breath and smile. "Normally I would jump right in to this week's review, but lately I've been thinking about the Duke and Duchess of Fairfax. We're all familiar with the epic love story of Monica Red and Prince Eddie. We've watched as this very unlikely pair fell in love after

Prince Eddie requested to meet Monica backstage at her London show. Their coupling was quick, and yet the public knew nothing about their affair until months later, when it was apparent the Grammy Award winner would be leaving show business behind to concentrate on her life with our tall, blond hero.

"Soon, wedding bells were in the air, and all of us—or almost all of us—fell for these two in the case of opposites attracting. Quiet, stoic Edward and the opinionated, fun-loving Monica became the couple of the century, flipping years of tradition and the royal family on its head.

"But even happily-ever-afters have bumps in the road, and as the media senselessly attacked the couple, with some reports of animosity coming directly from inside the royal palace, they bravely took a stand and said they were going to do things their own way. They were going to move on and make a new life for themselves as the Duke and Duchess of Fairfax. Now one can only wonder, what exactly does the future hold for these two? I, being a hopeless romantic, even though my love life has been anything but charming, can't help but root for their new chance at a happily-ever-after. But will their quest for privacy and anonymity ever become a reality? Is there such a thing as an HEA if the happy part isn't guaranteed? Come on, romance lovers, let's discuss."

Four

"FALAFEL?" CYNTHIA ASKS, POKING HER HEAD IN THE classroom doorway, her brows raised expectantly.

I'm already getting out of my chair and grabbing my purse.

Lunch hour just started, and today feels all over the place. Tomorrow is Friday, the last day of school before summer vacation begins, and it's hot and strangely humid, and the kids are absolutely zooey, with zero attention span. As a result, I'm frazzled with no place for my focus to land, so going into town for twenty minutes is probably the right course of action.

"Want to do coffee instead?" I ask Cynthia as we head down the hall. "I think I've had nothing but falafel and chips all week."

Ted's Falafel and Chips is the island's oldest food truck, located right across from the elementary school and the high school next door. There's always a huge line of teenagers outside, but when I'm pressed for time, it's literally the closest place to grab a bite on days I forget to bring my own lunch.

This week, that's been every day. I don't know if it's because it's the last week before vacation or what, but my mind has been *scattered*.

"Sure, I could grab an iced coffee," Cynthia says, and then her eyes light up. "And a cinnamon bun!"

With that, I know we're heading to Salty Seas Coffee & Goods, where I already stopped this morning for my pre-class fix. They have the gooiest cinnamon buns imaginable; they're melt-in-your-mouth and caramelized and almost crispy. I'm drooling already.

But as we're walking down the street, past the kids and teens lining up at the chip stand or getting slushies from the gas station, Cynthia mentions how much busier this place is going to get this weekend, when kids are out of school across the country and the island swells up like a balloon, and then my mind backtracks to two weeks ago.

It goes back to Monica and Eddie.

It goes back to Harrison.

That fateful encounter with the PPO was the last I'd heard of them being on the island. I never saw him again. They never moved in. The town very quickly, within a day, went back to normal, and all the British paparazzi vanished.

As for my podcast, well, it ended up being my most listened to episode, with it spreading all over the romance community. Tons of people messaged me, wondering who I was and where I lived, while an equal amount said I was lying and full of shit. The joys of anonymous comments and all that. I think listeners were disappointed when my next episode went back to reviewing romance books and I didn't mention the royals again.

"Hey," I say to her as we take a side street to the coffee shop. "Can I tell you something weird?"

"Weird?" Cynthia asks. "I love weird."

I know she does. She's wearing this necklace that looks like it's made of tiny animal bones sloppily painted in neon colors.

She says a student gave it to her for Christmas, and she hasn't taken it off since, even though I think those bones belong to a frog and that the child may have cast a curse on her or something.

"Okay, so two weeks ago, when the duke and duchess were in town, well, I went straight home because you told me it was chaos in town, and you were right. Except when I went home, there was a PPO blocking the road."

"What's a PPO?"

"Like the royal bodyguard." She gasps, her hands to her mouth. I go on. "Not just that, but *the* royal bodyguard. The sexy one. The brooding one."

The asshole one.

"*No way.*"

"Uh-huh. He had to escort me to my house."

"No! Piper. He escorted you to your house? Please tell me you let him do a strip search on you."

"No," I say, feigning disgust. His big, strong hands all over my naked body? I, uh . . . "*No,*" I repeat, more for myself. "He was controlling and a total prick on a power trip. Anyway, the whole point is that Monica and Eddie were looking to rent the place next to me. Obviously it would be perfect for them."

She gives me a questioning look. "I've never been to your house. I don't even know where you live."

"Scott Point."

She purses her lips. "Well la-di-da. Scott Point on a teacher's salary."

"It's a long story, but believe me, it's not what you think. I live in the old servants' quarters, and there is no view. And anyway, he was all concerned that I would be a threat to their safety. I mean, *me.*"

She nods, taking that in. "That's true. You're the least threatening teacher on the faculty."

"That's what I thought."

"Why didn't you tell me this earlier?"

I shrug. "I guess because he told me I couldn't tell anyone and then I kind of forgot with all the end-of-school madness. Turns out, I never saw them again, and it all died down. It's like it never happened."

"I guess he really *did* think you were a threat," she says, an amused smile on her hot-pink lips, which match her neon bone necklace. "Miss Piper Evans, the most feared teacher on SSI."

I attempt to elbow her, but she moves her lithe body out of the way. "Hey, apparently he thought I was someone to reckon with."

She laughs, shaking her head. I'm only five foot three, so any ferocity I have can be likened to a chihuahua's. "I can't believe that happened to you," she says with a sigh. "What a shame, huh? How cool would that have been?"

"I don't know," I admit as we approach the coffee shop and I hold the door open for her. "I talked to Bert, the head of the RCMP, and it seems a lot of people wouldn't have been all that happy if they moved in. Crisis averted."

"More like opportunity wasted."

"Hey, it wasn't my fault," I tell her, and then bring my voice down to a whisper once we enter the shop. "There could have been a million factors as to why they didn't settle here. Honestly, I couldn't really blame them. This can be a strange place."

Being lunch hour, there's already a line, so I briefly consider going to another coffee shop and skipping the cinnamon bun, but who knows what the line will be like over there.

We're almost at the counter when a woman sitting at the corner table loudly exclaims, "No!" and her friend leans over to see whatever it is on her phone.

She gasps.

They both gasp.

Then I see someone running past the shop.

And another person.

And another person.

Heading in the direction of the harbor.

My first thought is that there is some sort of emergency.

But then the woman and her friend jump to their feet and she quickly says, "Prince Eddie and his wife just arrived by seaplane!"

That's all it takes for nearly the whole coffee shop to abandon their cinnamon buns and lattes and run outside, joining the pack of people already running to the harbor.

"This is insane!" I exclaim, looking around. "Everyone has lost their mind."

Cynthia turns to me and gives me a pleading look with puppy-dog eyes.

"What?" I ask incredulously. "You want to join the mob and run down there too?"

"My mother is obsessed with Monica. It would make her day if I could send her a picture. Maybe she'd finally come and visit me."

"Fine, go," I tell her. "I'll get your coffee for you."

"And the cinnamon bun!" She grins at me, and then she's running out of the shop too, her necklace swinging.

I shake my head, and suddenly I'm the next in line since everyone ahead of me ditched out. I look at the barista with her pale silver-purple hair and nose ring. She's staring longingly at the door, her phone in her hand, mid-text.

"I'd take over for you if I could," I offer.

She smiles begrudgingly and rings in my order for two oat-milk lattes.

I snag the last cinnamon bun for myself.

Afterward I walk back to the school, hoping Cynthia can tear herself away from the mayhem before the lunch bell rings. Every now and then another person runs or speed walks past me, and I have to wonder what the hell is going through their heads. Maybe it's because I'd already had that meeting with Harrison, but I don't understand the obsession. This is like Beatlemania for the twenty-first century.

That said, there is a smaller version of myself, adorned with furry devil horns, perched on my shoulder and whispering in my ear, "They're back, the royals are back. They might be your neighbors after all."

That version of me sounds a little too excited, so I flick her off my shoulder and try to regain my composure. The whole town is going nuts for these royals, not me. Besides, just because they're back doesn't mean anything, and it certainly doesn't mean they'll be my neighbors.

My thoughts become reality. Aurelie Lamont, the French teacher, is leaning against the main entrance into the school, staring off into the distance. She's from Quebec, so there's something about her pose that's even extra dramatic, her dark hair flowing around her.

I give her a quick smile, about to make some passing small talk such as "Hot day, eh?" when she says, "They're buying a place on Juniper."

I stop in my tracks. "Sorry, what?"

She looks at me idly. "The duke and duchess. They're buying a place up on Juniper. That big house behind the gates. Used to belong to Randy Bachman. The Guess Who. '*Femme Améri-caine.*' '*Pas de sucre ce soir.*' You know."

"Really? Where did you hear that?"

She gives a light shrug with one of her shoulders. "A student told me. She lives in the neighborhood. Don't worry, I made her tell me in French."

I just nod at that and walk inside. I hate to admit it, but there's a flutter of disappointment in my chest. It's almost as if I secretly wanted them to move next door to me, even though I just spent my lunch hour chastising the idea. I guess having them as neighbors would have made me feel . . . special. Sounds silly and so stupid, but it probably would have been the most exciting thing that ever happened to me.

I shake it off. I have to. It's dumb, and earlier today the whole thing seemed like a distant memory anyway.

Before I know it, it's time to go home. I never regained control of my kids after lunch, so I pretty much just let them run wild in the classroom, so long as no one got hurt and no one puked in my bag again. Cynthia never even came to get her latte, so I ended up drinking both of them, and when I get inside the Garbage Pail, my hands are shaking from the four shots of espresso.

That doesn't prevent me from munching away on my cinnamon bun on the drive home, one hand on the wheel, one hand in the delicious gooey mess.

I'm almost at my house when I see him.

A black Range Rover physically blocking the driveway and Harrison Cole standing outside it, leaning against the door and facing me, arms folded, aviators on. Another sharp-looking suit that fits him like a glove.

My heart does something strange, like skips a beat, and I blame it on the caffeine.

I roll to a stop and then stick my head out the window.

"Excuse me, I'd like to get by now," I say in my best *Wayne's World* Garth Algar impression.

Harrison, naturally, doesn't get the reference.

"I'm going to need to see some identification, miss," he says to me in his raspy British accent as he walks toward my car.

I stare at him, openmouthed, until I realize I have sticky cinnamon bun all over my face. I can't believe his nerve, and yet I'm also trying to subtly clean my face at the same time.

"ID? You know who I am," I tell him.

"I'm afraid I need to see your driver's license," he says, stopping right outside the car, his Hulk-ish frame extra imposing from this angle. "Or is it still missing?"

"So you *do* remember me."

"I wish I could forget," he replies dryly.

I frown.

Dick.

"Then you know I live right there and you're blocking my own driveway."

"I can't let you pass until I see some ID."

I'm still staring at him. Is he serious? I mean, he looks serious and I think he's always serious, but how dare he ask for ID when he knows who I am? What gives him the fucking right to prevent me from going home?

He cocks a brow expectantly, staring down at me. I wish I could rip those aviators off and run them over with my car.

I let out a huff of anger and try to get my driver's license out of my purse. I'm lucky that it came in the mail two days ago. I'm not so lucky that I had the photo taken during my lunch hour, right after gym class, when Eunice dumped Gatorade over another kid's head after a game of basketball and I got most of the blowback. A partially drowned rat with smudgy mascara is forever immortalized in black and white.

"Here," I tell him, trying to hand over the ID, but of course it's a sticky cinnamon bun–smeared mess.

Harrison scrunches up his nose distastefully as he takes the card from me. He raises it to his nose and sniffs the substance. "What is this?"

"It's the remains of a baked good, what do you think it is?"

He sniffs again, seems to think about it, and then peers at the photo and then back at me. "These photos are never very flattering, are they?"

"Are you done?"

"Not quite, Ms. *Evans*," he says, pronouncing my name like it's some sort of alias before giving me the license back. "The duke and duchess have decided to rent the house."

"I was told they were buying Randy Bachman's house. You know, the Guess Who?"

"That was a decoy house to throw people off, at least at the beginning. They've decided that this is the place for them after all."

"Are you serious?"

He nods. Dumb question, really.

"I expressed my concern over you, but they didn't seem to be that bothered by it."

"Excuse me?"

He goes on as if he didn't just say that he told the royals that I was a security concern. "The gate will be going up as soon as possible. We're installing cameras, and there will be a passcode that only you and your mother will be given access to. Until then, I'll be parked here blocking the way, and my men will be in the trees."

"Men will be in the what?"

Suddenly I hear a sharp whirring sound on either side of me, and I look up in time to see a man in camouflage gear rappel from the top of a hemlock straight down to the ground.

"Holy shit!" I swear just as another man comes down a tree on the right side of me. Tree men! Secret agent tree men!

Harrison just lifts his hand up, as if to tell them to stay back. "This is Isaac and Giles. They'll be here temporarily. And if not, you'll get used to them. But until the gate goes up, we have to ensure the couple's privacy. I also have someone patrolling the water from a boat, just in case you see them." He pauses, studies me.

His gaze is unnerving, even covered by his sunglasses.

"What?" I ask.

"You have pastry in your hair."

My hand shoots up, trying to figure out where, when suddenly it becomes stuck and I know that I must have a huge blob of sugary goo in my hair.

Meanwhile, I swear I see a smirk on Harrison's mouth, the corner of his lips turning up a millimeter. If he wasn't so fucking aggravating I might actually find his lips quite lush and sexy, but that would only make things worse.

"At any rate, Ms. Evans," he says briskly, "I'm going to need you to sign a nondisclosure agreement."

I practically growl at him, my patience seeping out as I also wrestle with my hair. "An NDA? Why?"

"For obvious reasons."

"And if I don't?"

I don't know why I'm arguing with him over this. I mean, of course I'll sign an NDA, if it makes them comfortable, and I have no doubt that most islanders would band together to try to let them have as much privacy as they want.

But everything that comes out of his mouth pisses me off.

He looks behind him briefly at Isaac and Giles, who are similarly stone-faced, dressed in camo gear like it's no big deal, their rappelling ropes leading back into the trees.

Then Harrison looks back to me. "If you don't sign the NDA, things will get very difficult for you."

"Is that a threat?"

"Does it sound like a threat?"

"Everything you say sounds like a threat," I grumble. "Yes, of course I'll sign it."

"And have your mother sign it."

"Yes." I sigh loudly at that. I don't know how *that* is going to go down. I'll probably just have to forge her signature or something. It'll be hard enough to explain why there's a giant security gate going up, plus secret agent men in trees and officers patrolling in boats. She doesn't leave the house very often, usually just goes for walks in the neighborhood when she's feeling especially energetic or aggravated, but throwing all of this stuff into the mix isn't going to be easy. I'm going to have to have a real talk with her and hope she listens and learns that the royals are not the enemy.

God, I hope they aren't the enemy.

Harrison's face remains forever grim. "British Columbia has a privacy act that protects people from the media, that specifically creates the right to sue if privacy is being invaded. That's one reason why they chose this place instead of anywhere else. Keep that in mind."

"Are you done for real now? Can I at least go home?"

He nods. "Sure. Might want to take a shower too."

"What does that mean?" This guy gets worse and worse.

"Your hair," he says, nodding at my gooey, frazzled blond mess. I make a mental note to get a blowout for the next time I see him.

Then, to my surprise, he fucking smirks. "I'll be seeing you later to drop off the papers."

He turns, gives the other men a nod as he opens the door to his SUV, and gets in.

The men begin to go up into the trees again.

Harrison drives out of the driveway, giving me just enough space for the Garbage Pail to sneak through.

I start the car and rev the engine to make the small hill that goes up the driveway, and I'm bouncing forward, glaring at Harrison as I go.

By the time I'm parked in my spot, I'm livid. Having the royals next door isn't going to be fun at all, not if Harrison is going to be running the show.

I head into the house, and this time Liza comes barreling toward me, her tail wagging, tongue hanging out of her mouth. Judging by how excited/desperate she is and the silence in the house, my mother is asleep and Liza needs to go out.

I quickly take her through the woods and down the steps to the dock, stopping at the top just in time to watch a small dark speedboat slowly cruise past me.

I wave at the man, who then stops the boat and stares back at me.

He doesn't wave back.

Instead, he presses into his earpiece and says something I can't make out. He's wearing glasses identical to Harrison's, so I can't see his expression, but I know he's looking at me the whole time. Finally, after a staring contest that must go on for minutes, he looks away and the boat continues on.

I head back to the house with Liza, hating the fact that even being outside on our property is starting to make me feel watched, judged, and overall uncomfortable. Once I'm inside, I find myself pulling the curtains and blinds closed, and it dawns on me that I'm one step closer to turning into my mother.

It's just after dinner, with my mother still sleeping (don't worry, I checked on her), when there's a knock at the front door. Liza starts barking like crazy, which scares the shit out of me, and I'm an angry barrel of nerves by the time I rip open the door.

No surprise, it's Harrison. It won't get dark here until ten at night, but even so I'd bet he'll still be wearing his sunglasses.

He doesn't have any papers in his hands, though.

"Yes?" I say to him.

"Are you busy?" he asks me.

Now my brows are raised. "Am I busy?"

"The Duke and Duchess of Fairfax request your company."

Oh. My. God.

"Now?" I practically stutter.

He steps back and gestures to the path. "If you please."

I could easily close the door on him and say hell no. I'm not at their beck and call, I have a life to live and a podcast to upload.

But I slip on my shoes, close the door behind me, and follow Harrison down the path toward my new neighbors.

Five

HE'S GOT A NICE BUTT.

I frown at the thought in my head, mentally swatting it away. One minute Harrison is demanding I immediately drop everything and go and meet my new neighbors, as if it were an order, not a choice. The next I'm ogling his butt as he walks in front of me down to where my driveway intersects with theirs.

But it really is a nice butt. His suit jacket just skirts the top of it, but there's no denying how perky and muscular it is, like he does a lot of lunges, or . . .

As if he can hear me, he shoots a sharp glance at me over his shoulder, and I immediately still my thoughts, bringing my eyes up to meet his. Or, his sunglasses.

He jerks his chin down toward the road, where a bunch of flatbed trucks with planks of wood and other building materials in the back are parked in the cul-de-sac.

"They're all ready to go, once you sign a few papers," he says gruffly.

Jeez, that was fast. I should stop being annoyed at everything Harrison is throwing my way, but it irks me to think that he's got all these builders at his beck and call, as if they know I'm going to sign the papers, as if everything from this point onward is predetermined, and I have no say in it.

"What makes you think I even want a gated entry?" I ask him.

"Believe me, you will," he says over his shoulder as we start up the driveway to the mansion. "I take it you've never dealt with the British press before."

I don't have anything to say to that because obviously he's right, of course, and I've seen on Twitter alone just how intrusive, rude, and downright cruel they can be. If the duke and duchess are moving in here, then I'm probably going to want that fence.

I don't have a lot of time to think about the fence and the gate, because soon we're approaching the front of the house.

I'd be lying if I said I'd never seen it before. Many a time I've scrambled up the slight slope through the ferns and hemlock to take a look-see. But I've never gone farther than the driveway, even if I knew no one was staying there at the time.

Even now, it feels kind of wrong, but from the way Harrison and his nice butt are marching forward, I need to follow.

The mansion at first glance seems smaller than it is. The paved, tree-lined driveway does an elegant swoop into a massive A-frame three-car garage that's attached to a one-level made of bricks of pale stone. But the closer you get, you notice that the bulk of the mansion is behind that one-level, sloping down to the ocean in sections.

Harrison goes straight to the ornately carved front door, which looks like it was cut from a massive tree, and rings the bell. As we wait, his posture goes straighter, his hands clasped behind his back. I want to ask him where he's living, since he's ringing the bell and not walking right into the house, but then I see a shadow pass through the narrow windows at the side of the door and suddenly I'm nervous as hell.

It finally hits me what's happening. I'm actually going to meet Prince Eddie and MRed. Right here, right now.

This is absolutely insane.

And then the door opens.

I hold my breath.

A petite woman in her early fifties appears at the door, dressed in a gray shift dress and flat shoes, her graying hair pulled back into a neat bun.

She nods at Harrison and then gives me a small smile. "You must be the neighbor," she says in a crisp British accent. "I'm Agatha, the housekeeper. Please come right in."

Harrison walks in, and I follow him into the foyer.

"Should I take off my shoes?" I ask, reaching down for my boot, even though Harrison has strolled in without taking his off.

"That's quite all right," Agatha says. "The floors can be a bit cold at the moment. They're supposed to heat up, but I think we need an electrician in here to fix it."

"Well, good luck getting a reliable electrician on the island," I blurt out with an awkward laugh. "They only show up when they feel like it, like you're a huge inconvenience for hiring them."

I'm not exaggerating. There's a faulty baseboard heater in my room, and I called the electrician about two months ago and he still hasn't shown. Keeps texting me, saying, "Hope to pop by soon," but that "soon" never comes.

But from the firm smile on Agatha's face, perhaps it's not my place to joke about that.

"We will be hiring from off-island," she says.

"Of course," I say back, matching her smile. I should figure they've got all this worked out. It accounts for how they've got trucks full of building materials out front, ready to go.

"It will be nice for the duke and duchess to have you next door,"

Agatha says as she leads the way across the marble floors through the first level, which is sparsely decorated with some art prints of the Pacific Northwest. "We're all a bit fish out of water at the moment."

"That's what I'm here for!" I say, way too enthusiastically. "Anything you need, any questions at all, I'm your gal."

"I'm your gal"? This isn't a forties screwball comedy, Piper.

I really need to dial it down a notch.

I glance up (way up) at Harrison, who has fallen in step beside me, expecting him to be giving me a look.

And he is. He looks rather amused.

But what's catching me completely off guard is that his sunglasses are up on his head.

Which means, for the first time ever, I can see his eyes.

And . . . dear lord . . . am I in trouble.

Harrison's eyes are this gorgeous blue, a color that flirts between the sky and smoky sage green. At the moment they're crinkling slightly at the corners, yet I can tell how quickly they'd change in intensity. No wonder I could feel his gaze even beneath his glasses.

I swallow hard, unable to take my eyes away. At least until he raises his brow, those beautiful blues seeming to smirk at me.

They seem to ask, *Which do you prefer, my eyes or my ass?*

To which I'd say, *That's an impossible choice.*

"Watch your step," Agatha says quickly.

I look down in time to see that I'm in the middle of stepping off a landing.

Harrison's arm shoots out and grabs me by the elbow with so much force that I'm practically frozen in mid-step before he pulls me back.

"Oops," I say, giving him a quick, red-cheeked smile. Shit. I nearly ate it just because I was caught up looking at his eyes. I can only hope he doesn't bring that up or else I'll probably never stop hearing about it.

He lets go of my arm and gives me a nod, and still, there's that amusement in his expression. The kind that says he's laughing internally at me.

"Here we are," Agatha says, leading me over to a living room type of area with a see-through gas fireplace in the middle and floor-to-ceiling windows. The room looks over their sloping backyard, a spacious tile patio among a cultivated rose garden and sun-bleached brown grass beyond that. There are a few massive fir and arbutus trees and a stone-worn path that leads down to the private dock where a fifty-foot powerboat is tied up, sea-green waves crashing against the hull. In the distance, a ferry passes.

It's stunning. Absolutely. But in the back of my mind I can't help but notice that this would be our view if it weren't for where my house is situated and the trees that block it. It's like I'm realizing for the first time that my mother and I really do live in what used to be a very rich family's servants' quarters. We're buried in the trees, forgotten; they're up here in the open with the sun and the waves.

"Please sit," Agatha says, pointing to a modern-looking wing-back chair beside a polished wood coffee table. "I'll let them know you're here."

She walks off, and I half expect Harrison to walk off too.

But of course not. He wouldn't leave a potential "threat" alone in their house. He's standing in front of me, as if I'm going to make a run for it and start rummaging through Monica's underwear drawer or something, though his attention is out the window.

"Do you have the same view?" I ask him. I'm too nervous to sit down, so I just stand awkwardly by the chair.

He looks to me and gives me a strange look. Now I can see that laser focus in his eyes. It's almost unnerving, like they're seeing right through me. Maybe it would be better with his aviators back on.

"I beg your pardon?" he asks, his brows together in that formidable line.

I nod at the windows. "I was wondering if you had the same view. If you lived here with them."

His face is like a mask. "I will be living . . ." He pauses, clears his throat. "I live above the garage. Agatha lives in the lower level."

"Was it like that back in the UK? Did you live with them?"

"I had a cottage on the compound."

"So this is a big change for you too."

He shrugs with one shoulder. "I can deal."

But I'm staring at his shirt collar. When he shrugged, it moved over a little, exposing the skin above his collarbone. I swear I saw a tattoo.

I'm about to ask about it (because clearly I have no filter when it comes to him) when I hear footsteps behind me.

Harrison immediately drops his chin, his hands clasped in front of him.

I turn around, and there they are.

Prince Eddie and Monica.

In the flesh.

They both smile at me, and suddenly I have no clue what I'm supposed to do.

Curtsy? Right?

Or bow?

So I end up doing a curtsy-bow hybrid that makes it look like I have stomach cramps.

"How do you do?" I say to them as I straighten up, keeping a smile on my face while wincing internally at how ridiculous I must look.

"Monica," MRed says to me as she comes over, her hand extended, a beaming smile on her face.

I'm in a daze as she shakes my hand, focused on how damn pretty she is. I mean, this is the woman I watched accept her Grammy for best new artist; this is the woman in the infamous burlesque R&B video that had her in a blond wig, grinding against Zac Efron; this is the woman on *People's* 50 Most Beautiful People list (who should have been on the cover instead of Blake Shelton). I even watched her wedding on TV.

And she's standing in front of me, giving me a genuine smile and a hearty handshake. She's so much more beautiful in person. I didn't think that was even possible. Her dark skin is even-toned and glowing, her curly hair piled into a messy topknot, not a lick of makeup on, and yet she looks like she's ready for a photoshoot, even though she's just wearing leggings and a flowing tunic that gives her this boho chic vibe.

"Hello," Eddie says in a quiet voice, his accent as proper as can be, bringing my attention to him. "I'm Eddie."

Again, I'm drowning in disbelief here. Eddie is only a few years older than me, and as I grew up, I watched as he grew up. His face and the face of everyone in his family have been constants in my life, whether I was paying attention or not. I mean, his father is on our twenty-dollar bills.

In person, he's also better-looking. Compared to his older brother, who most people fawn over, Eddie is an unusual-looking guy with a piercing stare that says way more than he ever verbalizes, but he's still handsome. He just has a way about him, and right now, I'm picking up on that quiet kind of charm. It helps that he's wearing dark jeans and a navy polo shirt, a lot more casual than the Eddie I'm used to seeing in the press.

He shakes my hand, firm and warm, and I must be having an out-of-body experience right now, because I don't think I feel the floor beneath my feet.

"You must be Piper," Eddie says.

"We've heard so much about you," Monica adds.

I give her a nervous smile. The only way she knows anything about me is because of that big oaf standing behind me. I don't dare turn around and meet Harrison's eyes. I can only imagine what he's said.

Still, I say, "All good things, I hope."

Which in turn makes a moment of uncomfortable silence fall between us, Eddie's eyes darting over my shoulder to Harrison.

"Of course!" Monica exclaims, flashing me her pearly whites. "Here, why don't you sit down and get comfortable." She gestures to the seat while she looks over at Agatha. "Can you bring us some refreshments?" Monica looks back to me. "Would you like something to drink? Sparkling water, tea, a glass of wine?"

I'm never very good in these situations. I should say I'm fine, I don't want anything. Maybe a glass of water.

But because I'm nervous, and frankly I'm curious to see what kind of wine they drink, I say, "A glass of wine would be lovely."

"Red or white?"

"Either is fine. Whatever you have open."

"Are you sure?" Monica asks. "It's no bother. We have everything."

So much pressure. Everyone is staring at me to make a choice.

"I'll have a glass of white," I say. "Since it's finally summer and all."

"Hmmm, I think we only have sauvignon blanc chilled," she muses, looking to Agatha.

"There's a pinot grigio in the wine cooler in the cellar," Agatha says.

Monica then looks back to me for my opinion. This feels like it's already turning into a to-do. I shouldn't have said anything.

"Whatever is easiest," I tell her. "I'm not fussy."

Monica nods and gives me a small smile, probably picking up on how uncomfortable I'm feeling. "Agatha, can you get a glass of sauvignon blanc, please?"

As Agatha walks off, I look at Monica in surprise. "You're not having any?"

Perhaps it was the wrong question, because she looks uncomfortable for a moment. "No, uh, it doesn't agree with me."

"Agatha," Eddie quickly says after her, "make that two glasses." He gives me a wide grin. "I've been drinking too much beer lately; it's probably time to switch." He grabs his nonexistent belly in demonstration.

"Please, have a seat," Monica says again, gesturing to the chair as Agatha goes off toward the kitchen.

I quickly sit, feeling like I'm being a pain in the ass. I'm also still in disbelief that this is happening, like perhaps my mother put those magic mushrooms that grow in our yard in today's tea and now I'm on a hell of a trip.

Monica sits down on the love seat across from me, while Eddie sits casually on the arm of the plush couch. Harrison moves back toward the windows, though his gaze is tight on me, intense and suspicious. I do my best to ignore him.

Monica, though, must have noticed the look I gave Harrison, because she leans forward, her expression becoming warmer. "We really appreciate you coming over. I know that this all must be such a big change for you, and we want to work with you to make sure that this whole transition goes as smoothly as possible. We want to start off on the right foot, be good neighbors."

"So far, so good," I tell her. "Though, to be honest, I think we're all a little surprised that you picked this island when you could live anywhere you want."

Monica exchanges an amused look with Eddie before she smiles at me. "We get that a lot. To be honest, we're surprised that people are surprised. I mean, look at this place. It's absolutely gorgeous." She gestures to the view. "Where else in the world could you get this out your back door?"

I can think of a million places. "It's pretty now, but wait until winter comes. We don't get a lot of snow in the Pacific Northwest, but we do get months and months of rain and gloom. I'm from Victoria originally, and it took a few winters to get used to how dark it is here. When you're away from the city lights and the hustle and bustle, you really realize how alone it can feel. No wonder half the town either disappears to Mexico or Hawaii."

Oh god. I'm rambling.

"I actually like the gloom," Eddie says. "Monica here is the sun bunny."

"That's because you turn into a lobster in the sun," she points out. "So, Piper, how long have you lived here?"

"Five years. My mom and I moved so I could take a teaching position at one of the elementary schools."

"Aww." She breaks into a wide grin. Holy girl crush activated, Batman. "Which grade?"

"Second. Still sweet and innocent."

"That is so sweet. I would have loved to go into teaching if, well, you know, music didn't happen. So your mother, does she still live with you?"

People always tend to act funny when I tell them I live with my mother (though it's more the other way around, but I digress), but Monica merely seems curious.

"She does. She's got some neurological issues, so she lives with me and I pretty much support her. My father skipped out when I was a teen, so I'm really all she has."

To her credit, Monica doesn't look like she pities me. "That's admirable," she says. "I hope I can meet her soon."

I give her a polite smile, secretly hoping that never happens. My mother can be unpredictable, to say the least, and a situation like that might just set her back. She's been doing good lately but still refuses to see a therapist, and her medication seems to work half the time (probably because she forgets to take it if I don't remind her). Her whole life has been one step forward and two steps back.

Agatha appears with a tray holding two glasses of white wine, which she hands to me and Eddie, and a plate of tiny slivers of cucumber sandwiches, which she places on the table.

"If you're hungry." Monica gestures to it.

I'm not at all, but I take a sandwich, just to be polite, even though it has cream cheese, which tends to turn my stomach upside down.

"Well, it's good to know that about the winters," Monica says as I absently nibble on the sandwich sliver. "To be honest, I'm not sure how long we'll actually be here for. That's why we're renting. We're just kind of . . . figuring things out as we go along. We thought this island would be a good place to do that. Compared to back at home, the media so far has left us alone."

"You say that," I tell her, "but I've been in town, and people are losing their minds about this."

"In a good way or a bad way?" she asks, frowning. I probably should keep things positive, so I'm not sure why I'm telling them this.

I shrug. "The locals here can be . . . fussy. It's a big island, but it's a pretty odd, tight-knit community that tends to keep to themselves. I've been told it's because no one lasts very long here for one reason or another, so locals don't want to get attached. It can be . . . challenging making friends with people who gel with you. But I'm sure you'll have no problem. You know, if that's what you want."

"To be honest . . . ," she says, looking like she's trying to find the right words. She and Eddie exchange a glance. "We're okay with that. Not only because we're not sure if we're here for long, but because we really just need a break. We just want it to be the two of us. We've been shared with the public for so long, especially Eddie . . ."

"I totally understand," I tell them. "And I'll do whatever I can to help keep it that way. I'll protect your privacy. If you need someone to run errands or help out in some way, I can do it. I have summer off anyway."

"Oh, we could never expect that of you," Monica says, leaning forward and placing her hand on my knee for a second. "We have plenty of help here."

"Though it wouldn't hurt to get to know some of the island," Eddie says. "Through the eyes of someone who lives here. I know that what we crave is a step back from the limelight and some privacy, but I also know my wife, and she's going to get cabin fever pretty soon. Being locked up in here with me isn't as fun as it sounds."

Monica laughs, and from the way they're gazing at each other, it's apparent how in love and in sync these two are. I wish I could write something up about them or do another podcast, just to prove to all those tabloids and nobodies on Twitter who keep insisting that it's all a sham, that she's using him, that he's whipped or whatever misogynistic bullshit they keep spouting, that they are so far off the mark, it's not even funny.

Of course, being a good neighbor means keeping my mouth shut, as hard as that's going to be.

"The offer stands, anytime," I insist. "Anything you need, I would be happy to help."

"Well, thank you," Monica says. "You're too kind."

Harrison suddenly clears his throat, bringing our attention over to him. "There's still the matter of the NDA."

"Of course," Monica says quietly. She gives me a sheepish look. "Honestly, I hate that we have to even bring this up. I know things are going to be strange for you, especially once the media figures out where we are . . . hopefully not before the fence goes up. And really, there's no pressure for you to sign it. It would just make us feel a lot better."

"I get it," I tell her. With her asking me directly, it makes it an easy decision. Better than Harrison, anyway.

Harrison disappears into another part of the house, and then as I finish my glass of wine, Eddie asks me a few questions about outdoor activities, the best restaurants, that sort of thing. And even though I haven't for a moment forgotten who I'm talking to (a bloody prince of England!), the two of them have such an easy, zen way about them that it feels a little like talking to old friends.

Soon the sun is low in the sky, turning the water into gleaming gold, and Harrison produces the documents, placing them on the coffee table.

There's a lot of paper, and I do my best to read through each one. I don't think I need a lawyer to review anything, it seems pretty standard (I mean, I'm guessing, because I've never had to sign one of these before), although I do notice there's a little part about the fence and the gate, and I have to sign that I have no objections to either on my own property line.

When I've reached the end, I'm surprised to see another set of papers at the bottom.

"It's for your mother," Monica says. "I'm sure we'll be running into her eventually. Again, no pressure at all."

I just take the papers and smile politely, sensing that my time here is wrapping up. I'm not sure how much of this visit was to get to know me and how much was to make sure I'm not a loon. I think I may have seemed normal, but in the end, I still signed the papers. "Well, thank you so much for having me over. It's a beautiful place. Oh, and for the wine and food."

I get to my feet, and Monica does the same, her hands clasped together at her middle, as if she's not sure what to do with them. "Thank you so much for coming over. We promise we'll do our best to keep things normal around here."

"I'll show Ms. Evans out," Harrison says, walking toward the landing, as if he expects me to follow. And after I nod my thanks again to Eddie and Monica, my mother's papers firmly in hand, I walk right behind him, somehow used to him being my escort.

He opens the front door for me like a gentleman at least, slipping his sunglasses back. As we walk down the driveway, he's not talking, and I don't even do my nervous blabbering.

I'm about to say, "They seem really nice," when suddenly the sound of a drill blasts through the air. We round the corner of the driveway, and down at the bottom, where all the flatbeds are parked, there are at least a dozen construction workers, all carrying two-by-fours and digging a fence line.

"What the hell?" I say. "That was fast! How did they know?"

"I texted them the moment you signed the papers," Harrison says, nodding a greeting to one of the workers before we turn into my driveway. "The duke and duchess are used to efficiency."

"I think *you're* used to efficiency," I tell him, walking in step beside him. "They actually seem pretty chill and normal." I mumble under my breath, "Can't say the same about you."

When he doesn't say anything to that, I stop, which in turn makes him stop.

"So is this the end of this?" I ask him. He frowns in response, so I go on. "Your around-the-clock surveillance of me?"

"We've been here less than twenty-four hours," he says, folding his arms across his chest. His very wide, very manly chest. "I hardly call that around-the-clock."

"I guess I'm concerned this will be a constant thing."

"You signed the papers," he says. "And once your mother signs hers, I'll lay off."

"Oh, so now you're admitting that you're being a bit much."

"I'm not being a bit much. I'm doing my job."

"You're walking me home. You're not doing that because you're a gentleman."

His frown deepens, and he raises his chin. I think that remark may have gotten to him. "As I said, it's my job to protect them."

"Seems like you do a lot more than just protect them. I saw your pal out there on the boat earlier. I know there are men up in the trees."

I glance up to make a point, then gasp loudly when I notice a hand waving to me from high up in a Douglas fir. I can't remember if that's Isaac or Giles.

But it doesn't matter which tree man it is. I continue. "Who knows how many other security officers are about. The point is, I think you're more like their manager than anything else."

He stares at me for a moment, giving me plenty of time to focus on my reflection in his sunglasses. My hair is a bit ratty, and I wish I could have been wearing something a little nicer to meet the royals for the first time.

Finally, he says, "I'm whatever the duke and duchess need me to be. Maybe in your world you've just got your teaching, with some Tic Tac–eating tendencies thrown in there, and that's it, but in mine, it's possible to wear multiple hats at once."

Did he just try to insinuate that I have nothing going on in my life other than my job? "Hey, I wear many hats too," I tell him, unable to keep the bite out of my voice. "Maybe to you I'm just some island hick schoolteacher, but I take care of my mother when no one else will. I provide for her, I keep this house going, I've sacrificed a hell of a lot in order to stay with her and make sure she's okay. I'm a teacher, and I'm a caregiver. And I'm a daughter. And I have interests and hobbies and a rich inner world that you don't know anything about. So don't try to paint me into a box, because I don't fit in one."

My heart is pounding from all that, making me feel both alive and a little sick. I can't believe I just let that all out there like that.

Harrison continues to stare at me, then swallows. "I won't paint you into a box if you don't paint me into a box," he says, his voice low and gruff, the kind of voice that would send shivers up my spine under any other circumstances.

And he's got a point. I can dish it out, but I can't take it. Apparently that was a sore spot for me.

"Okay," I tell him, my pulse still wild in my neck. "Do you trust me enough to let me go, or do you have to walk me to the door?"

He tilts his head for a moment and then nods. "I trust you. Good night, Ms. Evans."

He then turns on his heel and marches away, disappearing around the bend.

Six

"CAN YOU PASS ME THE SAGE?" MY MOTHER ASKS, WRIST-deep in sticky dough.

I grab the sachet of herbs she'd been drying on the deck all week and sprinkle some of it out on the counter for her.

She takes a pinch and throws it into the mixing bowl, continuing to knead, her brow furrowed in concentration.

Baking is a new hobby for my mother, but it's something I wholeheartedly support. She's not the best at it yet (and neither am I, so I'm not judging), but it's edible, and it seems to really calm her down and give her something to focus on. She tends to start to follow a recipe before then throwing it out the window, choosing to get creative with flavors, herbs, and spices.

Today she's decided to do focaccia for the first time, and while I think she probably should nail down a simple bread recipe first, I'm interested in seeing where this goes.

"Can you get the buttermilk out of the fridge?" she asks me, really beating down the dough.

I pause. I'm not sure buttermilk belongs in this recipe.

"And the raisins," she adds.

More pausing.

But I get her the tiny container of buttermilk and a packet of raisins and let her have at it. Can't be worse than the savory carrot cake she made the day before.

It's been four days since the royals moved in next door, and my mother hasn't left the house once. Normally I'd be encouraging her to take a walk and get some fresh air, but this is for the best. The fence and gate are already up (I got a note on our door on royal stationery, giving us the passcode; I suppose that Harrison got the hint and is trying to put some distance between us), and a couple of media vans have already parked outside on the cul-de-sac. I've only gone out once for groceries, and that was enough to make me never want to leave again. Some reporter leaped out of the van and was practically chasing me. The Garbage Pail couldn't move fast enough.

The last thing I want is for my mother to go through that, though I know I can't avoid it forever. Just as I can't avoid giving her the papers to sign. There just doesn't seem to be a good time to tell her that the carefully crafted world she's buried herself in is becoming unearthed in a major way.

"I really think the savory quality of the sage will help bring out the sweetness in the raisins," she says to me, giving me a quick smile. I know from the look in her eyes and the way she's moving with a lot more gusto that she's swinging to the upside of her mood. Dealing with someone with BPD means erratic personality changes, far beyond what most people think of as bipolar or manic-depressive. Today she's been in a good mood, high energy, but I know her well enough to know that she's going to burn out soon. All I can do is be ready for it and try to encourage her as well as I can to stay in the moment.

"I'm sure it will taste great," I tell her genuinely. Sometimes when I try to placate her, she's quick to call me out on it (she picks up on emotions like you wouldn't believe) and it will often make things worse, sending her into a spiral. But right now she seems to believe me.

And then there's a knock at the door.

Shit.

She pauses and stares at me with big eyes. "Who could that be?"

"I'm not sure," I tell her, walking around the kitchen island toward the door. My mom is already rattled, and I have a feeling I know who it is, since we now have a buzzer at the front gate that no one has rung yet.

"Maybe it's that handsome neighbor," she says after me. "The one that looks like one of your mistakes."

I don't say anything, because it probably is Harrison, wanting those papers signed, though I would argue that none of my exes ever looked the way Harrison does.

I take in a deep breath and open the door

It's Monica, dressed in a floral sundress and ballet shoes, holding a bouquet of pale cream roses. Behind her is Harrison, same as always.

"Hi, Piper," Monica says, giving me an apologetic smile. "Sorry for barging over like this. I realized we didn't have your phone number."

I take a moment to revel in this moment. It doesn't matter that I was just with her at her house the other night, the fact that an honest-to-god princess is at my door doesn't fail to shock me.

"Who is it?" my mother asks warily from behind me.

And I'm not quick enough to close the door.

I look over my shoulder to see my mother peering at Monica and Harrison suspiciously.

This probably won't go well.

"It's the new neighbors," I tell her brightly. "This is Monica."

"How do you do?" Monica says, coming forward toward my mom, her hand extended. "I brought you flowers."

My mother stares at her, at the flowers, at her hand, then back to her face again.

My mother squints her eyes and then wipes her dough-covered hand on her apron in a rough manner, before shaking Monica's hand.

Oh god!

But Monica takes the doughy hand in stride and gives her a hearty shake.

"Thank you . . . ," my mother says to her, releasing her grip as Monica hands her the roses. Then my mother looks over at Harrison. "And you, you're back."

Harrison just nods.

"I didn't want to intrude," Monica explains. "I had met your daughter the other day and thought it would be nice to get to know you too."

Now my mother is giving me the full-on stink eye. She looks like she's seconds from blowing up. She hates not knowing things, and she's going to take this as a betrayal.

"I thought I would just drop by," Monica goes on, and it's apparent from her expression that she's worried this isn't going over well. "Eddie is in a meeting, well, a virtual meeting, with his advisors back home and—"

"Who is Eddie?" my mother asks, and oh wow, she really doesn't recognize Monica at all.

"Eddie is my husband," Monica says, not rebuffed in the slightest. "We only moved in next door a few days ago."

"Then who the hell is this guy?" my mom asks, jerking her chin at Harrison.

"He's our PPO, personal protection officer. Don't worry, his bark is worse than his bite."

And that's when it all seems to come together for my mother. She looks at Monica, looks at Harrison, looks back to Monica, and then finally to me, her brows raised.

"This isn't . . . They aren't . . . ," she says, pointing at Monica.

"Mom," I tell her calmly, putting my hand over her accusatory finger and lowering it, "this is Monica, the Duchess of Fairfax. She and her husband, Prince Eddie, have moved in next door to us."

My mom goes silent. Mouth clamped shut. This could go so many ways. She feels things so deeply that if she feels blindsided or rattled at all, she might explode in an angry rage, the kind of anger I've seen consume her countless times before.

I have no idea what's going to happen next.

Then she lets out a huff of air, like she was holding her breath too, then breaks into the biggest smile, clapping her hands together.

"I can't believe it!" she cries out. "I heard on the news you were in the area, but I never thought you would move next door to us!" She reaches out and smacks me playfully (and hard) across the arm. "Piper! Why didn't you tell me? This is amazing." She gestures to the house. "Please, please come in."

Oh no.

"It's quite all right, I don't want to be a bother," Monica says, shaking her head, but I know she's doomed. My mother won't stop.

"I insist, I insist," my mother says, and then she reaches down and grabs Monica by the elbow and pulls her up the stairs, leading her inside.

Harrison immediately springs into action, but I manage to

step in front of him, putting out my hands. "It's okay. She's a lot
to handle, but she's okay."

He doesn't seem to listen, instead brushing past my hands
and following Monica and my mother inside.

I exhale, pushing my fingertips at my temples in a futile attempt to steady myself, then follow them all inside.

My mother is at the sink, washing her hands, while Monica is
crouched down in the hallway, getting sloppy kisses from a very
happy, wriggly Liza.

"Oh, she's adorable," Monica says, even as Liza attempts to
jump up on her.

"Liza, get down," I tell her, coming over and grabbing Liza by
the collar and trying to haul her away. "I'm so sorry, she doesn't
realize who you are."

Monica laughs, still petting her. "I rather like that. Now I
know it's genuine."

Liza continues to lick her, then turns her attention on me.
Then notices Harrison lurking in the corner of the living room.

The hair on Liza's back raises, and I can tell she's ready to
bark.

"Shhh," I tell her, whispering in a soothing voice. "It's okay,
Liza. That's just Harrison. He looks creepy and constipated, but
as the duchess said, his bark is apparently worse than his bite."

"Constipated?" Harrison repeats, his brows raised.

I quickly look at Monica, knowing that I just insulted her
PPO, but she's biting back a smile.

"Okay, I'm ready now," my mom announces, coming over to
us. "How about a tour?"

"Mom, this *is* the tour," I say, letting go of Liza and straightening up. I gesture to the house. "This is it."

"Nonsense," my mother says, and she walks over to the sliding doors to the deck, beckoning for Monica to follow. "Come see our deck."

Monica obliges, stepping out onto the shady deck covered in pine needles, the deck with no view. Liza runs after them.

I stay put, leaning back against the kitchen island, trying to ignore the mess behind me. I didn't really notice until now, but there is flour absolutely everywhere, like the bag exploded. Broken eggs, herbs, and spilled salt are scattered along the counter.

You know how when people really tidy their house, people joke about the Queen coming to visit? Well, we have an actual duchess in our house, and it looks like a disaster zone.

I sigh at the mess and turn back around to see Harrison still standing in the corner. "I'm surprised you're not running out to the deck to make sure Monica doesn't get a splinter or something."

He grunts. Like a caveman in a suit. Then comes walking over to me.

I stiffen, wondering if I've taken things too far, though I can't imagine what he'd do. Can he arrest me for being a pain in the ass? Can he arrest anyone? And why can't he wear his sunglasses inside? His eyes are far too distracting.

He stops a foot away, close enough for me to smell that woodsy, fresh cologne of his, the kind of cologne that makes my stomach do a curious flip, then looks over my shoulder at the kitchen. "What's happening in here?"

"My mother's attempt at baking," I tell him.

"She any good?"

I don't want to throw my mom under the bus. "Sure is." I pause. "For a beginner."

He nods, and to my surprise, he walks past me over to the counter where the baking science experiment is. "What is she making?" he asks as he peers into a bowl. "Scones?"

"Focaccia bread." I walk over to him, my arms crossed and already defensive.

He cocks an eyebrow, his forehead wrinkling. "I see." He looks over at the buttermilk. "I hope she didn't put that in there."

"Why? Maybe it's her secret ingredient."

"It'll make the dough too wet. She should be using honey if she needs a bit of sweetness. Has she added the yeast yet?"

I stare at him. "Since when do you know anything about baking?"

He gives me a wry look. "Let's not repeat our little argument from the other day about being able to wear many hats."

"So you're a bodyguard, a royal consultant, and a baker?"

He gives me a small smile. "It's just something I used to have an interest in."

I look him up and down, my eyes coasting over his well-suited, mammoth frame. "You don't look like you'd have baking as a hobby."

"I'm sure this is no surprise to you, but looks can be deceiving, can't they?"

"Oh dear!" my mother cries out from behind me. I turn to see her, Monica, and Liza stepping back into the house. My mother comes over, flapping her hands anxiously.

"It's such a mess, I'm so sorry," she says.

"It's quite all right," Harrison tells her. "I was just curious about your baking process here. Seems very creative."

Thankfully, to Harrison's credit, his voice is warm and genuine.

"Oh," my mother says, blushing. "Well, I'm just trying new things. I like to keep busy, you know, new hobbies. Last month it was crochet, I made a sweater—want to see?"

"Mom," I warn her, but it's too late and she's scurrying off to her bedroom.

"Sorry," I apologize. "Once she gets her mind set on something . . ." I look at Monica. "And sorry about the tour."

"There's nothing to be sorry about, Piper," she says. "Your mother is delightful. Actually, the reason I came over was to invite you both to dinner tomorrow night. If you're free. And want to, of course."

I blink at her. Even after all this she's inviting us to dinner?

I glance at Harrison, but he merely nods.

"Well, yeah. Of course. We would love to," I tell her, trying to keep my enthusiasm at an acceptable level.

"Great," Monica says, and then takes her cell phone out of her pocket. "Can we exchange numbers? Might be easier than me having to show up at your door. And vice versa of course."

Unless I felt like being attacked by one of her tree guards.

Regardless, I can't believe she wants to exchange numbers with me. I tell her my phone number, and she quickly sends a text. My phone beeps from the living room table.

"And now you have mine," she says with a bright smile.

"I found it!" my mother cries out, carrying what looks to be a heap of dark green material. "I made a sweater."

My mother is slightly overweight and on the short side, and when she unravels the sweater and holds it up, the arms and shoulders are way too broad for her. "Here," she says to Harrison, pushing the sweater into his hands. "You take it. It will fit you."

"Uh," he says, totally caught off guard. "I can't accept this."

He tries to give it back, but my mother pushes it away. "I insist! You're a new neighbor too; this is my gift to you." She looks over at Monica. "How about I bake you something for tomorrow? Don't get any dessert, it's on me."

"Mom," I whine under my breath. "Please."

"Oh, it's no bother, Piper," she says. She blinks at Harrison. "You're taking the sweater, right?"

Harrison shoots Monica a quick glance. An impish smile plays on her lips, and she gives him a faint nod.

"Of course," Harrison says, folding the sweater under his arm. "I'm honored to accept this gift."

"Good, good," my mother says, clapping her hands together. She's positively manic right now. "Oh, can I make you tea? I make my own teas. All kinds, all from my garden."

"That's quite all right," Monica says. "We actually have to head back. I'm wanted on the back end of that meeting."

"Are you sure?"

"*Mom . . .*"

"Sorry again to intrude like this," Monica says, heading to the door along with Harrison. "But I'm so glad we were finally able to come over and meet you. I look forward to dinner tomorrow."

She gives me a wave goodbye, and I can only smile back, all of this feeling like I'm stuck in a whirlwind.

"Oh, me too," my mother says, walking after her, Liza on her heels. She pauses at the door and watches as they walk off. "Have a good day, Princess!"

She closes the door, and I'm already shaking my head.

"She's a duchess, Mom, not a princess." Even though I've been calling her a princess in my head.

"Oh whatever, it's all the same," she says, turning to me with a huge grin, her eyes as wide as saucers. "Piper. Piper, can you believe it? I can't believe it. Oh, I haven't been this excited about anything in years."

I shouldn't feel slighted by that, but I do. "Not even my wedding?"

She waves her hands at me dismissively. "No, no. We all knew that was going to end in heartache. That Joey is a rat bastard."

The mention of Joey makes me stall, old pent-up feelings flooding me like a raging torrent that I'm unable to keep back. "Oh, you knew, did you?" I know I should keep my mouth shut and stop myself from spiraling like this in front of my mother, especially when I know it won't go anywhere good. But I can't help myself. "Did you know he was going to cheat on me the night of his bachelor party? Did you know I'd leave him at the altar? You knew all that?"

She gives me a pleading look. "Please, Piper, let's not rehash this now. What's done is done. You didn't marry him, and it was for the best. Focus on the positive. We have royals for neighbors. We're going over to their house tomorrow for dinner. Oh my god, I have to figure out how to make a cake!"

At that she whirls back into the kitchen and starts making a mess of things. Meanwhile, my own heart is feeling a bit of a mess, so I go out onto the deck and stare at the trees, glimpses of the ocean and the light breeze managing to come through.

I really shouldn't dwell on my past, not now of all times. But I guess I can't help but feel it's all tying together. The duke and duchess are my neighbors now, they have my phone number and I have theirs, I've been invited over for dinner, but the truth is, I'm nowhere near being worthy of any of this. All it took was one little reminder of my past to bring me down into an unworthy shame spiral, something I thought I'd gotten better at avoiding, but I suppose not. I'm pretty much, as Harrison said, a Tic Tac–popping schoolteacher. One who had to leave her fiancé at the altar in front of the whole damn town. I'm in no way prepared to be hanging out with royal company.

And yet you are, I tell myself. *And they don't need to know all the gritty bits about you. Even if Monica is just being nice for the sake of being nice, this is still happening to you.*

I know when that positive inner voice pops up, it's all because of the work I've done with my therapists. I've also learned to embrace that voice instead of pushing it away, instead of thinking I'm not deserving of it.

So I listen. I straighten up my shoulders, walk back into the house, and prepare to help my mom with this cake for tomorrow.

Seven

THE NEXT DAY I WAKE UP EARLIER THAN USUAL, NEEDING a walk to clear my head.

I slip on my leggings and a hoodie, since it can sometimes be chilly in the mornings near the water, and head out of my bedroom.

Liza sleeps with my mom most nights, and the door is open, my mom snoring like a rusty chainsaw. She crashed pretty early last night, after we played around with a few cake recipes (all of them looking like a Pinterest fail, but hey), and I hope that her energy carries through today. I wouldn't be at all surprised, though, if she backed out of the dinner—and the cake—at the last minute.

I pick up Liza's leash, and that's all she needs to come running out of the room, her tail going Mach 5. We head out of the house, enjoying the quiet of the morning, peppered with lapping waves and the calls of Gary birds (not their actual name, but it sounds like they're constantly yelling for Gary).

The serenity is ruined the moment I step through the new pedestrian gate.

"Who is that?!"

"It's their dog walker!"

"It's the help!"

The cul-de-sac is filled with cars and news vans, and to be honest, it looks a bit like a campsite. There are fold-out chairs, collapsible tables with checkered plastic tablecloths, propane stoves, and barbecues. Seconds earlier, the reporters and camerapeople had been hovered around a giant French press, pouring coffee into tin mugs and paper cups.

Now, they're all running toward me, fumbling for their cameras and phones, coffee sloshing over the cups and splattering on the pavement.

Meanwhile, sweet Liza is in full-on panic mode. The hair on her back is raised, and she's growling. I'll admit, I normally hate it when she does this. She's not dangerous in the slightest, but she looks like she is, and pits already have a needless bad rap. I'll usually soothe the people we pass on our walks by telling them the truth, that she's a rescue, that she's a sweet girl, but she has people issues (I mean, don't we all?). But now? I know that the dog is all that's keeping these vultures from swarming me.

"What's your name?" a petite woman with severe blond bangs asks me, thrusting out a microphone while warily eyeing Liza.

"Do you work for the duke and duchess?" asks a man with a cigarette dangling from his mouth, the ash a mile long, while he aims his phone at me.

I immediately put my hand in front of my face, shielding it from the camera, just as more reporters start recording me. With Liza's barking and my hand in front of my face, at least I'm not giving them any good material.

Except . . . shit.

This *is* good material, isn't it? The mysterious, flustered girl with bedhead that rivals Cousin Itt, caught outside the secret royal house, having just come through the gate with her out-of-control pit bull.

"What is your name?" someone else asks.

I know I shouldn't answer, but I need them to leave me alone.

"Piper!" I cry out, tugging back on the leash. "And this is Liza, and we'd very much like to go for our morning walk without being harassed by the paparazzi."

The cigarette man snorts, the ash finally breaking away into the wind. "Paparazzi? Ma'am, I work for Channel 6 News. We're local."

I squint at him briefly. He does look familiar. It doesn't matter, though.

"Then you should know that *I'm* local," I tell him, and jerk my thumb to the gates. "I live there and share a property line with the duke and duchess. I'm just a schoolteacher, for crying out loud."

"So you admit it!" the blonde says, her appearance morphing into that of a cat about to pounce on a mouse. I'm quite obviously the mouse. "The duke and duchess live there!"

And now I've said too much.

"Uhhh," I mumble, and then spin around, my back to them, changing my focus to Liza. I'm wondering if I dare keep going for my walk or just run back to the property like the coward I am.

But before I can make any panicked decisions, the automatic gates start to open and excited chatter begins to spread among the vultures. They forget me and start swarming toward the gate, just as a black SUV comes cruising down the driveway.

It goes through the gate, cameras recording its every move, and then the back door opens wide and Harrison is in the back seat, staring at me with his usual gruff expression.

"Get in," he says, a total command.

I quickly glance down at Liza, who seems more in shock now than anything, and before anyone can get one more picture of us, I'm scooping her heavy weight into my arms and practically throwing her into the car.

I scramble inside after her, slamming the door as the vehicle pulls away, the cameras still recording.

"What the bloody hell was that?" Harrison says to me as I fiddle with my seat belt.

I pause. My eyes go wide, brows to the ceiling. Even Liza, who is crammed in between us, looks aghast.

"What do you mean?" I practically hiss. "I was taking Liza for a walk and suddenly it was a paparazzi free-for-all out there. I'm fine, by the way, thanks for asking."

He's not wearing his sunglasses yet, but even so, he turns his head away, looking out the window so I can't see his eyes. Silence fills the vehicle.

I frown at him, feeling anxious and all out of sorts, then try to get a better look at our driver in the rearview mirror. He's wearing square glasses and has thinning gray hair. He reminds me a bit of Anderson Cooper. He gives my reflection a stiff smile and then goes back to driving. Of course, I have no idea where we are going or why. I'm just glad to be out of that situation, even though this one doesn't feel that much better.

Safer? Yes.

Less awkward? No. Definitely not.

Meanwhile, Liza is shaking next to me.

"Poor girl," I whisper to her, pulling her upper half onto my lap and holding her. "That wasn't very fun, was it?"

I run my hand over the top of her head, trying to calm her, and feel Harrison's eyes on me as he shifts in his seat.

"It's okay, girl," I say, continuing to soothe her.

"She doesn't do well with new people?" Harrison asks.

I shoot him a sharp look. "I don't think anyone does well with being accosted by the media the minute you step outside your property. Not her, certainly not me."

He stares at me for a moment, his brow furrowed, as if what I just said confused him somehow. "I told you you'd be grateful for that gate."

"Do you expect me to be grateful that I need that gate to begin with? No."

He raises his chin and looks forward. "You signed the papers."

"As if I could prevent you from moving there."

One brow raises, but he still faces forward. "None of this was my choice. You knew this was going to happen."

"Yeah, well, doesn't mean I have to like it," I tell him. It doesn't escape me that I was quite okay with Monica and Eddie moving here up until this very moment, but that whole encounter with the media really rattled me.

I turn my attention back to Liza, who is calming down now, apparently not too worried that we're being whisked away somewhere. "Where are we going, anyway?"

"To town."

"Do I have a choice in this?"

He finally looks at me. "My apologies. Shall I have Matthew pull over and let you out?"

"So I can walk right back into that again? You know, I was trying to tell them that I'm just a local schoolteacher. Now they've seen me get in your car—they're not going to believe it."

"I suppose I could have just left you out there," he says with a sigh, briefly examining his nails, which in turn makes me gawk at his hands. Damn him for having such nice hands.

I open my mouth and close it again. He did just save me from a brutal situation, but it's a situation he's put me in, inadvertently or not.

Instead of saying anything to that, I go back to stroking Liza. "So why are you heading to town?"

He clears his throat, looking back out the window as we drive out of Scott Point and pass by a ferry terminal. "Groceries."

I stare dumbly at him for a second before I fight the smile on my face. "Groceries? They're making you get the groceries? Isn't that Agatha's job?"

"She's busy with the house, and I didn't want to disturb her this morning," he says curtly. "So I volunteered."

I don't know why I find it so funny. Perhaps because I can't imagine Harrison in his pressed slick suit perusing the aisles of the Country Grocer at eight thirty in the morning. Then again, he did surprise me with his knowledge of baking yesterday.

His posture is stiff now, his shoulders held tensely, his jaw set on edge. I probably only find it funny because it seems to bother him so much.

I clear my throat. "Might I ask which grocery store you're going to? We have two."

"The one by the marina?" he asks, sounding unsure.

"It depends on what you're getting."

He makes a gruff sound of resignation and pulls out a slip of folded paper from his breast pocket, sticking it out with a flick of his fingers.

I reach over and pluck it from him. I unfold it and quickly read it over.

It's written on royal stationery.

Organic apples.

Saltine crackers.
Leg of lamb.
Rosemary.
Potatoes.
Tetley tea.
Ingredients for a charcuterie board.

I flip it over. The list goes on and on. Seemingly not just for tonight's meal, but at least a full week's worth of groceries for at least four people.

"Okay, well," I tell him, handing it back, "you're going to want to go to a few different stores if you want it good enough to please the royals."

"I'm sure they won't be too picky."

I give him an amused smile. "I think you've forgotten who you work for. Even if they aren't picky, isn't it your job to find them the best of the best?"

He stares at me, and his eyes are as unreadable as they are when he's wearing his sunglasses. I'm sure he doesn't appreciate my telling him what his job is. Oh well.

"Fine," he grumbles after a moment. "You lead the way."

My pleasure. I get the driver to take us to the two big grocery stores, as well as the smaller all-organic one (picture Whole Foods, but somehow more expensive and smells like palo santo). After I convinced the driver that Liza would be fine to hang out in the back seat as long as he stayed in the car, I became somewhat of a foodie tour guide for Harrison. As we walked down the aisles, quiet in the early morning, I grabbed a lot of local delicacies—basil and truffle goat cheeses that melt in your mouth, sweet-and-spicy fruit jams like raspberry habanero, delicate smoked salts, and luxurious old-fashioned ice cream. I showed Harrison the best butcher to get our famous Salt Spring Island lamb, and the best organic produce from nearby farms.

Finally, after we loaded up the SUV with the bags, I asked if I could buy him a coffee.

"I beg your pardon?" he asks me as he closes the trunk.

"You drink coffee, don't you?" I ask. "Oh wait, it's tea. Can I buy you a tea?"

Since we've been outside, his sunglasses are back in place, but judging from that frown, he's totally perplexed by this idea.

To be honest, I am too. What am I doing?

"I drink coffee," he says after a minute, as if it took him that long to put it together. I'm about to tell him to forget it, lest the rejection start to sink in, but he nods. "I would love one."

"Oh." I mouth the word and then give him a crooked smile. "Right this way."

We walk through the parking lot and down the street toward Salty Seas Coffee & Goods. The streets are a little busier now, the tourists having woken up in their "charming and rustic" Airbnbs, ready to infiltrate the town to look for food and hot beverages.

"Your mother isn't going to think you've been kidnapped?" Harrison asks as we cross the one-way street. "Took the dog for a walk and never came back."

I hesitate before giving him a quick smile. "She'll be asleep for a while. Meeting Monica was a bit much for her."

"Is she going to be okay for tonight?"

I cross my fingers and hold them up to him. "Hopefully." I quickly add, "I'm sure she will be." I don't want Harrison to think that this dinner is for nothing.

It's busy this morning at the café, with the line snaking out the door. I'm about to tell Harrison we should go to another one when I spot their sandwich sign announcing they have donuts today.

"Ooh yay, donuts!" I let out a squeal loud enough for the people in the line in front of us to turn around and look at me. Then they look at Harrison. I've seen this look from people all morning. It's the "Who is this tall, handsome, built-like-a-truck man in a suit?" Followed by the "And why is he with this frizzy-haired Oompa-Loompa squealing like a pig about donuts?"

To Harrison's credit, he doesn't seem fazed. He's most likely used to me by now.

"Donuts?" he asks calmly.

"The best donuts," I tell him, ignoring the people still watching us. Probably tourists, anyway. "Almost as good as their cinnamon buns, but they only make them once every few weeks."

He nods. "Ah yes, the infamous cinnamon bun."

My cheeks go hot at the memory of it all stuck in my hair. Really ought to start wearing a ponytail when I'm around sweet and sticky pastries.

"Tell you what," he says. "You buy me a coffee, I'll buy you a donut."

I can't help but grin up at him. "You have yourself a deal, mister."

A strange giddiness flashes through me, and I have to check myself. I get giddy about a lot of things in life (I mean, look at me and food), but the fact that Harrison is buying me a donut shouldn't be one of them. It's a bad, terrible, no-good sign to feel giddy because of something a man does. Something that Harrison does.

And yet . . .

I temper my smile as the line moves and we find ourselves inside the coffee shop. My mind wants to focus on him next to me. I want to inspect him closely, look for those signs of the hid-

den tattoos, figure out if the bracing sea scent is from his cologne
or body wash, study the faint scar on his cheekbone, half hidden
beneath his stubble.

I'm about to remind myself that I'm staring, and that he definitely knows it, when I hear my name being called.

A shudder runs through me. I don't even have to look to know.

In fact, I make a point of not looking until Harrison nudges
me with his elbow.

"I believe this man knows you," he says.

I sigh quietly and turn to see Joey standing by the cash, a coffee and a pastry bag in his hand. Joey is smiling at me expectantly, in that way of his, as if I'm just some buddy he happened
to run into and not his ex-fiancée.

"Hey," I say to Joey, giving him a polite smile and nod, the
bare minimum. I don't want to get into a conversation with him,
especially with Harrison here. In fact, I lean in a little closer to
Harrison, hoping that Joey will assume we're together or something and just leave.

Alas, he does not. He leans against the coffee table across
from the cash, much to the annoyed detriment of the woman sitting there and reading a guidebook, and gives me the once-over.

"You're looking good, Pipes."

I cringe. So many things to unpack here. First of all, he called
me Pipes, which was his nickname for me, something no one else
called me (for good reason, because it's stupid); second of all, the
way he's looking at me and the way he dropped that compliment
makes it obvious that no one thinks Harrison and I are together,
let alone him, and somehow that stings.

"Thanks," I say stiffly, just as the person in front of us finishes
their order and then I'm up next at the cash.

My relief is short-lived. I open my mouth to put in my order, hoping that by putting all my attention on the barista, Joey will leave.

But instead, the barista is Amy Mischky. She's the sullen, gossipy, twentysomething daughter of Barbara Mischky, who is famous for her letters to the editor that somehow always get printed in our newspaper, often in the vain of "But who will think of the children?" And if I, a teacher of the children, think she's a pearl-clutching charlatan, then that tells you all you need to know. In short, both Mischkys love to know your business, spread it around, and slander you with it.

"Oh my god," Amy says in her low, dry voice. "This is soooo awkward."

My brows go up. "What?"

She looks over at Joey and then back at me, her small lips quirking into a smirk. "I haven't seen the two of you together since you left him at the altar."

My cheeks burn again, and I feel Harrison stiffen next to me, no doubt shocked by this. Or maybe not.

"Oh, that was ages ago," Joey speaks up, walking over so he's right beside me, now leaning against the counter. "Let bygones be going on."

"You mean let bygones *be bygones*?" I say.

He chuckles like an idiot. "And that's why you're the teacher." Then his gaze goes over my head to Harrison. "What's up, man? You new here?"

It takes Harrison a moment to reply. "Just visiting." Those two words sound crisp and authoritative coming from him.

Joey seems to pick up on it. He nods. "Well, cool. Hope you like the island. Tell Piper to take you to the Blowhole. Next Friday should be good." He looks at me. "You'll come, won't you, Piper? You always said you loved the band—well, the band is better than ever. Tell you what, I'll give you a free drink ticket. On the house."

"Oooh, well, well, well," Amy says, her eyes darting between us with a look of wry contempt on her face. "The two of you seem to be on the mend. You know, I would have thought you'd stay enemies until the end of time. Or at least until you decided to pack up and leave, Piper."

I blink at her. Pack up and leave? She thought I'd pack up and leave?

"But," she continues smoothly, her eyes twinkling at Joey, "guess that's not the case. How nice. It's good to have a real sense of community here, isn't it? I mean, just because you left him at the altar like that and ran away doesn't mean you'll continue to run away from all your problems."

I hate that she's said that, because her words are making me want to turn on my heel and run. In fact, as my gaze drops away from her triumphant one, I feel my body starting to turn.

Except Harrison steps closer to me, his body blocking me.

"Is this how business on this island is usually run, with a side of gossip?" Harrison asks Amy. His voice is so stern and commanding that she blinks up at him, her mouth dropping a little. "Shouldn't you be taking our order?"

Flustered, Amy hastily tucks a strand of her long brown hair behind her ear and looks down at the cash, avoiding Harrison's gaze. "Yes, of course. What will you have?"

"I'll have two donuts and an Americano, large," Harrison says, then, to my surprise, gently rests his hand on my shoulder. "What will you have, Piper?"

I clear my throat. Having his hand on me is making me feel

even more off-balance somehow. "A donut and a lavender oat-milk latte. Please."

Amy nods and puts the order in with the other workers.

Harrison gives my shoulder a squeeze.

I can feel the strength coming back to me. I take in a deep breath through my nose and exhale slowly. Harrison is already paying and I'm not about to make a fuss about it here, the fact that I was supposed to buy him a coffee, not the other way around, and I bring my eyes over to Joey.

He's staring at me unsurely, like he wants to ask me something else but can't find the words.

When Harrison is done paying, he puts his hand at the small of my back and guides me over to the wall to wait for our coffees, while the next people in line step up to order.

Joey watches us for a moment, then shrugs and heads out of the café without saying anything.

"You good?" Harrison leans in and whispers to me. His tone is gruff, but I appreciate his asking all the same.

I nod, pressing my lips together into a thin smile. I have too many thoughts to process, too many feelings, none of them good. It feels like the whole café is staring at me, even if they aren't, and I hate that even though I keep to myself as a self-proclaimed hermit, my situation with Joey is what I'm most known for on this rock.

It feels like forever before our order is up. Harrison isn't one for small talk, and it's not until I'm outside in the fresh sunshine that I feel myself relax even a little.

"Want to talk about it?" Harrison asks me as we cross the road to the parking lot.

I stare at him in shock. "About what?"

His brow raises. "About what happened in there?"

I shake my head. I should explain what happened between Joey and me, what led to my leaving him at the altar, but it suddenly feels too raw.

"It's none of my business," he says quickly. "I understand."

"It's not that . . . ," I tell him, but we've already reached the car, and he's opening the back door for me. His expression is grim and made of stone, back into bodyguard mode.

Conversation over.

Eight

"OKAY, THE MOMENT OF TRUTH IS UPON US," MY MOTHER says, wiggling her fingers together like Mr. Burns. "Are you ready?"

"As I'll ever be."

My mother bends down and opens the oven, sticking her mitts in and pulling out the cake.

I'm prepared for the worst, so when I see that it's retained its shape and looks brown and fluffy, I sigh in relief.

"It looks lovely," I tell her.

"Doesn't it?" she asks proudly, sliding it onto the rack. "The hard part is yet to come."

She brings out the icing she had made earlier, icing that had hardened slightly into chunks in the fridge. "Hmmm, seems a little stiff," she says. Then shrugs. "No matter."

I watch as she frosts the cake, but I'm no longer thinking about the fact that the frosting is spreading on like chunky concrete, and more about what happened earlier.

After we got our coffees, Harrison had the driver take us back home. The cul-de-sac was swarming with more of the media, and we pulled in through the gates just as Bert in his RCMP vehicle showed up, hopefully to get everyone to move.

When the SUV dropped us off on our driveway, Liza seemed beyond confused. The weirdest, longest non-walk she'd ever been on.

Harrison then said, "See you at seven."

And that was it. Door closed. Off they went.

When I got back in the house, my mom was just starting to get up. I didn't want to worry her with my paparazzi woes, so I said I had just taken Liza for a walk. Then she brought up the fact that I needed to go into town to get ingredients for the cake.

The last thing I wanted right then was to leave the premises, so I told my mother we could easily make do with whatever ingredients we had left over in the house.

So if the icing looks a little chunky, and if the cake tastes a little weird, it's probably my fault.

My mother, thankfully, is in a great mood, which is why she's happily slapping that frosting on without a care in the world. She's not nervous at all about the dinner, just excited, which she's told me at least every hour.

"Shouldn't you go get ready?" she says to me. She has frosting on her cheek.

I motion for her to wipe it away, but her attention goes back to the cake. She's right, anyway. Despite the frosting on her face, she's wearing a nice beaded blue tunic with matching slacks, and her hair is smooth.

I, on the other hand, am still wearing what I was wearing earlier. It wasn't a good look for running into my ex, and it's not a good look for dinner at the royals'.

I go into my bedroom and stare at the clothes in my closet. I know I was over there just the other day, but this feels more formal, seems more special. Eventually I settle on a yellow maxi dress with tiny white flowers, a flattering neckline, and billowy sleeves. If I pull my hair up into a topknot and wear some makeup, I might just look elegant, enough to fool them anyway.

When I'm ready, I throw Liza a treat to keep her occupied while we're gone, and we head outside, my mother holding the cake. It isn't until we're at the fork of our driveway that we're able to see the cul-de-sac. I see the cop car, but I don't see any of the media, so maybe Bert scared them away, or maybe they'll only stay away as long as he's there. My mother doesn't even look that way, keeping her eyes focused on the landscaping as we head up their driveway, oohing and aahing at the flowers.

Obviously I can't hide the media chaos from her forever, and she's not stupid. She's going to understand and most likely expect all of that to come with having royals next door. But even so, I'm protective over her, maybe when I shouldn't be, and just want to keep everything about our lives at an even keel for as long as possible.

Even though we're about to have dinner with British royalty.

"I never got a good look at this place before," my mother says in awe. "It's beautiful. And it's so light and airy." She briefly turns around and aims her face at the evening sun, her eyes closed. "Hard to believe we live just a few feet away."

Seeing my mom outside like this makes me want to take her on more hikes, get her out of the house more often, even if we have to deal with the paparazzi when we do so. Maybe Bert could be an escort or . . .

Before I can vocalize this to her, the door opens and Agatha appears.

"Good evening," she says to us. "Please come in."

My mother and I take off our shoes in the hallway and then follow Agatha down the steps to the living area, where Monica and Eddie are standing beside each other, smiling.

Monica, of course, looks gorgeous in a pastel-orange dress not too dissimilar to mine, her hair pulled into a smooth low bun, her face with barely any makeup, and Eddie is wearing a navy polo shirt and dark jeans. I exhale when I realize that this dinner isn't going to be too fancy for us.

"I am so glad you came," Monica says, clasping her hands at her stomach, looking at the both of us.

But my mother is starstruck, this time by Prince Eddie.

I mean, how can she not be? He grew up before her very eyes on the television, and now he's standing right in front of her.

"She baked you a cake," I say, taking the cake from my mother's hands and handing it to Monica. "Sorry, she's catatonic."

Monica laughs. "I'm used to it. People are always so enchanted when they first meet Eddie. Can't say I blame them. I felt the same way." She pauses and gives him a sweet smile. "Still do."

Argh. They are the *cutest*.

"It's a pleasure to meet you, Mrs. Evans," Eddie says, reaching out. He grasps my mother's hand between both of his, looks her warmly in the eye, and gives her a hearty shake.

My mother died a little inside. She makes a squeak that sounds like "thank you."

"Now if you will pardon me," Eddie says, "I have to tend to the lamb. I hope that's all right with you? I made a vegan casserole if not."

Oh my god. This prince is full of surprises. "You did the cooking?"

He grins. "I had a little help, don't worry. With some luck, it will be edible."

Eddie walks off to the kitchen, while Agatha waits patiently beside us.

"What would you like to drink?" Monica asks, gesturing to the chairs.

"Whatever you're having," I say, noting the glass beside her.

I swear she blushes. "This is just sparkling water. Do you drink wine, Mrs. Evans?"

"Please call me Evelyn," my mother says. "And actually, I'll go for a sparkling water too."

I'm proud of my mom. She's not supposed to drink on her medication, though she often reaches for wine when she gets upset or nervous, and it hits her hard and makes everything that much worse. Tonight she's showing restraint, which makes me think I should do the same out of solidarity.

"I'll have the same," I say.

"Piper," my mom quickly says. "Please. Have your wine. I'm fine; so is Monica."

"A nice cab sav would go really well with the lamb," Monica says.

"Then I'll have it with dinner," I concede. "Sparkling water is fine for now."

Agatha goes off with our order, and I glance up and down the halls. "Where is Harrison?"

Usually he's hovering over me by now.

"He's down by the water," Monica says. Her face softens. "I heard about what happened today. Harrison told me."

"What happened today?" my mother asks. "You've been home all day."

I glance uneasily at Monica, who looks slightly embarrassed. I guess it serves me right for keeping secrets from my mother.

"Actually, it happened this morning. When I took Liza for a walk . . ."

My mom waits expectantly for me to go on. I look down at my hands, not wanting to look at her or at Monica, who must feel bad for bringing it up. "There was a media circus outside the house. On the road. I was lucky that Harrison was heading to the grocery store at that time. Was able to rescue me, I guess."

"I feel awful," Monica says. "I know how the press can be, and for you to be subjected to that . . ."

"It's okay," I tell her quickly, giving her a reassuring smile. "I'll get used to it. And just now I saw Bert's car out there, the cop. It was just him, no one else was there."

"Why didn't you tell me this?" my mother asks softly, obviously hurt by the omission.

"Because I didn't want you to get upset."

"But I'd find out eventually, wouldn't I? Is that why you didn't want to go back into town? You were afraid?"

"Really, I'm so sorry," Monica says. "When we decided on this place, I didn't think that it would affect anyone but us. I had hoped the media would stay away."

I give her a wan smile. "You're the biggest news to happen here, ever. More so than when a pod of orcas swam into the harbor, or when someone's herd of llamas got loose and took over the town."

"Don't forget the Fall Fair, when Buzz McClaren grew that giant watermelon," my mother points out. "Bigger news than *that*."

"I'll deal, is what I'm saying," I tell Monica. "Besides, so far they all seemed local or at least Canadian. They were annoying, but I can't imagine they're any worse than what you had to deal with back home."

"And I'll gladly tell those buzzards to go fly a kite," my mother says. She's on her best behavior now, so when my mother says go fly a kite, what she's really going to say is *fuck off.* The media will go nuts with that.

"I think I should talk to all the neighbors on this road," Monica says, looking flustered, her brow knitting together with worry. "I would hate for this to become a problem for them too."

"I'm sure everyone can handle themselves," I tell her. Since I don't know the people on this road very well, I have no idea if that would be a good idea or not. "I'm sure things will die down."

"I hope so," Monica says after a moment, giving Agatha a stiff smile as she hands us all sparkling waters from her tray.

"Well, cheers to this, to my new neighbors," Monica says, raising her glass. "I'll try to keep the conversation lighter."

But as we finish our drinks and then head over to the dining room table, with candles glowing from gilded cages and a driftwood centerpiece, and Agatha starts to bring out the food, the conversation turns serious again.

"So, Eddie," my mother asks between bites. "Sorry." She gives him a quick smile. "Prince Eddie."

He gives her a dismissive wave and smiles. "Don't worry about it. My closest friends call me Eddie, not Prince Eddie. I prefer to hear the former these days. Makes me feel like we really did escape from that world."

My mother nods. "I was curious as to, well, if you miss anything about back home?"

"Not yet," he says. "But give it some time."

"The press has been awful to you, especially you, Monica," she says. "Bunch of racists."

"Mom," I warn her. "Let's not talk about it at dinner, please."

"It's okay," Monica says. "Really. There are lots of microaggressions in the press—"

Eddie lets out a derisive snort.

"What?" Monica says. "It's true."

"Some of the tabloids are just out to fucking get you, my dear." A flush of anger comes across his fair cheeks. "My apologies. I should be used to it. I am used to it. But not this. Not the way they hound you, write slander about you, all because you don't fit what their idea of a bloody royal is."

"Sounds like a lot of them need to catch up to the current century," my mother comments.

"You can say that again," Monica says. "But I knew it would be like that. I may be new to the monarchy, but it's not my first rodeo when it comes to the press and the public's expectations of you. Racism, microaggressions, it's nothing new, and I still decided to be with Eddie because our love is worth all that strife."

"But we also deserve a damn vacation," Eddie says. He gestures to the view. Then he gestures to my mother and me. "And we deserve to have a good dinner with new friends. How about we make another toast, then?"

We raise our glasses.

Soon after, dessert is served. My mother's cake actually turned out okay, considering, and both the royals eat at least half of theirs. I finish the whole slice, just so my mother won't have a complex.

I get up, head over to the window, and see Harrison down at the dock, the sun reflecting gold off the water. His back is to me, his hands clasped behind him, and he's facing into the distance. I know he has a job to do, but it doesn't feel right to have him all the way down there, especially after we had that beautiful meal, one that he contributed to in some way, even if it was just to get the groceries.

"Is it against the rules if I bring Harrison some cake?" I ask, turning around.

Monica laughs. "The rules? No. I'm sure he'd appreciate that."

"The man has a sweet tooth like you wouldn't believe," Eddie says with a boyish smile.

Interesting.

I head into the kitchen, where Agnes is putting dishes away, and she helps me put a slice of cake onto a plate. I slip out of the sliding doors onto the deck, then go down the stairs to the stone path that weaves through the sun-browned grass to the dock.

He still hasn't turned around, even as I step on the dock and it jostles a little from side to side, water splashing as I walk.

"It didn't seem right," I say, stopping a few feet behind him.

Slowly he turns around and glances at me, then at the cake in my hands. Not surprised to see me at all. Guess there's no sneaking up on him. Probably recognizes the sound of my footsteps or some weird shit like that.

"What didn't seem right?"

I gesture with the cake toward the house. "You not being there at dinner. Usually you're all up in my business, tailing me like I'm a shoplifter."

He looks back to the water. "Have to keep my eyes here. With the police up on the road, the media will try new tactics."

"How long is Bert supposed to stay there?" It sounds like an easy gig, but it's not like this island is free of crime. There's definitely a dark underbelly to this place.

"As long as he can. We're bringing another member from London over to take that duty, but it will be a few days."

"Jeez. How many people do you even have here already? It's hard to keep count, you're all so sneaky." Like, hiding-in-trees level of sneaky.

"Enough," he says firmly.

"Am I bugging you?" I ask. "I mean, am I distracting?"

He lets out a rough chuckle. "You're definitely distracting."

Even though he laughs, I have no gauge at how serious he is, since he's always so damn serious.

"Should I go? I just came to bring you cake."

He turns slightly, and though I can't see his eyes beneath the sunglasses, I can tell he's eyeing the cake. Or maybe he's looking at me.

"That's for me?"

I raise it up in his face. "They gave me permission and everything. I checked—it's not forbidden."

At that I see the corner of his mouth lift, and I'm momentarily transfixed by his lips. They're so full and pouty, and I'm . . .

Jealous. Jealous of his lips, that's all. Not at all turned on by them, not at all wondering what they'd be like to kiss, not at all wondering what they'd feel like on my—

"I see," he says. He reaches out and takes the plate from me. "Shame it's not forbidden cake. Always find it tastes sweeter that way."

From the rough sound of his voice, I'd swear he's making innuendo.

And then he dips his long forefinger into the frosting and pops it in his mouth, sucking on the finger briefly. I can see his tongue roll inside against his cheek, and my entire body flushes, warm and fizzy from head to toe.

My god. That *is* innuendo.

I can't see his eyes. I can only see my reflection in his sunglasses, and my mouth is open.

I abruptly close it.

"This your mum's cake?" he asks.

Okay, and the moment has passed.

I clear my throat. "Yeah. It's actually pretty good."

"Icing could use some work," he comments, delicately smacking his lips together and looking off. It's like watching a sommelier tackle some old Bordeaux, but in this case it's my mom's take on Betty Crocker. "Too much sugar. Definitely not the right consistency."

I fold my arms across my chest, feeling defensive. "Please tell me you were a past judge on *The Great British Bake Off*."

"Oh, that show is rubbish," he says. "None of it's real, you know."

I give a mock gasp. "You could get kicked out of Britain with that opinion."

"Good thing I'm not there, then," he says, slicing the tip of the cake with his fork. "So you're just going to stand there and watch me eat cake, is that it?" He nods up at the house. "Shouldn't you be up there?"

"You mean watching over my mom?" I ask uneasily. My eyes narrow.

"I mean conversing with the Duke and Duchess of Fairfax." He pops the forkful of cake in his mouth.

"We've done a lot of conversing," I tell him, wondering if he's trying to get me to leave him alone. If so, I'm being purposely obstinate. "Guess I felt like doing a nice thing."

He chews, and I can feel him watching me as he does so. I stare right back at my reflection. I know what I see in them, but I wonder what he sees.

"I appreciate it." He swallows, his Adam's apple bobbing. "May I ask you a question?"

"Sure."

"Why did you leave that guy at the altar?"

I stare at him a moment as he has another bite of cake. On the one hand, I didn't think he'd bring it up again. On the other hand, how could anyone not want to know what happened?

"That guy was my ex, Joey," I tell him with a heavy sigh. "And, as was the case with all the guys I dated, he was an asshole."

"You couldn't tell that from his name?"

I laugh, though Harrison looks totally serious. "I should have known. And I should have known given my track record. But I didn't, because I'm an idiot. And I went for the emotionally unavailable type because that's what I do, and I looked the other way far too many times, until I found out he slept with another woman on the night of his bachelor party."

Harrison stops chewing.

"Anyway, I didn't find out until my wedding day. Just as I was getting my hair done. A friend of mine texted me and told me what she'd heard. My poor hairdresser, she was trying to do this elaborate updo while I was crying and texting and calling everyone I knew, everyone who was supposed to be at the wedding in a few hours. They all confirmed it. There are a lot of secrets on this island, but that one came to light at the eleventh hour."

"Shit," Harrison swears. "I'm sorry."

I shrug. "I had no choice. I had to call off the wedding. And what that Amy chick, the barista, what she said wasn't true. I didn't technically leave him hanging at the altar. I told his family I was calling it off. They told me I was being irrational. They're one of these families that have been on the island for decades and decades, amassed a lot of land, a lot of friends, and a lot of power. They didn't want to lose face by calling it off. I thought they would have shut it all down, so I left. Turns out they all proceeded like I was supposed to walk down the aisle. Those assholes made me look like the bad one. Obviously to this day, people still think that, still talk about it."

"They must know what he did. Gossip travels fast in small towns."

"They know," I tell him in a huff. "They know, and they don't care. Easier to vilify me. Me, who keeps to herself, who doesn't quite fit in. I'm the one who gets the blame, not their golden boy."

"Golden boy with a blowhole," he comments.

I can't help but laugh. "That's the name of his pub. It's the only pub in town, so if you want to go out for a fun night, you have no choice. Then his shitty band plays shitty songs and you're trapped."

"So I take it you won't be going to his show next Friday," he says.

"Absolutely not," I say. Then pause. "Unless you care to come with me."

Another small smile flits across his mouth. "You boldly assume I have Friday nights off."

"Do you get *any* nights off?"

"My job is round-the-clock," he says, bringing his attention back to the water. I suppose I have been distracting him with my cake nonsense.

Still. "What if I asked Monica to give you the night off?"

"Don't you dare," he says sharply.

"She seems pretty understanding," I goad him, "and you just said you have even more people coming to help."

"I'm not taking any time off, not to go to some Blowhole pub with apparently shit music."

I nod, pursing my lips. "Ah, I see. It's because you have nothing to wear. Only suits. Tell me, what do you sleep in? I bet it's pajamas with a breast pocket and a handkerchief you never use."

He frowns, and I know his eyes must be blazing. I really need to stop getting such joy out of pissing him off.

"It would be inappropriate if I told you what I slept in," he says. "And I'd rather not go, because if I did, I'm pretty sure I'd end up breaking your ex-boyfriend's nose."

Whoa.

Did . . . Harrison just get all macho possessive on me, or . . . ?

"Don't look so shocked," he says. "I have a low tolerance for wankers. What he did to you means he deserves at least a jab in his face. And the last thing I need is to get in trouble outside of my job."

I should keep my mouth shut. Turn around and go. But I can't help it.

"You'd get in trouble for me?"

"I'd rather not."

Then he jerks his chin behind me. "You better go back. Been out here long enough."

He's back to being the Harrison I know.

Though, come to think of it, I know nothing about this man at all.

Other than the fact that he wants to punch my ex in the face.

Which is, well, actually kind of sweet.

"Okay," I tell him.

I turn around and walk down the dock, my heart beating fast for no reason at all.

"Thanks for the cake," he says. I look over my shoulder at

him, and he's raising the plate in the air. "Tell your mother she did good."

I give him a soft smile and continue on my way back to the house.

That giddiness threatens to rise up inside me, but I squash it down once again.

Nine

IT RAINED LAST NIGHT. THE AIR IS SWEET, AND SPAR-kling water droplets sit in the curved bow of the hostas like stick-on rhinestones. The sun barely makes it through the overlap of the hemlock and fir, just enough to make everything glitter.

I knew my mother would need a few days of rest after the hul-labaloo over at the royals', so I'm in her garden, weeding. I hate it. I hate how it hurts my back, I hate how tedious it is, I especially hate how blackberry bushes seem to take over when you're not looking. But the work is rewarding. At least that's what I tell my-self when I'm picking thorns out of my fingers.

The last few days have been pretty easy. With my mom on her downward spiral and keeping to her bedroom, I've been able to clean the house, record a podcast on a paranormal romance I've been reading (bear shifters are all the rage right now, and I'm not complaining), do lots of cooking, and . . .

That's about it.

Even though I told Monica it was fine that we have to deal with the media, I still didn't leave the house until late last night to do a grocery run. I didn't see any media, but I did see a black SUV parked on the side of the road, and I have to wonder if it was

Harrison in there or the new person who supposedly came in from England. Either way, it's kept the media away for now.

In keeping to myself I haven't seen anyone but my mother since the dinner the other night. I thought maybe they'd drop by or send a text, but nothing. It probably means nothing at all, just that they're busy, but I can't help but wonder if there was something I did wrong. Maybe they discovered my mother and I are too nutty to have as neighbors. Maybe Harrison told Monica I was being distracting and inappropriate. After all, I brought him cake when he was on duty.

But he was the one who ate that cake like it was foreplay, I remind myself.

Unless I'm only seeing what I want to see, which has always been the case with me. It's how I've ended up with my heart broken every single time.

And why am I even thinking like this?

I shake the thought out of my head and get prepared to yank out the final weeds when I feel a presence behind me.

I whirl around and see Harrison.

Three guesses as to what he's wearing?

"What are you doing there, you creeper?" I cry out, getting to my feet.

"Sorry, I thought I was being loud," he says, looking slightly embarrassed.

I roll my eyes. "If that's your loud, I can't imagine what you're like when you're really trying to sneak up on someone."

"I'm not a secret agent, you know," he says wryly.

Well, at least he finds me amusing this morning.

"How would I know? You said you wore many hats."

His brows come together, and I can't tell if he's looking at me or the garden. "Let me guess, you're a gardening expert too?" I ask.

He takes a few steps forward, until he's right in front of me, and then reaches out for my face. I try not to flinch as he runs his finger lightly along my cheekbone.

"You have dirt on your face," he says in a low, gruff voice, before he takes his finger away.

My heart is pounding so loudly in my chest, I'm afraid my ribs aren't enough of a barrier.

"Oh," I manage to eke out, and then quickly rub my forearm along my face.

"And those are blue angel hostas. They get bigger every year. In a couple of years, these two will compete for space."

I give him a steady look, even though my skin is still tingling from where he touched me. Man, I really need to get laid or something, because I should not be feeling this way from a simple touch.

I clear my throat, hoping to appear normal. "Did you come here to nitpick my gardening skills?"

"Actually, no," he says. "I was wondering if you knew someone who had a boat."

"A boat. We're on an island. Nearly everyone has a boat. Why? You have a giant one docked right over there."

"Eddie wants to get away from the house, but they aren't comfortable going into town yet. They thought getting out on the water might be good. However, they don't want to go out on their boat either. People will recognize it."

"You came all the way here to ask me that? Monica could have texted me."

He doesn't say anything for a moment. "Guess I came by to distract you."

"Well, unfortunately for you, I'm done weeding for the day. And yes, I know someone with a boat. Bert has one. I'm sure he'd be more than willing to lend it to you."

"Please contact him and see."

I sigh and shrug. "Sure."

I mean, I'm not friends with Bert; it's not like I often call up the head cop and ask him how he is. But I'll do it for the royals.

Not for Mr. Bossy Pants.

"Thank you," Harrison says, and then he turns and leaves, walking back down the driveway, as silent as a mouse.

"Weirdo," I mutter under my breath. But the moment I say the word, I feel my face flush and a strange fluttering feeling in my gut. Oh great. Seems not only do I like to annoy him, but I like it when *he* annoys me.

THIS IS A first.

Despite growing up by the ocean, my experience with boats has been limited. I know, I should be banished from the Pacific Northwest forever. But boats are expensive, and we never had a lot of money, even when my father was around.

That said, since I know the area, and I've had experience driving thanks to going out on Joey's parents' speedboat a few times, I've been delegated as captain.

Bert was more than happy to lend us his vessel and was vocally disappointed that he couldn't take time off work to accompany us on our little adventure. I think he should have, since he was the one who drove his boat all the way to the royals' dock, getting a ride into town after with the royals' driver, but I suppose there was some drum circle in the middle of town that he had to go break up.

"Are you sure you know what you're doing?" Harrison asks me.

I turn around and smile at him. "I'm fine," I say, giving Monica and Eddie a reassuring look. They don't actually look all that worried, though; they're both grinning into the wind and pointing at the scenery as we head down Long Harbour.

But Harrison is watching me like a hawk.

Not that that's unusual. However, today he's not wearing his sunglasses, which makes me feel like I'm getting a rare glimpse at a secret side of him.

"I'm fine," I tell him again, but my hands momentarily slip from the wheel, and the boat starts to nose in toward the shore.

I whip around and grip the wheel hard, straightening the boat.

"You're sure?" he asks.

I nod and keep my eyes on the water ahead, though I can feel him smirking behind me.

Harrison did offer to command the small speedboat—I suppose PPOs have to know how to drive everything, just like James Bond does—but since I'm the only one who knows where we're going, I figured it was best this way.

That said, I don't have much of a plan. Long Harbour is aptly named, a narrow inlet that stretches past a ferry terminal and yacht clubs, all the way to a lagoon at the back I nicknamed Creepy Lagoon for obvious reasons.

I decide to take them all the way back there, the water so narrow and shallow in one passage that cedar branches scrape the side of the boat and you can see crabs scuttling along the green-blue bottom.

Monica and Eddie ooh and aah at the sights, waving at people who are sitting on their docks and enjoying the sunshine, probably having no idea just who is passing by. The last thing locals would expect is to actually see the royal couple out and about.

While Monica has always had a smile on her face, both she and Eddie seem to be at peace for the first time since I've met them. I guess it helps that they're exploring like tourists, not royals, and not confined to their house. No matter how nice their house is, it must feel like a prison sometimes.

Finally, after we tour the lagoon and go past some of the nicer houses along the water, I take them back toward the opening of the harbor, stopping at an island in the middle, near the ferry terminal.

"I love coming here," I tell them as I try to pilot the boat toward the shore. Joey and I used to come here a lot (we also had sex on this island, but that's neither here nor there). "Makes me feel like I have my own private hideaway, like I'm Robinson Crusoe. Or Tom Hanks from *Castaway*. Minus the volleyball."

"You can't get enough of one island, you have to come to another?" Harrison asks wryly, leaning over the side and observing the bottom as the water gets shallow. "Watch out for that rock."

He's pointing to the left, so I swing the boat to the right and accidently gun the engine. Everyone is thrown back with a collective "Whoa!" and I manage to get the nose of the boat right onto a patch of white shell beach and kill the engine.

"Sorry!" I exclaim, turning around to give everyone a sheepish smile. "I'm so sorry."

Harrison is just shaking his head, but Monica is laughing.

"Woo, that's the most excitement I've had in a long time," she says, pressing her hand against her belly. She's been wearing long and flowy shirts and dresses every time I've seen her, though now that I'm staring at the small bump on her stomach, I'm starting to realize why.

I look to Eddie and notice him staring at me in concern.

I quickly turn around, blinking.

My god.

Is Monica . . . *pregnant*?

Or is that just a food baby? Because lord knows I get that after I eat a bunch of cheese (doesn't stop me from eating cheese, of course, nothing will ever stop me).

I decide to mind my own business. If she's pregnant or bloated, it's never anyone's place to ask, and I'm sure if she's the former, it will come out in due time.

"Okay, let's get out," I say, trying to ignore it. I go to the bow and attempt to climb over it onto the shore, but Harrison has already jumped off the boat, narrowly missing the water, and he's standing below me, holding out his hand.

"Here," he offers.

"I'm fine," I tell him, trying to push his hand away. I wish my legs weren't so short, because this looks like quite the leap. Perhaps this wasn't a good idea.

But Harrison has his own plans. He reaches over and grabs me by the waist and literally hoists me in the air like I weigh the same as a bag of feathers instead of a sack of potatoes.

He gently places me on the ground, and there's a brief moment when I'm up against him and he's staring down at me and I swear there's a glint of something fiery in his eyes, a tic along his jaw. Then he quickly looks away and steps back, clearing his throat.

"Need help?" he asks Monica, going to her as she comes to the end of the boat.

What was that? I swear that look was *something*.

"Be extra careful with her," Eddie warns Harrison, and something silently transpires between them, adding extra fuel to my little theory.

Mind your own business, Piper!

Harrison plucks Monica off the boat in the same manner, checking to see if she's okay, and I start heading farther onshore. It's a steep scramble over barnacle-covered rocks before an ascent up scrubby, dry hillside to a grove of arbutus trees at the top. Normally I wouldn't have thought twice about it, but now with what I *might* know about Monica, I'm a little worried.

I stop and turn around before I climb the first rock.

"Is this going to be okay?" I ask.

"Why wouldn't it be?" Monica asks.

Eddie and Harrison exchange a look over her head.

She notices and frowns at them. "What? I'm not an invalid. I'm fine."

"Perhaps this is a little dangerous," Eddie says gently, putting his hand at her elbow. "Maybe we should stay by the boat and let the two of them explore."

"I'm fine," she insists, giving me a weak smile.

"This is probably a bad idea," I say.

"Why?" she asks again.

Eddie gives her arm a squeeze. "Monica, dear, I think we should tell her. She's going to find out eventually. Everyone in the whole world will."

She stares at me, and I can see her weighing options in her head.

Tell me, tell me, tell your friend Piper.

She licks her lips and then nods, looking up at Eddie, smiling gently. "Okay." She nods at Harrison and then over to me. "I guess you'll figure it out sooner or later. Piper . . . I'm pregnant."

I burst into a grin. "I knew it!"

"You did?"

"I mean, I only figured it out in the last five minutes, but yeah, I knew it!"

Monica laughs. "Okay then. Well, the secret is out." She places her hand on her baby bump. "Shit, it feels good to finally tell someone!"

"Of course, this will stay secret until they're ready to tell the public," Harrison says in that ultra-stern voice of his.

"She signed an NDA, Harrison," Monica chides him. "Besides, I trust Piper completely."

I beam at that. Not that I could legally talk even if I wanted to, but I don't want to. I feel pretty damn important being entrusted with this secret, and I'll guard it with my life.

"I won't tell a soul," I assure her. "This is so exciting!"

The royals are having a baby!

"I know," she says, matching my grin. "It's one of the reasons why we moved here, so I could go through my pregnancy in peace. We'll head back to England for the baby, I'm sure, but for now I just wanted to be here with Eddie and really sink into the experience. We're not far along, and I don't even know the sex yet, but I'm just enjoying being pregnant."

"And I'm enjoying being a father-to-be," Eddie says, wrapping his arm around her waist. "Not that I do anything."

She pats him on the chest. "You do plenty," she says. "Holding back my hair during morning sickness, that was something."

"I do that when she's had too much champers too," he says, winking at me.

Harrison clears his throat, and we all look to him.

"I'm just wondering if we should get back on the boat," he says, his gaze going up the sharp sides of the island. "Not only do I think it might be too dangerous . . ." He then looks to the ferry terminal behind us, where the big ship is pulling away from the dock. "But that ferry is about to pass. In fact, it's probably for the best if we get back in the boat. All those tourists on the deck have their cameras out already."

"Aw," Monica whines. "This was our first real trip out of the house."

"I know," Eddie commiserates. "But perhaps Bert will let us do this again."

"I'm sure he would," I tell them. "And I won't take you back here. There's a really cool white sand beach in the next harbor over. It's called Chocolate Beach. I'm not sure why, but it'll make you feel like you're somewhere tropical, even if the water is freezing."

"Then I must insist Piper isn't the captain," Harrison says.

"Hey," I say to Harrison, glaring at him. "Not nice."

"In fact," Harrison goes on, a faint twinkle in his eye, "I'm commandeering the ship as of now."

"It's practically a dinghy, Harrison," Eddie says with a good-natured rolling of his eyes.

"Doesn't matter. I've seen her drive."

"And you always get where you're going in one piece," I shoot back.

"I chalk it up to luck." The corner of his mouth twitches.

Funny guy.

"Suit yourself, then," I tell him, walking past him to climb back in the boat.

This time I don't want any help, which means I'm struggling to pull myself on for a good few minutes as the three of them watch my futile attempt to even swing one leg up on the side, my ass in their faces. Monica is trying not to laugh.

"Oh, Harrison, go help her," she says. "Please."

Next thing I know, Harrison is doing that caveman thing

again where he has me by the waist and is hoisting me up, and I am doing what I can to pretend I'm not actually enjoying this. Damn if it isn't the sexiest thing being picked up by him, and even though I know he's just being helpful, his hands against my body feel absolutely delicious.

I have to tell myself to chill out as I take my seat at the back of the boat. Monica gets on the same way I did and takes a seat next to me, while Eddie and Harrison push the boat back off the shore.

"So I assume your family knows about the baby," I say to Monica as Harrison goes behind the wheel, Eddie acting as skipper.

"They do," she says, nodding slowly. "My parents are thrilled, of course. They want to come visit at some point."

"And Eddie's parents?"

She gnaws on her lip for a moment. "They're happy. Of course they are. It's just . . . you know, I'm used to people telling me how they feel, I'm used to emotions being on display and all that, and with them . . . it's like getting blood from a stone. It's actually quite hard being around them, because there is so much poise and tradition and distance that's bred into them, like everyone is wearing a mask except me. I suppose that's what makes me an easy target."

"You're too real," I point out as Harrison starts the engine and we start reversing.

"Not *too* real. Just real enough. I don't think I'll ever fit in with them. I definitely tried at the beginning, you know. I tried to wear the right clothes and carry the right bags and greet people the right way, but my true self kept slipping through, and I was breaking protocols left and right and up and down."

"Sounds exhausting," I tell her. "I could never do it. I would fail right away. There's no hiding who I am."

Okay, so there's a little bit of hiding with my saucy romance podcast, but Monica doesn't need to know that.

"I know. That's why I think we get on so well," she tells me.

Now I'm smiling the cheesiest smile. I'm so hopeless.

"By the way," she adds, "another bodyguard has just arrived. His name is James, and he'll be sharing duties with Harrison. Once news of the baby gets out, you can bet we'll need to step up our security."

"Is he like Harrison, or is he normal?"

Monica bursts out laughing, and I look to the front of the boat to see Harrison glaring at me.

I give him a look like, *Well?*

He turns back around, and we speed away.

Ten

THE NEXT DAY I FEEL LIKE I'VE GOT A PRECIPITOUSLY placed cork in me, barely holding the contents of a bubbling secret inside.

I can't believe Monica and Eddie are having a baby.

Furthermore, I still can't quite believe that they both entrusted me with that information. They don't even know me, and yet they somehow trust that I'm not about to run to the tabloids with this information. Even with the NDA signed, I have no doubt that I would be paid a lot of money for the tip, and it's obvious that my mother and I aren't exactly swimming in the dough. And yet they confided in me, and as a result, I've been pulled into their world.

Maybe they're just good judges of character. I would never even dream of doing such a thing, and perhaps they see that.

But at the same time, whoo boy, it's a little unfair, only because I don't know if I'm allowed to tell my mother or not, and even though I obviously have hidden many secrets from her, this one feels hard. But it's not my business to tell, and so I keep that cork firmly pushed in place.

My mom is in a good mood this morning. She's in her own

little world, making more tea and talking to herself, leaving the kitchen a mess of different dried herbs and flowers. Occasionally she'll shoot me a question about flavor combinations, but the rest of the time she's happily muttering away and doing her thing.

I'm on the couch with Liza curled at my feet, trying to read the next book in this bear-shifter series so I can move on to this octopus erotica (don't judge, it's a thing), when there's a knock at the door.

Startled, I drop the book, and Liza starts barking.

Without seeming too concerned, my mother heads over to the door and opens it.

Harrison is on the other side.

My first thought is that I'm glad to see him. My second thought is a swift correction, that I shouldn't be glad to see him.

"Well, good morning, Mr. Harrison," my mother says, and then gestures inside. "Please, come in."

"Actually, it's just Harrison. My last name is Cole." He looks over my mother's shoulder and at me. "And I was wondering if I could have a word with you, Piper."

Ah, here it comes. He's going to get me to sign an NDA over the whole pregnancy thing. Figures that this is the only reason he seems to show up, when he wants something from me.

Obviously. Why else would he be here? the voice in my head asks, always keeping me in check.

I get up and go to the door, stepping outside and shutting it behind me.

Harrison towers over me, dressed in his usual suave body-guard attire, while I've got on my leggings and a long cream tank top that's a little more low-cut than I normally wear.

He has a clear view of my cleavage, but it's not like I can tell where his eyes are focused.

"Here to threaten me into silence?" I ask him with a tired sigh, leaning against the house.

His brows raise. "Pardon?"

"I assume you're here to make me sign another nondisclosure agreement over what Monica told me. And no, don't worry, I haven't told anyone. Not even my mother."

He gives his head a light shake. "No, that's not it. I do what Monica asks. She hasn't said anything about that . . ."

The way he trails off makes me think he might bring it up with her now.

"Well, good," I say, feeling a little stupid for jumping to conclusions. "So why are you here?"

He rubs his lips together for a moment, and I realize it's probably the first time that I've seen any hint of trepidation or hesitation on his face. Like, ever.

"I need to go off island, find a Costco or something comparable, so we don't have to keep running to the grocery store every other day." He pauses. "We don't have a Costco card."

"So you assume I do?"

"Do you?"

"Well, yeah. Groceries are crazy expensive here. Costco is always worth the trip."

"Would you be willing to go now?"

I stare at him for a moment, feeling like maybe, just maybe, my proximity to them and my understanding of their situation is being taken advantage of. "As a favor to Monica and Eddie? Sure. I can do that. I mean, it does take a big chunk out of my day, and there are ferries to consider."

"We'll compensate you financially," he says. "Whatever your price."

"Just pay for my gas and the ferry and we'll call it even." I bite my lip. "And I request that you come along."

"Me?"

"You just said *you* need to go off island, and I'm not doing this by myself."

"I have a grocery list."

"I'm sure you do. But this will take all day, and I'm not going to do it alone, especially if I'm shopping for a duke and duchess. I don't want to cause a scandal because I accidentally subbed oat milk for almond milk or didn't get the right cut of meat. That's going to be your responsibility, not mine."

He doesn't say anything for a moment, but that crevasse between his brows is deepening. "I have to run it past them," he says warily, like I'm really twisting his arm here.

"Didn't Monica say your other dude is here? You know, the spare bodyguard."

"James isn't a spare," he says. "He's part of the team."

"Either way, you ask them, because I'm not going without you. Either you come with me or *no one* is going to Costco."

He stares at me for a moment. "You drive a hard bargain, Ms. Evans."

"And you're the one asking big favors."

He exhales in a low huff and takes out his phone, quickly sending a message.

"So you can text?" I comment wryly. "Ever thought about doing that instead of showing up at my door or in my yard at random hours?"

"As I said the other day, I take great pleasure in distracting you."

The way he says *great pleasure* is borderline lewd, his voice rich and silky, and I actually have to look away from his non–eye contact. I hate being flustered in front of him, and seeing that reflected in his sunglasses, and I especially hate this sexy act with his words and the way he eats cake.

He doesn't seem to pay me any attention and looks down as his phone beeps. "It's fine. Shall I drive?"

I should let him drive. Let him do something, especially in one of those nice SUVs. But because I'm already inconveniencing him, I decide to inconvenience him more.

"I'll drive," I tell him, giving him a borderline evil grin. "Let me get my keys."

Before he can protest, I head inside the house, grab the car keys and my purse, and tell my mom I'm going to Costco and to text me if she wants anything. Then I'm closing the door behind me and smiling at Harrison, taking extra pleasure in his discomfort.

"Shall we?" I say to him in a singsong voice as I walk over to the car.

He grumbles something under his breath, then catches himself and gives me a decisive nod. I'm really getting under his skin now.

I get in the Garbage Pail while he tries to fit himself through the passenger side. Much like before, on our very first meeting, his knees are almost rammed up against the dash, and the seat adjustments are taking him for a ride.

And like before, I find it beyond funny. As the seat jerks back and forth, I'm giggling, unable to hide it.

"This is why you insisted on driving, isn't it?" he asks me, his voice peppered with annoyance.

"Maybe you're not the only one who likes to be in control."

That makes him pause. Then the seat locks in the right position and I'm starting the car. He's so damn imposing, his shoulders so wide, that the car feels way too small for the two of us. I can't tell if this was a good idea or a bad one.

The new annoying thing is that I don't have a remote gate opener, so I'm totally prepared for Harrison to get out and enter the code, but to my surprise he pulls a fob out of his pocket and aims it at the gate. It opens slowly.

"How long have you had one of those, and why the hell don't I have one?" I ask him.

He shrugs with one shoulder. "Guess it slipped my mind. Here, have this one," he says as he opens the glove compartment to put it in there.

A million Tic Tac boxes come pouring out onto his lap, along with insurance papers, school papers, and a historical romance I'd thought I lost.

I can't help him. The gates are open, and I'm driving the Garbage Pail through, the cul-de-sac empty except for an SUV parked at the mouth of it. James, I assume.

When Harrison finishes struggling to get everything back into the glove compartment, he says, "Let me guess, you get your Tic Tacs from Costco."

"I do," I admit. "But I don't eat them as much in the summer. Less stress. Though with the way the media is taking over, maybe I should get some more."

"I don't see anyone," Harrison says, looking around as I gun the gutless car up one of the undulating hills. "With James stationed there now, it seems to be doing the trick."

"Yeah, well, from the way Monica talks about the media, I wouldn't be surprised if things get worse. So far it's just been local press. What happens when the Brits get here?"

"We'll handle it," Harrison says gruffly.

"I sure hope so," I tell him. "Because the more I learn about them, the more I'm horrified by them. Monica and Eddie don't deserve any of that."

"They don't," he says. "But it comes with the territory. Eddie is used to it. He doesn't know any different. And Monica is too, to a degree."

"I remember when Monica was MRed. I loved her music, honestly. Sure, TMZ would occasionally talk shit about her, and maybe some crappy tabloid would take a picture of her at the beach and point out cellulite, as if she isn't allowed to have any. But she wasn't treated like the way she's treated now. It just enrages me that they can be so cruel and vicious because she's not a royal, not an aristocrat, not white. Meanwhile, Eddie's older brother gets to gallivant around, having numerous public affairs with models and actresses and socialites, and no one says anything bad about him or the girls. Double fucking standard."

"He's gotten some flack; don't think he's gotten off easy," Harrison says.

"I suppose you would know more than I do."

"I do," he says, adjusting himself in the seat. He seems so uncomfortable, I almost feel bad.

"So, how long have you been doing this? I mean, your job. For the duke and duchess?"

"I've been working for Eddie for six years," he says. With his stiff posture and the way his mouth is pressed firmly closed, I know he doesn't want to talk about anything to do with him. But that's all the more reason to make him talk. He's my prisoner in this car for a reason. I don't have a problem going off island to do an errand—it's good for your mental health to get off this rock. But a chance to actually have quality time, one-to-one, with the mysterious British bodyguard? You can bet I won't pass that up, and I'm not going to let this opportunity go to waste.

"So, tell me, how did you get the job? Did you see an ad in the classifieds or . . . ?"

He glances at me sharply, as if I'm serious, and I quickly have to clarify, "I'm joking. But seriously . . . how does one become a royal bodyguard?"

Silence fills the car. Well, that's not true: the sound of the raggedy engine fills the car, but my question has caused him to clam up, and there's tension between us. Sometimes I really wish I could know what he's thinking and why just asking simple questions seems to piss him off so much. Perhaps he's not even allowed to talk about it.

I hadn't considered that, and I'm about to tell him to forget it when he clears his throat.

"I met Eddie in the army," he says. He leans back against the seat, his focus out the window at the passing houses nestled in the trees, lightly drumming his fingers on his left knee. "We became fast friends. After he left, I stayed on. Got injured, my leg. Had to leave. Eddie and I were still in touch; he was adamant that I come work for him. I told him I had no experience in being a PPO, but he didn't care. He said he wanted someone he could trust. So I went, and I learned how to protect him. I've never looked back."

So Harrison was in the British Army. I am so not surprised.

"Is that when you got your tattoo?" I ask.

He turns to look at me, frowning as he shifts in his seat. "How do you know I have a tattoo?"

Against my better judgment, I take my hand off the wheel and reach out, tugging at the sharp end of his white collared shirt. "Sometimes you can see it."

"Hands on the wheel," he says, wrapping his fingers around my wrist and placing my hand back there. "Eyes on the road."

I laugh, even though my skin is practically buzzing from where he touched me. His hands are warm. "Don't worry, I'm not going to risk my life to ogle you."

He grunts.

"So, your tattoo," I press.

A long moment passes. "I got my tattoos a very long time ago. Before the army."

Tattoos. Plural. Another snippet of information. I'm unsure how to lead the conversation, how to keep him talking. I'm gobbling it all up like candy.

"How many do you have?"

He shrugs. "Ten, eleven. I'd have to think." His voice is clipped in a way that tells me he's not about to think on it.

"Do they all mean something?"

"I take it you don't have any tattoos," he says.

I shake my head. "I don't. Nothing against them, I just . . . not sure what I would want mine to say. So the one near your collarbone, what is that?"

"A raven."

"For what?"

"'The Raven' by Edgar Allan Poe."

Interesting. "When did you get it?"

"When I was young and fucked up," he says. I'm pretty sure this is the first time I've heard him use the F-word, because the ferocity behind it catches me off guard.

I'm not sure I want to keep bugging him. I press my lips together and concentrate on the road as it winds through town, heading to the Fulford Ferry Terminal.

After a few minutes pass, I say, "You really don't like to talk about yourself."

He snorts softly. "You're very astute."

"Why is that?"

A sigh escapes his lips as he begins tapping his fingers on his knee again. "I don't know. Why is it that you *like* to talk about yourself?"

"I don't like to talk about myself," I protest.

Another soft chuckle. "Right. That's why within minutes of meeting you I knew you were a schoolteacher, knew that your mother had several neurological conditions, knew that you like to read romance novels. Furthermore, you told me about your past relationship."

"You asked!"

"Yes, and you answered. Not right away, but you eventually did."

"Believe me, I'm not an open book."

He glances at me. "I didn't say you were. I just said you talk to me."

"Is that so bad? Me talking to you?"

"Not even a little," he says.

Hmmm. Well.

"I'm not an open book," I repeat, quieter this time. "I guess I just . . . Look, I don't have many friends on this island. I keep to myself. I like it that way. Things in my life . . . they're complicated. My past, my present, it's far from perfect; it's just this evolving mess, a wave that I can't get in front of. It's . . . sometimes harder to open up to the people you know, the people you call friends, because the judgment can hurt. But you . . . a stranger. The judgment doesn't hurt as bad. Maybe I tell you things because there's nothing at stake."

But the moment I say those words, I know they're not true.

Because believe it or not, there is something at stake now.

I like Harrison. It's why he's in this car. It's why I'm trying to learn as much about him as I can. I like him, and beyond that, I *don't fear his judgment.* I'm not sure why that is.

"You still think of me as a stranger?" he asks. The drumming of his fingers has paused, and there's this weight to his tone.

"Not anymore," I admit. "Though I can't quite call you a friend either."

"What can you call me?"

I take my eyes off the road for a moment to look at him. My reflection in his sunglasses is distorted and quizzical. Kind of how I feel.

"Someone I would like to get to know better," I tell him, feeling strangely vulnerable. "And on your terms. If you don't want to talk about yourself, you don't have to talk about yourself. I can fill in the silence."

"Or we could just sit in silence."

I can't tell if that's his way of getting me to shut up, that he's tired of hearing from me. "Of course," I tell him.

Here's the thing about me: I hate silences. Not the ones that I have between me and my mother, nor the blessed silence of quiet time at school, but the silence between two people that feels fraught with awkwardness. It happens all the time to me, the fact that I have to just keep blabbering to fill the space, to the point sometimes where I don't realize I'm talking over people and dragging the conversation where it shouldn't go.

This silence with Harrison is no better. I'm so acutely aware of every movement he makes, every sound, from the way he scratches his stubble to his fingers drumming on his leg. His smell. Try as I might, it's delicious and intoxicating and seems to get stronger by the minute. There's something so unbearable about all this that it almost makes me want to pull over, put down the windows, do something.

"So why did you move here?" Harrison asks suddenly.

I nearly jump in my seat.

He goes on. "I recall you telling Monica that you moved here from Victoria. That's where we're headed right now, isn't it?"

It can be confusing. There's Vancouver, which is the biggest city in British Columbia and part of the mainland. Then there's Vancouver Island, which is huge (larger than Belgium). That's where Victoria, the capital, is. Then there's Salt Spring, which is part of the Southern Gulf Islands, nestled right up against it at the bottom. Between us and the mainland is the Georgia Strait. So we're taking a ferry from one island to another, Belgium-size island.

I nod. "I moved here for work. To be honest, since I'm kind of in charge of my mother, I thought it would be a better place for her. Victoria is lovely, but it's still a city, and I wanted someplace quiet and peaceful."

Harrison grimaces. "I guess it's been anything but that lately."

"Not really. But I suppose a little change never hurt anyone."

"And your father? I remember you saying he left when you were a teenager."

I swallow thickly and nod. It doesn't necessarily hurt to talk about it, but it's not my favorite subject. "He did. I was fourteen."

"Amicable divorce?"

I laugh bitterly. "No. Otherwise I wouldn't have said he skipped out. Because that's what he did. Just straight up one day didn't want to deal with me or my mother anymore. She was too much for him, always so dependent and paranoid. In some ways I don't blame him, but he took a vow for better or for worse, and when she got worse, he decided to leave us. I mean, he knew when he married her what she was like. My mother has always battled with her mental issues. Her own parents were abusive; I don't even know them, never met them. So it wasn't like my dad didn't know what he was getting into."

"I'm sorry."

"It's not your fault. It is what it is."

"Sisters, brothers?"

"Only child. So taking care of my mother became my responsibility. You can imagine that after that, she took a turn for the worse. Meanwhile, my dad is now remarried and lives in Toronto. My stepmother, his new wife, had kids from a previous marriage, so he's just busy being a father to them and not to me. Whatever. I'm over it."

I can feel Harrison's eyes on me from behind his sunglasses. "Not an easy thing to get over."

He's called my bluff. Obviously I'm not over it. All the therapy sessions I've had, and I'm still not over it.

The scenery along the road changes from the dark, towering hemlock and fir to open fields and vineyards. The sky widens above us, this saturated blue, as the car coasts down the hill past olive groves and pastures dotted with sheep. This is probably my favorite part of the island.

I roll the window down and breathe in the air, wind messing with my hair. I grin, press my foot to the gas, and the car zips down faster. It feels like I'm flying.

When we finally get to the bottom, zooming past the turnoff to the local brewery, I glance over at Harrison. He's staring at me.

"What?" I ask him.

"Nothing," he says after a moment.

We get to the ferry terminal just in the nick of time. They don't leave every hour and I wasn't sure we'd make this one, but we manage to roll onto the ferry a minute before it's due to leave.

This ferry is small with an open car deck. There's nowhere really to go except a small lounge area and some outside upper decks, but that's okay since it's only a thirty-five-minute sailing.

"Want to take a walk?" I ask him once we're parked and the ship starts to pull away.

"Yes," he says, and I can hear the relief in his voice. He manages to unfold his large frame from the car and get out.

I get out from my side, and we work our way through the lanes of cars, the ferry packed at this time of year, and then head to the upper deck. We stop by the railing and stare out at the harbor as the ferry chugs along, passing immaculate, secluded houses with ocean views and tiny scenic islands that make up the thirty-five-minute passage.

The wind messes up my hair, making it swirl around my face, but I don't care. I close my eyes and breathe in the fresh, salty air.

Then I feel Harrison step closer to me.

His fingers brush against my cheeks, gently pushing my hair back behind my ears until I can see again.

And all I see is him.

"You looked like you needed some help," he says. He says it so simply, it's like he has no idea that his touch unleashed a kaleidoscope of butterflies inside me.

"Hey!" a sharp, obnoxious voice yells, shattering the fragile moment between us.

I turn to see some heavyset, thirtysomething guy with a camera approaching me, trucker cap on backward. "You're that girl!"

I stare at him, my heart racing because he's coming up pretty loud and pretty fast, and I have no idea who this man is.

Harrison spares no time. In a flash, he's putting his frame in front of me, one hand reaching back, signaling for me to stay behind him.

"Back off," Harrison growls at the man.

"She's the girl! She's one of the royals."

Despite the situation, I can't help but laugh. "I'm a royal? You must be blind."

"You don't have to say anything," Harrison says to me over his shoulder.

"Let her talk," the guy says. "I've seen the pictures, she's everywhere with them. As are you."

"I'm their personal protection officer," Harrison answers. His words are calm and cold. A warning.

"So then why are you with her? Obviously she's a royal. I just want a picture, just a picture and a word."

"If you even try to take a photograph, I will take that camera and throw it over the edge."

"And then I'll call the police."

"The police that are entrusted with the same job I have? Go right ahead. You'll find out that they aren't on your side."

"Miss, please, I just want a word."

I see the man peering around Harrison, raising up his camera.

Harrison steps forward, snatching the camera from the guy's hand and then holding it up high in the air, aiming it toward the water that's rushing past the ferry.

"I warned you," Harrison says.

The man lets out a squeal that has the whole ferry looking our way. He attempts to jump up to get the camera, but Harrison's height and bulk are big enough obstacles, and all Harrison has to do is stick his palm straight out, keeping the man at arm's length.

"You can't do this to me! I have a right to make a living."

"And I have a right to protect the ones I'm sworn to protect," he says, and with those words, Whitney Houston's "I Will Always Love You" comes blaring into my head, making me feel dizzy.

"Now," Harrison continues, oblivious to the scenes from *The Bodyguard* that are flashing through my brain, "I'll give you the camera back if you promise to turn around and go back to the hole you crawled out of."

I crane my neck around Harrison and see the man glance at me, bitterness and defeat clouding his features. He's lost.

Finally he steps back and grumbles, "Fine."

Harrison takes a moment before lowering his arm and handing him back his camera. "Now, politely, do fuck off."

The man slinks away past the rows of seats and down the stairs to the main deck. Harrison's head turns to follow him, and I can feel the intensity in his expression. Maybe that's why he wears sunglasses all the time. Otherwise he'd cause people to burst into flames.

"I . . . I can't believe you did that," I stammer. It's only now that I realize how hard my heart has been pounding. I lean against the railing, my grip tightening on it.

"Why not?" Harrison asks, fixing his focus on me, one brow quirked up. "You think I won't protect you?"

"It's not your job."

"It doesn't matter. I've now made it my job." He tilts his head, examining me. "Do you have a problem with that?"

Do I have a problem with this man protecting me? Hell no.

I shake my head. "No." I give him a shy smile. "Thank you."

"As I said, it's my job," he says dismissively. "Shall we go back to the car?"

I nod. I hate that this has now become my reality, whether I like it or not. But I'm grateful to have him.

And, well, if we're being honest here, it's more than just being grateful.

I'm swooning over him. Just a bit. Just for that.

Nothing else.

I swear.

Eleven

THE DRIVE FROM THE FERRY TERMINAL AT SWARTZ BAY to the Costco outside Victoria is about an hour with traffic, which meant plenty of silent driving. That is, until Harrison reached over and turned on the classic rock station, satisfied with Black Sabbath riffing "War Pigs."

"I didn't peg you for the heavy metal type," I tell him.

"What kind of music do you think I listen to?" he asks, sitting back in his seat, his fingers drumming along the edge of the open window.

"I don't know. What do soulless people listen to? Dave Matthews Band?"

He turns his head to look at me, and I feel his glare beneath his sunglasses. "I would rather stick broken glass in my ears," he says firmly.

Whoa. Okay, so definitely not a DMB fan.

"What music do *you* listen to?" he asks after a moment.

I place my hand on my chest. "You're . . . you're asking questions . . . about *me*?"

His mouth moves into a firm line before he says, "I'm always asking you questions."

"Ha! No, sir, you don't. Maybe you do in your head, but that mouth of yours never opens to speak."

"I'm speaking right now."

"I know. It's shocking."

"So?"

I shrug. "Music? I like all kinds. Except country. I will take that glass you have in your ears and jab it in mine if I hear any sort of twang accompanied by some dude singing about his lost dog. I mean, why are you singing about it? Go out and put some Lost Dog posters on the telephone poles or something."

He laughs. He actually laughs.

I gawk at him. "What's the date today?"

"It's July 6," he says. "Why?"

"Because I want to remember it as the day I made Harrison Cole laugh. I'll celebrate it every year by making offerings to the Holy Saint of PPOs, leaving tidings of aviator sunglasses and stiff upper lips."

He's shaking his head at me. "And you said *I* wasn't normal."

"It takes one to know one."

He's trying hard not to smile, I can tell.

IS IT WEIRD that I get excited every time I go to Costco? I mean, the place is generally chaotic, but there's something about buying in bulk that makes me feel like an accomplished adult. Or maybe it's just the fact that you need a membership card. I've wanted to belong to an exclusive club ever since I read The Baby-Sitters Club.

"Have you ever been to a Costco?" I ask him as we grab a cart and wheel it into the store, one of the staff checking my card to make sure I'm a member. I wave it at him with satisfaction.

"No," Harrison says, taking off his sunglasses and slipping them into his front pocket. He looks around the giant store with its towering aisles. "First time for everything."

"Okay, but you're going to need to have a hot dog."

His brow quirks up in amusement. "A hot dog?"

"Yes. They do awesome hot dogs."

"You bloody Americans and your hot dogs."

I smack him across the chest. "You're in Canada. You're going to get a poutine dog if you're not careful."

"Dare I ask what that is?"

I shake my head. "You're not ready for it."

We walk through the aisles, Harrison reading groceries off his list. Because I'm not used to frequenting Costco as much as my local Country Grocer, I forget where things are, so there's an awful lot of going back and forth across the store. Of course, I also want to stop at every single station that's handing out free samples.

The first time around, Harrison stood back as I munched on some kind of chutney and crackers. With his lip curled, he looked utterly disgusted at the idea of someone just handing out food like this. But by the time I got on to the chocolate chip cookies, he was intrigued enough to have some too.

I watch as he munches on the tiny crumbles, his eyes lighting up.

"Perhaps we should grab a bag of these cookies," he says, eyeing the display beside the person handing out the samples.

"See, this is how they get you," I tell him, reaching over and grabbing a bag and tossing it in the cart.

"I feel victimized," he says. "They bait you first with the free samples, then they swindle you into buying it."

At that, he reaches over and takes yet another sample from the station, giving the person a wink.

"You know it's one sample per customer," I whisper to him as we walk away. "If word gets out that the royals' bodyguard is trying to game the Costco sample system, it won't look good."

He leans into me, and I find myself holding my breath. "It will be our little secret, then."

Then he straightens up and I'm slowly exhaling through my nose. Sheesh, he oughta warn me when he comes in close like that; it's like I freeze and go into shock. If I breathed in his scent, my eyes would roll back in my head.

The rest of the shopping trip goes normally, with Harrison back to avoiding the samples again, and it feels like we've gotten everything we needed, and then some.

Though sometimes, just sometimes, I get this feeling that there's heat in his gaze. The way I caught his eyes drifting over my chest when he thought I wasn't looking, how his fingers brushed against mine as we both reached for the Kirkland bacon, how he guided me out of the store with his hand at the small of my back. Not to mention the peonies he picked up. Two for Monica and Eddie, but one bouquet for me.

I didn't find that out until I drove through the gates back home and parked in front of the royals' house.

"These are for you," he said as he reached into the back seat and handed me one of the peony bouquets.

I stared at him for a moment in disbelief, then at the pink flowers in my hand. He continued by saying, "It's a thank-you. For being so helpful and understanding."

Aka don't get any wrong ideas about this ten-dollar purchase.

But still, even as a gesture, it was sweet.

Then I popped the question.

"You know how you can really show me your appreciation? Come with me to the Blowhole on Friday."

He looked offended at the suggestion. "Why would you even want to go to that?"

"To show them all I'm not afraid." I hesitated. "I'd feel safer if you were there."

"Do you want me to go as protection or as a friend?"

"As a friend."

He gave me a curt nod. "I'll see what I can do."

IT'S FRIDAY AFTERNOON and I haven't seen Harrison all week, which is kind of strange. Same goes for Monica and Eddie. The mysterious James PPO in the SUV seems to have done a great job of keeping the media away, so whenever I've walked Liza or gone on a coffee run or a hike, I haven't seen them either. It's been completely and utterly peaceful.

And, I have to say, a little boring. All I've been doing is reading and doing podcasts, more so than normal. All this time I wish I could talk about Harrison and Monica and everything that's happening here, but I've managed to keep it just about the books this time. Luckily, I've been able to read a bunch of books featuring a "cinnamon roll hero" (which, no, has nothing to do with those gooey treats from the café and more to do with romance heroes with a soft center), enough that I have a good segment for my listeners, who seem to grow in numbers by the day.

My mother isn't particularly good to talk to these days either. She'll happily go on about Monica and Eddie, but if I bring up Harrison at all, she gives me that look, the look she's given me in the past whenever I started dating someone. I know it doesn't matter that I'm not dating Harrison, that the thought hasn't crossed my mind (not to mention isn't viable whatsoever), but she gives me that look all the same. Maybe because she *thinks* she knows me, thinks I'll get some silly idea and start falling for him.

I am *not* falling for him. Not even close. Not even a little.

But I am spending the day pacing the house, wondering if I should gather up the courage to text Monica just to check in, just to see if Harrison comes up. I'm wondering if Harrison totally forgot about our non-date at the Blowhole. I'm also checking the front door constantly, thinking he might randomly turn up. But then again, why would he? He's a PPO. His job is to protect the lives of the duke and duchess. His job isn't to go on a faux date with some small-town schoolteacher as a favor, of all things.

By the time dinner rolls around and I'm helping my mom make a stew, I've mentally given up. There's no way I'm going to the bar by myself. It was either I go with Harrison or not go at all. And I'm very aware that my motives for having Harrison there are on the petty side, but I think he knows that too.

I've physically given up too, resigned to sweatpants and a ratty flannel shirt, my hair pulled back into a tangled nest, as we sit on the couch, slurping on the stew as my mom flips through channels on the TV.

I'm trying my best not to be in a foul mood, especially since my moods, particularly my negative moods, tend to transfer to my mother. There's a reason why I seem peachy keen most of the time—I've trained myself that way. Another thing that my therapist unveiled when we discussed my C-PTSD (or complex post-traumatic stress disorder). A lot of the time my negative emotions get buried because there's no safe place for me to express them, and it's been that way since I was a kid.

Even so, I know that this week reminded me of what my life is normally like: boring. And how much excitement the royals injected into it. Though my conversations with Monica and Harrison have been somewhat few and far between, just having that interaction with them makes me realize how badly I actually need a friend or two in my life.

I'm contemplating giving Cynthia a call, even though I've never really hung out with her outside of school, when Liza starts barking.

My mom and I both swivel our heads toward the front door seconds before there's a knock.

My heart leaps in my chest.

It can't be him.

I get up and go over, acutely aware of how awful I look but still hoping it's Harrison all the same. I mean, who else could it be?

I open the door.

It's Monica, looking sweet and elegant as usual.

"Hello, Piper," she says, looking apologetic. "I'm so sorry for just stopping by and not texting. It just seemed silly when you live so close." She looks past me to my mother on the couch and gives her a quick wave. "Good evening, Evelyn."

"Princess, come on in!" my mother hollers. "I made stew!"

"We just ate, but thank you so much for the invitation," Monica says. She fixes her deep brown eyes on me. "Harrison had mentioned earlier in the week that you wanted him to accompany you to the local bar tonight."

Uh-oh. Even though Monica seems amiable, I can't tell if I'm in trouble or not.

"Yeah, I might have mentioned that," I say uneasily. "Should I not have done that?"

She breaks out into a grin and gives me a friendly tap on the arm. "No, no, I think it's great. I mean, I really do. That's why I'm here. Harrison mentioned it in passing, as if he either expected me or wanted me to say no. I just wanted to talk to you first, to make sure the offer was still there and you were serious."

"Definitely. I thought it would be fun."

"Good. Then I'll tell him he has to go."

I put my hand up. "Wait, wait. I don't want him to *have to* go. I thought maybe he wanted to."

She cocks her head and gives me a wry look. "He doesn't know what he wants or what's good for him. Listen, I'm close with Harrison, and there's a few things you should know. He has never, ever asked for time off. Even when Eddie insists, Harrison is still *on* in some aspect. He's never had a vacation. He's never dated anyone, not in a serious relationship, anyway."

"I'm not dating him," I interject. "This isn't a date."

"One-night stands, maybe," she goes on, ignoring me. "I don't talk to him about that."

"It's not a date or a one-night stand," I repeat, even though the thought of him having a one-night stand with someone else makes my chest feel all flustered.

"Oh, Piper, I know that. He knows that. I'm just saying, he doesn't go out and doesn't get to live his life. *We're* his life. And I know that's the way he thinks it has to be because of his job, but it's not true. One of the reasons we insisted on Harrison coming with us when we moved is because we thought this would be good for him. He had to be at the height of surveillance in England. There were threats everywhere. We knew coming here was the only chance for all of us to breathe."

"I take it he's like family to you."

"He is. And if I'm being his meddling substitute mother right now, I don't care. Just tell me when you want him to come by."

"Monica, Duchess, with all due respect, I don't want Harrison to come if he's going to be miserable."

"If you haven't noticed, he's always miserable. At least he'll be out of our hair. Don't we deserve a break too?"

What can I say to that?

"So what time?" she presses.

"Uh, I guess in a half hour? An hour?"

"He'll be here in a half hour."

And with that she gives me a quick wave and then leaves.

I give myself exactly three seconds to mouth *what the fuck* to myself, and then I'm hurrying back inside the house.

"What did she want? Why didn't she come in?" my mother asked.

"Can't talk, gotta get ready," I tell her as I run straight to the bathroom. I run the shower and hop in, the old pipes groaning loudly as the hot water kicks on. If this is actually happening, there is no way I'm showing up to the Blowhole looking less than a one-hundred-percent fine-ass bitch. If I'm showing up to the bar and Joey with Harrison at my side, I'm going all out.

At the very least, I need good hair for once, so I spend what feels like forever blow-drying it straight, then quickly put on some makeup, a little heavier on the eyes this time, with shining highlighter you'd be able to see across a bar. Then I'm scrambling in my towel across the living room, over to my bedroom, and quickly riffling through my clothes. I slip on skinny jeans and am just pulling a slinky black tank top over my head when there's a knock at the door.

I've been rushing so fast, I haven't even had time to feel anxious, but now it's hitting me like a freight train. I know I have no reason to feel nervous, but my body is just full-blown butterflies at this point.

It's not a date. He's doing this as a favor. He doesn't even want to go.

I take in a deep breath even though it does nothing to calm my racing heart, and I head over to the door.

Of course my mother beats me to it.

"Hello?" she says as she opens the door. "Mr. Cole. You seem different. My goodness. Your tattoos. Look at them all. Why would you do that to yourself?"

Oh god.

I can't see Harrison from where I'm standing, only hear him. "Is Piper here?" he asks, his voice as cool and calm as ever, even with my mother running her mouth off about his tattoos (she hates tattoos so much, it's a wonder that I never got one out of spite).

My mom frowns. "Yes, she's here." Then she turns and looks over at me standing outside my bedroom, and her eyes narrow as she looks me up and down. "You're all dressed up. Where are you going? What's happening?"

"Just going to the bar. Don't worry about it," I tell her.

"You can't drink and drive."

"I'm having one drink, I promise."

"Is this a date?"

Oh. GOD. Did she not hear the conversation I had with Monica?

I shake my head vehemently and gesture for her to get away from the door. "No. Not a date. We're just going to the bar. Okay?"

She exchanges a glance with Liza and then sulks away, back to the couch.

I go to the door, ready to run before she says something else.

And I hardly believe my eyes.

Harrison is wearing a fitted black T-shirt that shows off the tattoos on his arms and charcoal-gray jeans and dark work boots. He's so ruggedly dressed down that I hardly recognize him, though of course he's wearing his aviators. He wouldn't be Harrison without them.

To say he looks hot is an understatement. He looks ridiculously hot. Like, a whole other level of handsome, a whole other league of gorgeousness. For once I'm looking at him not as a bodyguard extraordinaire to the royals but as a man who has turned my ovaries into a ticking time bomb, a man who makes me want to climb him like a jungle gym, turn him into a ride I never want to get off.

Except that I do want to get off.

"Hi," I say brightly. Too brightly. It's like he's hypnotized me with his sex appeal. Sexnotized me.

He doesn't say anything back for a few moments. It's long enough to be noticeable, and I wish that damn sun wasn't still out even though it's seven at night, otherwise I'd be able to see his eyes. Does he like what he sees? Or does he think it's all a bit garish?

"Well, shall we go?" I say awkwardly.

"Yes, of course," he says with a start, shaking his head slightly, as if to snap out of it.

I step outside and close the door, heading over to the Garbage Pail.

"Are you sure you want to drive?" he asks.

I open my door and give him a smile. "You're sick of my driving already? You did so well the other day."

He reluctantly walks over to his side. "I thought you might want to have a few drinks."

I shake my head. "I'm fine. Get in."

He grumbles quietly and gets in his side. I take a moment to stare up at the trees above and take in a deep breath, bringing my brain back on track.

He's doing me a favor, it's not a date, he doesn't even want to be here.

I repeat that and get in the car, but my nerves fire up again once I realize how different it feels to have him so close to me when he's wearing less clothes. Yeah, it's a T-shirt, but compared to a suit he's practically naked now. I can clearly see the tattoos on his forearms and his biceps and . . . oh lord, his forearms! His biceps! They're so huge, the muscles hard-won and rippling and taut, and I can't even focus. Maybe I shouldn't drive. He's more intoxicating than any drink.

And then there's his scent, like sea salt and lime and something woodsy and sweet, and the heat generating off him, his shoulder so close to mine, and . . .

"Are you okay?" he asks.

I blink. I have to blink. I think I've been staring, no, *gawking,* at him without blinking, like a fucking lunatic.

"Yes," I manage to say, feeling my cheeks burn. I start the car. "Just lost in thought."

He nods at that though we're just past the gates when he says, "Weird seeing me like this?"

"Super weird," I say, even though weird doesn't begin to explain it and I'm not about to. I clear my throat. "Thank you for coming, by the way. Monica told me that you didn't want to, so I appreciate it. But I mean, I don't want to force you to either."

"No one is forcing me to do anything," he says, sounding all grumbly. "It's taken some consideration, that's all."

"She said you need to get out more."

"She's the one who needs to get out more. Not me. Luckily, I have complete faith in the team, so I know they'll be fine." He pauses, glancing at me quickly. "Me, on the other hand . . ."

"You'll be fine," I tell him. "Do you have a curfew? Are you going to turn into a pumpkin if I don't get you home in time?"

I don't have to see his eyes to know he's glaring at me.

"Apparently, thanks to you, I have the day off tomorrow," he says.

"Well, if I'm driving, then you're drinking. No excuses."

He doesn't say anything to that. Frankly I don't care if he drinks or not. I just want the guy to relax for once. After what Monica said about him being so busy and devoted to his job that he doesn't even date or seem to have a personal life at all, it's given me a bit of insight into a man who's notorious for clamming up.

It's only a ten-minute drive to the pub, situated at the edge of town and at the base of a large marina. There are people standing outside the entrance and smoking, and I immediately scan them to see if I know them. I may not have a lot of friends, but I know a lot of people, not all of them good. I exhale when I don't recognize anyone. Probably tourists.

"You going to be okay?" Harrison asks as we trundle along the gravel lot and park.

"Sure," I tell him.

He's staring at me, I think, and now that the car isn't moving and I don't have to concentrate on driving, I'm even more aware of how crammed we are in this small space.

I reach over and place my fingers on the edges of his sunglasses and gently pull them off his face.

He blinks at me, his eyes the color of the water here when the cedar reflects off it, intense as anything.

I have to take a moment to find my breath.

"You can't wear these inside," I tell him. "You'll look like a douche."

He squints. "I guess I should be happy I don't already look like one. I feel like one."

I hold out his sunglasses, and he takes them from me, his fingers brushing against mine, sending sparks up my arm, to the base of my neck, and down the rest of my body.

I am in trouble.

"You look great," I tell him, my voice small, like I'm holding back what I really want to say. "Not at all douchey."

Just ridiculously, sinfully hot.

He seems satisfied with that, though his eyes hold mine for what seems like eternity, the tension between us growing thick and heavy. My god. Is this how he always looks at me?

I have to look away. I clear my throat and smile bashfully at my steering wheel, at nothing, at anything but him, and then I get out of the car.

Twelve

THE WARM SUMMER AIR AND THE SUDDEN DISTANCE between us lets my brain stop focusing on him so much, but unfortunately that means it starts focusing on the pub.

Harrison gets out of the car and walks around to me.

"Are you going to give me a rundown of what to expect?"

I shrug as we walk across the gravel lot. "It's just a small-town pub."

"I figured that," he says. "But in regard to your ex. Isn't that why I'm here?"

He's right. But he's also here because I want him to be here.

He goes on. "If you're wanting it to look like we're together, like a couple—"

"No, no, no," I say quickly. "That's not it at all."

"Because I don't think that's a good idea," he adds, and some tiny part of my heart is crushed. "People know who I am. Maybe not in that pub, but elsewhere in the world, they do. I can't be in there, my arm around you, pretending you're my girlfriend when the media could easily get wind of it. My credibility would be destroyed, and they would drag Eddie and Monica through the dirt. They're always waiting for the first opportunity."

"I totally get it," I tell him, even though I'm reeling a bit. "So you're never allowed to date anyone, ever?"

He gives a quick shrug with one shoulder. "I'm free to do what I want. But I have to face the consequences. And if I was seen with you in that way, when it's likely known by now that you're a local, and a neighbor, it wouldn't be good. It would seem highly unprofessional to them, regardless of how I'd personally feel about it."

My eyes widen. *And . . . how do you feel about it?* I want to ask. I want to shake him and yell at him and get an answer, an answer to a question I didn't even know existed.

Instead I just nod, pausing outside the doors and out of earshot of the people smoking. "I don't want anyone to think anything. I just want to show up because I never do. I've lived here for long enough, and yet I barely belong. I've been sheltering myself because I've been too afraid of getting to know people, of letting them know me. Even when I was with Joey, I had made him my world and no one else. It's what I do when I'm in a relationship, and maybe that's normal, but when you're in a toxic relationship, it's unhealthy. I don't think I've ever been in a healthy one . . ." I trail off, looking down at my flip-flops, the chipped aqua nail polish on my toes. "I know this probably doesn't make a lot of sense to you. It barely makes sense to me."

"I understand more than you think," he says. "Come on. Let me buy you a drink."

He opens the door for me, and I walk in.

The place is packed. The opening band has already started, playing a cover of "Pour Some Sugar on Me," and waitresses are bustling past us with trays of flat beer and fish and chips.

"Where do you want to sit?" I ask Harrison, having to raise my voice over the music, noticing that a lot of people are looking over at us, women in particular. I don't look at them long enough to see if I know them.

"Wherever you like," he says.

With the live music, most of the patrons are crowded near the stage in the upper portion of the pub, but being here is more about making an appearance, not being subjected to the drunk and sweaty masses, so I head toward the patio overlooking the marina, where I spot a table for two in the corner.

"Wasn't the point of coming here to be seen?" Harrison says as he pulls out the chair for me to sit down. I mean, who does that? The English might.

"Thank you," I say to him, touched by how ridiculously gentlemanly he's being. I sit. "The loud music gives me anxiety. Being out here still counts."

Particularly when I see none other than my favorite person, Amy Mischky, by the server station. I guess she has two jobs, and if I left the house more often, I'd have known that. She's staring at me and Harrison before she gathers our menus.

I quickly smooth my hair around my face and give her a big, bright smile as she comes over.

"Hello," I say to her.

"Hey," she says, frowning at me, then ogles Harrison. "Didn't think you'd show up."

Ah, see, there's the rub.

"Who could pass up the invite?" I say with a happy shrug.

She purses her lips for a moment, studying me, probably thinking lots of unkind thoughts. "Know what you're having to drink?"

"The menus would be a helpful start," Harrison says.

Ha! I love snarky Harrison.

Amy narrows her eyes at him for a split second, then pastes a very phony smile on her face. "Of course." She drops the menus on the table and walks away.

"Love that you said that," I say to him.

"If she's as bad at serving as she is as a barista, this is going to be a long night."

I take a menu. "That's a sign that you haven't been fully integrated into island life. Island life means that it's everyone's first day on the job, always. Just be happy they show up."

He shakes his head, a touch of an amused smile on his lips as he looks over his menu. "To be honest, I'm not sure how you do it."

"To be fair, it's not like you have to deal with the public much."

"Even so, the lack of efficiency is excruciating to me."

"You get used to it. Just gotta go with the flow. That means stop worrying about things you can't control."

"I'm not worried. Controlled is a preference."

"I think you're getting preferences and needs mixed up."

"I know the difference," he says mildly, flipping the menu over. "Can't remember the last time I had a beer."

"Really? You make a pretty poor Brit."

"Rightly so," he says, twisting in his seat to wave over Amy.

She comes over reluctantly and stands in front of us, her hand on her hip. "So, what will it be?"

Harrison nods at me to go first.

"I'll have a water and a Corona Light," I say.

"I'll have a brown ale."

"Just the drinks, then," she says, reaching to take the menus away.

Harrison places his palm down on them. "Haven't decided

yet," he says in a polite yet firm voice, adding a flash of a smile at the end.

Amy's either stunned by his smile or intimidated by his direction, and she blinks at him for a moment, her mouth dropping open until she manages to say, "Of course."

She goes on to another table, Harrison watching her with a sneer to his lips. "I don't like her," he says, turning back to me. "She's bad news."

"Well, she comes from a long line of bad news," I tell him. "Her mother is one of those people who writes editorials to the local newspaper, complaining about tourism or protesting against cell phone service or that a man she doesn't even know is cutting down too many trees on his property. I'm actually shocked that she hasn't written about you guys yet. I can't imagine your being here has been a smooth transition for everyone else."

"I hadn't considered that," Harrison muses, squinting at the sun. I know he's dying to put on his sunglasses, but for some reason he hasn't yet. "I'd just been so focused on you."

I'd just been so focused on you.

That's what he just said.

I hate that some part of me is absolutely melting, just the notion that someone has been paying attention, and that that someone is him.

His gaze goes over the marina. "I guess staying holed up at the house, we haven't really been out and about to see how people feel about us."

Okay, so either he's skirting over it, that he's been focused on me, or he doesn't realize what he's said. It's hard to get a read on him because his eyes are taking in the boats. He doesn't look exactly relaxed, but then again, he never does.

"All I know is, there is more media here because of you."

"Well, I don't see them here tonight," he points out.

I look around. That's true. Wherever the media hides out, it isn't here.

"Maybe they all left. With Bert and then James patrolling out there, and with Monica and Eddie never leaving the house, maybe they gave up."

"That's what they want you to think," he says, tapping his temple. "Tricky bastards."

Amy comes back with our drinks and plunks them down in a hurry, doesn't bother to ask us what we want, which is just as well, since I haven't even looked at the menu.

"Cheers," I say to Harrison, squeezing the lime slice through the bottleneck and then holding up my beer. "Here's to a night on the town."

That gets a smile out of him. "Cheers to that."

We clink, and I manage to maintain eye contact with him as I sip my beer. Then someone by the doors catches my eye.

Shit.

It's Joey.

I mean, I obviously came here hoping to see him, but more like I hoped he would see me from afar and be like, *Oh, Piper, she's obviously not afraid to be out and about, guess I didn't ruin her like I thought.* Something along those lines. And then he would just play his awful music and stay away.

But no, he's walking over to me, not staying away.

I sit up straighter, put a stiff smile on my face, and it's enough that Harrison looks behind him. When he looks back at me, his brows are raised expectantly. I recall what Harrison said on the dock about wanting to break Joey's nose and hope it hasn't come to that yet.

"Pipes," Joey says, standing in front of our table, his arms crossed. He's got this cheesy, smug look on his face, and I have to wonder why I ever found him attractive. Oh right, it's because he was an aloof commitment-phobe and I figured that was what I deserved.

"Joey," I say to him. Then I smile and point my beer at Harrison. "This is Harrison. I don't think you were formally introduced last time."

"Oh right, hey, man," Joey says, holding out his hand. "You're the visitor."

"That's me," Harrison says, shaking Joey's hand and absolutely crushing it.

Joey is trying so hard not to wince, I cover my mouth with my beer to hide my delight.

He pulls his hand away, offering a crooked smile. "Wow. That's some handshake." Joey looks at me. "Where did you find this guy, Pipes? The MMA?"

Intensity radiates from Harrison's eyes. "Not quite," he says in a low voice, the kind of voice that should tell Joey he's on thin ice.

"Do they even have the MMA in Britain? You're British, right? Would have expected you to have more of a Jason Statham kind of voice. You know. Like this." And he proceeds to do a terrible impression of Jason Statham, like Michael Caine on steroids.

Oh Joey, please shut up.

"No, I don't know," Harrison says carefully, staring at him now with full-on menace. "I'm sorry, what's your name again?"

"Joey."

"And you're Piper's . . . what, friend?"

Harrison knows what he's doing. Joey blinks at him, taken aback, like he can't believe I haven't told Harrison about him. I can see he's thinking back to the café, wondering if Harrison had overheard the part about me leaving him at the altar, but I love that Harrison is pretending otherwise.

"No," he says, and then shoots me a glance. "Well, yes. I'd say she's my friend. We have a complicated history."

"I see," Harrison says. "It's good to meet Piper's friends. I hope they all treat her as dearly as I do."

"Right," Joey says slowly. "Anyway, my band is playing a set in ten minutes or so. You should come inside and see. Don't worry, Amy will hold your table out here."

"We'll see," I tell Joey, and then wave at the water. "It's just so nice out here, shame to be inside."

Joey looks disappointed. Good. He walks away, and I sigh.

"Please don't tell me you still have feelings for that wanker," Harrison says, finishing the rest of his beer in one gulp.

A choked laugh escapes me. "Are you kidding? No. Hell no."

Harrison seems to brood over that for a moment, then gets up.

"Where are you going?" I ask, fearing he's leaving.

"Going to go place an order at the bar. I don't trust our waitress. What would you like?"

"I'm not drinking anything other than this," I say, waving the beer bottle at him.

He lightly taps the table with his fist. "Be right back."

I watch as he walks off into the pub. I really hope he's not going in there to do something stupid. Not that he's ever struck me as the brash and reckless type; he's been the opposite. But he is drinking when he doesn't seem to normally, and maybe there's a side of Harrison that comes loose.

So I sit there, nursing my beer, watching sailboats dock and tourists going to and fro, and trying not to worry about him.

Finally he returns, double-fisting two dark beers. Instead of looking triumphant, however, he just looks annoyed.

"Took you long enough," I tell him.

"I had a shot of whisky," he says, sitting down, the beers spilling over the edge of the glass.

"You what?" I stare at him.

"I had a shot of whisky," he repeats, fixing his eyes on me, almost as a challenge. He doesn't seem like he's had a shot of whisky and a beer already; his gaze is as sharp and as clear as ever. But I'm still surprised he's taken this turn.

"Making up for lost time?" I ask.

"Something like that," he says. "Your ex is up onstage. Sure you don't want to go in there and watch?"

"No, thank you," I tell him. "In fact, when you're done with those beers, we can leave."

He frowns at me, his blue-green eyes growing more intense. "So soon?"

"You actually want to stay?"

He shrugs and palms his pint. "Why not? You dragged me out here, I've had the first drinks I've had in months. Dare I say I'm actually enjoying this?"

I wave my fingers at him. "*This* is you enjoying something?"

He gives me a crooked grin and then has a hearty gulp of his beer. "You can't tell?"

Well, since he wants to stay and I've got him mostly alone and feeling a little looser, I decide to start my investigation into Harrison's secretive backstory.

"So, tell me," I begin, sitting back in my chair. "When was the last time you had a day off?"

He sips his beer and ponders that for a moment. "I honestly can't remember."

"I'm guessing when Monica and Eddie asked you to come with them to Canada, you didn't have many reasons to say no."

"Not particularly."

"Any family?"

A darkness washes over his eyes, and he averts his gaze from mine, staring down at beer #2. Something tells me that wasn't a harmless question.

"A mother. A younger brother and sister. They're back in London."

"Did your father skip out too?"

"I never knew him. But yes. Knocked up my mom and that was it. Then my mom got knocked up by two other guys, had my siblings. None of them stuck around, so it was up to me to help my mom raise them."

"Oh. I'm sorry."

"No need to be sorry. I'm not. It's just life. Managed to finish high school, then went straight to the army. Figured it was the easiest way to support everyone."

"They must be very proud of you."

He shrugs lightly, his brow furrowing. "Maybe. I wouldn't know. It's hard to keep in touch with them, but I try. And send them money too, my mum particularly. She's had a tough go with life."

"So you were in the army a long time."

He nods. "Was the best decision I ever made. It kept me in line, made me stand up straight and take responsibility. You probably wouldn't believe that I was a bit of a wanker when I was young. Shit disturber, always in trouble. Drinking, drugs, you name it. I suppose it was me rebelling at having to act like a father at such a young age. Going into the army kept me from a dark and dirty fate."

Every little piece of himself that Harrison reveals feels like a gift and a revelation. It all makes so much sense now. His cool, calm, and collected demeanor, his need to be in control. He couldn't be better suited for his job, but it might explain why he's so devoted to it. He's afraid to slip up.

I hope he's not slipping up now. He's just finished his second beer and is halfway through number three. Maybe eating something is a good idea.

"Have you ever had duck wings before?" I ask, picking up the menu. "They're amazing here. So is their fish and chips. Freshly caught halibut."

He gives me a wry look as he takes his menu. "You getting paid to say that?"

"Hey, I'm big on food. If a place has good food, I'll shout it from the rooftops."

His eyes flick over the menu. "Then I'm surprised that you're not out and about here more often."

"I guess you can say both of us desperately needed a night out, then. Maybe I'm coming to realize I can't stay a hermit forever."

"Can't live in fear," Harrison says, his voice dropping a register. "But that's easier said than done. Isn't it?"

I mull that over while Harrison flags down Amy again and we put in an order for a pound of duck wings, plus another beer and a highball of Scotch for Harrison. I've decided I have zero business telling him what he can and can't drink. He's a grown man. He makes his own decisions. And I was the one who insisted he come with me, and he did.

Besides, I'm still thinking about what he said. About the fear. And that there's a moment when fear no longer serves you, no longer protects you. It harms you and holds you back. I might be at one of those thresholds, where my desire to keep myself and my mother safe from harm, specifically the harm of others' opinions and thoughts, might actually do more damage in the long run. I can't speak for my mother and how she feels, but I think it's healthier for me to put myself out there, even if there's a chance doing so might hurt me.

Amy comes back with the beer and whisky first, and by the time she brings the duck wings, Harrison is already done with his drinks and is ordering another round.

And he's starting to look a little drunk. His eyes have lost that intensity, seem a little unfocused.

"Don't worry about me," Harrison says, his brow lined as he looks me over. "I see your worrying all over your face."

I try to make my face look as smooth as possible. "I'm not worried," I say brightly, lying. "Maybe you're not used to me wearing this much makeup."

"You're right. I'm not." He doesn't sound happy about it.

"Let me guess: You think I look better without all of it?"

"I think you look beautiful either way."

Whoa.

My eyes go round, but he doesn't seem to notice what he's said.

He's drunk, I remind myself.

Though don't drunk people speak the truth?

Beer goggles, I counter.

And then Joey comes out of the pub, striding across the patio toward us.

"Duck wings, nice," he says, nodding at the plate. "Always a favorite." He gives me a pointed look. "You didn't come to see me play, did you?"

"I didn't even notice your band was playing," I tell him honestly. "Sounded a lot like the band before."

I can practically see his hackles go up. That bothers him. He hates the cover band, thinks it's beneath a musician to cover other people's music, even though I know he plays a few covers as well.

He looks to Harrison. "Hey, you know what? We were just talking about you. I know who you are."

Harrison glances up at him, squinting. "And?"

"You're the bodyguard. To the prince and princess or whoever they are. On Scott Point, right beside Piper. This all makes so much sense now."

"What do you mean?" I ask sharply.

Joey laughs and points at me and then at Harrison. "I mean, come on. I knew you guys weren't a couple; that made no sense at all. Figures that you're her bodyguard or something, though honestly I don't know why anyone would bother pestering Piper here. She's just a schoolteacher, no one important."

There are so many infuriating things to unpack with that spiel that I can't even say anything and just stew in my burning, indignant anger.

"Why wouldn't we be a couple?" Harrison asks, his voice so steely and calm that any sane person would hightail it out of here.

Not dense, ignorant, righteous Joey. "Well, sir, I don't normally compliment another man, but you're definitely out of her league." He shoots me a faux sad look. "No offense, Piper. You're just, you know, and he's just . . . well, I don't think you'd be leaving him at the altar like you did to me."

And there it is.

His words hit me like a slap in the face and then sink to the pit of my stomach, turning over in knots, then fire back up like I'm a fucking volcano.

I jump to my feet, the chair knocking back, and yell, "You're the one who cheated on me during your bachelor party! I didn't leave you at the altar. I called it off earlier because I found out that you were a cheating asshole!"

"Sure. Keep telling people that. No one in this town believes you. Except maybe this guy, if he's dumber than he looks." He jerks his thumb at Harrison.

And Harrison is quicker than a lightning bolt. In one fast, smooth move, he reaches out and grasps Joey's thumb with one large hand, squeezing it, ready to snap it in two.

Joey lets out a squeal, and now everyone on the patio is looking at us.

"Is this how you treat all your customers?" Harrison snarls at him, the venom in his voice and in his eyes unmistakable. "By calling them dumb? Is that how you run your business?"

"Let go of me," Joey pleads, sniveling and pathetic. "Let go of me. You have no idea who I am, who my family is."

"I don't give a flying fuck who your family is," Harrison says. "But I will let go of you." He releases Joey's thumb, and Joey snatches it to his chest, cradling it. "And if you ever insult me or Piper again, or any other customer who has come in here on a Friday night to give you business, then I'll make sure the world knows about it. See, your island is small. But my world? It's bigger than you can even imagine. Now, if you want to save your bloody pub, I'd apologize, and mean it, and then wipe our bill clean."

With everyone here watching, and knowing that the pub is full of tourists who don't give a rat's ass about his family's history on the island, Joey is trapped.

He looks at me, and I glare right back at him as he says, "Sorry, Piper."

He can barely make eye contact with Harrison. I don't blame him. "And I'm sorry to you. The bill is on me. Whatever else you want is on the house." Joey waves Amy over. "Amy will take care of you."

"Better late than never," Harrison mumbles under his breath

Joey then walks quickly out of the patio, avoiding the eyes of the customers as he passes by. Amy, on her best behavior and with a nervous smile plastered on her face, takes Harrison's order for a double of Scotch.

When she leaves, I let out a long, shaky breath, staring at Harrison with a mix of trepidation and awe. "I thought you were going to kill him."

Harrison closes his eyes and breathes in deeply through his nose. "I wanted to."

"You stayed in control."

He nods. "Barely." He opens his eyes and looks at me. "He deserves so much worse than what he got."

"I know. But humiliating him is just as good."

"The nerve he has to talk to you like that . . ."

"Like I said, I know my assholes."

"I don't understand how you could have been engaged to him."

I give him a tight, sad smile. "I didn't understand until my therapist explained why. Since then, I've been single. Guess I'm too afraid of making the same mistake. Too afraid of being attracted to the wrong people. Least I know the warning signs now."

"And what are those?"

"Someone who's handsome, controlling, emotionally unavailable."

Something in my words must strike a chord with him, because he flinches slightly. "That sounds a lot like me. Especially the handsome part."

"At least you can admit you're emotionally unavailable."

"Just what I've been told," he says, and then starts looking around. "Where is that drink?"

With that slightly awkward blip over, the rest of our night at the Blowhole passes uneventfully. I talk a lot about my mom, and the other assholes I dated, and the work I did with my therapist, and my complex PTSD and everything like that, while Harrison listens and drinks. And drinks, and drinks.

Soon I know it's time to leave. He's slurring his words and wavering slightly in his chair.

"Okay, time to go, I think," I tell him softly, getting to my feet.

Harrison grumbles something and then gets up, and for a moment I think he's about to keel over. I go to him and take his arm, pulling him across the patio and leading him out of the pub.

It takes a bit of effort to get him in the car. It's feeling more and more like I'm trying to see how many clowns can fit in a Volkswagen, and while I'm driving us home, he passes out, his head against the window.

Shit. What a night. Never in my wildest dreams did I think it would end up like this, with Harrison getting shitfaced and threatening to break Joey's thumb and ruin his restaurant. In a way I'm glad it happened, because Joey needed to be put in his place, especially after he was so insulting to the both of us, but I can't help but feel a little uneasy that this is going to come back to bite us in the ass in some way. In small towns, but especially on an island, word travels fast.

A little too fast.

With the gate fob at the ready, we pull past the SUV and then up the driveway, Harrison suddenly stirring.

"No," he says, slurring. "Don't take me back. I don't want them to see me like this."

I pause and then reverse back down the driveway and turn left into mine, coming to a park.

"You just need to sleep this off," I tell him, getting out of the car. "Come on."

I go over to his side, open the door, and start to pull him out of the car. He doesn't come easy. When he gets to his feet, there's a lot of his weight leaning on my shoulders, his arm around me for balance, and it feels like I'm trying to stop a giant boulder from rolling down the hill.

We stagger up to the house and open the door. My mother's bedroom door is closed. Liza is probably in there with her, which is good. She doesn't need to see this and worry.

We make our way to my bedroom, and I lead Harrison to the bed, where he keels over facedown.

I then unlace and pull off his boots, noting his brightly colored yellow socks, and take a throw blanket from the easy chair and toss it over him. I get a glass of water and some Advil from the kitchen and put it by the bedside table. He's already asleep and snoring lightly.

I pause, taking a moment to really look at him, his massive frame making my queen-size bed look like a single. This mysterious broody man, my next-door neighbor, finally feels like someone I could really get to know.

I just hope that tonight doesn't change him, doesn't make him take two steps back to make up for this one tiny step forward.

I close the door. I grab extra blankets from the linen closet, then go to sleep on the couch.

Thirteen

I WAKE UP WITH A START.

Something rattled me awake, put my hair on end, even before I figure out where I am. What is it? What's happening?

It's dark, almost black save for the power light on the TV. I'm on the couch, tangled in the fleece blanket, and there's something going on.

There it is. A choked cry.

But it's not my mother.

I get to my feet, stumbling across the dark living room, running my shin right into the cedar coffee table. I wince, seeing stars for a moment (that's gonna leave a bruise!), and then I open the door to my bedroom, rushing inside.

My eyes have adjusted. Harrison is on his back on top of the covers, his head moving back and forth, mouth open. Another doomed cry comes from his lips as his face contracts in anguish.

"Hey," I whisper. "Hey, hey, you're okay."

I put my hands on his shoulder, barely touching him, not wanting to scare him. When he doesn't seem to wake, I shake him a little harder.

"Harrison. Harrison Cole. Wake up. You're having a nightmare."

His head stops moving, and his eyes slowly open, his breath labored. He blinks into nothing for a moment and then looks at me, visibly shaken.

"What . . . Where, where am I?" he gasps.

I keep pressure on his shoulder, hoping it's more soothing than restrictive. Not that I could restrain him. I can feel the power and muscle beneath my hand.

"You're okay, it's me, Piper. You're in my bed. You were having a nightmare."

In the dim light I see his shining eyes finally focus on me. He takes in a deep gulp of air, his body relaxing slightly under my touch.

"Piper," he manages to say, licking his lips. If the situation weren't so worrisome and dire, I'd be more distracted than I already am by the fact that he's licking those lips and he's lying in my bed.

"It's me," I tell him, giving his shoulder a squeeze. "You fell asleep on my bed."

He blinks a few times at me and then seems to remember what happened.

"Fuck," he swears, his voice still thick with sleep. "That was unreal."

I sit on the edge of the bed. "What were you dreaming about? Do you remember?"

"Yeah," he says, nodding, his eyes still looking a little wild. He swallows. "Yeah. It's always the same."

He seems in such a wild, fragile state that I don't want to press him too much.

"Do you want to talk about it?"

He shakes his head and sits up. His eyes pinch together, wincing. "No."

"Here," I tell him, fetching the water and pills from the bedside.

He shakes his head again, brushes the glass and pills away. "I'm okay. I need to go back. They're probably worried."

"It's the middle of the night. They're probably asleep. Just stay and sleep for a bit. You can go back in the morning."

But he's already getting out of bed. He's unsteady on his feet, and I leap up to press my hand against his chest in case he topples over again.

Here we are. In the dark. In my bedroom.

I'm pressed right up against him. His chest feels as hard as a rock beneath my fingers. He's staring down at me, his breath raspy. I keep my focus on his chest because I'm afraid to meet his eyes.

"I need to go back," he says, his voice low and rough, and at such close proximity it sends shivers down my spine. "But thank you."

I dare to look up at him. In the dim light his eyes are fixed on mine, the line between his brows deepening.

Our faces are so close. If I stood on my toes, I could kiss him. I won't.

But for the first time, I'm consumed by how much I want to.

It was easier to ignore before. It's impossible to ignore now.

Is it the same for him?

Does he feel this? The tension that crackles like a live wire, the pull that I feel toward him like a planet orbiting the sun.

"Thank you for what?" I whisper.

He swallows.

"Taking care of me." His eyes search mine, glittering in intensity, seeming to wrestle with something. "It's been a very long time since I've had that," he murmurs.

Then he reaches out and brushes a strand of my hair back, tucking it behind my ear. Keeps his palm pressed against my cheek.

His face dips down an inch, and I suck in a sharp breath as his gaze drops to my open mouth.

Oh my god.

I'm frozen in place, frozen in time, knowing that Harrison is about to kiss me and . . .

He pulls back. Clears his throat. "I better get going."

Then he walks around me, leaving me feeling cold.

He sits on the end of the bed and slips his boots on and I want to say something, anything, but I can't. My skin feels alive where he touched me, my heart aching for that kiss that never came. I'm confused and tired, and damn it, I'm *yearning*.

"I'll see you later," he says to me once his boots are on, not bothering to lace them up. Then he's walking to the front door, and then he's gone.

I stand there for a few moments and then slowly lower myself on the bed.

I don't think I'm going to fall back asleep anytime soon.

DESPITE WHAT HARRISON said about seeing me later, I didn't see him at all yesterday, nor today. It's back to quiet in the house, which gives me time to start working on my lesson plans for the first week of school this fall (just because teachers get summers off doesn't mean they don't have work to do).

It also gives me a lot of time to think about what happened on Friday night. It made me realize that I can't let the fear of what other people think of me rule my life. I've never been that social, mainly because it's been ingrained in me to stay home and look after my mother, but I wonder how much of that is really needed and how much of that is misplaced guilt.

I decide to spring the question on my mom on Sunday night, when we're sitting around on the deck, waiting for the sun to set, a sweet breeze coming off the water beyond the trees. She's wrapped up in a crossword puzzle. I'm trying to read a book, but I've basically been repeating the same sentence over and over again.

Finally I put the book down.

"Mom?" I ask.

"Mmm," she says absently as her pencil hovers above the squares.

"You know how I went out the other night."

"Mmhmmm."

"Were you okay with that?"

She puts down her pencil and peers at me. "What do you mean?"

"Did it bother you that I went out?"

"No. Of course not." She tilts her head, considering. "Okay. I have to say I was a little concerned that you went with Mr. Cole."

"Why?"

"Because I know your type."

"I'm not dating him."

"It doesn't matter," she says, shaking her head at me. "I see the way you look at him. I've seen that look many times before, Piper."

I cross my arms, feeling defensive. How am I looking at him? I can't control what my face does. "I'm not . . . We're not . . . We're just friends."

"You want to be more than friends."

"Well, so what?" I say in a huff, throwing my arms out. "So what if I want to be more than friends? It hurts only me. I know we can't be together for a million reasons, so obviously whatever feelings I have will remain buried, locked inside me forever."

"No need to be so dramatic," she says, as if she's not usually the queen of self-created drama. "I'm just pointing something out to you. You say your therapist does the same thing. You haven't gone to her in a while, so maybe someone has to step up."

She's right. I talk a big game about therapy, but I haven't been in at least six months. I guess I kind of felt like I was done, but I'm starting to think that therapy doesn't have an expiration date. You're never cured. There *is* no cure. There's just a way to cope. Only you know when you're ready to move on, but you also have to know when you should go back.

Maybe I should go back. Maybe everything I'm dealing with hasn't resolved itself.

I gnaw on my lip for a moment, pulling the plaid blanket I have wrapped around me tighter. "Maybe you'd like to go with me?" I ask quietly, bracing for the impact.

"To therapy?" my mother questions. Her eyes are wide and unblinking. She's pushed back against this so many times before that I know it's pretty much futile to even ask, but I figure I might as well try.

"Yeah. I think it would be good for both of us to go together, don't you?"

Now she's blinking rapidly. Tears are forming at the corners of her eyes.

Shit.

"Why . . . I thought I was doing well," she says. "I've been doing well, haven't I? I've been good."

I reach out and put my hand on top of hers. "You've been so great."

"Then why would you say that? Why would you say that to me?"

I've made a mistake. I wanted to talk to my mother about how perhaps I'm not as needed at home as I think I am, that maybe I ought to stop using her as a crutch, as an excuse to withdraw from society. But now I've mentioned therapy and she's upset and on the defensive, just as she always is.

"Forget it," I tell her.

A tear spills down her cheek. She will not forget it. She will dwell on this for days.

"I've been trying so hard, Piper. I really have. With them moving next door, I feel like I have to be on my best behavior, and I've been so afraid of screwing up. I don't want them to judge me. I want them to like me."

This breaks my heart. I squeeze her hand tighter until she pulls it away.

"Mom, please. You're doing fine. I promise they aren't judging you and that they like you and you're handling this change so well. I just thought that maybe if it's time for me to go back, you'd come with me. Not so much for yourself but for me. I . . . it would be nice to have the support."

But she doesn't believe me and won't hear me, that much I know. Once she has something in her head, all the convincing in the world won't change her mind.

She gets up, crying now, and heads inside.

I sit there, my heart sinking. I fucked up this time, I really did. This is how it's always gone when I mention therapy. She's so resistant to it that it's like a reflex. The same goes for medication. She should go to the doctor a lot more than she does, and I have to be the one on top of her refills. She'll happily run out of pills and won't tell me for weeks. Sometimes I wonder if she's so afraid of society judging her for her mental illness that the stigma contributes to her denial. Or I think that maybe my dad had something to do with it. I was young, but I remember many arguments between my parents, my dad often saying that my mother could change if she wanted to, and that there was no such thing as borderline personality disorder. Hell, he's the type to believe that depression is just a case of the blues as well. I wonder how much he contributed to the way my mother is now, you know, aside from the fact that he left her high and dry for the very reasons he told her didn't exist.

Liza, who has been lying on the deck, gets up and walks over to me, looking up at me with questioning eyes. She's so sensitive to both our moods, which is one of the reasons why she's such a great girl to have around. Even though she's not an official emotional support animal, she acts like one anyway. Maybe her upbringing, being found as a stray, most likely escaped from an abusive home, makes her know just what it is that people in pain, emotional or physical, need.

"Hey, girl," I say to her, feeling choked up myself. I stroke the top of her head. "Go check on your grandma. She needs you."

Liza stares at me for a moment, but she knows what *grandma* means. She trots off into the house, presumably to go be by her side.

As for me, I know the damage I've done and that going after my mother and trying to explain and apologize isn't going to get me very far. It will only make things worse. The only thing I can do now is give her space and hope that she'll come around soon.

Tomorrow is Monday. It's a great day to call my therapist and make an appointment for myself.

MY THERAPIST IS getting more than she bargained for.

I slept in a little this morning, feeling tired and melancholy, and eventually ended up making an appointment for next week (my therapist is in Victoria). My mother stayed in her room with the door closed, and I only opened it when I heard Liza scratching at the door to be let out.

On our second walk of the day, I decide to check the mail. Our mailbox is farther up the road, but luckily the cul-de-sac is empty save for that SUV. I don't want to stare too hard, but either James never sleeps or he's not in the SUV at all and it's just for show. Either way, it's been keeping the media away.

I grab the mail, which is just an envelope and the local newspaper, the *ShoreLine*, and then take it back to the house.

Where I unfold the newspaper on the kitchen table.

And stare at the front page.

It's a picture of Eddie and Monica, with Harrison in the background, taken in England at some time.

The headline?

"Royal Bodyguard Involved in Altercation at Local Pub."

Followed by the first line: *If the Duke and Duchess of Fairfax are expected to be our new residents, how long can the peace last?*

The article itself is a very long, waxing piece of mumbo jumbo. I've already read it two times, and I'm currently sitting on the couch and trying to read it again, because it doesn't make a lot of sense.

I'm not named in the article for some reason or another, but I have been given the title of "local schoolteacher who is neighbors with the royals." It starts off by saying there was an altercation at the pub over the service (a damn lie and they know it) and that

Harrison Cole reacted in an aggressive manner toward the owner. The article goes on to talk about Joey himself and his family and their island legacy, before going into the negative impact the royals will have on the island. It says that the island so far has been peaceful, but when the royals become news, the media will come out in droves again.

That part is most likely true. However, the article then veers into fearmongering, talking about how the royals might be bad for the island long-term; how the island doesn't need negative publicity, since the royals' appearance in Canada alone has brought out resentment from taxpayers; that we're far too small and humble for the likes of celebrities like them, etc.

Basically it's just one long, big bashing, using Harrison's incident as an excuse for it.

I don't recognize the name of the person who wrote it, but that doesn't matter much anyway. They think a certain way, and I'm sure Barbara Mischky and others are apt to share the same complaints. I think it's ridiculous that this hateful drivel was actually allowed to be printed, and on the front page, but sometimes I suspect the people at the newspaper might not be as unbiased as they claim.

I'm still stewing over this when, surprise, there's a knock at my door.

This time I have no idea what to expect. Is it Monica, here to get mad at me for what happened at the pub (after all, the outing was my idea)? Is it Harrison . . . here to get mad at me for what happened at the pub? I mean, the possibilities are endless.

I open the door.

A tall and lean man in a suit, with a strong jaw, black hair, and dark eyes, is standing on my steps.

PPO James.

"Good afternoon," he says in a Scottish brogue. "I hope I'm not bothering you. The duchess is wondering if you'd join her tonight on the dock."

"Am I being forced to walk the plank?" I ask.

James smiles. He has a nice smile. Proof that not all bodyguards need to be as moody and broody as Harrison. "Not at all. She said she was due for a girls' night and was hoping you would join her. I believe she'll have drinks and food set up. You don't have to bring anything."

"Why did she send you here?" Why didn't she send Harrison? "She could have just texted."

"She would have come here herself, but she's gone off island with Eddie. To the doctor."

"Oh my god, is something wrong?"

Another quick smile. "Not at all. It's routine."

Ah, for the baby. Of course.

"Okay. Sure, I would love to have a girls' night. Do you know what time?"

"I'll be back at seven p.m. to get you," James says. Then he touches his forefinger against his forehead in a sort of salute and walks off down the driveway, the fallen leaves of the arbutus tree crunching beneath his boots.

Interesting. He said that *he'll* be back to get me tonight. Not Harrison. I figured the reason Harrison wasn't here delivering the invitation was because he was off island with Eddie and Monica. But if that's the case, then wouldn't he come get me later, not James?

Unless Harrison is embarrassed to be around you. The way he acted, how drunk and vulnerable he was, the nightmare. He's probably seen the newspaper. Maybe he realizes he needs to take a step back. Maybe whatever you had between you, that beginning of a friendship, maybe that's officially over.

I usually tell the negative side of my brain to shut up, but I don't have a good counter to it this time. I think I'm right.

AT TEN TO seven, I'm wearing skinny jeans, a white tank, and a long cardigan, since evenings can get cool, and waiting for James. My mother is in her room still, only coming out briefly to get some water and snacks before going back. She's avoiding me, and as much as it hurts, I know I just have to let her have her space.

At seven on the dot, there's a knock at the door.

James is outside and nods when he sees me. Seems all the bodyguards are equally as punctual.

I walk with him to their house, glancing at him curiously. In some ways he seems the same as Harrison: big, broad-shouldered, a body that looks like it has no problems being lethal if it has to be. And even though James is quick to smile around me, there's a sadness in his eyes. He looks like an old soul.

"Where were you working before you came here?" I ask him.

"I wasn't," he says, giving me a soft smile. "I was on sabbatical."

"Oh. Well then, is it good to be back to work?"

He nods. "Yes. Especially here. It's a lot easier to do the job when you're on an island in the middle of nowhere."

"I wouldn't say it's the middle of nowhere."

"Compared to England, yes. But that's not an insult. I love the peace and quiet here. Gives me time to think about my next moves."

"Are you going to stay with them the whole time they're here?"

"Probably. But I'm not sure where I'll go after that."

"Why were you on a sabbatical?"

Another quick smile; this one doesn't reach his eyes. "It's a long story. But we all need a break sometimes, don't you think?"

I couldn't agree more. Being a teacher is perfect for that, even though I still have a lot of work to do during the summer to prepare for the upcoming school year.

I decide not to pry any further, and we go around the side of the house, down a set of stairs that leads to the back hillside, and follow the sloping path down to the dock where the yacht is tied up.

At the end of the dock are a couple of Adirondack chairs with throws over the back and a log-stump table in between them. It looks like a gorgeous spot to just sit and relax and watch the world go by.

Except now I'm noticing that there are quite a few boats out there. Little speedboats and Zodiacs that are just sitting on the waves, not going anywhere. Odd. There's a lot of traffic at Scott Point, with the ferries heading out of Long Harbour or out of Active Pass, sailboats, fishing boats, and whale watching tours heading in all directions between Salt Spring, Galiano, and Pender Islands. The difference here is, these boats aren't moving.

I'm just about to say something to James about it when a speedboat comes roaring out from around the corner, the same speedboat I saw when they all first moved in. The boat cuts right in front of the dock, between us and the waiting boats, and it's only then that I realize that it's Harrison behind the wheel.

If he's noticed me at all, he doesn't show it. He handles the boat with grace as it zips past and does a quick turn, getting closer to the waiting boats this time.

"What's going on?" I ask James as we stand outside the yacht, the dock now moving underneath us as the waves from the speedboat crash against it.

"The press," James says with a sigh. "They've been awakened with that newspaper article." He glances at me. "I assume you've seen it?"

I nod. "Yeah."

"Well, news travels fast, especially online. I have a feeling that these are our dear British tabloids that have finally shown up, late to the game and doubly frustrated that they can't get close to the house."

Monica pokes her head up from inside the powerboat, looking tiny against its massive size. "Piper," she says. "Come aboard."

She's smiling as always and seems cheery, so that relaxes me somewhat. Doesn't stop me from feeling like all of this is my fault, however.

I get on board, while James walks to the end of the dock and sits down on one of the chairs. Harrison is still going around in the speedboat, though he's slowed down now and the wake isn't so bad.

Monica waves me inside the boat, and I follow. The interior is slick but a little cold and austere, with zero personal touches. "Nice boat," I tell her.

"I'm not a fan," she says, and then laughs when she sees my expression. "It's okay, it's not our boat. We chartered it for the time we're here. It was the only one this big that was available for such a long time. Here, have a seat. Want some wine? I've at least got that. And please, don't decline because I'm pregnant. I need to live vicariously through someone. I am missing wine like I'm missing a limb."

"Well, in that case, yes, please," I tell her, sitting down on one of the plush chairs by an oak table. "You know, I've heard doctors say that it's okay for pregnant women to have a glass of wine every now and then."

She pulls a bottle from the fridge and laughs. "That applies to most women, but I don't fall in the 'most women' category. Word would get out somehow, and then my unhealthy habits would be splashed across every tabloid across the planet. When my child grows up, if there's anything less than perfect about them, then you can guarantee a million fingers will be pointing my way, and at that one glass of wine."

"You're right," I tell her as she plucks a wineglass from the shelf and brings the bottle over, filling the glass with a generous amount of pinot blanc. "I never thought of that."

"Unfortunately when you're me, you have to think of everything," she says with a tired sigh as she sits across from me. She leans forward, her elbows on the table, and steeples her fingers under her chin, looking at me thoughtfully. "You'd think I would be used to it by now, but sometimes, whoooo boy . . . it's like the rug is pulled right out from under me. Today is a good example of that. I had originally thought we could have a little girls' night here on the dock, but once those boats started showing up . . ."

I cringe. "I'm so sorry about that."

"It comes with the territory," she says with a shrug, sitting back in her chair and resting her hands on her bump, which is looking more pronounced than ever.

"But it's my fault."

She frowns at me. "Come on. It's not your fault. How is it your fault?"

"I'm the one who invited Harrison."

"And I'm the one who made him go," she says. "Besides, I'm not concerned about what happened. I heard Harrison's side of the story, and I'm sure yours is the same . . . He said he was defending you."

I nod. "He was."

"From your ex too. I tell you, if I were there, it would have been ugly. I have a temper that comes out at the worst times. Or perhaps just the right times. But it's all bad news when everyone is watching your every move." She pauses and gives me a small smile. "I'm glad you had Harrison with you. Don't think otherwise."

I take a sip of my wine. It smells of green apple and honey, and it's so crisp and divine, I immediately relax. "I wouldn't have gone without him. I don't think I've been to the local bar since . . . well, a long time."

"Not your scene?"

I shake my head. "Not really. I mean . . . sometimes I feel like I'm missing out. In fact, just being there made me feel a little more connected to where I live. I don't necessarily like some aspects of the community, but I like feeling as if I'm part of something, and I guess, I don't know, hiding here in the trees makes me realize that I'm hiding from a lot of things."

"Such as?"

"I don't know." I shrug. "Life?"

"You're a schoolteacher. That makes you a part of the community. You're responsible for the well-being and teaching of the community's children."

"I know. But it feels disconnected. It's so much easier to bond with my students. Easier than making friends among the teachers. I've lived here for so many years, but I made the big mistake of getting involved with Joey, with my ex, right off the bat. Everything was about him, and whatever friendships I had were shallow as a result. By the time they could develop into anything really meaningful, we broke up and I was left at the wayside, an outcast. People made their decisions about me without even knowing me, and I knew I had too many hardships in my life that they wouldn't be too understanding of. I wanted to protect myself, protect my mother."

"You know, you're describing my own life," Monica says. "Back when I was doing music, the press was different. I was just a Black singer to the media. No one cared enough to dig deep about my own family. Yes, my parents are very lovely people and they're still together in Seattle. But my father cheated on my mother when she was young, and I have a half brother that a lot of people didn't know about; my mom, like yours, has struggled with mental illness. It's a story like so many, but people only cared about my singing and my body and my dancing. Shallow stuff. Then I met Eddie and . . . it all changed. Suddenly everything was on the table. Every bad thing I ever did, every ex I dated, everything I said when I was drunk. The tabloids found it and exploited it and did what they could to mount a campaign against me. We couldn't hide our relationship for long; I was thrown right into that fire. Believe me, I know what it's like to have shallow friendships, to feel like you don't belong, to feel that you'll never be accepted as you are. I know it because I'm living it too."

Okay, now I feel a little silly, because as bad as I think I have it, it's nothing compared to what Monica has had to go through.

"Then how do you do it?" I ask. "How do you get out there? If I were you, I'd be hiding all the time."

"What do you think I'm doing now?" she says through a dry laugh. "I'm hiding. We're literally inside a boat because I wanted some time away from the house, the other place I'm hiding in, because the media is just outside there with their telephoto lenses. We came here to hide because I didn't *want* to do it anymore. I know that this is the life I chose, that I chose Eddie and everything that came with him, and I have no regrets. But it doesn't mean I have to like it or that I have to put up with it *all* the time. It doesn't mean my heart doesn't race and I don't lose my breath every time I step out in public. I know I'm strong, but it's impossible to be strong all the time, and as much as they said we were running away by coming to Canada, they were right!"

"And yet they're still here."

"I know all of this seems bad to you. I know that seeing those boats out there, or being accosted by the media outside your house, or being written about in your local paper, is aggravating and depressing. It is bad, and you don't deserve any of it. You're just an ordinary citizen. But believe me when I tell you, it can get worse. And no matter what happens here, it won't ever be as bad as it was for me back in the UK."

"Do you think you'll end up moving here forever?" I ask.

She rubs her lips together in thought, folding her slender hands in her lap. "I don't know. I just know that I want this time to be barefoot and pregnant. Time to be alone with Eddie. Time to figure stuff out. I'm sure I'll be back in London for the birth—the Queen would disown Eddie if our child wasn't born on British soil."

"What's she like?" I can't help myself.

"The Queen? She's . . . she's okay. I admire her a lot, you know. She had to go through so much growing up and at such an early age. She's always been kind to me, though there's a lot of distance between her and her family. It's nothing personal. Just the way you have to be when you're a monarch."

"If Prince Daniel doesn't have any children, does that mean Eddie will have to take up the throne? Is that something he even wants?"

"Eddie would be amazing at it," she says quietly. "And I would support him one hundred percent. That's the deal I made when

I fell in love. You can't choose who you fall in love with, but you can choose to be with them, and that was my choice."

I mull that over as I have another sip of my wine, and she studies me carefully.

"Can I ask you a question?" she says.

"Of course."

"Why are you still single? What happened with your ex wasn't recent."

I feel my cheeks flush. "Guys just don't know what a catch I am."

"Oh, I'm not suggesting there's something wrong with that," she says quickly. "I was just curious. Please, I'm sorry if I offended you."

"I'm not offended. It's true. It's hard to get to know people if you're hiding away most of the time. It's not like I'm hitting on any single dads who come for parent-teacher interviews." Though there was this one dad last year who was pretty damn cute. I didn't do anything about it because of my own parent-teacher codes, and now I'm not even sure if he lives here anymore.

"Besides," I add, "I have the worst taste in men. I figure it's just easier to be by myself."

"You know," she says slowly, "there are photos of you on the internet."

My chin jerks back. "What?!"

She nods. "Nothing bad. From Friday. I guess someone at that bar knew who the both of you were."

"Oh," I say slowly, wondering where she's going with this.

"You looked really happy," she says. "And so did Harrison."

"Well, Harrison was drunk," I tell her.

She smiles. "I know. I think that's good for him too, to let off some steam. But there's a photo of the two of you, you'd swear you were on a date and enjoying it."

Uh-oh. My pulse starts to quicken. Is this the reason for the girls' night?

"It wasn't a date," I say as casually as possible.

"I know it wasn't. So does he."

"And *I* know it wasn't," I fill in. "You know I just wanted protection, a buffer."

"You wanted to upstage your ex in a way, I get it. And I'm glad you did it."

And yet I can tell she wants to say more. I want to say more too. To deny, to tell her again that there's nothing going on, because there truly isn't.

"Look," she says, pressing her fingers against the table. "I'm not going to tell you what to do or what not to do. You're a grown woman, and Harrison is a grown man—"

"Whoa, whoa, whoa," I tell her, holding my hand out in front of me, my palm out. "You're so mistaken here. There's nothing going on between us."

"He didn't come home until very late."

"Well, did you ask him what happened? He didn't want to go home, so I took him to my bed. I slept on the couch. That's what happened."

"He's skirted the question . . . as he often does when it's anything personal."

"Nothing happened between us." I'm practically pleading.

She nods. "Good. I was worried for a moment there."

Wait. Wait, why was she worried?

"Why would you be worried?"

She gives me a wry smile. "Because I like you, Piper. And Harrison is like a brother to me. And knowing him, and knowing you, it would be a disaster if you were to get together."

A disaster? I mean, I never thought it would be a good idea, but *disaster* is a pretty strong word.

"It would be bad for him and bad for you," she goes on. "And perhaps bad for Eddie and me too. I just . . . look, it's not really any of my business, but I just wanted to make sure we were all on the same page."

"Of course," I tell her. The same page being it would be a disaster. Well, if I wasn't on it before, I am now. No one likes to be told that.

So much for my motherfucking feelings. And to think I thought he was going to kiss me. Thank god he didn't.

"Want another glass of wine?" Monica asks as she gets up, and it's then that I notice I've finished mine. "The TV in here gets Netflix. We could watch something. Have you seen that new rom com with Keanu Reeves? You can never go wrong with Keanu, am I right?"

I nod yes to the wine and yes to Keanu Reeves. The girls' night is continuing.

But inside I'm focusing on that very big and final *no* to Harrison and me.

Fourteen

IT'S WEDNESDAY, AND I'M IN HIDING.

My mother is still not talking to me, though she's out of her room more often. As a result, I've started hanging out in my bedroom. Trying to avoid looking at the internet and social media, because I know people are talking about me in some way. The other night, after Monica told me she saw my picture, I spent hours going through every single article or post there was about me online.

Yeah, my name is out there. Local schoolteacher Piper Evans. I'm pretty sure someone, aka Amy, tipped them all off to who I am. Luckily, none of the posts seem to focus on the fact that it looked like a date; they are more concerned with what happened next, when Harrison grabbed Joey's thumb. A lot of the comments are about how Harrison is hotter than ever (I told you that he had a huge online following), and that the jerk Joey deserved it. Then again, a lot of people despise Monica and everyone associated with her, so all the comments from those people say that Harrison should be charged with assault and that everything Monica does is a disaster (Eddie's name is rarely mentioned).

Anyway, none of that was good for my mental health. I'm just glad I destroyed the newspaper before my mother could see it and that she's not one for being on the internet. In her paranoid, vulnerable state, this would really set her back.

Alas, I'm starting to realize that hiding out isn't doing me any favors either. Part of me wants to hide out for the rest of the summer and not emerge again until the school year starts in September. The other part of me doesn't want to be intimidated any longer. Why should my fear of what people will say about me control what I do with my life? Why give people that power over me? After all, they're going to think what they want whether I'm inside the house or not.

So I decide it's a good day to go into town. I'm going to go grocery shopping, get a coffee, go have lunch alone at the Treehouse restaurant (I mean, I'm not dumb enough to go back to the Blowhole). I'm going to do the things that scare me because I don't want to be afraid anymore. If someone recognizes me and takes my picture, I'll deal with it. I don't need Harrison to protect me (not that I've seen him since he was patrolling in that boat, and even then it was from a distance).

It's . . . not so bad.

I take the Garbage Pail to the grocery store and do a big shop for the week. It's packed, a lot of tourists and seniors, our two competing industries here, and people are nice and friendly. I know I should go to some of the other coffee shops in town, but the idea of a cinnamon bun is too enticing, and as much as it would suck to see Amy again, I know I can't avoid her forever.

As it goes, Amy is working.

I get in line, and she doesn't see me until I'm right there.

I give her a sugary-sweet smile. "Hi, Amy. Cinnamon bun and a large lavender oat-milk latte, please."

She stares at me for a moment and then looks over my shoulder, as if expecting Harrison.

I continue to smile, though it's turning more wicked than sweet as she slowly puts in my order.

"I'm surprised to see you," Amy says after she yells the order to the barista in the back.

"Oh? How so?"

"I thought you would be too embarrassed to show your face. Making the front page of the local paper, not a good look."

"Hmmm. I didn't see it," I lie as I swipe my debit card in the machine. "But I do love publicity. I'll have to hunt down a copy somewhere and frame it."

She flinches. That throws her game off.

"It's nothing to be proud of," she says under her breath, handing me my pastry, which is mashed inside the paper bag, icing spilling out and onto the counter.

"Don't worry," I say to her quietly, wiping the counter off with a napkin and tossing it at her chest. "I'm sure one day someone will care about you enough to write you up in a newspaper. If not for being a bitch, maybe for being a shitty server and barista."

And then I walk over to the wall to wait for my coffee.

She's so stunned by what I just said that she stares at me for a few moments before the tourists waiting in front of her start waving impatiently in front of her face.

Then I get my coffee, the barista handing it to me with a sly, cheeky smile, and I'm out of there.

I grin and laugh to myself all the way to the harbor, where I find a bench under a cherry tree and enjoy the view, my heart racing, adrenaline pumping. I can't believe I just told Amy off. That girl has had it a long time coming, but I really didn't think I'd be the one to do it.

I have to say, it felt good. She probably expected me to smile forever or hide forever, but I am tired of faking it, being nice, and trying to get people to like me. Fuck them if they don't.

I happily munch on my squished cinnamon bun, feeling like I've won something for once. Maybe my own respect for myself. Maybe I've owned the fear.

So I sit there for a bit under the sunshine, the fresh sea breeze in my hair, watching the tourists walk to and fro, smiling and happy to be in such a beautiful place, and I'm hit with the feeling that this beautiful place is my home and I'm not going to let anyone make me feel like I don't belong here.

When I'm done with the sticky pastry and on a sugar high, I decide I don't even need lunch after all. I did what I needed to do. So I go peruse one of the local bookstores for any new romances, pick up a copy of an enemies-to-lovers one set on a cruise ship, then get in my car and head back to the house.

I'm unpacking my groceries from the trunk when I hear a throat clear from behind me.

I know it's Harrison. Trying not to sneak up on me this time.

I still don't turn around.

He clears his throat again for good measure.

When I finally turn around, I do a double take. He's carrying a loaded laundry basket in his arms. Dressed back in his usual, including his shades.

"Uh," I say, "that's not for me, is it? Because while I like to think I've been a good neighbor, doing laundry is below my pay grade."

"The dryer is broken," he explains. From the stiff tone of his voice, it sounds like this is the last place he wants to be, which makes me feel a little sad. "I was wondering if I could use yours. If it's not too much trouble."

"So they have you getting groceries and doing the laundry. Jack-of-all-trades strikes again."

"Do you think this makes me doubt my own masculinity?" he asks idly.

No. Not even a little.

He continues. "You wouldn't expect Agatha to walk all the way over here, across your rough and weedy land, with a heavy basket of laundry in her hands, would you?"

"'Rough and weedy'? Those are ferns."

"Your driveway has potholes that nearly swallow your car every time you drive on it."

I roll my eyes. "Fine. Sure. The laundry is below the deck. Come on, I'll show you."

I walk past the car and down the side of the house, which, yes, is rough and weedy. There are some stone steps, but they are rather sporadic, and I could totally see Agatha losing her footing and having an accident here.

Under the deck there's something like a basement, which has a big freezer where my mom likes to stockpile chicken breasts "just in case," as well as some gardening equipment, tools, and old paint cans, and of course a washer and dryer. It's actually not as creepy as it sounds, and we've tried to dress it up a little with some paintings and rugs and a heater in the corner to keep things dry and toasty.

But my focus isn't on the décor. It's on Harrison, who follows me down the path and into the room.

I don't know if he feels it or not, but the tension between us is high. I mean, it's probably in my head, but since it's been nearly a week since I saw him, and I last saw him under strange circumstances, things feel strained and raw and weird.

But if he feels it, he doesn't show it. In his professionalism, he strides toward the dryer and starts throwing the laundry in.

"I'm going to go unload the groceries," I tell him.

"Need any help?" he asks, pausing.

"No. Just do what you have to do here . . ."

I leave the room and head back out onto the path and up toward the car, feeling uneasy. Not in a bad way, per se, but after everything, and especially after what Monica said, I feel like whatever strange and fleeting relationship we had before was . . . just that. Strange and fleeting. And that it won't ever go beyond that.

And that doesn't stop me from being foolishly disappointed for the way my feelings went. I never believed I had a chance with Harrison, never really thought he would be interested in me, definitely didn't think that something would or could happen between us even if he was. But I still had feelings all the same, and there's really nothing I can do about them except suck it up and try to forget about it.

It's just hard when he lives next door. Even harder when he has to come by to do the laundry.

I'm heading back for the third paper bag full of groceries when I see Harrison going to the trunk of the car and scooping it up in his arms.

"I've got it," I tell him.

"Oof, it's heavy," he says, ignoring me and brushing past me to the house. "What did you buy?" He pauses by the front door and peers inside. "A million bags of flour?"

"Shhh," I tell him, trying to wrestle the bag away from him, but he's not having it. "It's a surprise for my mom. She's . . . not doing too well."

Harrison's face softens. "I'm sorry."

"It's okay, but please, let me have this." I hold my arms out for the bag. "I don't think it's a good idea if she sees you in the house." Another thing to set her off.

He nods, handing the bag to me, then anxiously rubs his fingers along his scruffy chin. "Yes, of course."

I take the bag and head inside, placing it on the counter.

Then I head over to the door to close it, but Harrison is still there.

"Can I . . . talk to you?" he asks. "Somewhere private?"

I swallow. I don't know what I'm expecting, but it can't be good.

"Sure," I tell him, trying to smile. "How about the dock? I mean, my dock. It's half-sunken, but as long as no media are out and about, we should have it all to ourselves."

I close the door, and he follows me the other way around the house, past the garden (which I eye with disdain since the blackberries have returned), and down the rickety wooden steps that lead to the dock.

Even though it's the afternoon and it's north facing, there's still a bit of sunshine left. I would usually feel relaxed the moment I step here, but with Harrison with me, there's no chance of that. I sit down on the more buoyant edge of the dock and stare out at the narrow isthmus, the fancy houses that line the shore on the other side.

Harrison stands beside me for a moment, seemingly not sure what to do. Then he finally sits down on the dock beside me, crossing his long legs. Probably doesn't want to get his suit dirty.

"So . . . what's up?" I ask him, trying to keep my tone light. "Haven't seen you for a while."

"I know," he says, clearing his throat. "I wanted to come by earlier and talk to you, but . . ."

I wait for him to finish. Ahead of us on the water a fish jumps. "I just wanted to apologize."

I turn my head and squint at him. "What for?"

"For a couple of things. But what it really comes down to is that I'm sorry for being a wanker."

"You aren't a wanker—"

"No." He shakes his head vehemently. "No, you're wrong, Piper. I was a wanker. I got drunk and did things I shouldn't have done. I acted like a bloody fool, and I embarrassed you, and I'm sorry."

"You didn't embarrass me!" I exclaim. "Honestly, you didn't."

"I did. If I hadn't been . . . If I hadn't lost my temper around that cockweasel, then I wouldn't have made front-page-fucking-news. And you would have been spared."

"They didn't name me, and anyway, I don't care. I was there. I know what happened. You stuck up for me."

"Yeah, well, maybe I shouldn't have."

Ouch. Now that's a blow to the chest. "But . . . I'm glad you did. You don't know what that meant to me."

"I acted like an idiot. Like I had no control. I just . . . lost it, at a time I shouldn't have."

"But you defended me," I press on. "You defended me against a man who destroyed me, who made me feel gaslit, who made me feel like I had no place here or anywhere. You stood up for me, and you're you and I'm me and . . ."

It meant more than you'll ever know.

He frowns, and I see my reflection in the aviators. "What do you mean, you're you and I'm me?"

I shrug. "You know. You're . . ." I gesture to him and then wave at myself up and down. "And I'm . . ."

"This guy did a real number on you, didn't he? *Gaslit* is the right fucking term. You sound just like him."

I sigh. "I just mean, I've never had someone so . . . worldly and successful and smart and strong and respected go to bat for me. I'm used to having no one. To have it be you . . ."

I trail off and look down at the water sloshing rhythmically against the dock. I'll say too much if I don't shut up now.

"Then that isn't right," he says, his voice low, adjusting himself slightly to sit closer to me. "Because any man, any person worth their salt, would see how good you are. How sweet you are. How fun. You have a very pure, very big heart, Piper, and anyone who doesn't see that isn't worth your time. Sure, you run your mouth off a bit, but it keeps people on their toes. I know you keep me on my toes."

"I *annoy* you," I tell him. "There's a difference."

"You don't annoy me," he says. "You . . . transfix me."

Transfix? Does he really know the way to my heart? Is he purposely going the Mr. Rochester route?

"Is it like staring at an eclipse?" I ask, half joking.

"Something like that," he says after a moment. "Look at me."

When Harrison tells you to look at him, you look at him.

He puts his glasses up on the top of his head so I can see his gorgeous eyes squinting at me. This feels like something big here, like this means something. A man who keeps his control behind a barrier is now baring himself for me to see.

Or maybe that's what *I* want to see.

"I think you're . . ." He licks his lips, and I watch, entranced. "A rare and precious thing. And it pains me to know how easily you've been discarded in the past, that others haven't treated you with the respect that you deserve. And that's why I need to apologize to you, because the last thing I wanted was to disrespect you or cause trouble for you. I fear I did that by not only making a scene in public when I should have been on my best behavior, behavior that was always supposed to reflect on you, but I got drunk and made you take me to your room. You put me to bed when I was a wasted shitbag; you took care of me. Were at my side when I had a nightmare, of all things. You did all that despite the trouble I put you through, and . . . well, my apology won't ever seem like enough."

I blink at him, still stuck on him calling me a rare and precious thing. I clutch that phrase to my heart.

"It's okay," I whisper, my throat feeling thick. "It's really okay."

"And I avoided you all week because . . . I was too afraid to face you."

His eyes are downcast. Instinctively, I reach over and put my palm to his cheek, his skin hot from the sun, his stubble rough. "You're facing me now. Please know that I always want you around, no matter what. And I accept your apology, even though I don't think you needed to make it. I'm just so happy that you came with me. It meant a lot."

"I really fucked that up," he says, his eyes lifting to mine, his face turning just slightly so he's close to kissing the palm of my hand.

Put your hand away. Stop touching him.

Remember what Monica said.

I relax my palm to let my hand fall, but he reaches out and envelops the back of my hand with his, pressing it against his cheek, holding it there. His eyes are searching mine, something very alive and anguished running through them. My palm tingles against his skin.

He closes his eyes and then moves my hand over to his mouth and places a kiss in my palm. Warm, fiery shivers cascade through my entire body, a fizzy, weightless feeling in my core.

Now *I'm* transfixed.

I just know that those lips against my palm are turning me inside out, and if this man were to ever kiss me on my mouth, I might not survive it.

He pulls my hand away from his mouth and lowers it, giving it a tight squeeze before letting go.

"I should go check on the laundry," he says, his gaze leaving mine and staring across the harbor.

I'm certain that the laundry isn't dry yet, but he obviously wants out of this situation. He gets to his feet and stares down at me. "Are you staying here?"

I shake my head. It's so nice on the dock, but I have groceries to put away.

He puts his hand out and I put my hand in his, and he effortlessly lifts me to my feet.

With the dock slanted and unsteady to begin with, I rock a little on my feet, and his other hand shoots around to the small of my back, holding me in place.

Holding me against him.

His other hand lets go of mine and then slides into my hair, fingers gently working in through my strands, cupping the back of my head.

Friday night plays through my mind again, except this time we're not in the dark of my bedroom in the middle of the night and he's not disoriented and drunk. We're on the dock, in the bright open sunshine, and judging by the scaring clarity in his eyes, he's sober as anything.

"I don't know what to do about you," he murmurs, his eyes drifting across my face, settling on my cheekbones, my nose, my mouth.

I have a hard time swallowing. "What do you mean?" I whisper, afraid that if I talk anymore, any louder, that I'll break this spell.

He presses his lips together, as if to keep the words inside. He shakes his head slightly, his brow crinkled. "If I were a lesser man, I'd kiss you right now."

I blink at him, my lips burning at the suggestion, my stomach doing flips.

My god.

"If I were a lesser man, I'd gladly lose control," he goes on, his voice low and rough and aching. "I would throw all caution to the wind, and I would give in and never look back." He gives me a faint smile. "But I don't want to be that man. That's not who I am; that's not who I've worked all my life to be. You deserve the best, Piper, but I can't give you the best, can't give you what you really need. It's better if I stay away."

Wait. Wait, what?

"Stay away?" I whisper, his fingers making a light fist in my hair, and oh god, it's impossible to keep steady.

"I like you a lot," he says, closing his eyes, still pressing me against him. "I like you more than I can come to terms with right now. It's . . . a foreign feeling. But it's not one that I can afford to feel. Especially when it comes to you."

He leans in and kisses my cheek, slow and lingering, and then pulls back.

Lets go of me.

I am bereft without his touch.

"What if it's not up to you?" I say quickly as he turns around, feeling panic claw through me. "What if I feel something for you too? Doesn't that make a difference? Don't *I* make a difference?"

He stops and glances at me over his shoulder. "It makes all the difference, Piper. And that's the problem."

Then he walks over to the stairs, leaving me on the dock with my heart at my feet and an aching emptiness in my chest.

Fifteen

HARRISON WASN'T KIDDING WHEN HE SAID HE WAS going to stay away.

It's been nearly two weeks since I've seen him.

In that time, I've hung out on the boat with Monica twice (and it's always James who fetches me), I've been to Victoria to see my therapist, I've gone into town nearly every day, just to be there and take up space and enjoy the summer (my therapist agrees that it's something worth doing just to get more confidence).

And my mother has come back around.

At least, we're on speaking terms again, and her mood is steadily improving each day. My therapist gave me some helpful reminders about how to deal with her, and those have been working so far. There's a thin line between being supportive and being aggressive to my mother, and I know it's a line I cross too often when I get impatient. Even if it comes from a good place, my mother doesn't see it that way.

I like that I feel closer to Monica, and she seems to want me around (though I remind myself it probably has something to do with my being the only friend she has here), and I'm grateful for that. It's a slow-building friendship, but I'm in no hurry, and I often forget at times just who she is. We have a lot in common regarding our families, and even though I'll never understand what it's like to be a royal, let alone famous, I can still relate to her.

All that is to say, I miss Harrison. I miss him showing up at my door. I miss having him around. My life is too simple and quiet and boring without him in it. Which seems ironic, considering his quiet demeanor. But he brings out a side of me that makes me feel more alive, and at the end of the day, isn't that what everyone wants? To feel like they're getting more out of the short lives we've been given? To feel like they're participating in life instead of just being a bystander?

All I know is, the feelings are still there, and even with the distance, I don't think they're going anywhere. Truthfully, I've never been with someone who made me feel good about myself.

Not that I'm with him. Not that I was with him.

But damn. The way he looked at me. The way he kissed my hand, my face. The words he said.

That was *something*.

That was everything.

And I could tell that it was something to him too.

Something that scared him.

To say I haven't been replaying that scene on the dock over the last two weeks would be a lie. It's all I think about. The burning intensity in his eyes, the rough yearning in his voice, the way his large, strong hands felt around the small of my waist or cupped at the back of my head. His lips. Those damn beautiful lips that didn't even touch mine and yet felt more erotic, more intimate, more meaningful, than any deep kiss.

And that's all you'll get, I tell myself as I pull the Garbage Pail into my parking space. *A non-kiss to fantasize about for the rest of your life.*

I sigh and look around, my heart always beating a little faster when I get home, hoping for a glimpse of him. Obviously he's never to be found.

I get out of the car and smooth out my dress. Today I decided to go into town with a book and sit down on the patio at the café to read, sip iced coffee, nibble on a cinnamon bun, and take my sweet time enjoying the hot weather, all while I knew Amy was inside glaring at me through the windows. On the advice of my therapist to do things that make me feel confident, I put on one of my favorite summer dresses, a yellow-and-white gingham pattern with spaghetti straps and fitted at the bust, the kind of dress you can twirl in.

I grab my straw purse and head inside the house. My mother is on the deck, snoozing in a deck chair, her chin tucked into her chest. Liza is splat on the ground at her feet, her belly rising with each breath. It rarely gets scorching hot on the island thanks to the constant ocean breezes, but today is one of those days when our lack of air conditioning really shows. I go around opening up all the windows to the house to get fresh air in, and by the time I'm done, beads of sweat are on my brow.

I decide it's probably a good time to escape the heat and do laundry. The basement is always cool no matter what. I grab my laundry basket from my bedroom, tossing my paperback on top of it, and then head downstairs and down the side of the house to the bottom back door. It already feels cooler here.

I open the door and step inside, and just as I realize I must have left the light on at some point, I see Harrison standing by the dryer. I come to a dead stop, the laundry basket nearly falling from my hands.

"What are you doing here?" I exclaim, sounding more accusatory than I mean to.

Harrison's eyes are wide, not covered by his aviators. He shifts from one foot to the other, seeming wary and unsure, two qualities I never see in him.

"I'm sorry," he says. "The dryer still isn't fixed, so I came by and your mother was home. She said it was no problem if I used yours again."

I raise my laundry basket higher and walk across the concrete floor toward him, my flip-flops smacking noisily. I wish he didn't look like he was caught red-handed.

"I suppose it was a relief when you found out I'd gone," I tell him, putting the laundry basket on top of the washer. I fold my arms across my chest and lean back against it, looking him in the eye. I'm not going anywhere.

"I didn't have a choice," he goes on, looking away and skirting past what I said. "The guy that was supposed to fix the dryer never showed up. He's been supposed to show up for the last five days."

I give him a dry smile. "Island life strikes again."

"I wouldn't have come if I'd . . ."

He wouldn't have come if he'd known I'd be here.

". . . Monica is very grateful that you've been so generous."

"So I guess this ends your two-weeks-of-avoiding-me streak." I turn away from him and open the lid to the washer. I make a tsking sound. "And you were doing such a good job."

He doesn't say anything to that; instead the room seems to hum with tension. I dare to look at him, and though he's stone-faced, there's a spark in his eyes. The thing is, he *was* avoiding me. He told me he would stay away. There's no way he can deny the truth.

I shove the clothes in the washer and slam the lid shut, straightening up to turn the dial to the right settings.

Without saying a word, Harrison starts walking off.

What the fuck?

I march over to him and grab his arm, pulling him to a stop.

"That's it?" I ask him, feeling irate. "Now you just walk off without saying anything? Is that what you're going to do every time you see me now?"

He turns to face me, his brow furrowed, eyes blazing. "I'm just doing what I can." His voice is rough, borderline angry. Why is he angry? I'm the one who is angry here.

"You don't have to be a dick about it."

"How am I being a dick?" he snaps.

"You had no business telling me all those things you told me," I say, and I hate how shaky my voice is and how vulnerable I feel. I fold my arms across my chest, as if I can protect myself that way. "You said some of the sweetest, nicest things that anyone has ever said to me; you told me that you *liked* me. And then you walked away and stayed away, just as you're trying to do now. Is this how it's going to be? For how long?"

"For as long as I'm here," he says gruffly. His jaw muscles clench, and I can tell how badly he wants to leave. But I won't let him go easily.

"Oh really. So, for at least the next six months, you're going to just pretend I don't exist? Why?"

His eyes narrow, nostrils flare. "You know why."

"I don't. I don't, okay? You gave me some vague mumbo jumbo about me deserving better and if you were a lesser man you'd lose control and that you can't afford to feel the way you do about me. Well? Do you feel something still or not? Has it gone away? Has it magically disappeared because you haven't seen me? Out of sight, out of mind, is that how easy it is to forget me?"

He presses his lips together in a hard line and looks away.

"Hey," I tell him, taking a step closer, until I'm right up against him and really in his face, about impossible to ignore as I'll ever be. "Now you're just being rude. Look at me."

With reluctance, his eyes meet mine, and they're as intense as I've seen them, burning, practically smoldering.

"I'll say it again, okay? You don't get to tell me nice things and then act like it never happened. You don't get to pretend that I don't exist. I don't know what we have between us, but there is something between us. You said as much yourself. Maybe it scares you, but it scares me too, and yet I'm not about to pretend it doesn't exist or that it isn't real. I just . . ." I shake my head, surprised that I'm still talking, that I'm going *there*. "You said you'd be a lesser man if you kissed me. I think you're a lesser man for running away."

His nostrils flare at that. It's a sore spot.

And I decide to poke at it again.

"You need to fucking man up," I add snidely.

Something in his eyes snaps. The greens and blues ignite, and I know I've crossed a line that I can't come back from.

It happens so fast, there's no time to blink.

The space between us disintegrates, and then his hands cup my face, his fingers pressing into my skin as his lips crash angrily against mine.

I'm still so full of fire that it takes me a moment to realize what's happening, that it's *his* mouth on mine, hard and soft all at once and unrelenting in his pursuit. His hands are large and warm, and it's not just that they hold me in place—they pull me to him, until I'm unsteady on my feet. I feel like I'm standing precipitously on a rock that juts out into an ocean storm, waves crashing on either side of me. I have a choice to surrender to the chaos or head back to shore.

I choose to surrender.

My mouth opens against his, my hands grasping his shirt in a ravenous, delirious way, as if I'd been starving all this time and only realized it now. Heat floods through me, like stepping into warm, sweet bathwater, and I make the fists in his shirt tighter, as if that will give me some control.

A groan escapes from his lips, reverberating through me, a sound filled with so much frustration, want, and need that I feel it in my core, this wicked flame that causes my legs to squeeze together.

This is happening.

My brain can barely conjure up the thought. There are more thoughts that want to follow, to fill my head, to make me second-guess everything, but they have no place here, not now. For once, I just want to feel and not think.

I let go.

This kiss lives in the marrow of my bones. Each sweep of his tongue against mine is the cumulation of unsaid words. As his mouth opens against my lips, hungry and frenzied, growing more passionate and rough by the second, there are weeks of pent-up feelings coming to light and burning away.

We stumble backward across the room, one of his hands sweeping up under my hair, his fingers curling around my strands, pulling with just the right amount of pleasure. He's breathless already, and I'm not sure I'm breathing at all. If it weren't for my heart trying to beat its way out of my rib cage, I'd wager that I'm not even alive. Died and gone to heaven, or caught in some fevered dream.

But if I'm dreaming, I don't ever want to wake up.

My ass hits the dryer, and we come to a stop.

He pulls his mouth away from mine, a greedy little gasp escaping my lips, and rests his forehead against mine, his breath raspy. His eyes flutter closed, his forehead wrinkled in some form of anguish.

Please don't let him stop, I think. *Please don't let him apologize, get cold feet, turn, and walk away.*

"Harrison," I whisper to him, my voice thick with lust. I put my hands on either side of his face and then let my fingers trail to the back of his head.

He shakes his head slightly, his eyes still closed, and I can feel it, this cord, this connection between us. It's been snapping and crackling like an electrified whip, but it's starting to wane, to stretch, threatening to break.

He's going to pull that walking-away shit, isn't he?

"Harrison," I say again, licking my lips, my mouth already bereft without the heat of his. I run my thumbs under his eyes, marveling at how I can touch him like this. Wanting to touch him more.

Emboldened only by determination and the fact that I've never been this turned on before, I let my hand fall from his face, run my fingers down the middle of his collared shirt. I start undoing buttons, stealing a glance at his skin, the tattoos, a hint of chest hair. I can feel the heat radiating off him.

Then my fingers get impatient and I let my hand drift down, down, down, until I pause at his belt buckle.

He swallows audibly, and his eyes open, staring right into mine, a look of warning flashing through them.

I take that look as a challenge.

I start undoing the buckle, then yank down the zipper.

The sound of it unzipping echoes in this room.

Keeping my eyes locked with Harrison's, I slip my hand into his pants until my palm presses against his boxer briefs and the long, thick width of his hard-on.

Wow.

I've never been this bold before.

Then again, I don't think I've ever ached this much for someone in my life.

I bite my lip, unable to stop from giving his dick a firm squeeze, feeling the heat and desire crash over me like a tempest.

Holy shit, I'm in trouble.

An involuntary groan comes out of him, flooding me with even more desire than before. "Piper," he murmurs, pressing himself into my hand. "I'm this close to unraveling."

"That makes two of us," I tell him, releasing my hand momentarily and then slipping my fingers underneath the elastic waistband until his bare skin is in my palm, hard as concrete, yet soft like warmed velvet.

"Fuck," he whispers, breathing in through a gasp as I make a fist, reveling in his size. "You don't know what you're asking for."

Then he's putting his hands at my waist and lifting me up onto the dryer.

"I know perfectly well," I tell him, because this is what I've been asking for, even if I've been too afraid until now to say it. "I—"

His mouth crashes against mine, sealing off my words, his hands going to my thighs and hiking up the hem of my dress. His hands are rough and hot as they travel up my legs, gripping at my hips, a thumb hooking around the lace edge of my underwear.

Then my underwear is being pulled down until it's dangling off one foot and his lips continue their hungry journey from my mouth, down my jaw, nipping and licking until they reach my neck.

I moan loudly, unashamed at how vocal I am, and as he sucks roughly at my tender neck, his palms go to my inner thighs and spread them. Hands hook around my ass and shrug my body closer to him. I eagerly wrap my legs around his waist, wanting so much more of him that it seems I can't get close enough. The intensity is wild, a visceral thrill, and I'm already wet between my legs with this ridiculous need for him.

His hands trail up to my shoulders, slipping the spaghetti straps off, and he places hot and impatient kisses along my shoulders, nipping across my collarbone.

I'm impatient too. I reach between my legs for his cock, wrapping my fingers around it and giving it another hard squeeze.

"Piper," he ekes out against my skin, pulling down the neckline of my dress.

I love the way he says my name. Like it's a way to hold me to him, as if I'm something magical and unreal and ready to float away.

His lips and tongue make a path down my chest until my breast pops free, my nipple immediately hardening. He takes it in his mouth, a sharp, wet suck that causes my body to shake and burn, as if pure fire has been poured into my veins.

"Harrison," I hiss. Now I'm saying his name in the same way.

As his mouth works at me, the pleasure radiating outward from his fervent lips and teasing tongue, my neck arches back, eyes to the ceiling.

"Are you protected?" he asks, his mouth pulling away, wet and slick.

"I have an IUD, if that's what you mean," I tell him, catching my breath. "And I'm clean. It's been . . . a really long time." Like . . . I hate to admit it, but the last person I slept with was Joey.

I quickly shove that awful image out of my head.

"Same for me," he says, his eyes searching mine. "And also a long time. Ridiculously long." He swallows, giving me a hint of a smile. "I apologize in advance if I'm unable to hold back for long. I will still make it worth your while."

And at that he moves back and dips his head between my legs.

Oh wow. Oh, Harrison.

This is happening.

I tense up from the feeling of his rough stubble scraping against the tender skin of my inner thighs, my fingers curling over the edge of the dryer.

My legs part, and then the long sweep of his tongue glides over me where I'm already wet and willing. Nerves leap at the contact, and I instinctively press my thighs around his head.

He moans into me, causing me to gasp, my back arching.

Holy shit.

I try to relax into him, his tongue wide and hot as he licks at me, soft and hard all at once, and my heartbeat feels like it might just break through my rib cage. I start to lose my train of thought, forgetting where we are, forgetting everything except us. Only we exist here.

"Fuck," I cry out as he swirls around my clit, one of my hands shooting to his head, tugging on his hair. I'm trying to bring him closer, because even as I feel the pressure building and swirling inside me and I'm close to coming already, it's like he can't get close enough. I want so much more of him and more than this. I want him inside me.

"Harrison," I try to say, my words coming out heavy and hoarse. I tug at his hair again, but he's a man on a mission. Who am I to get in his way?

So I let him bring me to the edge. I let myself fall over.

There's the free fall, and then my orgasm comes up like a rocket ship, blasting through me and into deep space until I don't know my name anymore. I moan loudly, my body quaking, my thighs squeezing around Harrison's face until I slowly come back down to earth.

Dear Lord . . . that was . . .

I can barely think, barely talk.

And Harrison doesn't leave me any time to catch my breath.

He grabs me by the back of my head, pulling my face toward his, his lips crushing mine. I taste myself on his tongue, mixed with the sweat from his exertion in this now hot room, and I open myself to a kiss that seems to turn me inside out, a kiss that makes my soul ache.

I place my fingers at the back of his neck and pull back just enough, our mouths wet and open, our breath heavy in unison. He rests his forehead against mine, his eyes searching my eyes. There's a flash of worry in them, the way he's frowning.

I think he thinks I'm about to tell him to stop.

I'm about to tell him the opposite.

"Come inside me," I whisper.

He stares at me in faint surprise.

It lasts just a moment before a raw, primal heat makes his eyes simmer with lust.

And then he's kissing me again. I'm lost to him, and we're wild, messy, lips and teeth and tongues that grow more ravenous by the second. He reaches down between my legs, positioning himself at my entrance, and I grip his strong shoulders just as he pushes himself inside.

I gasp loudly, my body in shock. As I said, it has been a long time since I was with someone, and that someone was definitely not built like Harrison.

"Are you okay?" he murmurs, pulling away from my mouth to stare at me in concern.

I nod, trying to breathe, trying to swallow.

"I'll go slow," he says, placing kisses along my jaw, over to my neck, as he slowly pushes himself in to the hilt.

Good lord. How am I going to survive him? I don't mean just now. I mean after this. How will things go back to normal after I know what it feels like to have him so deep inside me, to have him make me feel so full?

"Better?" he asks, before his tongue drags across my chest, sucking my nipple into his mouth. I close my eyes, my mouth falling open in a low moan.

"Yes," I manage to say, holding tight as he slowly withdraws and then thrusts back up inside me. "God, yes."

My body starts to mold to his now, surrendering to the decadent push and pull as he pumps inside me, and hot, wicked flames start to burn deep, a fire that will soon consume me as every drag of his cock feels like a match about to strike.

We have a rhythm now, easy, sweet, and indulgent, but now I want more, need more. I don't want him to hold back anymore. I want him to let loose, to overtake me, to set the wild beast inside him free.

"Harder," I say through a groan, my nails digging in through his shirt. "Please."

He grunts in response, picking up the pace as his hips start to slam against mine. The dryer rocks beneath us, but it doesn't slow him down. I hold him tighter as everything inside me starts to wind around itself like spools of electricity, frayed and vibrating and promising relief.

Harrison continues to piston his hips against me, his thrusts deeper and harder, and I stare up at his gorgeous face, the heavy lids over fiery eyes, the hard set of his jaw, the lines in his forehead where sweat is pooling from the way he's working me. Because it is work, the way he's so determined to fuck the life out of me.

Then he slides his hand down between my legs, his fingers rough over my slick skin, and I'm crying out his name, the live wires inside me threatening to break me.

"Oh god," I practically whimper, "I'm close."

But I am closer than I thought.

With one rough pass of his thumb over my clit, it yanks the rug out from under me and I'm falling again, into him, into this wild, crazy, unadulterated bliss.

My legs wrap around him tighter, I'm clawing at him like I've lost my mind, and my head goes back, the world spinning out of control.

"Fuck," he moans, and I fight through my orgasm to stare at him, taking in the sight of Harrison as he's losing control. His face contorts in pleasure and pain, and then he's making a fist in my hair and tugging it as he comes, his body shuddering as he releases inside me.

"Piper," he cries out, his face burying in my neck as his pumping slows. "Piper."

He doesn't have to say anything else. I feel it all.

We stay like that for a while, our hearts slowing, our breath returning.

He pulls back and stares at me, brushing my wild hair off my damp forehead, and gives me the sweetest smile. His eyes are sated, his body relaxed even as he's still inside me. I don't think I've ever seen him at peace like this, like he's a completely different person. No longer in control, he's succumbed to me, and we're together in the aftermath, realizing that it's okay to break every now and then.

I just hope that he knows he's always free to break with me.

"That was . . . ," he begins, licking his lips.

I smile. "I know."

He lets out a low chuckle and shakes his head. "I'm not sure what came over you."

"Does it matter when you came inside me?" I say, joking.

Another rough laugh escapes him. He leans in and kisses me softly on the lips. "You really are something, you know that?"

"I've been told."

And please keep telling me.

He lets out a long exhale, resting his forehead against mine for a moment, and then reaches down and pulls out. I feel bereft at his absence already.

"Made a mess," he says, eyeing the dryer.

"Good thing we're in the laundry room," I tell him.

I move my legs to the side, and then he wraps his large hands around my waist and gently lifts me down to the ground. I grab a towel from a laundry basket and quickly wipe away the mess we made.

"You know those are royal towels, right?" he comments.

I stare at the towel, with its logo of the Fairfaxes. "Whoops."

He grins. "It'll be our secret." Then he pauses. Clears his throat, his eyes turning serious. "You know, this should probably stay a secret between us."

I swallow, nodding. "I know." I want to tell him about what Monica had said, that she disapproved of the idea of us together, but decide against it. We already seem to be on the same page. "I can keep a secret if you can."

He gives me a wry smile. "You know I can. I'm a vault." He pulls up his pants and buckles his belt. "It's not that I'm ashamed, though. I don't want you thinking that. It's not about Eddie or Monica either. I . . . I just need some time to . . ."

"I get it," I say quickly. "You don't have to explain. I know you have a job to do, and I know things might get complicated. But we'll figure it out. Right?"

He nods. "We'll figure it out."

And I'm going to have to trust him on that.

Sixteen

"PIPER." MY MOM'S IMPATIENT VOICE BREAKS INTO MY head. "Can you please pass the sugar?"

My head slowly swivels toward her, and I blink.

There's cornstarch in her hair as she stands at a saucepan on the stove, wearing an impatient look on her face.

I absently reach for the bag of sugar beside me and pass it to her.

"No," she says, shaking her head. "You're supposed to measure it. One cup. Where is your head at?"

Where is my head at? Good question.

It's been one hundred percent compromised by Harrison.

Specifically, what Harrison and I did on that dryer.

It's been about twenty-four hours since Harrison and I consummated our strange relationship in the laundry room, and I haven't recovered even a little.

After he left, I spent the rest of the day in a daze, hiding from my mother like I was sixteen all over again, having lost my virginity to my loser of a high school boyfriend, Mark. I felt like if she took one look at me, she would know. I mean, when I looked in the mirror, I thought it was painfully obvious. My lips were swollen (the ones on my face, but also . . .), my eyes were bright, my cheeks flushed. I looked like I was brimming with life.

I had all night to replay it over in my head, bringing out my vibrator to give myself an encore. I won't lie—I'd used it many times with Harrison in mind, but now that I had the real thing to compare it to, my old fantasies didn't stand a chance.

Today, the feelings from last night are still coursing through me. My mother hasn't noticed anything is off, well, aside from my silence, but she doesn't know it's because Harrison has become the subject of each and every thought I've had. I can still feel his rough stubble between my legs, still see the way his face contorted with pleasure moments before he came, the look in his eyes afterward as he gazed at me, a peace to them I'd never seen before.

It was everything I'd wanted and more.

But I was at a loss as to how we were supposed to move on from here. He said we'd find a way, he said he wouldn't leave it at just that, just that moment. I'm unsure of how we're going to keep it going. Will we see each other once in a while? Is that sustainable? Is it even fair?

I've never had a purely physical relationship with someone. I've been a serial dater in the past, always monogamous but always quick to rush into a relationship. I form attachments easily, especially after sex. I don't know how to deal with my growing feelings for Harrison, nor how to proceed when everything is so . . . secretive.

The funny thing is, Harrison really doesn't seem to care either way. I would have assumed he would have been the first to make this all stay hush-hush, but his fear is more to do with him, and what he can give me, rather than his job or his relationship with Monica and Eddie.

It's my relationship with Monica that has me worried. I know she warned me about this on the boat; I know that a relationship between Harrison and I would cause me to break a girl code. And as someone who has struggled to make friends, I don't want to do anything to put our friendship in jeopardy.

At the same time, it feels wrong to have to hide it from her.

Same goes for my mother. There's no way she'd understand, but for totally different reasons.

My mother is watching me like a hawk right now as I awkwardly dump sugar into a measuring cup and hand it to her.

"What is with you?" she asks as she pours it into the saucepan and stirs with a whisk. "You've had this look on your face all day."

"What look?"

Please don't say pathetic puppy dog eyes.

"I don't know. Daydreaming. You're somewhere else. Don't tell me you're bored."

"Bored? I'm making a lemon meringue pie with my mother—how could I be bored?"

She gives me a pointed look as she whisks away. "Don't be cute, Piper. Why don't you do another podcast?"

I wave at her dismissively. Doing a podcast is the last thing on my mind right now, as is reading. I can't seem to think of anything else but Harrison.

"I'm fine." I clap my hands together. "What else do you need me to do?" Being distracted is probably key, because if I dwell on this too much, my mind is going to start running away on me and create something bigger than reality.

"You can . . ." She trails off as the saucepan bubbles on the stove, and starts skimming over the recipe on the iPad. "Oh, *shit*."

"What? Did you miss a step?"

She closes her eyes and makes a grumbling noise.

"What?" I repeat, reaching for the recipe. I take the iPad and look at it, unable to see what the problem is.

"The piecrust," she says, looking at me after a moment. "The recipe only gave the recipe for the meringue and the filling. I forgot I needed a crust!"

"Maybe you don't?" I say, looking over the recipe. But there it is. "'Pour mixture into your pre-baked piecrust.'"

Uh-oh. My mom looks on the verge of losing it. She's been doing so well, and baking is usually her happy place, no matter what happens to the final product.

"Hey, it's okay," I tell her, going to the stove and switching off the burner. "We'll come back to the filling after. Let's start on the crust. Do we have what we need for that?"

"I have no idea," she whimpers, throwing her arms in the air. "I have never made a piecrust."

"Okay, okay, I'm sure it's easy. Don't panic. It will be fine."

I pull up a piecrust recipe and start reading the ingredients. "Flour. We have plenty of flour, right?"

My mom opens a cupboard and pulls out a bag and plops it on the counter. It's not even closed, so flour flies out into the air.

I ignore the particles gathering on my shirt. "Okay, so that and salt, water, and we just need either butter or shortening or lard."

"I have butter and shortening, I think," my mother says, opening the fridge.

While she looks, I start measuring out the two-and-a-half cups of flour, which naturally gets everywhere. I'm definitely no better than she is when it comes to not making a mess.

"Which one should I use?" she asks, pulling them both out.

I'm about to tell her I have no idea when there's a knock at the door.

We look at each other in surprise, just as Liza comes charging from around the corner, barking and heading to the door.

I walk over, dusting my floury hands on my black tunic, then open the door.

It's Harrison. Suit, aviators, hands behind his back.

My heart does a triple axel.

A stupid grin spreads on my face as my body tingles, muscle memory from everywhere he touched me.

"Hi," I say. "You're here."

A ghost of a smile flits across his lips. "I am."

"Mr. Cole?" my mother says in the background. "Need to use the machine again? Liza, come here."

Liza has already given up on barking, but now she's doing circles around Harrison's legs and sniffing him, getting her hair all over the fine material of his suit.

He clears his throat. "Actually," he says, louder so my mother can hear, "the duke and duchess were wondering if you would join them for dinner on Friday."

Not gonna lie, my stomach sinks a little with disappointment, as if I really thought he was here to see me.

"Friday?" my mother says. "Sure. Say, you wouldn't know how to make piecrust, would you?"

"Mom, don't bug him," I chide her.

"It's not a problem," Harrison says to me. He removes his sunglasses and slips them in his jacket pocket. "I would be happy to help." He takes a step forward and pauses, his eyes drifting to my lips and up to my gaze. "If that's okay with you, of course."

I make a squeak that means "of course" in fluttery crush language and step aside as he walks in. He brushes past me, his scent filling my nose and making those butterflies take flight, my knees feeling weak.

I close the door and follow him into the kitchen, where he observes the mess.

"So what happened here?" he asks mildly.

"Argh," my mom says. "I was trying to make a lemon meringue pie and forgot all about the crust. Now I'm stuck on whether to use butter or shortening."

Harrison watches her and nods. "I see. Well, you can use both. In fact, that's what I prefer."

"Both?"

"Here, let me," he says. He takes off his suit jacket, and I hurry over to take it from him, hanging it up by the front door. He then rolls up the sleeves of his white dress shirt to his elbows, his tattoos on display. "Can you get me a larger mixing bowl?" he asks.

My mother grabs a bowl and hands it to him, while I lean against the kitchen island, taking immense delight in the sight of him in my kitchen, helping my mother. It's like when she was making focaccia, but it shows how far our relationship has evolved.

Man, if I only knew back then that I'd end up sleeping with the man. I was so innocent.

"Need any help?" I ask him.

He glances up at me and gives me a soft smile, warmth in his eyes. "I've got it."

Grabbing the measuring cups and a knife, he starts cutting out the butter and shortening. "See, the shortening is needed because it has a high melting point. It creates flakiness. That tender melt-in-your-mouth feeling you get from a good crust. And the butter, well, nothing beats it. It gives that rich, unmistakable smooth flavor. Now, generally you want your butter in the freezer, especially when the temperature outside is hot, but if I work fast, it should be okay."

I have no idea what he's talking about but I'm fascinated, watching the muscles in his forearms as he works. "Why is that?" I ask.

"Because you want your dough as cold as possible. That's why you have to use cold water."

"Shit, I probably would have used warm," my mother says, also watching him like I am.

"Common mistake," he says, giving her an assuring smile. "We want the dough cold so that the fat from the shortening and the butter don't melt while you're working on it. They need to melt in the oven, where the steam created will help separate the crust into those flaky layers you want."

"Okay, you have to tell me how you know all this," I say. "Don't tell me it was the army."

"Actually," he says, "it *was* the army. We had downtime, and that's what I did. Improved morale, got my mind off of what was happening, and was a nice change from the bloody awful food."

"You need your own cooking show," my mother says.

He laughs quietly, with a genuine smile that lights up his whole face and makes me dizzy all over again. "I definitely do not need that. But I am happy to help out when I can. Now, I need to work fast. Do you have a pastry cutter? Two forks will do."

"I just ordered from Amazon," my mother says proudly as she hands it to him.

We watch as he starts using it to cut up the butter and shortening into small chunks, and then we help by adding ice to the cold water and adding it a little bit at a time as he stirs with a spatula. With flour liberally applied to the counter, he rolls out the dough until he's made a few dough discs that he wraps in plastic and then puts in the fridge.

"How long do we have to wait?" my mother asks.

"Two hours at the very least," he says. He nods at the saucepan. "Don't worry, you'll be fine with the rest of the recipe."

My mother grabs his arm firmly, looking him in the eye. "I don't know how to thank you. You've been so kind."

Harrison looks mildly embarrassed. "It's not a problem, Mrs. Evans."

"Please, call me Evelyn," she says. "And let me make you a cup of tea."

She turns around and starts ransacking the cupboards for tea. All the boxes are empty, which means the bags are all over the place, complete chaos.

"It's all right," he says.

"He likes coffee, anyway," I tell her. And since I know she's now going to insist that he has coffee, I say, "And if you're making any, I'll have some too."

"No problem," she says. I know it makes her feel good to do simple things for people, especially after Harrison just helped her with her baking.

While her back is turned and she brings out the coffee canister, I take my time staring at Harrison.

My god, I'm freaking lucky. Not that I have any claim to him, per se, but I still can't believe what happened. After playing it over and over in my head and now having him here in front of me, it's like a fantasy come to life.

Harrison Cole.

The bodyguard.

The man I never thought I would get to know, the man I never thought would be mine, has become so much more than what I had imagined.

He stares right back at me too, his eyes soft, his expression warm. No longer guarded, no longer worried. We don't even have to speak to each other to know what the other is feeling—we can just be. Sure, I don't want to gawk at him when my mother is watching, but these stolen glances and hidden moments, they mean the world to me already.

Good lord, I want to jump him.

"I have dark roast, is that okay?" my mother says, turning around, and we both whip our eyes toward her.

I clear my throat. "It's fine. Right, Harrison?"

He nods. "Did you know that dark roast actually has the lightest caffeine content?"

"I don't think that's true," my mother says. "But we'll find out when we're all bouncing off the walls, won't we?"

She gets the coffee going and then leans against the counter, looking at Harrison. Specifically at his arms. "Why do you have those tattoos?" she asks, not hiding her disapproval.

"Mom," I chide her. I look at Harrison with an apologetic look. "I'm sorry, she hates tattoos."

He chuckles. "I'm used to it. But the reason I have them is because they all tell a story. They remind me of moments in my life. They remind me of who I was then, and they tell me to keep trying to be the man I'm supposed to be."

"That's sweet," she says hesitantly. "What does your mother think about them?"

Oof. So nosy.

But Harrison takes it in stride. "My mother has tattoos herself."

"Oh?"

He nods, running his hand through his hair. "Yeah. I may look like I come from the well-bred portion of British society, but I assure you I've come from the bottom. My mother raised me alone, after my dad fucked off somewhere. I had to help her raise my siblings, and then I got into the mean shite on the streets. It wasn't a pretty life for me back then. I got tattoos to remember those moments. Of course, some of those moments are just me high as a bloody kite and getting a friend to ink me, but most of these tattoos serve a purpose. I suppose even the ugly ones do, just like the ugly moments in life remind us of where we're headed."

My mother blinks, stares. I know for a fact she's never heard him talk this much before, not to mention the fact that he's let out something that I know he keeps tucked away, whether out of shame or guilt. I have to say, I'm shocked too that he would let my mother in like this. Shocked but grateful.

My heart swells, feeling warm and impossibly full that he trusts her like he trusts me.

"My goodness," my mother says after a moment. "I had no idea."

He lifts up a shoulder in a shrug. "I don't talk about it. Even the media doesn't know, which I'm grateful for. I know I'm just their PPO, but in the UK, they'll go digging up dirt on absolutely everyone who even says hello to them. I've always been able to spare my mother and my brother and sister that intrusion."

"Well, you can trust me," my mother says, making a show of crossing her heart. "I swear it. I won't tell a soul."

"I know you won't." He gives her a sweet, beautiful smile. "That's why I told you."

Oh fuck. I am falling so hard for him, so fast. I swear if I'm not careful, I'm going to blurt out something really stupid.

I clear my throat and nod at the coffeepot. "Coffee is ready."

My mother turns around and pours the coffee into two mugs, and I briefly reach out and touch Harrison's pinky with mine, trying to convey with my eyes how much that whole exchange meant to me.

Then she pivots toward us and gives us both a mug.

She grins at him, clearly as happy as I am that he was so honest, and then clears her throat. "Now if you'll excuse me," she says, "nature calls." She walks off to the bathroom and closes the door.

The fact that we're alone weighs so heavily on me that I think I might just crash through the floor.

I swallow, staring at Harrison, wanting to say so much, do so much.

He rubs his lips together and stares right back at me.

"I should probably head back," he says after a moment, having a sip of coffee.

"Do you have to?" I whisper. I nod at his mug. "At least finish your drink."

Something in his eyes softens, the lines on his brow deepening "It's not coffee that I want."

He puts the mug down and comes around the island and places a hand at my waist, holding me there firmly, his other hand going to my face. He gently brushes his thumb over the tip of my nose and smiles.

"You've had flour there this entire time."

I blush, my cheeks burning.

He runs his fingers under my chin, holding my face up to meet his. "It took everything in me not to kiss it off."

Oh boy. Here come the swoons. Here come my hormones.

He leans in and whispers in my ear, his breath tickling my skin, "I haven't been able to stop thinking about you. I've been going mad."

He places a kiss beside my ear, then my cheekbone, then . . .

The sound of the toilet flushing in the washroom causes him to pull back abruptly, his hand dropping away.

He takes a step back, his expression both wistful and apologetic, and walks over to where his suit jacket is hanging just as my mother comes out.

"You're not leaving now, are you?" she asks. "What about your coffee?"

"It was fabulous, but you know what, I think I'll be bouncing off the walls when I don't need to be."

"But the dough," she protests. "I know it's two hours, but I could use your help."

"You'll be perfectly fine on your own," he tells her, putting the jacket on. "I have full faith in you."

"You will come over for pie later, won't you?" she asks. "You could bring some to Monica and Eddie."

"I'll swing by tomorrow," he says, his eyes catching mine for a moment, trying to tell me something. But I can't figure out what it is, and then he's gone, nodding goodbye to the both of us and closing the door.

Tomorrow. He'll be back tomorrow.

But will he be here to stay this time?

Or are all our meetings in the future going to be fraught with anxiety and stolen kisses, forever having an audience?

There's always laundry, I tell myself.

Seventeen

THE NEXT DAY I WAKE UP TO A KNOCK ON THE DOOR AND Liza barking her head off.

"Liza!" I yell from the bedroom, slipping on my robe over my flimsy camisole before heading out into the living room, where she's barking furiously at the door.

"Stop losing your little doggy mind," I say, stepping between her and the door. I shoo her away toward my mother's room, but she doesn't budge, stubborn as anything.

I put my hand on the doorknob, knowing I'm going to see either Harrison or Monica, and I'm at that stage now with both of them where I don't really care if I have crazy bedhead and sleep in my eyes.

Actually, scratch that. I don't want to look like a total troll if it's Harrison. Just because we had sex doesn't mean I'm about to let myself go.

I attempt to smooth down my hair, tighten my robe around me to make sure I don't have a wayward boob slipping out from my camisole, and then open the door.

My heart leaps in my chest, doing that fluttery thing.

It's Harrison.

And he's smiling at me.

"Good morning," he says, pushing his sunglasses to the top of his head. His eyes take me in, startling in their clarity, and holy hell, I am an absolute fool for this man and I know it. Think he might know it too.

"Good morning to you," I tell him, leaning against the door. "You're up early."

"Part of the job," he says. "I'm sorry if I woke you up, though." He glances at his watch on his forearm. "It's eight a.m. already."

"You know, normal people wake up at eight a.m."

"You're calling yourself normal?" he asks with a sexy smirk, the kind I want to wipe off with my lips. Man, it's like all the sexual tension since we slept together is only getting worse as the days go on, an itch that desperately needs to be scratched.

But I have a feeling Harrison isn't here for a secret early-morning booty call, as much as my body is wishing he was.

"Speak for yourself," I tell him.

"Listen, I'm heading into town today to pick up some things . . . thought maybe you'd like to join me."

"You don't even have to ask, you know. Just assume that whatever it is you're doing, I'm on board. Want me to drive?"

He grins, making my stomach flip. He's never going to stop having that effect on me, is he? "I have to say, it makes life a little more exciting when you do, love."

Love? Did he just call me *love*?

Be still my heart.

I swallow, feeling goofy, giddy, all the good things. "I would have thought you'd want a break from excitement, being a body-guard and all."

He looks around him, the calm breeze ruffling the arbutus,

the nuthatches chirping from the branches. "Yes, this place is nonstop excitement, isn't it?"

"Let me get changed," I tell him, about to head back inside. I pause. "Unless you want to help me?" I ask sweetly, batting my lashes.

He runs his tongue over his teeth, seeming to think. "I better not."

"You sure about that?"

I flash him a coy smile and then open the door wider, gesturing for him to come inside.

He hesitates, eyeing Liza, who is sitting on the couch, staring at him. Then he cautiously walks inside after me, slips off his shoes. I gently close the door as his eyes flit to my mother's bedroom, the door closed.

"She's still sleeping, it's fine," I whisper to him, beckoning with my finger for him to follow me into the bedroom.

I close the door behind me, and as I'm turning around, Harrison's hands go to my waist, holding me there, his lips pressed against mine. I'm back against the door, my mouth opening to his, the slick, hot pass of his tongue making me feel molten inside.

With fumbling fingers I latch on to his suit jacket, gripping the lapels with a quiet sort of desperation, the need inside me spurred on as the kiss deepens and deepens.

"Oh god," I whisper against his mouth.

How I've needed this.

He grins, his hand slipping underneath my robe and camisole, large rough palms sliding up against my skin. An explosion of shivers rolls through me, making my thighs press together.

His hand goes to my bare breast, squeezing gently, his thumb brushing over my nipple until I'm letting out a deep moan. I swear this man has the ability to conjure sounds out of me that are borderline animalistic.

"God, your greedy little sounds," he murmurs against my mouth, pulling away briefly to stare at me with languid eyes. "You're nothing but trouble, Piper Evans."

"Trouble?" I say, already feeling breathless as he starts kissing my jawline, my neck. I grip his jacket tighter, wanting him closer, as insatiable as ever. "How am I trouble?"

"You make me want to do things I've only dreamed about," he says gruffly.

Dear lord.

Feeling emboldened by his words, I reach down and place my hand against his crotch, feeling the large, thick outline of his hard-on. He says I'm trouble, but he's the one walking around with that weapon in his pants.

But before I have a chance to tell him that, we're cruelly interrupted by Liza barking.

"Fuck," I swear as Harrison pulls away, breathing hard. "She better not wake up my mom."

Face flushed, my heart hammering in my chest, I quickly open the door to see Liza on the other side, sitting down like she's totally innocent, seeming to smile at me.

Then she barks again.

She's now an official cock-blocker in my book.

"Liza," I hiss at her. "Shhhh."

Bark. Bark.

And now I hear my mother stirring in her bedroom.

"Oh shit," I swear. I look over my shoulder at Harrison standing behind me and hastily push him back in my bedroom, even though he weighs the same as a boulder. I shut the door on him just as my mom shuffles out of her room.

"What's Liza barking at?" she says through a yawn.

Bark. Bark.

Barking right at my door.

"She's just being weird," I tell her, watching my mom as she makes her way over to the bathroom. Once the door is shut, I fling open the one to the bedroom. To my surprise, Harrison is trying to escape via the window. He's already removed the screen and is hoisting himself up in an impressive feat of strength.

"She's in the bathroom," I whisper. "Just go out the front door."

He lowers himself to the floor and gives me a sheepish smile. "Always know your exits." Then he hustles past me, grabbing his shoes, and steps outside, hopping around on one foot while he tries to slide a shoe on.

Just then, my mother steps out of the bathroom and looks over at me right as I'm about to close the door on him.

"Harrison?" she asks, squinting. "You're over early. I didn't even hear the door knock."

I pause. So, so close.

Harrison and I exchange a look like, *Okay, be cool,* and then I open the door wider.

"Yes, Harrison," I say to him, stepping back. "Why are you over here so early?"

He clears his throat, his gaze volleying between my mother and me. "Is it early? I had no idea. I, uh, was hoping Piper could accompany me into town."

My mother stops halfway to the kitchen and narrows her eyes at us, her suspicion piqued. "Oh really? Is that so?"

I gulp. Uh-oh. She's on to us.

"It's not because you wanted to come over and try the pie?!" she exclaims happily.

Whew. Saved by the pie.

Harrison gives her a cocky grin. "Well, I suppose there's no point beating around the bush, now is there?"

"I knew it," she says, waving him over. "Here, come on in. I'll make you some coffee, and you can have pie for breakfast."

I raise my brow at Harrison, expecting him to hurry off or remind my mother that we need to get going or something. But instead he surprises me yet again by saying, "I'd love that."

Damn this sweet man. That's twice in a row now that he's shown compassion and interest in my mother without humoring her.

He steps inside, and luckily her back is already turned, so she doesn't notice he never had a chance to put on his shoes. He quickly places them on the floor, and as I shut the door behind him, I give his sleeve a quick tug.

"You're amazing," I whisper to him.

The corner of his mouth lifts, a warm spark in his eyes as we stare at each other for a moment. I don't know if he can feel what I'm feeling, but I'm pretty sure I'm just radiating happiness right now, straight from my heart.

The pie actually turns out to be good, and of course Harrison insists that it was all my mother's doing, as if he didn't save the whole thing himself yesterday. While the two of them chitchat in the kitchen, I quickly get changed, and then Harrison and I are off.

"You are unbelievable, you know that?" I tell him as the car putters in the driveway, waiting for the gates to slowly open.

"Not sure what you mean," he says as we drive through. Though James's SUV is parked in the cul-de-sac, the media hasn't shown up yet. "But I won't refute it."

"You know what I mean," I tell him, briefly reaching down

and squeezing his hand, which is resting on his thigh. My god, it's taking everything in me not to maul him here in the car, but judging by his body language, that might be totally inappropriate. "The way you are with my mom. It means a lot."

He glances at me, frowning as his eyes search my face. "This isn't the first time you've said that to me. I have to say, it enrages me to think how the both of you have been treated, if showing any kindness has been an anomaly in your house." He looks away, gnawing on his lip. "Can't say I haven't been through it myself. Growing up, I knew what people thought about me, my siblings, my mum. I was told I was right trash all the time, to my face. When you're at the fringes of society, when you're not considered normal, whatever the fuck that really means, it just gives people an excuse to shun you. I won't ever look the other way with you, Piper. Not with you, not with your mother. You're both the loveliest people; you're *my* kind of people. It's society that needs to get fucked."

I don't hear Harrison swear that often, but the word *fuck* sounds exceedingly good with that accent.

"No wonder Eddie and Monica trust you with their lives," I tell him after a moment, slowing down as a deer crosses the road. "They're the first royals who have pushed back against the monarchy, to embrace being imperfect. I know when Monica made that speech about mental illness last year it meant a lot to people, to have someone from that family actually speak out for once."

"It also ruffled a lot of feathers," he says. "But then again, that's the part of society that needs to go fuck itself."

"Say *fuck* again," I tell him, grinning.

He gives me a wry glance and then slips on his shades, running his tongue over his bottom lip. Damn if I don't get butterflies again.

It turns out that Harrison needed to go into town to pick up a few books for Monica, which was fine with me since I never pass up a chance to look at books.

"Not that I'm complaining about the outing, but are you sure she can't just buy books on her Kindle?" I ask him as we step inside the town's bookstore. I give a polite nod to the owner behind the till. She's used to me coming in once a month and berating her over the shop's lack of a romance section, so I can't blame her for stiffening when she sees me.

"She says she prefers to read paperbacks," Harrison says, peering over his sunglasses at the new-releases section. "And something about how the house feels empty as it is and she needs to start filling the shelves."

"She's probably nesting," I tell him, before I realize I'm in public and I need to keep my voice down. There's no doubt the bookstore owner knows who Harrison is, especially since she's pretending to read a thriller, even though her eyes are constantly ogling him. Thankfully she's too far out of earshot to have heard me or even know who we're talking about.

"Anyway," I say quickly, coming over to Harrison, "what did she ask for?" I lower my voice and lean in. "I hope it's not anything baby related, because that's going to tip a lot of people off."

"She didn't really say," he says, pulling out a Stephen King. "She just wanted me to bring back books. Think she'd like this?"

"Well, does she like horror?"

"I don't think so."

I sigh. "Come here."

I walk around the shelf to the other side and gesture to one row of books, my meager victory for the romance industry. "Here. Pick any of these."

"This is the romance section?" he asks warily.

"Oh come on, don't lose all the brownie points you've recently earned with me. She likes romance; she's said as much herself. Bring her some of these. Plus, the more they sell here, the more the store will order."

"Okay," he says, reaching for one with a bare-chested man on the cover. "Hmmm," he muses, flipping it over. His lips move as he silently reads the blurb. Finally he says, "It's supposed to be a moving story about life and love. The cover tells me otherwise."

I hastily pluck it from his hands, raising my chin. "I've read it. It's about life and love, but also lots of wild sex and even some pegging thrown in there."

His forehead wrinkles. "Do I dare ask what pegging is?"

I laugh, shaking my head in mock sympathy. "Oh, you poor innocent man. I have so much to corrupt you with."

"I wouldn't mind being corrupted," he says quietly, his voice gruff, eyes glinting with the kind of heat I felt this morning.

"Well, I *tried* to do that this morning," I remind him.

"I'm going to blame your dog for that one."

"Can I help you?"

We both look up to see the store owner smiling expectantly at us.

I gesture to the romance. "Just showing a friend your most awesome romance section."

"You know, we have some other books that may be more of interest to you," she says to Harrison in a knowing voice.

"How do you know I didn't find exactly what I'm looking for?" Harrison says to her, standing his ground. He takes the book from my hand and shows it to her. "A riveting story about loss and love and pegging."

The owner purses her lips together and backs up slowly while I turn away, choking on my laughter. Oh, she *definitely* knows what pegging is. Perhaps she's not as anti-romance as she seems. I file away a mental note for a future podcast theme.

I grab a few more books for Monica from the shelf, still giggling, while Harrison flips through the pages of the pegging book. I have no doubt he's looking for a sex scene, and I know he's found one when a hint of pink starts to creep up his cheeks.

He clears his throat and hastily puts the book on top of the stack I'm holding. "I think I see where you get your, uh, voracious appetite from."

"Are you complaining?" I tease, walking past him.

"Not at all," he says roughly as he follows me to the till. "Just wish we had more opportunities."

You and me both.

But the truth is, Harrison and I don't have a lot of time to be together, and definitely not alone. After we buy the books for Monica, we pick up some groceries, and then we're heading back to the compound so Harrison can go back to being a bodyguard and I can go back to trying to work on some lesson plans for the fall.

It's a fruitless effort, though. He says goodbye to me in my driveway, and even though no one is watching, we keep our distance from each other. Then I go to my bedroom, lock my door, and decide to spend the afternoon pretending he's with me.

Eighteen

"YOU KNOW, I WOULDN'T MIND IF MR. COLE CAME OVER more often," my mother says, her voice casual and high pitched for extra innocence.

I glance over at her, my brow raised in surprise.

We're sitting on the deck sipping iced blueberry tea. It's only ten in the morning, but it's a scorcher already. A couple of hot days in a row is pretty rare here, even in July, but it's been a consistent heat wave all week long.

There's no way Mom hasn't caught on, I think to myself.

"Why would he come over?" I ask, trying to sound blasé.

"I don't know, Piper." She says this in a way that suggests she very well does know. She takes a satisfied sip of her iced tea. "He's here to do laundry quite a bit." Her eyes twinkle at me. "And I know my pie is good, but it's not that good."

Don't fall for it. It's a trap.

I shrug. "I'm sure their machine will get fixed one of these days. And it is that good. You could open up your own bakery by now."

It's been a couple of days since Harrison stopped by the house and then took me into town. I would have loved to have seen him that night, but figuring out how to be with each other without raising suspicion has been a pain in the ass, plus his schedule doesn't leave a lot of freedom.

Yesterday he came by again, except he wasn't alone. Monica came with him, apologizing for their taking over our laundry room and to invite us again for dinner on Friday. Harrison then went down below to do more laundry, but with Monica and my mother chatting in the kitchen, it wouldn't have looked right if I had suddenly left them to go check on the laundry or something.

The dinner is tomorrow. At any rate, I don't think I'll be seeing Harrison today, but you never know. My stupid, stupid heart is holding out for the best, even if I berate it for being so hopeful.

"You know," my mother goes on, "I was wrong about him."

"What do you mean?"

My mother? Admitting she was wrong? What is this world?

"At first I thought I knew who he was. I had him figured out. I thought I knew his type because I'd seen that type so many times before. You'd bring them home all smitten, and they were the type of boys to make my skin crawl. I'm sure you thought I was being paranoid and judgmental, but I knew none of them were good enough for you, Piper."

"Yeah," I say softly, watching the ocean breeze move the branches of pine at the end of the deck. "I should have listened."

"You didn't. Because they were your mistakes to make. All I can say is thank god you found out about Joey when you did. I know that it was so tough for you, sweetie, and I know it was embarrassing. But that was worth it, wasn't it?"

I nod. "It was. And I know I've made mistakes. But I also know how to look out for them now. I know my personality. I know I've . . ." I don't want to mention trauma, because it's trauma she's helped generate, and I'm not trying to play the blame game, not when we're finally talking like this. "I've been through things that have shaped me, but I also know how to dig deep and get better. And you know why? Because of my therapist. She helped me see why I was doing the things I was, and she gave me the tools to change it."

I expect my mom to shut down at the mention of therapy, but she only sighs and leans back in her chair. "I really hope you find the right man one day, Piper," she says. She rolls her head to the side to look at me. "And that's what Harrison is. He's a man. He's not a boy. He's not here to play games with you. That's why I like him. He comes from a strong, earnest, kind place. I know that now. I can feel it."

I swallow thickly. She's right. He is a man. Everyone else was just a boy, as fragile and slippery as a leaf in the wind.

"You know we're not . . . ," I start. "He's just a friend."

"I know," she says. "I know that's what you keep saying. I know it's what you both want to believe. But I've seen it on your face from day one, and now I see it on his. Chemistry is hard to fake and even harder to hide. You have it in spades. And even though I'm your mother and the last person you want to confide in, I still know you. That man has your heart. Maybe it's time you admit it, if not to me, to yourself. And to him."

No. No way. My heart . . . what even is my heart? It's been this beating, aching creature in my chest, hiding behind my ribs, afraid to bare itself lest I get hurt again. I've kept it tucked away, having no reason to let it free. And yet with Harrison, it wants to be free. It wants to. And I think, no matter what I do, I'm going to eventually fall in love with him.

But what good is that when there is no relationship to speak of? All we have between us is a stolen moment of passion and kisses few and far between. I don't even know if he feels the same way I do, and I wish it wasn't important, but it is.

"I'm fine," I tell her begrudgingly. "It's just a crush."

"Well, whatever you want to call it, I just want you to know that I approve. However you guys make it work, I'm behind you one hundred percent." She pauses and smiles devilishly. "Besides, the man can *bake*. That pie was the best I've ever had all because of him. He's a keeper."

"You just want delicious pastries," I tell her.

"Don't you?"

I laugh. The fact that Harrison can bake is a bonus. I'm sure there are a million bonuses about him. And if I'm lucky enough, I'll get to know them all.

The two of us sit on the deck for a little longer, but the heat is starting to become unbearable.

"I think I'm going to go to the lake and cool off," I tell my mother as I go inside. "You interested?"

She shakes her head, her eyes closed. I can tell she's heading in for another nap.

I go to my bedroom and slip on a yellow bikini before pulling on a loose linen dress on top. I grab a towel, place a wide-brimmed hat on my head, slip on my sunglasses and flip-flops, and I'm out the door.

I throw the towel into the back seat and am about to get in the car when I glance up through the trees at the tiny glimpse of the royals' roof.

Hmmm.

Why do I have to wait around for Harrison? Why can't I make my own things happen?

I head up through the brush that separates our properties, my legs scratched by the salal bushes and ferns, not even bothering with the driveway, and head across to their front door.

I knock and glance around, expecting the men in the trees to rappel down at any moment and accost me with their polite but gruff British ways. I've never come here on my own without being invited, and there are so many massive trees they could be hiding in.

Luckily the door opens before the tree men make an appearance. It's Agatha, looking surprised.

"Ms. Evans," she says. "I wasn't expecting you."

"I know. I'm sorry. I was heading to town and wondered if you needed anything." I mean, I'm not really heading to town, but I'm hoping my ploy works.

"Let me ask, just a moment," she says, closing the door on me. I try not to take offense, knowing it must be protocol.

A few moments later, the door opens again.

Harrison.

"Piper?" he asks.

"Surprise," I say, throwing my arms out and jutting my hip to the side.

"Agatha said you were going to town?"

He sounds all business, which bothers me a little, even though I know he absolutely has to be all business right now.

"Yeah, I just wondered if you guys needed anything. Or if you needed me to take you somewhere." I say that last bit a little lower.

His brow cocks up. He gets it.

"Sure," he says. "I take it you're driving?"

I nod.

"I bet there are some errands I can run," he says. "Meet you at your car."

He closes the door, and I walk back across their driveway, grinning to myself, then doing a little skip.

A flash of movement catches my eye from up above.

The wave of a hand.

From up in a tree.

I can't see the rest of him, but I smile and wave back. I don't care if he caught me skipping and looking like a fool. I am what I am.

I head to the car and get in the driver's seat. It feels like forever until I see Harrison's shadow, having not heard him approach at all.

"Hi," he says to me, getting in his seat.

"Hot day," I tell him.

He buckles in, and I start the car. It purrs like a broken cat.

"It is," he says. "Guess you wouldn't believe it if I told you the air conditioning broke."

I laugh as we pull down the driveway, pause as the gates open. "That whole house is falling apart. Let me guess: Going to be a while before you get a repairman for that over?"

He shrugs. "He said he'd be here tomorrow. Though that's what the dryer person's been saying for days, and I'm starting to suspect they're the same person. Roscoe's Heating and Cooling and Roscoe's Repairs, seems like too much of a coincidence."

I giggle at him. "Don't forget Roscoe's Electrical Services. Still haven't fixed a baseboard heater in my house."

He lets out a small laugh, and I let the trippy, happy feelings flow through me for a moment before the more awkward ones resurface.

The funny thing is, though, aside from the sexual tension between us, which is very taut and thick and real, I don't feel that incessant need to blab. The silence is comfortable. Being in his presence both speeds up my heart rate and calms me at the same time. These feelings are a paradox, but I'm grateful for them all the same.

When we drive past the town, though, he turns to me. "Where are we going?"

"Nowhere," I say, briefly sticking my tongue between my teeth.

He focuses on that for a moment, then looks me in the eye. "Why did I have a feeling?"

"Because I was tired of waiting for you," I tell him.

His expression falters. "Sorry. It's not exactly easy to get away. Especially since I came by to do laundry yesterday. There's only so much."

"I know, I'm just giving you a hard time." I wink at him. Innuendo and all that. "Or at least, I hope it'll be hard."

His brows raise. "So where are you taking me?"

"A place where we can be alone and escape the heat."

He chuckles. "That sounds like an oxymoron to me."

"You'll see," I tell him.

I take the Cranberry Road exit heading past the sign to Mount Maxwell Provincial Park. It's a long and winding drive up past forests and farmlands, more hidden nooks of the island. Harrison's attention is rapt on the scenery. "There's so much here that I haven't seen. And I've seen more than Eddie or Monica."

"Doesn't that bother them? I mean, I know they came here to escape, but even with that big house, cabin fever has to be getting to them too."

"I think they're just so focused on the baby," Harrison says. "Then again, I'm just going by what I hear. I think Eddie might be getting a little annoyed, but it's hard for them to go anywhere."

"We could always go for a hike somewhere," I tell him. "In fact, we're about to go for a little one right now. Except if they came, they could get in trouble."

"In trouble?" he repeats. "Okay, what do you have planned? I don't trust that expression in your eyes."

I give him a saucy grin. "Relax. Go with the flow. Island life, remember?"

It's not long, though, until we're on the bumpy mountain road, avoiding potholes that threaten to swallow the car whole. To his credit, Harrison doesn't say anything else, but I can tell he's wary about this whole thing.

Finally I pull off the road and park at the foot of a hidden driveway, baby birch trees growing along the edges. I get out of the car and grab my towel, then point across the road to where the dust from my car is still lingering in the hot air.

"What?" Harrison asks.

"We're going in there," I tell him.

"Into where? Those trees?"

"Mmhmm. It might be time for you to leave your jacket behind. It's going to get torn up."

Now he looks panicked. "Where are you taking me?"

"Don't worry, it's an easy hike. And anyway, I don't know how on earth you can wear that suit in this weather. Don't you have some formal secret agent shorts or something?"

"Not a secret agent. And no, we don't have shorts. What a ghastly sight that would be."

I grin and wave him forward. "Come on."

I cross the road and head into the forest, Harrison following. I point to a tall chain-link fence that ends a few feet away before walking through the brush that skirts around it.

"That fence didn't use to be here, but the fire department put it up to stop us from using the lake."

"Wait a minute, you're taking me to a lake?"

"Where did you think I was taking you?"

"I don't know," he says. "Perhaps an old abandoned hunting lodge with a bed in the corner."

I laugh and look at him over my shoulder. "My god. I have higher standards than that."

"Do you? You're taking me on what seems like an illegal excursion to a lake."

"It's not illegal. They just tried to, you know, dissuade people. This lake is gorgeous, and for whatever reason they decided they didn't want people to use it. Someone complained, probably Barbara Mischky, or one of the houses on the lake. They say it's because it's a reservoir, but a lot of the other lakes on the island are reservoirs, and you don't see them fenced off."

"Uh-huh."

I look at him again. He's marching through the undergrowth with ease, branches from the hemlocks tugging at his shirt as he passes by.

It's about fifteen minutes of bushwhacking before we see the lake.

Just as I suspected, there's not a soul here, and from where we are, tucked into a small bay, you can't see the houses at the end of the lake either. It's just us, the gleaming jewel-green water, the sun-dried moss that covers the slopes of granite and quartz that lead to the shore, the tall, wavering fir and cedar.

"Shit. It's a beauty," Harrison says.

I waste no time.

I immediately pull my dress over my head and throw it to the side along with my towel, then scamper down toward the shore in my bikini, kicking off my flip-flops just before I carefully climb onto a couple of rocks that jut out into the water.

"Piper!" Harrison calls, but I ignore him.

I get to the last rock, find my balance on the sun-warmed surface, and then launch myself into the lake.

And by launch, I mean cannonball. Any attempt at diving would result in a belly flop, and besides, I'm like five years old at heart.

The water is cool, shocking me awake as I hit with a big splash, my arms wrapped tightly around my shins. I open my eyes to the bubbles and then kick up to the surface, bursting through to the sun on my face.

I tread water and look over at Harrison, who is on the lake-shore, his hands on his hips, frowning at me. But there's a smile on his lips too, just as I'm grinning widely at him.

"Come on in, the water is just fine," I say, splashing around.

He stares at me for a moment, then starts to unbutton his dress shirt.

I am here for this.

I keep treading, my eyes focused on each sliver of skin that's slowly revealed.

Yes, I've had sex with Harrison.

But I never got to enjoy his body the way I would have liked to.

This is my first look, and I am going to *look*.

He reaches the last button, then removes his shirt.

Damn.

I watch as he folds his shirt neatly and places it on the moss beside him, my eyes drawn to every bare inch of his torso, from the wide expanse of his chest, to his rock-hard shoulders, to his literal six-pack abs, all of which are covered in tattoos, tattoos that mean something to him, tattoos that tell the story of Harrison.

I am determined to read that story as far as he'll let me.

Of course, he doesn't stop undressing.

His pants come off next.

Socks.

Shoes.

Then he's just in his boxer briefs.

And then . . .

He's completely naked.

Head to toe.

Completely naked and standing in a sun-dappled forest, looking like some kind of Celtic warrior with his brawny muscles and mysterious tattoos, decorating him like runes.

It takes me a moment to bring my eyes away from his appendage and up to his face, where he's taking off his sunglasses, because of course they were the last thing to go.

He carefully folds them and places them on top of the rest of his folded clothes. I look at my messy discarded pile for contrast, and he strides into the lake, getting up to his knees before he dives in right beside me.

He's swimming underwater for a long time, his skin glowing against the dark water, until he pops up farther out into the lake. I swim after him.

"Impressive," I tell him, treading water.

There's a wet lock of hair on his forehead, and he shakes it loose.

"What is?" he asks. "My package or my diving skills?"

"Both," I say, biting my lip as I smile at him.

"I can only explain my diving skills," he says. "To be a PPO, you have to hold your breath for a long time. As for the other, we'll just chalk it up to luck."

"And how are you with treading water while holding on to someone else?" I say to him, swimming closer.

"Just try me," he says, reaching out underwater and grabbing my waist, pulling me toward him. "I'll never sink. I'll always hold you up."

I wrap my legs around his waist, holding on to his shoulders. "You promise?"

It's so strange to be with him like this, out in the open sunshine, our bodies wet, his completely naked, his dick pressing against me. I stare at his wet lashes, the drops of water in his arched brows, the warm curve of his smile.

"This is nice," he says, his voice low.

I lean in and brush my lips against his, then move my head back before he has a chance to kiss me.

"You're being a tease," he says. "Might need a spanking for that."

I laugh, unable to stop the thrill from running through me. "Yes, please."

He reaches down and grabs my ass, giving it a hearty squeeze. I yelp playfully.

"You know, when I woke up this morning, I didn't think I'd end up naked in a lake with you," he comments.

"I guess you never know what to expect with me."

"That's true," he says, almost wistfully. "You really are unlike anyone I've ever known."

"Oh come on," I say, looking away, my eyes squinting at the sun on the water. "I'm sure you've met a few kooky blondes in your day."

He shakes his head, frowning as he stares at me. "No. There's been . . . no one." He takes in a deep breath. "I've obviously been with women over the years, but maybe a night here or there. Nothing memorable. Nothing . . . significant. Because I just don't have the space for them in my life."

I swallow hard. *Oh. Present tense.*

He continues. "Piper, I'm going to be honest with you . . ."

Oh no.

"I don't know how to make this work."

Oh . . . no.

My face falls. I can't help it. I feel like letting go and sinking beneath the water.

He holds me tighter, giving strong kicks to keep us afloat, moving us toward the shore until he can touch the bottom. "Please, let me finish, because I am not finished with you." He puts his hand on my face, cupping my cheek. "I don't know how to make it work, and that's true. But that doesn't mean I'm not going to try. That we won't try to figure it out together. I'm . . . I just need you to know that no matter what happens, it's not going to be easy to be with me . . . if you even want to be with me."

"Of course I do," I say, my words coming out in a hush.

"Then you have to understand . . . I'm a bloody mess."

I stare at him for a few seconds, nearly dumbfounded. "A mess? *You're* a mess?"

He nods grimly.

"I don't understand," I tell him. "You're the opposite of a mess. You're stoic and in control and serious. I'm the mess here, with my crazy past and my mother and the pastries that get in my hair and my Tic Tacs. There's only room for one mess."

"Then you'll have to make room for me," he says. "Just because I am a certain way doesn't mean that's not the result of something else."

"What do you mean?"

He licks his lips and closes his eyes, his expression fraught, like he's battling with something. "You know I was in the army for all of my twenties, and then some," he says. "But do you know why I left the army?"

"Because you wanted to work for Eddie."

"Because I didn't have much choice. I left the army because of a mistake I made. A mistake that got someone killed. A friend of mine, someone I had taken under my wing, that I was sworn to protect. I injured my leg in the process, couldn't serve anyway. Was sent home. Eddie knew. Eddie reached out." He opens his eyes, and they're brimming with pain. "I don't know where I'd be if it weren't for him. The army gave me the structure I needed. Eddie gave me that same structure after I thought I'd lost it all. I am married to my work, Piper. For better or for worse, in sickness and in health, I have sworn to protect them, so that I will never fail again. So when I say I don't know how to do this with you . . . I don't. I only know my job. I only know my duty. There's been no room for anything else."

Damn. Poor Harrison. It's painfully obvious now how much his work has overcompensated for the guilt he feels.

I put my hand on his cheek. "You have to make peace with your guilt. You have to find your own forgiveness, your own redemption. You'll be working for Eddie and Monica until your dying day otherwise, and that's not much of a life. You still deserve to have one and live one and enjoy it."

And maybe there's room for me in it.

"That's easier said than done."

"I know it is," I say imploringly. "You're suffering from PTSD."

He looks away, gnawing on his lip.

"It's true," I tell him. "I assume that nightmare I caught you having, that it's not the first one. That you have them a lot. Right?"

His eyes are still focused on the water, on nothing. That says everything.

"You're reliving it in your dreams because you haven't dealt with it in real life. And look, I'm no expert. I would never diminish how you feel, and I know that what I've gone through with my mother and father is small peanuts compared to what you've had to go through. But I have been there. I have learned that the past can hold us and mold us, drown us in its depths. And the person who comes out of that past is a product of everything it was subjected to. But you can get past it, out of it. You can recognize your patterns and behaviors and stop blaming yourself. Just accept it. It sounds like that's what you're already doing. You *know* why you are the way you are, and you want to change it. You should be proud of yourself."

"Then how come I don't feel proud?" His voice is grave. It breaks my heart a little.

"Because it takes time. A lot of time. And therapy. Have you been to therapy? I assume that the army must have mandated it."

He shakes his head. "I said I was fine. I was deemed fine."

This explains so much. "But you're admitting you're not fine, right? I mean, if you don't think you have room in your life for another person because you're too devoted to your job, that's not normal. That's not fine."

"I don't want to hurt you, Piper. I don't want to mess up. You deserve someone better."

"First of all," I tell him, adjusting my grip on his shoulders, "you will hurt me and you will mess up. So will I. We're two messy people with different baggage, but baggage all the same. And second of all, I get to decide who I deserve. I've been around, I've had my heart broken, my soul crushed, and I've walked out of it. Maybe I have some scars, but they remind me of what I do deserve, and what I deserve is you. You'll have to trust me on this."

He gazes into my eyes, the blue green of his shimmering like the lake below. He looks . . . awed. "You're bloody amazing, you know that?"

I shrug, trying to play it off. "Well, I—"

And for the second time, Harrison cuts me off with a kiss.

Like the first time, I accept my silence willingly.

His hand tightens around me, gripping me close as his mouth presses hungrily against mine, all fire and need and desire. I'm both floating in the water and grounded by him, my legs wrapping around tighter.

I've needed this.

I've needed him.

His lips drop down to my neck, sucking at my skin, while I hold him to me, my hands disappearing into his hair, then grabbing his shoulder, then coasting down the hard, muscled plane of his back.

While he nips at my neck, a mix of pleasure and pain, I throw my head back and open my eyes to the blue, blue sky above. I think I see a plane, or maybe it's that I feel so free, it's like I'm flying, especially as Harrison takes his hand and lowers it down until his fingers are wrapping around the hem of my bottoms.

He pulls it to the side, taking a moment to adjust himself before he pushes himself inside.

I gasp, my voice carrying across the water, feeling every inch of him.

"Is this okay?" he asks, his voice hoarse with lust yet gentle and concerned. Always the gentleman.

I nod, making a groaning sound as my body adjusts to his, taking in a deep breath until he pushes in to the hilt.

I hold him tighter between my legs as he takes a commanding

stance in the water, and he starts pumping himself in and out, slowly at first, making sure I feel every blissful drag of him.

I can't believe this is happening. I know I keep thinking that, and the more that I think that, the less I feel it's real. But here we are in this beautiful lake, and Harrison is deep inside me, grunts and rough little noises escaping his lips as he works at me.

Occasionally he pulls back enough to stare at me, his brow furrowed with awe, like he can't believe this is happening, and then he kisses me hard, as if that will bring him proof.

All I can think of is how my body responds to his, how easily it bends and twists and molds to his movement, like we're synchronized swimming in one spot. I'm weightless and lost to him, to this moment, to everything he's brought into my little life.

This man.

This *man*.

I think he might be mine.

"Christ, Piper," he practically growls as his mouth drifts down to my breast, pulling my top aside and sucking at my nipple. "I don't know how much longer I can last."

I'm about to tell him that I won't be long either when he slips his hand between my legs, his finger pressing against my clit, and from the loud moan that pours out of me, I guess I don't need to tell him after all.

"I'm coming," I say through a gasp as his fingers continue to work at me.

There's no holding back.

Not with him.

Not anymore.

The orgasm sweeps through me like a wave. The kind of wave that you think you can handle, the ones that end up bigger than you thought they'd be. This one takes me out, makes me feel like I'm being spun around like a galaxy, and I'm opening wider and wider and wider, like an exploding star, spreading fire and ice until there's nothing left of me.

Harrison grunts as he comes inside me, his grip still tight while his pumping slows, his breath heavy and laborious.

We stay connected like this for a few moments, both of us catching our breath. I rest my head against his shoulder and can feel his heart pounding against his chest, competing with the drumming from mine. Slowly, very slowly, the world comes back into place, and I remember where we are and what we've done.

We need to get out of here.

"I hate to be one of those people who insists on leaving the scene of the crime," I tell him as I grip his shoulders and he slowly pulls out of me, setting me back in the water, "but I think we should vacate the area before some bored water department officer shows up."

"Good idea," Harrison says.

We both swim back to shore, giggling as we quickly slip on our clothes, feeling like a couple of teenagers who just snuck into a public pool after hours, high on life and sex and each other.

We run back through the forest, staying close.

Nineteen

GIDDY.

That's the only word to describe what I feel like.

It's probably one of our earliest emotions—I mean, what toddler hasn't gotten giddy after a first bite of ice cream? What child hasn't gotten giddy thinking about Disneyland? Or going on a pony ride? Or Christmas morning?

But as we get older, the giddiness fades. We become more cynical. The excitement, the increased heart rate, the swarmy, fizzy feeling in our stomach? It morphs into anxiety. We become nervous. The joy is removed, and all we're left with is worry. The joy is something that belonged to the past, to when we were more innocent, when we had things to get excited and happy about.

So this, this giddiness, makes me feel like a child all over again. Like I've been reborn, picked up and washed off and polished to a shine and then set back down into this world.

All I can think about is Harrison. He's taken over my thoughts and my heart and everything in between. But it's more than that, more than how I'm thinking. It's how I'm living. Like every waking moment I am bursting with impatient joy that's bundled up inside and dying to get out. I want to kiss him, have sex with him, hold him, listen to him, stare at him. I want so much, and the kicker is that for once, I'm going to have it.

This is happening.

"Okay," my mother says to me, appearing in my bathroom mirror as I'm putting on blush. It's like a horror movie jump cut, and I whirl around to face her, my heart pounding.

"Jeez, Mom, don't sneak up on a girl like that," I tell her. I then notice she's wearing a gauzy pink top with a statement necklace and black pants. "You look nice."

"*You* look nice," she says to me, nodding at my face. "A little too nice. You're smiling nonstop."

"I have to smile to do my blush." I turn around to face the mirror and do a close-lipped smile, propping up my cheeks. I swirl the blush brush on them.

"You have been smiling all day," she says, crossing her arms. "And yesterday too."

"It's summer. It's a beautiful day. We're both alive and in good health, we have this wonderful house, and the best doggo, and we're about to have dinner with the Duke and Duchess of Fairfax. Give me one reason not to smile."

She narrows her eyes as she studies me. "Uh-huh. What drugs are you on? You haven't upped your medication, have you?"

"No," I tell her, rolling my eyes.

"Didn't think so. So then I'm going to assume this is all because of Mr. Cole."

Do I have the strength to argue with her? No. I mean, I do, but I don't want to argue with her. I'm too fucking giddy.

So I just shrug and stare at her in the mirror. "Life is good right now."

"Because of Mr. Cole. Just look at you, Piper. You're glowing."

I look at myself. My eyes are wide and glossy and my skin looks alive, and it's not just the blush or the highlighter. I look happy. Really happy. I don't think I've ever seen myself look like this.

"Oh no. You're not pregnant, are you?" she adds, aghast.

"No," I say in a quick huff. "I'm not pregnant." I pause. "And why would you even think that? I never said I was sleeping with him."

Now it's her time to roll her eyes. "You think I'm a fool, don't you, dear?" Then she turns around and walks into my bedroom. "You better hurry up. We need to be there in ten minutes."

This is a change. Usually my mom has zero concept of time. Perhaps things are evolving for the both of us.

Tonight is the dinner, and while I don't think it will be any more formal than last time, that doesn't help quell the excitement and nervousness in the air, at least when it comes to my mother. While I'm practically floating above the ground (giddiness makes you buoyant), my mother has been so anxious that she didn't even bother making a dessert. We're not heading over there empty-handed, however. I did manage to bring a bottle of local blackberry wine for after dinner, something I had been saving for a special occasion.

And what's a better special occasion than this? Sure, it's a normal dinner to everyone else, but to me, and hopefully to Harrison, this feels like a next step. I know our relationship is still under wraps and I don't know how long it will have to stay that way, but I guess any excuse to be with him feels like something worth celebrating.

Which reminds me.

We're almost to the mansion's door when I pull my mom to a stop.

"Mom," I say to her, my voice low. "I need to tell you something."

"What?" she says in a hush. Her eyes widen. "Oh, you really are pregnant!"

"No," I say again. "I have an IUD, so that's not happening. But whatever is happening between Harrison and I, it's a secret, okay? Monica, Eddie, the housekeeper, none of them can know."

She frowns. "Why not?"

"Because," I tell her, "Monica specifically forbade it."

"She specifically forbade it?"

"Okay, so she vaguely warned me about dating him. Or being with him. She said it would be a disaster and would reflect badly on her. Which I totally understand."

Now that I'm saying this out loud, I realize what a shitty friend I've been to her. Because of course it would reflect badly on her. Everything does. If the media found out about Harrison and me, they would have a field day with it, and Harrison would get slammed for being unprofessional, even though it's in his right to date a citizen (I think), and Monica would get dragged through the mud for having hired Harrison. Everything would come out, maybe even a look into Harrison's past.

"Oh, sweetie," my mother says, putting her hand on my cheek. "Don't look so glum. I won't say a word. I promise."

I give her a quick smile of thanks but now find it impossible to shake off this feeling. There goes my giddiness. Shot down by reality in seconds flat.

I sigh, and we walk toward the door. I'm going to have to talk to Harrison about this when I get a chance. So far we've been so wrapped up in how we feel about each other and our own obstacles that I forgot that we might really hurt Monica by doing this, and that by doing this—sneaking around and keeping it a secret— we might be awful people. I know our conversation was meant to be between us, but even so I feel like Harrison should know what she said.

My mother rings the doorbell, and Agatha appears. We're led into the house and to the lounge where Monica and Eddie have gathered. I don't see Harrison, which makes me feel both disappointed and relieved.

"I'm so glad you were able to come," Monica says.

"Please have a seat," Eddie says, gesturing. "Agatha will bring you something to drink. What will you have?"

We settle in our seats, and both my mom and I ask for a glass of wine. My mother didn't drink last time because of her medication, but this time seems different. My eyes are boring into hers, hoping she'll give me some explanation, but she's smiling and fixated on the royals. I just hope she can handle that one glass.

"So I was talking to Harrison last night," Eddie says to me.

Oh god. Oh god.

"And he had mentioned that perhaps the both of us should get out of the house more. Can't say I didn't agree with him."

"Speak for yourself," Monica says. "I am quite happy in this glass-walled castle." She gestures with her glass of sparkling water to the view.

Eddie chuckles and squeezes her hand. "Okay. Then I will speak for myself. Harrison said you mentioned a few places we could go, where we probably won't be photographed, or at the very least, won't be harassed by people. I understand a few photos are inevitable; it's more about being given space and privacy."

Harrison didn't mention the lake, did he? Because that's not exactly a good place for the royals to go. I mean, we could have gotten in trouble yesterday. It's only luck that we didn't.

Agatha hands me my wine, and I have a sip first, swallowing

before I say, "I know of a few hikes and walks and quiet places to go. Some more adventurous than others."

"See, darling," Eddie says to Monica. "Doesn't even have to be a hike. Just a walk. I think it would be good for you to get out of the house."

"You know," I tell them, "even if you wanted to look around town, I don't think it would be the end of the world. I'm not sure if as much media is still here, and anyway, with James and Harrison, I don't see how anyone could get close to you. And the locals, as zany as they are, won't harass you, I know that much."

"Are you sure about that?" Monica asks glumly. "My mother has been following the news. She says she's seen a few interviews with the locals complaining about us being here. It's more than just some article in the local newspaper."

"But that comes with the territory," Eddie says.

"And people complain about everything," I tell her. "No one here likes change. That's why they move here. To get away from all the change and come to a place where they can just be. But they also don't realize, everyone needs to change. You can't stay stagnant forever. You have to evolve and become more than just a static figure in your own life."

Monica frowns, probably wondering why I'm getting philosophical all of a sudden. "Is that why you moved here?"

"Well, for the job."

"That's why I wanted to move here," my mother speaks up, already having finished half the glass of wine. "Living in Victoria, I felt too pressured to improve myself, to fix myself. Coming here, people leave you alone. It's an island in every sense of the word, letting you yourself become an island too. But I've come to realize, ever since you moved in, that you can't hide and shrink for the rest of your life. You have to embrace change and welcome it, or you'll never get better. If there's no push, there is no growth, and that is the damn truth."

I stare at my mother, openmouthed. I've never heard her say anything remotely like this before. I mean, this is pure Grade A therapy-speak here.

She gives me a quick look. "I'm allowed to have my own epiphanies, Piper," she says. "The last few years, the both of us have become so tightly wound that we've become dependent on each other. It's not just me being dependent on you. It's the other way around too. Only now, with you spreading your wings a bit, I've been able to find my own footing. You worry about me, sweetie, and I don't blame you. But you have to let me live and find my own growth too. On my own."

Silence fills the room. My eyes start to water. It means so much to hear my mother say that, as shocking as it is, and especially with an audience.

"You are so very right, Evelyn," Monica says gently. "I think we can all relate to that. I know I can. I am changing, in the biggest ways"—she rests her hands on her small bump—"to the smallest ways. And because I'm changing, I knew that would make me an easier target. But being here so far has made me realize I can't hide forever. As much as I want to, as much as it truly has been needed to find myself, to rekindle our relationship as a couple, to prepare for the baby, as much as stepping back has brought such peace into our souls, I know that peace is fuel for the future. That it will help us handle what will be thrown our way. I can't be afraid of change any more than you can."

"So is that a yes to the hike or not?" Eddie asks.

We all laugh.

"Sure," Monica says. "And Piper is right, maybe a walk through town will do us good. I've walked through fire; a little stroll can't hurt us." She bites her lip and looks down at her stomach. "Maybe it will be a good opportunity to tell the news."

Eddie lets out a low whistle. "You can still hide your bump. Let's think about that one first, because once word breaks out, then we'll never be left alone." He looks to me. "You say the locals won't harass us, but when there's big money for photos of a baby bump, things can change."

"I know. But maybe you need to have faith in the place you moved to. Believe me, it's hard at times, but I still know that most people are good. Once you feel comfortable here, once you start showing your face more, you'll feel less like an outsider. They'll see you as a local, as one of them—as much as you can be, anyway."

Eddie seems to mull that over. I don't know what the right answer is here, but I do know that there is a change in the air for every single one of us, change that has us second-guessing what we want and what the right thing to do is. But things are happening. Sooner or later we will all make our own leaps into the unknown and hopefully have enough faith to survive them.

Speaking of my own change, Harrison is still nowhere to be found. I don't see James either, which I guess means Eddie and Monica fully trust my mother and me, which is nice. We're no longer a threat; we're actually their friends.

And look what you're doing to your friend, I remind myself.

The guilt is hard to ignore.

Dinner turns out to be roasted Cornish game hen, which Agatha whipped up. Naturally, it's delicious and lemony, and Agatha insists it's an old family recipe on her mother's side.

My mother has had two glasses of wine now and is a little

loopy, but other than that, she's been behaving herself, though she's talking a lot.

"So, Piper," Eddie says between mouthfuls. "Are you happy to have summer vacation, or are you itching to go back to work?"

"A little of both," I admit.

"Piper never gets bored," my mother speaks up, even though that's totally untrue. "She reads a lot."

"Oh. A fellow bibliophile," Eddie says. "I love reading too. One good thing about stepping away from our royal duties is that I've found so much more time to read. What kind of books do you read?"

Here it comes. The question that every romance reader gets, followed by the internal struggle of whether to tell the truth, tell a lie, or water the truth down a bit. The romance stigma is still real, even with it being the most popular genre.

I decide to go for the truth.

"Romance," I tell him, straightening in my seat. "Lots of romance. Historical, contemporary, romantic suspense. If there's kissing and sex and swooning, I'm on it."

"Ah," he says. "I'm going to assume that's more than *Fifty Shades of Grey*."

"*Fifty Shades* opened up the doors for the whole industry. It got people reading. You can't ever fault that."

"Well, I like romance," Monica says. "Sophie Kinsella is one of my favorites."

I want to point out that even though I love Kinsella's books too, they're more women's fiction (oh, how I dislike that term) than romance. But it doesn't matter.

"Did you know that Piper has a podcast?" my mother suddenly says. "It's about romance."

My eyes go big. Oh my god, she didn't.

She knows that's a secret, doesn't she?

Or maybe I've just never had any friends to keep the secret from.

"Mom," I warn her. "Maybe you shouldn't have any more wine."

"Why?" she cries out defensively. "I'm fine, Piper. And why can't I tell them about your podcast?" She smiles at Monica, thinking she's helping. "It's a romance podcast, you see." Then she looks at me quizzically. "Actually, I was just talking about your podcast earlier, and I think I got the name wrong. It's *Romancing the Podcast*, right? That's what I told them."

If my eyes were wide before, now they are practically falling out of my head. "What?" I cry out. "What are you talking about? Who is *them?*"

Oh my god, oh my god, oh my god.

"Them? Didn't I tell you?"

"Tell me what?" I'm practically shouting. It's then that I notice Harrison enter the room, looking grave. He meets my eyes for a moment and frowns, and I can't read the look in his eyes. It's like he's worried about me and also worried about something else.

He pauses by Eddie while I wait for my mother to explain what the fuck is going on. It's one thing to have her admit that I have a podcast in front of Monica and Eddie, especially when I actually did a podcast about them; it's another to give the name so that they can check it out and allude to telling some "them" about it.

"Oh, I'm sorry, sweetie," she says, her smile faltering a little. "I thought I told you. I swear I did. Maybe you didn't hear me." She looks apologetically at Monica and Eddie. "Someone called me earlier today asking questions about Piper. They were very interested in her. They said they were from some news site, I don't remember who. I should have written it down."

"Who? Why? Why would they ask questions about me?"

I glance at Harrison, who is staring at me with a grim expression. Shit. Does he know what this is about?

Icy fingers work their way through my gut, that sinking feeling.

"I don't know, I'm sorry," she says. "I thought I was helping. They sounded so nice. I told them all about you, about your podcast, but I think I got the name wrong."

But she got the name right.

And podcast aside, why the hell is someone asking my mother about me?

"You told them all about me?" I ask incredulously.

"No, not everything," she says. "Good heavens, I know you've had your share of troubles with me and your past. I didn't say anything personal. I kept it all very light. I even told them that if they wanted to know more, they would have to talk to you. I gave them your number, but I'm guessing they didn't call."

My blood is whooshing so loud in my head that I barely hear her when she says, "I'm sorry, Piper. I thought I told you earlier. Guess I was so distracted about everything."

Monica is watching me carefully. "I suppose the real question here is why someone wants to interview Piper. No offense, but if nothing happened after that article in the paper, I can't see why someone would take an interest in you now."

Harrison clears his throat loudly, bringing all eyes to him as he stands by Eddie at the head of the table. "I'm afraid I know the answer to that question."

He gives me a look that says he's sorry, and those icy fingers are practically turning me inside out.

Oh. No.

This is going to be bad.

"Well, what is it?" Eddie asks. "What's going on?"

Harrison rubs his lips together and takes in a deep breath. That admission of vulnerability alone causes Monica to sit on the edge of her seat, her expression ping-ponging back and forth between us.

"There were some photographs published on Facebook this morning," Harrison says. "I didn't discover them until they were shared on TMZ." He adds, looking mildly ashamed, "I get news alerts from them."

"What photographs?" Monica asks.

But somehow I already know. I already know what he's going to say, and things are about to get so much worse.

"Yesterday," Harrison begins, "Piper took me into town. Except that she didn't take me to town. She took me to a lake."

NO. NO. NO.

"Okay," Eddie says slowly, clearly confused.

"We went swimming at this lake," Harrison says. "We were only gone for a couple of hours. Maybe we were in the lake for one." He licks his lips and looks at me, and I can see how hard this is going to be on him, let alone me. I'm practically gripping the edge of the table. "The lake seems private, but there are some houses at the end of it. I guess someone in one of those houses was nearby and we didn't see them. They took photos of us."

"And? So?" Eddie says. Then he chuckles, "Were you naked or something?"

Harrison swallows. "I was."

"Oh," Monica says softly. She looks at me, her brows up, but doesn't say anything.

"So they got a naked picture of you," Eddie says carefully, glossing over the fact that Harrison was naked around *me*. "That's not the end of the world."

"Eddie," Monica says, giving him a pointed look. "Harrison was naked. In a lake. With Piper. What do you think was happening?"

Eddie's brow furrows as he thinks that over, then his eyes go wide. He looks at Harrison with a mixture of shock and, well, amusement, of all things. "You . . ." Eddie then nods at me. "And you?"

I keep my mouth shut. This is Harrison's home turf right now, and I'm not about to open my mouth and make things worse.

"How long has this been going on?" Monica asks. She's not looking at me, which hurts.

"Not long," Harrison says, looking uncomfortable. "But I'm afraid our attempts to keep it a secret from you and the world haven't worked. They took photos of us in the lake, looking particularly, uh, amorous."

I put my face in my hands, wanting the ground to swallow me whole.

Pictures. Of me and Harrison. In the lake.

Having sex.

I mean, thank god they wouldn't have been able to see anything since we were hidden by the water, but even so, the pictures are everywhere now. TMZ!

"I suppose they identified the both of you," Eddie says.

"The original Facebook post was posted by someone who lives on the lake, angry that tourists were, uh, having sex in the lake. Though actually I feel they were more angry about us being in the lake in general, since we weren't supposed to be there."

"Oh, sweetie, you didn't take him to Lake Maxwell, did you?" my mother asks. "You know Bert has been very vocal about teenagers not going there." Never mind the fact that we obviously aren't teens, which makes it even worse. Adults who should have known better.

"Then," Harrison continues with a weary sigh, "someone identified the two of us. I hate to say it, Piper, but it was that troublemaking bitch."

My mother nearly spits out her mouthful of wine, collapsing into a coughing fit.

"Who?" Monica exclaims, looking just as shocked that Harrison called someone a bitch, as perfectly fitting as it is, considering I know he's talking about Amy.

"It's not important," Harrison says. "But they IDed us, and the rest is history." He clears his throat. "I understand if you both need a moment to come to terms with this," he says, looking between Eddie and Monica. "I also understand that I may lose my job over this, and I am prepared to handle the consequences."

"No," I cry out. "No, Monica, Eddie. Please. Don't fire him. He's not in the wrong. I'm the one who took him to this lake, I'm the one who invited him. It was all me."

Eddie gives me a long look, the corner of his mouth twitching. "Piper. I appreciate you vouching for Harrison, but it takes two to tango, and I find it impossible to think that you tricked him in some way, shape, or form." He looks at Harrison. "I'm not going to fire you, you arse," he says. "You're a grown man. And you're a good friend. I trust you with my life, which means I trust you in everything. There are no rules about who you can date or become romantically entangled with. You know that. Or perhaps you don't, because it's never come up. All the more reason why you probably needed this to happen."

Eddie then glances at me. "And I'm sure you knew the risks too, being with a public figure. I can't say I'm surprised that this is happening to you, but I'm still sorry for it all the same."

"It's okay," I tell him. "As I said, I shouldn't have taken the risk. I should have thought it through. I'm sorry. I'm so sorry." I look at Monica as I say the last bit, but she's still not looking at me.

"I'll say it again: this still isn't the end of the world," Eddie says, shrugging. "Perhaps the world could use a distraction in the form of Harrison's arse."

"How did you know they posted a picture of that?" Harrison asks. He then looks to me. "And while it may not be the end of the world for me, if someone is already calling up Mrs. Evans and asking questions, that means things might get a lot more complicated for Piper."

He's right, of course. But when it comes to pictures of me and Harrison together, I don't see how anything could harm me, except an invasion of privacy.

"Mom, are you sure you didn't say anything too damning?" I say to her. "You realize that the person who called was probably from a tabloid."

"I swear I didn't," she says. "I guess this all makes sense now. You're famous because of the pictures; now everyone wants to know who you are. You're the mystery girl, Piper."

Except that I wanted to stay the mystery girl. I'd been so focused on not upsetting Monica that I didn't for a second think about how my being with Harrison would affect *my* life.

But really, what can they say? "Local schoolteacher enjoys fling with royal bodyguard"? Other than the expected slut-shaming and a new focus on me as a person of interest, is this really going to change things for me?

"So how should we handle this?" Harrison asks.

Eddie shrugs. "Well, I'm going to finish dinner. Then we can all retire to the deck, open a bottle of champagne, and celebrate the fact that you've found each other." He looks to his wife with a smug look on his face. "I hate to say it, but, Mon, darling, you owe me money."

She gives him a small smile.

They bet on this?

Dinner is over fairly quickly, and as everyone prepares to head outside with champagne glasses, I pull Monica to the side.

"Hey," I say to her. "Look, I'm really sorry. I haven't . . . we haven't been sneaking around for very long, and I've felt so bad about keeping it a secret from you. I know what you said about us, and I should have run it past you first. I should have been open."

"Piper," she says softly, putting her hand on my arm. "It's okay. And I should have never said anything to you about him before. It wasn't my place."

"You said it would reflect badly on you, and now it might."

"I know what I said. But I was wrong to say it. I'm so used to thinking about myself that I didn't stop to think about you or Harrison. Whatever you guys are doing, however you feel about each other, it's okay. Whatever you do is your business, and if it reflects badly on us, then so what? People who hate will always find a reason. The both of you are great people who deserve someone great in your lives. I mean that."

"You're not mad?"

She shakes her head and plays with the pearl necklace around her neck, no doubt worth a fortune. "I'm not mad. But I do feel bad that you're going to be in the public eye again. Let me tell you, those first sex photos will haunt you for the rest of your life. I should know—I had quite a few back in my day, before I met

Eddie, of course." A wicked smile flits across her lips. "Hell, maybe just enjoy it. After all, how many people can say that they had sex in a lake with Harrison Cole? You know he's become quite the fan fiction hero."

A knowing look passes between us, and I have a feeling I'm not the only one who has read them.

Monica goes out to the deck, but I excuse myself to use the washroom.

To be fair, I just want to look at the pictures in private.

I sit on the toilet, pull them up on TMZ, and flip through them.

They aren't that bad. I mean, it does look like we're having sex, even though the shots are a little grainy and shaky, obviously taken from far away. My top stays on in these pictures, thank god, since I know my breasts were exposed on a few occasions. It seems they caught us at the end of the act.

And then there's the final picture, just as Eddie predicted, the both of us walking onto shore, Harrison completely naked, tattoos and bare butt on display. I have no doubt that if I checked Perez Hilton, I'd see him fawning all over Harrison's gorgeous body right now. I have to say, it makes me feel uneasy to know that he's being exploited, more so than I am.

The article is typical TMZ style, giving us much detail on who I am as possible. A local schoolteacher and next-door neighbor. Thankfully they don't say anything shitty, though I'm sure that's happening elsewhere in the world.

I exhale loudly and exit the page. It's a gross feeling to know that the world knows your business, and this is a giant leap from my mention in the *ShoreLine*. The only thing I can do is hold my head high and not let it bother me. I knew Amy Mischky would throw me under the bus the first chance she got.

But if this is the worst she can do, then I can handle the worst.
I decide to check my email while I'm at it.
And that's when I see a message from the school board.
My heart stops as I catch the subject line:
"You are under review."

Twenty

I STUMBLE OUT OF THE BATHROOM, MY PHONE CLUTCHED in my hand, and run right into Harrison in the hallway.

He immediately grabs me by the arms, holding me, his eyes anxiously searching mine. "Piper," he says gruffly. "I am so sorry."

I blink at him, unable to get my head on straight.

"I didn't know if I should have said anything about the pictures or not," he goes on. "I certainly didn't want to spoil your dinner. But I thought it would be best that we came clean. They'd find out sooner or later." He peers at me closer. "You've seen the pictures, haven't you?"

I nod, my lips moving, but it feels like forever before words come out, like everything is moving in slow motion. "I saw the pictures. But I don't care about the pictures. I don't care about what they wrote. I . . . I just got an email from the school board."

"The school board?"

"Yes. They said I'm under review."

"What?!" he exclaims, his eyes wide. "Because of the pictures."

"Yes. No. Here."

I pull up the email on my phone and give it to him, my hand trembling.

He reads it over, his frown deepening, his eyes blazing as he goes.

I'm in deep shit.

According to the email, someone filed a private complaint about me and my personal "hobbies," saying that I'm unfit to be a schoolteacher and that they don't feel comfortable with someone like me teaching at the school. The school board has to take the complaint seriously, so they've set up a meeting on Monday for me to state my case in front of everyone.

The reason?

It's not just the pictures. I could understand a little if it were the pictures. Even though it was a private moment, I was in an area where I shouldn't have been, and the press is painting me as a little wanton, which definitely doesn't help with the next part.

The next part being that my podcast is out in the open.

Whenever my mother did that interview today, the news got printed really fast. *Romancing the Podcast*, though not the subject of the article that I believe is in the *Daily Mail* (which is much worse than TMZ), was mentioned.

A romance podcast shouldn't be a big deal.

But whoever filed the complaint has made it a big deal.

Something something, a public schoolteacher shouldn't have a public podcast where she discusses sex and reads explicit sex scenes out loud.

Never mind the fact that it wasn't public until today, that it's been operated anonymously. I suppose I could just deny it's me, but I guess once you do know it's me, it's easy to connect the dots.

I'm fucked. And the funny thing is, this is exactly why I wanted to keep the podcast a secret, because I knew that someone somewhere would take offense at it and then call for me to lose my job over it.

And that's exactly what's happening.

Harrison finishes reading and hands the phone back to me.

"Sue them," he says angrily.

"I can't sue them."

"They have no right to fire you over something you do in private. Over sex? Over discussing sex? That's preposterous."

"They're looking for any way to vilify me, you know that."

"Not they," he says. "Someone. Someone who filed the complaint. The school board will side with you, once you state your case. Not that you should have to state your bloody fucking case; you're entitled to do whatever you want on your own time so long as it hurts no one, and this hurts no one."

"Except that someone wants to hurt me. They want to prove a point."

"It doesn't say who they are."

"No. But I have an idea. It's either someone from Joey's family or it's Amy's mother. The town crier. She's blocked a bike lane from being built, a bike lane that would prevent the dozens of accidents and collisions we have on our main drag every year, just because it would promote tourists to come visit. If she's that rooted in stasis, there's no way she's going to let this fly."

He sighs. "I guess we're going to have to wait and see. You know I'm coming with you, right?"

"I'll be fine."

He puts his hands around my waist and dips his head, looking at me sincerely. "It's for your own protection, and I mean it."

He leans in and kisses me gently. "I'm really sorry it had to be this way," he murmurs, running a hand through my hair. "I thought we had a little more time with each other before we were exposed."

"I did too," I tell him, kissing the corner of his mouth. "But I don't regret it. I don't regret it coming out, because I have to say, I was feeling pretty sick at the thought of keeping it from Monica. I would have kept the secret for you, but it didn't feel right. Now she knows and . . . I guess she's okay with it."

"She owes Eddie money," he says with a soft smile. "I guess he bet that one of us liked the other one. I wonder if she owes him double now that it ended up being mutual."

"Liked," I say. The word, though accurate, sounds so small and puny on my tongue. "I more than like you, Harrison Cole."

"And I more than like you, Piper Evans."

"And I think the two of you are the cutest thing since sliced bread," my mother's shrill, tipsy voice comes through, breaking us apart.

"Since when is sliced bread cute, Mom?" I say wryly.

"Since you cut a little happy face in it," she answers matter-of-factly.

The thing is, I should be mad at her because she's the reason that this shit is all happening. But I know it's not her fault. And the last thing she needs is to know that I'm being investigated by the school board. It's better I say nothing at all.

She gives us another approving look before she walks into the washroom and closes the door. I grab Harrison's hand and give it a squeeze. "I'm not going to tell her about the email, just so you know."

"Why not?"

"Because she'll blame herself. And rightly so, but it will send her on a downward spiral."

"But doesn't your mother have a right to know? You can't keep hiding all the bad things from her, Piper. You know it doesn't work."

He has a point, but he doesn't have my mother.

"I'm protecting her," I tell him. "You of all people should know what that's like."

He studies me for a moment and then nods. "Come on. Let's at least try to enjoy the night."

He gives my hand a squeeze and leads me to the back deck.

MONDAY ROLLS AROUND before I know it.

I did my best to try to slow the weekend down. On Saturday, Monica, Eddie, Harrison, and I went for a walk along a trail not many tourists know about, named for the Canadian astronaut Chris Hadfield. It takes you past old-growth cedar groves, then through a fairy-tale-like forest with exposed veins of quartz and moss, and along a gurgling creek that runs out into the ocean, to a grassy knoll where you can sit and watch the pleasure boats, seals, and sometimes orcas glide past.

We didn't run into anyone until the end of the trail, and they only gave us a second look and a smile and carried on.

On Sunday, Harrison spent the evening at my house.

A night off.

My mother decided to give us some privacy and said she was going into town, which was surprising but appreciated all the same.

I wanted Harrison to stay over, but he said he didn't want to push his luck. Even though he's a free man to do what he wants, we're both still trying to figure out the balance here. Obviously I'm okay with whatever, at least until school starts again after Labor Day (if I even have a job . . .), but Harrison has never had to balance a relationship and his job before. I know he wants to make sure he's doing right both ways, so he's taking his time. And so if that means he's not spending the night here yet, then that's okay with me. As long as I get some lovin' and some quality time before he goes.

But he does stay true to his word when it comes to protecting me.

So at nine thirty the next morning, he's knocking at my door, ready to take me to the meeting.

"Where are you going?" my mother asks from the couch, already engrossed in some soap opera.

"Just to town," I tell her. "Text me if you need anything?"

She gives me a once-over. I do look extra professional today. My hair is pulled back in a low bun; I'm wearing a white shirt and black pants. I look like a waitress.

I leave before she can say anything else, smiling at Harrison.

"You still haven't told her?" he asks.

"Shhh," I tell him, my finger to my mouth. "She has surprisingly good hearing."

"Piper . . ."

"This is for the best," I tell him. "Now come on, let's take my car. I don't want to show up in anything royal-related. I'll look like a pompous ass."

"You'd take Oscar the Grouch over a pompous ass?"

"Every time. Get in."

He gets in and then we're off, and suddenly I wish I wasn't driving because I'm gripping the wheel so hard that my knuckles are white and my palms are sweating.

"Hey," Harrison says gently, putting his hand on my leg. "It's going to be okay. You're going to do great."

I give him an incredulous look. "I know you've seen me when

I get nervous. I babble. I'm going to babble. I'm not going to say the right thing."

"You will," he assures me. "You will. Trust yourself. You're sticking up for yourself, your podcast, your habits, perhaps even your love life, if it comes to that, and I sure hope it doesn't. You know yourself the best, and you sell yourself the best. Anyone with a brain will be able to see your whip-smart mind and beautiful heart."

God. I'm melting here.

I give him a look full of longing, the kind of longing that makes me want to pull the car off the road and climb on top of him. "Please stop being so nice to me."

"I'll never do that."

"It's going to go to my head."

"If you know how amazing you are, the world will be a better place."

Where did I find this man again?

Oh right. The royals next door.

Harrison's kind words and pep talk, combined with the pressure of his soothing palm on my leg, keep my nerves in check for the drive, but by the time we pull in front of the elementary school, I'm a nervous wreck again.

Naturally, it being a Monday in the middle of summer, there aren't many cars here. I recognize the principal's station wagon, plus the electric car of the chairperson, and five other cars. I've never actually been to a school board meeting before, since I'm not on the board (and have never been in trouble), so I have no idea what to expect.

"You're going to be fine," Harrison says to me again as we walk toward the front doors, giving my hand another comforting squeeze.

It's so weird being here in the summer; it feels like a place from a dream. In a way it's best that I avoid the building on my months off and get back into the swing of things in the fall. Being here now feels like a mistake, like I've stumbled into some other dimension. It makes me realize how different I am in the summer, when I'm not working, than when I am. Not that either version of me is bad, but they do feel like different people.

We walk in through the doors and toward the first classroom on the right. The door is open, and there's a low murmur of voices.

I stop just outside and look up at Harrison. "Do you mind waiting here?"

"Not at all," he says, leaning in and giving me a quick kiss on the cheek. "You've got this."

I'm not sure what I've got. But I know I've got his support. And that counts for a lot.

I step inside the classroom and see seven heads swivel toward me.

I try to take them all in at once, but at the same time they're a blur, like I see nothing at all.

"Piper," the principal, Georgia Hopkins, says to me. She gives me a shaky smile and gestures for me to sit down at the front beside her.

I am so nervous I might just pee my pants.

It's hard to swallow, I feel like I'm almost choking, but I manage to walk across the room toward her without fainting or screaming.

Georgia has always been a great principal, beloved by both the kids and the staff, and I know from the apologetic look in her eyes that none of this was her idea. That puts me a little more at ease, knowing there is one more person here who has my back, even if the other person is waiting outside the door.

Georgia clears her throat and then looks to the unsmiling people sitting in the plastic chairs facing us. Maureen Portier, the chairwoman of the board, is the only person I recognize.

Then I'm introduced to Jerry Bluth, the vice chairman; Angela Kim, the union representative; Marty Howe, the secretary treasurer; Alexander LaCroix, who I'm told will be recording the meeting (and who I also know works for the newspaper); plus a trustee.

Barbara Mischky.

To be honest, I've never met the infamous senior Mischky in person, only seen her face posted many times in the paper's editorials, but in person she looks more like Amy than I could have imagined. A face that could be pretty if it weren't full of such spite.

And right now, all that spite is directed at me.

"Piper, I'm going to let Maureen speak since she is the one who called this meeting," Georgia says to me. "Just so you know, this is all a formality of what we must do for every complaint. I know this is your first meeting with the board, but this isn't a usual meeting and it's a closed one. Alexander is only recording it for transparency's sake."

Maureen clears her throat. I've only met her a handful of times, and she's a pretty stern lady with a pinched face and a close-cropped haircut, but she's not particularly unkind, just tough.

"Ms. Evans," Maureen begins, adjusting herself in her seat so she's sitting up taller, folding her hands in her lap over her notebook. "Thank you for coming here on short notice. I want to reiterate what Georgia said. This is an investigation because it's what we have to do when a complaint is lodged. We are here to tell you the complaint, why it matters, and then hear your side of the story. We are not judge, jury, and executioner, and the aim of this meeting is not over termination. It is merely a follow-through."

That should make me feel a little bit better, but it doesn't. I feel like a little kid up here, being judged and presided over anyway.

"Now, as was mentioned in the email, a trustee member came across several things that put your role as a schoolteacher here in question. I am going to read off the two things that we vowed to investigate. One is that pictures were published last Friday, between you and the bodyguard of the Duke and Duchess of Fairfax, whom we know are staying on the island. The photos taken were a breach of privacy on your behalf, and even if you were having an intimate moment with someone else, it is none of our business. However, the pictures were taken at Lake Maxwell, which has been sectioned off by the Island Committee and the Watershed District board. The lake is considered private property, and under BC law, you are subject to trespassing. So there is that."

"May I speak?" I ask, raising my hand.

She nods primly. "Of course."

"It doesn't say private property on those signs, and how could it be considered private property if there are houses that share it? Are you suggesting that all those houses own the property along with the waterworks department?"

Yeah, I know I'm kind of wasting my time here on this point—there are so many conflicting theories floating around the island about why the lake is sectioned off, it would take all day to unravel them—but I want them to know that I'm not going to just sit back and take a dressing down. I'm right too. There is a fence, there is a notice of no swimming or ATVing due to it being a watershed, but there are no signs about it being private property. Maybe it's a moot point, but I'm going to take it.

"Regardless," Maureen says, "the signs specifically tell you to stay back, and going around the fence doesn't avoid the issue. The point is, you are a schoolteacher of impressionable children, and to see you doing something like this reflects very badly on you and the school."

Okay. Fine. She's right about that, then.

I must have an air of defeat around me, because I catch Barbara Mischky smiling at me from the back row.

"Which then brings us to the second issue," Maureen says. "Which is the fact that you have a romance book podcast."

Jerry, the vice chairman, snorts at that.

I immediately give him the nastiest look I can muster.

He stops smiling.

"Now, what a teacher does in their private time is not an issue so long as it doesn't hurt anyone. But when faced with this, it was pointed out that if a teacher was promoting pornography outside the classroom, there would be very swift punishment toward them."

I nearly choke on a laugh. What?

"I'm sorry," I say, raising my hand again. "Are you suggesting that my romance podcast is akin to promoting pornography?"

Maureen's face goes red. She clears her throat again. "I am saying that perhaps it could be perceived that way."

"Well, have you read a romance? Better yet, have you listened to my podcast?"

She shakes her head.

My eyes bug out. "You're calling me up here to try to clear my name over something and you didn't even bother listening to the supposed evidence?"

Maureen clamps her lips shut and looks away.

I stare at everyone else. "Did any of you?"

"I did," Barbara says, her voice smug and tight. "I listened to one, and that's all I could take. You're an extremely crude and disgusting person and definitely not suited to be teaching the innocent children here."

I am so flabbergasted, so angry, that I don't even have the words. I don't even know how to proceed.

It takes everything inside me not to call her the same word Harrison used to describe her daughter.

"My podcast," I begin, my voice tight, "is directed to a mature audience. To the romance-reading audience. It's okay to read about sex. It's okay to have a book that's focused on both people falling in love and the woman's own pleasure. The genre has a lot of stigma attached to it, but only because some people are afraid of women's empowerment and sexuality."

"It's smut," she practically spits out.

"It's smut, and it's wonderful," I tell her. "What's so wrong with smut? What's wrong with a book that focuses on sex? On romantic relationships? And on top of that, in a respectful way. Why is sex in movies and in TV and in art and in music and in literary novels considered okay, but a romance novel isn't?"

She looks shocked. "It's wrong . . . It's prostitution."

She's really reaching now. "So now you're saying that a romance novel is akin to prostitution. Okay then." I look at Maureen. "Is this why you called me here? Because this is what you believe? That a romance novel, or talking about a romance novel, is the same as prostitution? Never mind the fact that I can also debate you about sex workers and the lack of support and care they get. I'll save that for some other time."

"No, of course not," Maureen says. "Look, this is all very complicated."

"Actually, I don't think it is," Georgia speaks up. "As the principal of the school, I think I should get a say in the matter." She gives me a supportive smile. "I know Piper is an excellent teacher. What she reads or does in her own time is her own business. But I will say you are making this out to be something it's not. Just because you have a prejudice against romance novels doesn't mean that what you believe is true. It means you've bought in to a dangerous, inherently anti-feminist narrative. I read a whole range of books, and some of them are romances. I wish I had known about Piper's podcast before, because I would have loved to have felt like part of a community, especially when so many of the readers get shunned for it. As it was, of course, Piper's podcast was anonymous until it was more or less doxed. Wouldn't you say that's correct, Piper?"

I'm trying not to smile at how she's going to bat for me, but my heart is being warmed over. "Someone called up my mother and asked her a few questions about me. My mother thought she was helping, but the podcast would have remained anonymous otherwise."

"Because you're ashamed," Barbara says.

"Because I knew that someone like you would have an issue with someone like me talking frankly about sex. That's why. But you know what, grill me all you want over this, try to shame me. I won't be ashamed, I will not retract, I will not back down. I am a proud romance reader, and I'm not ashamed of what I read or what I discuss with other readers. Nothing you can do or say will make me feel that way."

A loaded silence fills the room, and everyone stares at me, gobsmacked. I want to look over at the door to see if Harrison is still there, but I don't dare. Besides, I can still feel him.

Maureen clears her throat again. "Okay," she says slowly, rubbing along her temple. "You have made your point, Piper. But there is still the issue of swimming at the lake."

"There is no issue," I tell her. "You know why? Because it cancels out. I have a right to privacy. Those pictures were posted without my permission. Furthermore, it was Barbara's daughter, Amy, who identified me in the pictures, which makes me think this whole thing is a conflict of interest. Certainly Barbara here is biased."

"I am not biased," she says in a huff.

I ignore her. "I have a right to privacy. Maybe I shouldn't have been in the lake, but you don't have the right to preside over everything I do. Those photos should have never been published."

"It was in public," Maureen says.

"But it wasn't, according to you," I remind her. "Look, you gave me the two reasons why you called this meeting, and I argued my case on each one. But what it really comes down to is, you don't know me. You can't vouch for me. Only Georgia here knows me, and that's because I work with her. I've lived here for years, and yet I barely recognize any of you. That's partially your fault, for not getting to know your educators. It's also partially my fault for being a hermit. But why am I a hermit? Because I don't feel welcome here. I feel like if I'm myself, I'll be judged and pushed to the side. It's hard to see it when you're in it, but since I still feel like an outsider, I'll explain to you what I see, from the outside looking in.

"Why do people move to a small town or to an island?" I start ticking off my fingers. "They want peace. They want privacy. They want a sense of community, a place where they can both be themselves and belong. But that's not what they get anymore. There is no peace when there is no privacy, when people think they have the right to know everything about a person, purely so they can judge them. There is no sense of community when people are made to feel like outsiders. We should be protecting each other, looking out for each other, respecting each other. But that doesn't happen."

I point at the secretary treasurer, whatever his name is. "You. See, I don't even know who you are. We're told about community, but we don't even really know each other. Why do you think the duke and duchess moved here to this island? Was it for the weather?"

The man looks around for help, his eyes wide beneath his glasses. "Uh, no?"

"Do you think they moved here because they wanted a place to relax, to be themselves, to live their lives out from under that ever-present microscope?"

"Uh, yes?"

"Well, you're right. That's what they wanted. But that's not what they got. We should have been protecting them from day one. Instead, all you did was complain about the media circus. You complained about the people coming in, people, as if they don't contribute to the economy. You looked at them like they were outsiders, and you do that to a lot of people, not just them. And it's not unique to this place; this happens everywhere. We're so obsessed with our little bubbles that we become afraid to let other people in. We put blinders on, and we shut people out, and when we do finally look at them, we think we have the right to know everything. This isn't about getting to know your fellow neighbor; this is about finding ways to continually shun them. If we want to truly be a great community, we have to be inclusive, regardless of what someone does, or reads, or where they come from."

I'm tired now. My mouth won't stop flapping, and I'm babbling and off-topic, and I knew this would happen once I got going.

"All right, Piper," Maureen says after a moment. "Are you done?"

"Are you?"

She nods. "We'll deliberate and let you know."

I have to fight to not roll my eyes. After all that, pouring my soul out, defending my character, they still have to talk it over? Fucking bureaucracy.

I get up, giving Georgia a grateful smile, and then leave.

The moment I'm out the door, I practically collapse in Harrison's arms.

"Good job," Harrison says to me, holding me close, his chin resting on my head. "You were phenomenal, Piper. You really were."

"I feel like an ass," I mumble into his chest.

He chuckles warmly. "Well, you did not sound it." He pulls away and peers at me, holding me by the shoulders. "And nope, you certainly don't look it either."

"Is it too early for a drink?" I whine as he puts his arm around me and leads me out of the school.

"There's a cidery around the corner that I've been itching to try," he says. All the right words.

Twenty-One

I BARELY SLEPT LAST NIGHT. I TOSSED AND TURNED, MY mind full of thoughts that went nowhere and worries that multiplied. Oh, and copious amounts of cider. After the "hearing," Harrison and I plunked ourselves down on one of the picnic tables and drank a bottle of cider, then bought some more and headed back home and down to the dock. He had the day off, so we were able to just be alone and enjoy the sunshine.

I guess that's what kept my brain preoccupied, because as soon as I was alone in bed, that was when I started thinking and fretting.

Was I going to lose my job?

Did I say too much?

Did I say the wrong things?

How much power does Barbara Mischky have?

Was I too rude?

Was I too proud?

As a result, I didn't sleep at all until I started to see the light of dawn through my bedroom window, and that's when my body finally decided to rest.

I passed right out.

It's now noon, and my mouth feels like it's full of cotton balls and my head is heavy. I had that disoriented feeling of waking up late—it's like taking a nap, throws your whole day off.

I glance at my phone. There's a text from Harrison asking how I am, and yes, a simple text still makes my heart do backflips, but there's nothing else. I check my email, and nada. I would have thought they'd have made a decision by now.

I slip on a house robe and pad out into the kitchen. It's raining now, a freshness and relief in the air after such a hot week, and my mother is standing by the coffeepot. It's percolating, and the smell fills my nostrils. Even though I am a wreck, it's still awfully cozy here.

"Piper," she says softly. "I heard you stirring. I thought you could use some coffee."

"Thanks, Mom," I say, leaning against the island as she pulls the pot off the burner and pours me a cup. I hold it in my hands and take a sip, looking past the windows and out to the deck, where a dense fog has moved in, obscuring the ocean and making the trees look like ghosts.

"Piper?" she says again, her voice sounding raw. "Can I ask you something?"

"Of course."

"Why didn't you tell me what happened yesterday?"

I stare. Oh shit. She knows.

"What do you mean?" I play dumb, even though there's no use.

"The meeting. You were being investigated by the school board."

"Let me guess: Someone called you up and asked you about it?"

"No," she says. "I saw it online. On the *ShoreLine*'s website."

"You what? You saw it?"

"Yes. A video. My god, Piper, I've never been so proud of you."

While her admission warms me, it does nothing to abate the shock that's running through me. A video? A video of yesterday? My one-person defense over lake swimming, community, and romance novels?

I immediately dig my phone out of my robe pocket and go to the website.

Sure enough, front page is an article entitled "Local Teacher Defends Right to Privacy," which I suppose is the simplest way of putting it.

It's written by that dude with the key-lime mineral water name, Alexander LaCroix, and during a quick sweep of the article, I'm surprised to see that the whole thing is in my defense. In fact, it paints me very favorably. Maybe this is to make up for that article written about Harrison at the Blowhole and the subsequent royals smackdown, or perhaps he's tired of Barbara Mischky's editorial letters. But either way, he told the truth and made good points on how we need to band together as a community instead of looking for ways to keep people out.

And then there's the video.

I click on it and watch for a moment until it all becomes too much. First of all, I should have worn more makeup, because I look tired as hell; second of all, I make the absolute worst facial expressions; and third of all, I'm rambling. At least I think I am.

But no matter what I think, it doesn't matter, because that video is out there in the world now.

Somehow I've gone from a reclusive hermit to having paparazzi harass me, to articles written about me and my ex, to sexcapade lake pictures and then heartfelt speeches, all shown worldwide, all in the span of a summer.

It takes me a moment to realize the turn my life has taken.

Those damn royals, I think. And yet I'm not mad. Because there is change in the air for all of us, a fire that's growing. Sometimes you just need a spark. Sometimes you just need a new neighbor.

"Why didn't you tell me, sweetheart?" my mother asks forlornly.

I put the phone down and face her. "Because I didn't want you to worry."

"But you're my daughter."

"Exactly."

"But you're *my* daughter, Piper. I have the right to worry about you, especially if you're in trouble. I don't want you to keep me out of these things. I want you to include me. Even if it hurts."

"Mom, please, I just . . . you've been doing so good, I didn't want to—"

"Set me off? That's not up to you. Listen, sweetie, you mean well and you always have, but you can't protect me forever. You have to give me some breathing space, and you can't keep hiding things from me. First it was the duke and duchess moving in, then it was you and Harrison, then it's this. The fact that your very job is at stake. Let me be a part of these things. And if it hurts, let me hurt."

She's right. "In that case, you should know that the reason the school board found out about the podcast is because you spilled the beans to that reporter." Her face falls. "Look, I get that you get excited, but really, I expect my right to privacy as much as you do."

"I know. You're right about that. I'm sorry. I wasn't thinking."

"It's okay. Really. And I'm sorry too for being overprotective. I'll do better."

"It's not about doing better, Piper. It's about seeing me as a mother and a friend and not as my mental illness. I'll never be able to learn on my own if you're always there. I appreciate all you do for me, but as someone who is told they have dependent personality disorder, you seem to want to keep me dependent."

This goes back to what she said the other night at the royals'. That we've become too dependent on each other, and for all the wrong reasons.

"And since we're coming clean about things," my mother goes on. She immediately has me intrigued. "I have a confession to make."

"What?"

"Well, for one, I've been seeing an online therapist."

My mouth drops. "You have? How did that happen? For how long?"

"Oh, just a few weeks. I've only had three sessions. I figured this was an easy way to try it out without having to commit to anyone or go anywhere. You seem to think therapy was a hot-button issue for me, and you were right, but the more I thought about it on my own terms, the easier it got. I just wasn't comfortable meeting someone in an office face-to-face. But online? It's much easier. I almost . . . like it. It's like I'm a puzzle. Or, better yet, a cake. And I'm reverse baking, trying to figure out the ingredients that make me the way I am."

I am so ridiculously happy that I burst into tears. I go around the island and wrap my arms around her, pulling her into a hug. "Mom," I sob.

"Don't cry," she says, patting me awkwardly on the back. "This is all good."

"I know, I know," I say, stepping back and wiping the tears from under my eyes. "Ugh, I am such a wreck these days."

"Your emotions are all over the place," she chides me. "Who

can blame you? You've got Harrison now, your photos are every-where, your job is at stake. I'm guessing they haven't contacted you yet with their verdict?"

I sniff and shake my head. "No."

"Well, you know what, if they end up firing you, we can take them to court. I know more than enough people to vouch for your character."

"You know people?" I ask, half joking.

"Well . . . ," she says, looking awfully coy. "I know one person. Same person who helped me find the therapist."

I frown. "Monica?"

"Bert."

"Bert the bushy-mustached head of the RCMP?" I ask, wide-eyed.

She nods. "He's really the only one I know here. I thought I would ask about local therapists, and he told me that so many peo-ple on the island go to therapy online because it's more convenient."

Now normally I wouldn't think much of it. But the fact that she seems a little coy, her cheeks are a bit flushed, and there's a certain gleam to her eyes makes me think that Bert might mean more to her than she's letting on.

"Well, then I'm glad you can count on Bert as a friend," I tell her.

"Yes," she says, suppressing a smile. She turns her back to me and potters over to the cupboard just as my phone starts to ring.

I jump a mile and glance at it.

Local number.

With a racing heart, I pick up the phone and answer it, my mother watching curiously.

"Hello, Piper speaking."

"Piper?" comes Maureen's stodgy-sounding voice. "It's Maureen Portier from the school board."

My breath hitches in my throat, and I can barely say, "Yes?"

A moment of silence passes. It feels like it's strangling me.

Then I hear Maureen let out a heavy breath. "I want to start by apologizing to you, Piper. We should have investigated the complaint more carefully than we investigated you. You never should have had to stand before the board and defend your hobbies, particularly your interest in romance novels. That's no one's business, and you're correct in that the stigma against it has left many people with the wrong idea. Myself included."

"Okaaay." I hope there isn't a *but* involved here.

"We should have only brought you in with regard to your trespassing at the lake, and while I still wish you hadn't done that, the photos were printed without your permission, an invasion of your privacy. If you had posted about it yourself, it would have been a different thing, but in this case, it wasn't. We decided that the person who filed the complaint was biased and had an agenda, and she is no longer a school trustee. And with that, I wish to tell you that you will not be losing your job, or receiving any form of punishment, and that what you had to defend was punishment enough. I sincerely hope you accept my apology on behalf of the board. Georgia was right when she vouched for you. You're a good person and I'm sure an excellent teacher, and we are happy to have you, and in the future, we'll be lucky to know you better."

It takes me a moment to find my words. "Thanks."

"You're welcome."

"You know that the reporter for the *ShoreLine* shared the video on its web page."

She sighs. "I know. We had a debate about that. We feared

that perhaps the trustee we let go might try to slander you some other way because she didn't win this time. We're aware of her many contributions to that paper over the years, and Alex thought it would be better if he beat her to it. That way, there's nothing to hide." She pauses. "And if you've noticed yet, you've amassed a passionate following so far, just here in town. Perhaps a new sense of community will come out of this." She pauses again. "I hope so. At any rate, I look forward to seeing you again in the fall, but don't hesitate to reach out to me at any time. Goodbye, Piper."

I tell her goodbye and hang up, relief flooding through me like sunlight.

"So?" my mother asks. "You have your job, I take it?"

I nod. "I do."

And Mischky got the boot, without a leg to stand on now, thanks to that video. That was some quick thinking on the reporter's part. Nice to know the truth still matters to some people.

"So I guess we won't sue them after all," she says. "Though I bet you could, for the trauma they caused. Did I tell you how proud I am?"

"You did."

"Good. But I may just tell you again."

She pours herself another cup of coffee and walks out to the foggy deck, Liza jumping off the couch and following her.

I'm so relieved, I may just go back to bed.

LATER THAT EVENING, when I'm already in my pajamas on the couch with Liza, and my mom has gone to bed, I get a text from Harrison.

Good evening, Piper. May I come over?

May I come over? A most gentlemanly take on the "U up?" booty call if I've ever seen one.

Yes you may, I text back, grinning like a fool. I hold the phone to my chest for a moment, letting the giddiness that had been at bay these last few days come flooding back.

He's fast. In minutes the front door is slowly creaking open and Harrison is poking his head inside. "All clear?" he whispers. It's not that we're sneaking around my mother—I mean, I know she more than approves of us—but I also don't need her to know he's here, if I can help it.

I nod and get off the couch, motioning for him to follow me to the bedroom.

We're inside with the door closed in seconds, and then his hands are skimming over my body and his lips are on mine and we're moving backward onto my bed.

We waste no time.

There is no time to waste with us.

I take my clothes off, he takes off his, discarding everything on the floor like we'll never need them again. We're naked in no time, and he rolls on top of me, all muscle, all man.

I stare up at his tattoos and trail my fingers over them, feel his taut skin, his temperature rising, and then his lips are on mine in a bruising kiss that makes my toes curl.

After everything that I went through these last two days, the one constant was Harrison by my side. But right now, it's not enough to have him by my side—I want him deep inside me. I need to feel that connection between us, the one I'm so afraid of losing.

Because in the end, I want him more than anything.

Our mouths are moving together in a deep, searing kiss, frantic, hungry, all-encompassing. I run my fingers down his forearms, feeling the sinewy muscles as he holds himself above me, then I brush my hands back up to the hard planes of his shoulders, feeling the heat of his skin.

He pulls his mouth away, damp from our kiss. "Piper," he whispers, staring into my eyes, fevered with desire. I stare up at his lips, so lush and perfect. "I'm so proud of you."

I give him a small smile, heat flaring inside my chest, tightening around my heart. "Proud of me?"

He reaches down and brushes his thumb under my lip. "Yes. From the moment I saw you, I knew you were going to change my world in some way. I knew that you were strong. That you were going to go places."

"Technically I'm not going places. I just didn't lose my job, that's all, and all you knew was that I was stubborn as shit."

He smiles and places a kiss at the corner of my mouth. "That last part might be true. But don't sell yourself short. You're able to do whatever you put your mind to. I think everyone on this island should be grateful that you're the one teaching their kids, so that they can believe in themselves the same way."

I swallow, feeling uncomfortable with the compliments. "I don't always believe in myself."

"No. But you do enough, because you know when you're right, and you have the strength to follow through. And I believe in you. It may not matter for much, but I do."

"Harrison," I tell him, my hands resting on the back of his neck. "It matters more than you know." I pause, giving him a wicked smile. "Now, are you going to fuck me or what?"

He blinks, clearly taken aback at my bluntness. Oh well. The Brit can deal.

Then he's kissing me again, hungrier this time, adding fuel to the fire.

His hands coast down my body, sliding between my legs where I'm wet and waiting for it, and he slides a couple of fingers inside, groaning when he discovers how ready I am.

"What am I going to do with you," he murmurs as he sucks down the length of my neck, over my collarbones, across my breast.

"Anything you want," I manage to say before I break off into a moan as he sucks my pert nipple into his mouth, heat and electricity radiating outward through my body, snaking through every vein.

My god, I don't think I've ever been so turned on.

"I need you inside me," I tell him, my voice raspy and thick.

He grunts in agreement and presses his hand against my inner thigh, holding my legs open as he pushes up deep inside me. Shit.

I gasp, feeling the air leave my lungs, and then he pushes my legs back together again so I'm tighter. As he pulls out and thrusts back in, I feel *everything*.

I dig my fingers into his shoulders, holding on, and his body matches the slow rhythm of mine as he thrusts his hips forward, his cock driving deeper and deeper inside me. Every nerve in my body is being pulled inward, swirling into a hard knot, live wires buzzing and tangled and begging to be unraveled.

I'm captivated by watching him. When I slept with Joey, I never made any eye contact whatsoever, but with Harrison it's completely different. I *want* to stare at him. When his eyes meet mine and he stares back, I feel a thrumming connection deep in my veins, something inside me telling me that he's mine and I'm his and he can see me. Really *see* me.

With each thrust, he pushes himself in deeper, and that connection amplifies, like puzzle pieces sliding into place. My eyes
drift down over his body as it moves, the way his abs clench as he
thrusts inside, the sweat on his brow. His tattoos seem to come
alive right now, all of them whispering their secrets to me.

I can never get enough of him.

I don't think I ever will.

I don't want him to leave me. Ever.

"Harder," I whisper, and Harrison wastes no time in pushing
in deeper.

So deep, my eyes roll back in my head.

"Fuck," I gasp, feeling the emotions swirl inside me. My head
drops back, my eyes closing in shock as I surrender.

This man is mine.

And I am his.

Nothing else matters.

Even if he has to leave me, nothing else matters.

But, god, please don't let him leave me.

The thought sets off a tidal wave in my core that's slowly
building in strength and size and speed, wanting to take me under. I welcome it. I want to drown in my feelings for him.

"Please," I whisper, my voice shaking with my sudden need
for him, like I've gone absolutely mad for Harrison Cole and
nothing else will do. The fear of what happens next, the fear that
my heart might be lost to him forever, is making me into an insatiable woman. "I need more."

His eyes nearly roll back in his head at that, and he responds
instantly.

With a low, rough groan, he starts thrusting harder, deeper,
one hand making a tight fist in my hair. He presses his chest

against mine, our skin damp with sweat, and kisses me, lips tasting like salt. My mouth is wild against his, the need inside me growing restless, reckless.

The muscles in his neck are corded as beads of sweat roll off his forehead, and his eyes are lost to desire. The sounds he makes are primal, raw, and I feel utterly devoured as he works at me.

I want to feel this way forever.

I want Harrison forever.

"I'm coming," I cry out softly, my voice raw, trying to keep our eye contact. He stares back, his eyes watching in fascination as I give in.

Then I'm twisting and turning as the orgasm crashes over me again and again, and I'm swept out to sea, floating there, warm and blissed-out and full of joy. Nonsensical sounds fall from my mouth as I swirl around in place.

Harrison isn't done quite yet. His labored breathing, the rough sound of his groans, the slap of his damp skin against mine, all fill the air. I can only hope we're being quiet enough.

Then he lets out a long, raw moan that he tries to bury, his arms shaking from the strain as he comes.

His movement slows, his body relaxes.

He collapses against me, his gaze drifting over my face, his breath heavy.

A tear escapes the corner of my eye, everything I've been feeling and trying to deal with, all my wants and needs and fears, it's all coming to a head now. I can't hold back.

"Are you okay?" he whispers, his breath heavy, his words kind.

I nod, pressing my lips together for a moment, trying to regain my breath. "I'm fine. I'm just . . . I'm happy."

He frowns at me for a moment, the line between his brows deepening, and then he smiles. "I'm happy too."

It sounds like such a simple emotion when you hear it, but when you feel it, really feel it, you know it's anything but.

I close my eyes, letting that wash over me.

Our happiness.

"Piper." Harrison's voice slides into the haze of my thoughts. I think I was close to drifting off in his arms.

"Mmmm," I say, snuggling into him deeper.

"What now?"

The question is so stark and loaded it makes my eyes fly open. I'm officially no longer asleep.

I twist in his arms to look at him, his arm now draped across my waist. "What do you mean, what now? Like . . . now, now? As in, do you go to sleep here or go to sleep in your own bed?"

He shakes his head, swallows. "No."

I completely turn around, and he props his head up on his elbow. I'm searching his face for any signs of anguish or bad news, but there's none to be found. His expression is quiet and thoughtful, plus a little bit sated from the sex.

"What do you mean?"

"I mean, for us," he says, reaching out with his other hand and brushing a strand of hair behind my ear. "Now that it's all out in the open—far more open than I ever would have expected, to be honest—don't you think we should figure out where we stand? Our future."

I worry my lip between my teeth for a moment. The fact that he wants to have this conversation, that he wants to know what our future is, means more to me than he can know.

"I realize I may be too forward," he goes on. The corner of his gorgeous mouth quirks up into a small grin. "But I don't really care. I'm not letting go of you, Piper. I'm not pretending that I don't want more for us, more than this."

I swallow thickly. "I want more too," I admit, feeling shy all of a sudden. "But I know you have your job, and the last thing I want is for it to come between us. You said it would take time to figure out how to make it work and balance, and I believe you. I'm by your side as it all gets sorted. I'm not going anywhere." I pause, hit with the sudden weight of realization. "But I suppose . . . you are. You're not meant to be here forever."

"We'll make it work."

"And I can't leave my mom, not now, even though she's starting to come around. And my job . . ."

"Piper," he says imploringly, holding my face as he stares into my eyes. "We'll make it work. No matter what . . . I can always stay here."

I blink at him. "Even when Eddie and Monica go back home?"

He nods. "Maybe a break will do me good. Maybe it will be more than a break. Look, I know this is all a bit fast and a bit much, but you have to understand . . . I've never felt this way in my whole entire life. You've opened up a whole new part of me, like . . . it's like I've discovered a whole new solar system. And I can't believe it's been out there this whole time, just out of sight, just out of reach. But now I have it. I have you. And I'll do anything not to lose you."

He leans in and leaves a searing kiss on my lips, one that makes my toes curl, a kiss that threatens to drown me in the most beautiful way.

I am so lost to this man.

"I am so in love with you," I say.

And then I realize I was only supposed to think it.

Not say it.

My eyes go wide, mortified, and my mouth clamps shut, and shit, shit, shit, I just fucking ruined everything, didn't I?

I just told Harrison I'm in love with him.

"I'm sorry," I squeak, attempting to turn away from him, but he grips my shoulders and holds me in place.

"What did you say?" he asks, his voice broken, the line between his brows deep. "Piper."

"Nothing, I said nothing," I say, and attempt to turn around again, but he won't let me.

I close my eyes and lie back, wishing I could just disappear.

"You just told me you loved me," he says.

"I didn't."

"You bloody well did."

I open one eye to look at him. "Technically I said 'I am so in love with you.'"

"And there's a difference."

"Well, yes. One is *I love you* and the other is *I am in love with you.*"

"I think they're both the same."

I close my eye again. "They're not."

"You're in love with me. That's the one that I want." I feel his lips against mine. "Piper," he whispers roughly against them. "Piper, look at me."

Hesitantly I open my eyes.

I'm immediately lost in the burning intensity of his.

"Piper, I love you, and I'm in love with you too," he murmurs.

He can't really mean that.

He's only saying it.

"I'm not saying it because you did," he goes on. "You just beat me to it. I am madly, aggravatingly, desperately in love with you. It's been frustrating to try to negotiate an emotion I've never felt before, but there's no mistaking it and no hiding from it. I'm not hiding from anything when it comes to you and how I feel about you." He runs his thumb over my lips. "You're it, Piper. You're everything. And so when I say that I'm going to make this work for us, I'm going to make it work."

Effervescent.

That's what this feeling is.

It's like that giddiness combined with clouds and rainbows and fizzing champagne bubbles that lift you higher and higher and . . .

Hell. Maybe this is just love.

"You love me," I whisper against his thumb.

"I love you," he says again, and I could literally hear him say it all day to the end of time. I know I'll probably replay it over in my head for years to come.

He loves me.

How the hell did I get so lucky?

I grin up at him, unable to stop from smiling, the joy radiating outward until it feels like it's swallowing us whole.

I pull him onto me, giggling, kissing, a mess of limbs and tangled hair.

A meeting of the hearts.

Twenty-Two

Three months later

"MISS EVANS, I THINK I'M GOING TO BE SICK."

I look up from my desk to see Cinder Graves approaching my desk, a hand at her mouth.

Yes, her name is Cinder. Short for Cinderella.

Yes, her older brother is my student from last year, Nicky Graves.

Yes, she's about to hurl. It runs in the family.

I quickly kick the wastebasket over to her and look away just before she vomits. It's gross, all right, but my handbag is safely tucked away (and actually it's a hand-me-down from Monica. Since she's moving away in a couple of days, she's been unloading a lot of her designer stuff on me. I promised myself I would keep them safe and not bring them to school, but this one is Gucci with butterflies on it, and it makes me happy).

When Cinder is done, I send her to the nurse's office, knowing she'll be back here in an hour, ready to learn. Some kids are allergic to school, I swear.

Me, though, I'm enjoying it more than ever. Not that I didn't before, but after this summer, I feel like I'm really hitting my stride. I'm bonding more with the students and their parents, trying to give them more individualized attention. Plus, I've been a lot more social. Oh, I'm still a hermit most evenings, just cuddling up with Harrison on the couch (you can still hermit with someone else, right?), but I've been spending a lot more time with both Cynthia and Georgia and become friends with some of their crew as well. As much as I complained about the lack of community and being an outsider, I knew that unless I was putting myself out there one hundred percent, I wasn't one to talk.

After the bell rings, I head over to Cynthia's classroom to say goodbye, making a date to have a girls' night at her house over the weekend, then I head across the school parking lot to where Harrison is just pulling in with the SUV.

Don't worry, I still have the Garbage Pail. Or should I say, it's at least in the family. My mom drives it when she feels like visiting Bert, who may or may not be her boyfriend. It's hard to tell. She says that after you get divorced, you're allowed to have friends without putting a label on it, and I think that's smart considering the hell she went through with my dad.

But I also know that when I mention his name, she gets that damn twinkle in her eye. It says a lot without her having to say anything.

I open the door to the SUV and get in the passenger side. Harrison, looking as sexy as ever in a black denim jacket and those ever-present aviators, leans over and gives me a lingering kiss.

"How was school?" he asks me as we pull away.

"Good, good. The old me would have had her purse puked in."

"Ah One of those days, then."

"Wouldn't trade it in for anything. How are you doing?" I ask.

He gives me a quick smile. "I'm all right."

While work has been great for me, Harrison's been going through some things.

The biggest one is that Monica and Eddie are moving back to England. Monica is six months pregnant and is set to go home before it gets too complicated to fly, so she can have her baby back there.

I'm terribly sad that they're leaving. Both of them, but Monica especially, have become such good friends over the summer that it's going to be hard not to have them next door. From weekly dinner parties with my mom—and then later with Bert—to Netflix and gossip sessions on the boat, to hikes and the occasional dinner in town (with the entire world watching), there was always something to do, always something to look forward to. I've been getting teary-eyed thinking about it these last few days, and I know it's really going to hurt when they're gone.

But for Harrison, it's far more complicated. Not only are Eddie and Monica his friends, and the people he had sworn to protect, but he's stepped down as bodyguard.

Actually, it happened about a month ago, when Eddie and Monica first announced when they were leaving. Harrison and I had a big, long talk about what to do next, and as much as I love him, I was fully prepared to have to say goodbye to him. I wasn't about to make him choose between his job and me, especially when so much of his guilt over his past was tied to it.

To my surprise, that's exactly why Harrison chose to stay. He said he didn't want to be tied to a job where he felt he was in it only to reconcile with himself and to make amends. That wasn't fair to himself, and it kept him in a never-ending cycle.

Besides, it's not what he wants to do with his life.

Harrison's dream shouldn't come as a surprise. He wants to open a bakery. In fact, he's been in talks with one of the more prominent bakeries in town, which is in the midst of selling. I'm not sure he can make this deal work, but he's been trying every day to find just the right place, then set up his business.

"No luck with the bakery?" I ask him. Their asking price is quite high, even for an established spot, so Harrison was hoping he could get them to come down.

He shrugs. "They said no. Might not be in the cards."

"You'll get there," I tell him. "Maybe that's not the space for you, maybe you're meant to have a better location. Maybe the timing isn't right."

"That's a lot of maybes, Piper."

"But you know it's true. It's going to happen. Just have faith."

He grumbles something and concentrates on driving.

Even if he doesn't have faith, I do. He's amazing at baking. He's been literally working on it nonstop, perfecting his technique, and I've gained a solid ten pounds because of it. Not that I'm complaining. I'll handle those ten pounds if I can keep eating the delicious treats that he makes. But honestly, he's good. He's a pro. He just needs the right shop and his business is going to take right off.

He often asks me how I can be so sure, but I just point to him and tell him he's got to start doing TikTok baking recipes. But shirtless.

He hasn't listened to me on that one yet. Doesn't matter, though: Harrison is a media darling, especially after the news of us went public. With my speech going viral, combined with the protective incident at the Blowhole and the whole sex-in-the-lake thing (and naked butt pictures), plus adding in the years of fanfic and people generally lusting over him, Harrison Cole is literally one of the most searched people on the internet. Even though his whole baking dream is a secret for now, once we get the business plan approved and buy the right place, people will be lining up at our door from all over.

And the locals too. That viral video of mine may have enamored the public to us as a couple, but it also made me a local celebrity. It gave a boost to my podcast, inspired me to start a romance book club at our very inclusive, super awesome local library, and helped create a sense of camaraderie on the island. Of course there are always going to be the naysayers, but they're less tolerated now that people realize that having each other's back is truly what makes this place sing.

We pull into the driveway, no more SUVs or media vans parked on the street (though things did get a little crazy after Monica announced her pregnancy), and drive up to the royals' house.

There's a large van outside that two movers in dark suits (I'm guessing specially hired British people) are moving furniture into. Monica had said they wanted to ship a lot of things via freight back home. I'm starting to think there won't be much left of the house after this.

"I wonder what's going to happen to this place?" I ask Harrison wistfully as we step out of the car.

He walks over to me and grabs my hand. "You don't see us living here one day?"

I give him an incredulous look and snort. "No. Do you?"

He nods, squinting at the house. "I do. You have to dream big, Piper. No reason why this can't be ours."

"Uh, because it costs millions of dollars."

"That's why I said to dream big," he says, pulling me toward him. He cups my face in his hands and peers at me with soft, inquisitive eyes. "You know I'll buy it for us one day. We'll move in here. Your mother will live next door."

"What about Liza?" I ask, touched by how sincere he is.

"She can run around and choose," he says. "We'll put doggy doors on each house."

I kiss the inside of his hand. "And where are you getting this money from? You never told me that being a PPO was so lucrative."

"It's not," he says. "But you did say that TikTok videos are the next big thing."

"You're kidding me!" I smack his arm.

He just grins. "As I said, dream big."

I think he's probably joking about doing his whole naked-baker thing, but you never know. At the very least, he's thinking to the future.

And he's making sure I'm in it.

We head over to the door that's already open and step through. There are boxes absolutely everywhere, and we catch a glimpse of Agatha scurrying in the background.

"Hello?" Harrison says as we make our way through the halls.

"They're just outside," James says as he steps in from around the corner, nodding at the deck. He lowers his voice. "Between you and me, I think the moving is getting to them. Monica has been a bit weepy all day."

"Thanks, mate," Harrison says, slapping James on the shoulder. Since Harrison stepped down, James stepped up. He was a natural replacement. Those tree guys are still somewhere, I presume, unless they headed home to London already. They have me wondering what they'll do with no giant firs and cedars to hide in. Rappel down old buildings and statues?

We head out onto the deck. It's mid-October and it's chilly, but there's something so cozy about it. The leaves on the maples have turned gold and orange; the grass is high and tan, flowing in the sea breeze like wheat; and fog hugs the shore. I wrap my cardigan around me tighter and go over to Monica, who is sitting down and buried under a million layers of fleece.

Her eyes are puffy—James was right about that—and she's so huge even at six months that she can barely get up.

"Stay," I tell her, putting my hand on her shoulder. "Are you sure you're warm enough?"

"She better be," Eddie says, dressed in a flannel jacket and toque pulled down on his head. "Otherwise we're heading inside."

"I'm fine," Monica snaps, and then adjusts herself. "I have a hot-water bottle at my back. It's doing wonders."

"Care for a glass of wine?" Eddie asks us.

"I'll take a red," Harrison says, heading for the doors. "Piper?"

"Yes, please. I'm off the clock."

"Harrison, please sit down. Agatha will get it," Eddie admonishes him.

"Agatha is running around like a chicken with her head cut off," Harrison says, disappearing inside. He only moved in with me a month ago, so he had a long enough time here, with this place as his home. It's normal for him to help himself to their always stocked fridge and bar.

"So how are you doing?" I ask Monica, perching on the deck chair beside her. "You doing okay?"

She nods, and then a tear runs down her cheek. She hastily wipes it away before resting her head in her hands. "I'm fine," she sobs.

I put my hand on her back and rub it reassuringly, looking to Eddie for advice.

"She's been feeling extra emotional," Eddie explains patiently, taking a sip of his wine. "It's the hormones; it's the move."

"I'm going to miss you so much," Monica wails, suddenly pulling me into a hug. I brace myself against the chair so I don't fall onto her.

"Mon, don't kill her," Eddie says.

"Sorry," she mumbles into me, not letting go. "I'm really going to miss you, Piper."

Okay, I hate goodbyes, so I've been pretending this whole time that she's really not going anywhere or that she's just going for a short while and will come back. But now she's crying and giving me no choice but to face the music.

Shit.

I'm crying now too.

"I'll come visit," I tell her, though honestly, how will that be possible? Are they allowed to have normal people as friends? It's not like I can just drop by the palace or wherever they end up living.

"I know, but it's not the same," she says, pulling back. She waves her arms at the ocean. "I'm going to miss this too. Miss being here next to you." She turns her head to see Harrison walking out with the wine. "And Harrison. Harrison, my man. How am I going to get on without you?"

Harrison seems a little taken aback to find us having emotional meltdowns, but he takes it in stride. He hands me my drink. "You're going to be just fine. You have Eddie. He does all right most of the time."

"Thanks, man," Eddie says.

Harrison winks at him. "You're welcome."

"But things back home are so scary," she says. "So busy. So noisy. I just want to stay in this fog forever."

"Look, the fog is lovely and October is always nice here," I tell her. "But soon it will be November, which is rainy and cold and awful. December is saved only by Christmas. Then there's January, which is the absolute worst. You'll pray for snow to break up the monotony of the rain and the gloom and the fact that it gets pitch black at four thirty p.m., but the snow never comes. Believe me, you are better off in the city with people and bright lights and all those things." I pause. "And, you know, you're royalty, and you'll be in a palace, so that helps too."

"Besides," Eddie says, "the other day you said you were craving noise and people and chaos. Which means it's the right time to go."

Monica sighs and wipes her tears with the heel of her palm, her lower lip pouting. "I guess so. Doesn't mean I'm not sad about it."

"We're all sad about it," Harrison speaks up. He clears his throat, looking thoughtfully at them. "The two of you are the only people I've really known for such a long time. There was the army, and then there was Eddie, and then there was you, Monica. To be honest, I'm having trouble myself coming to terms with what's happening." He glances at me and gives me a warm smile, the kind of smile that makes my heart leap. "I've talked about this with Piper a lot. She knows I want to stay. That I'm choosing my new life here. But that new life is still scary, and it's going to be different. And I wish you could stay here in this house for as long as you can, but I understand that you can't. You're doing what's best for you both, and what's best for the baby."

Monica sniffles. "Damn it, Harrison. Don't make me cry again."

"Technically you never stopped," he points out.

"Oh," she grumbles, waving him away dismissively.

"Hey, come on," Eddie says, walking toward us. "I didn't invite you both here so we could sit around and cry all night. I invited you here so we could celebrate. Say goodbye to the old times, welcome in the new beginnings. And get rightly smashed."

He raises his glass of wine.

We raise ours.

Monica raises her mug of tea.

"To the best next-door neighbors a girl could ever hope for," I say to them. "Despite the men in trees, and the paparazzi camping outside the gate, to throwing this handsome, grumpy, sunglass-wearing mystery man my way, I couldn't have asked for a more eventful summer. You changed my life. And it won't feel quite like home without you both next door. All I know is that I am immensely grateful that you brought Harrison into my life. At least I get to keep him."

Harrison puts his arm around my waist and kisses the top of my head. "You'll never be rid of me."

"He's not joking," Eddie says with a laugh. "The man will become your shadow—you'll never be able to shake him."

I grin up at Harrison. "I'm counting on it."

Epilogue

Two Years Later

"THEY'RE HEEEEEEEEERE," MY MOTHER SAYS, CHANNELING the creepy little girl from *Poltergeist*.

Except she's not holding on to a staticky TV, but poking her head out onto the deck where I'm sitting with Harrison, nursing a glass of wine. It's the middle of summer, the sun is hot and glinting off the waves below us, and the two of us have been out here all afternoon, getting sufficiently buzzed while waiting for the arrival of our favorite people.

You guessed it, Monica, Eddie, and baby Madeline have finally made it back to our rock on the Pacific. Honestly, when we first parted ways, I doubted I'd see them again. It felt like their fairy-tale presence was only for a brief moment in my life, perhaps just enough to bring Harrison and me together, like a pair of enchanted matchmakers. I mean, it feels absolutely unreal at times that Harrison and I are together (let alone engaged, but more on that later), the royal bodyguard and the small-town schoolteacher.

The last thing I expected was to still be friends with a duke and duchess.

And yet, here we are. I've managed to keep in touch with Monica, texting with her at least a couple of times a month. She listens to my podcast too—she says it helps her sleep, but whatever, I'll take it as a compliment.

Of course Harrison has kept in touch with them as well, talking to Eddie often. It just took two years for them to finally find the time to come here. They've tacked it on to a trip down to Seattle to see Monica's parents, but they haven't told anyone except us, so it's kind of secret.

Or at least that's the plan. I'm just waiting for the helicopters to start showing up.

"Bert got them okay?" Harrison asks my mother as he gets to his feet.

"Yes, they should be here any minute," she says just as the timer dings from the kitchen. "Oh, and the pie is ready."

"Mom, they just got here after an incredibly long journey. You think the first thing they're going to want is pie?"

"Oh, sweetie, don't be such a pastry hater," she says with a dismissive wave, heading toward the kitchen.

Harrison makes a tsking sound as he holds his hand out for me. "You know nothing interrupts our pie Sundays."

I put my hand in his, and he effortlessly hauls me to my feet, then places a kiss on the top of my head.

Pie Sundays are a thing now. Well, they have been since Harrison opened his bakery. I swear to god that job keeps him busier than being a royal bodyguard did. He's up before dawn, working crazy-long hours, and yet he still finds time to make a pie with my mother on Sundays, which I find incredibly sweet, since I know he just wants to relax and do nothing on his day off.

But it means something to my mom, especially since we got engaged. She really wants to make him a part of the family, which has been pretty easy considering she lives next door to us.

And us, well, we're in the mansion.

Naturally, a schoolteacher salary and owning a bakery does not buy a house of this magnitude, but what does is a tell-all book. Harrison wrote one (I helped, but that's neither here nor there), with Monica and Eddie's permission, of course. The thing is, the book wasn't really about the royals. It was more about baking, with some personal stuff interspersed in there.

And by *personal*, I mean it was really all about Harrison. He talked about his youth, his family, growing up, the army, being a bodyguard, and finally being a baker on a small island on the Salish Sea. Since he's such a private person by nature, it really pushed him out of his comfort zone to open up, especially about the nitty-gritty. But as he's said a few times before, fuck the part of society that doesn't understand, and I couldn't be more proud of him for being so honest and vulnerable. There's really nothing sexier.

It did extremely well. It definitely helped that I convinced him to do TikTok videos for a bit, which in part really helped promote the book, and it became a runaway success.

So now we live in the mansion, and my mother and Bert live next door to us.

They're officially together now. Not engaged or anything like that. I'm not really sure if either of them will take that step, even though my mom does seem to be warming up to the idea. But they're honestly the sweetest thing and so good for each other. Bert is a real take-charge, protective guy, which is perfect for her, and she's still going to her therapy and taking her meds. Sometimes there are setbacks, but with an arsenal of people who love her around, she always gets back on her feet. Of course, she has

Liza, who runs around on the compound, using the doggy doors to each house, just like we'd imagined.

"Shall we go meet the mini royal?" Harrison says, grabbing my hand.

"Of course." We step inside, and I yell at my mother in the kitchen. "When you're done fussing with the pie, can you get the white wine out of the fridge? That's what they're going to want first, believe me."

"Which one? You have a million bottles," she asks, staring at the fridge.

"The Garry Oaks Pinot Gris," I tell her. I don't normally have a million bottles in the fridge; it's just that we had a small party on Friday night, just me and Harrison, Cynthia and her new boyfriend, and Georgia and her husband. We try to do a couples thing every other week, just to keep me from going into my antisocial hermit zone, and I have to say it's really helped me stay connected to society, especially during the summer, when I'm not with the kids every day. I've made some deep, lasting friendships in this place, and, coupled with Harrison's business and working with the public every day, I no longer feel like an outsider. Just takes a bit of effort sometimes on my part.

Harrison and I walk through the house and step onto the driveway just as we see the gates open and Bert's RCMP vehicle pull up to the house. I cringe a little—for some reason I expected him to pick them up in a black SUV, and yet here they are, being deposited like they're being dropped off at a police station.

After an amused glance at Harrison, I can tell he's thinking the same thing.

Nevertheless, the doors open and they step out. Eddie, Monica, and little Madeline.

"Hey!" Eddie cries out, jogging over to Harrison and wrapping him in a tight hug before he does the same to me. He's dressed down in a polo shirt and jeans and looks as relaxed as he did the last time he was here. "We made it."

"Got them here in one piece," Bert says proudly as he exits the vehicle just as James, the bodyguard, gets out the passenger side. He gives me a polite nod as a greeting.

But I'm already looking at Monica, who is as beautiful as ever in a sundress. She's still glowing, so obviously that's nothing to do with pregnancy; it's just who she is.

"Piper," she says to me in a subdued squeal, and we have a quick embrace. "So good to finally see you." She smiles down at Madeline, who has the gangly limbs of Eddie and the dark hair of Monica. She's shy, barely making eye contact, but she radiates the same kind of calm energy that her mother does. "This is Madeline. Madeline, do you want to say hi to Piper?"

"Hello," Madeline says quietly.

It looks like what Madeline really wants to do is bury her head against Monica's leg, and I've never related to a kid more. I want to tell her that I get that way when meeting new people too, except this kid is a royal and she's been trained to push past that discomfort and put on a good face, something I need to learn.

"She's shy," Monica whispers to me. "Which is a challenge considering who we are."

"She's lovely," I tell her. "How was your flight over?"

"Well, Madeline slept for most of it," Monica says, reaching down and scooping her daughter up into her arms. "And I can tell she's still a little sleepy. I, on the other hand, was kept up by a book."

"What book?"

A sly smirk plays on her lips, her eyes dancing mischievously. "A book you bought me years ago."

I have no clue what she's talking about. "When did I buy you a book?"

"Well, it was Harrison who gave it to me, but I know you had something to do with it. At least I hope." She leans in close to me and whispers in my ear, "It was about pegging. I didn't even know what that was. I had to look it up, and oh boy."

I burst out laughing. "You read that on the plane?"

She grins at me. "Well, it gave me some ideas for Eddie, at least."

I don't even want to think about the two of them in a compromising position, but I'm saved by my mother appearing at the front door in her apron, proudly displaying her baked goods.

"I hope you're all starving, because it's pie time!" my mother exclaims, grinning at us before disappearing into the house.

"Don't worry," I say to the royals as we head inside. "There's wine and beer too. Figured that's what you really need."

"No wonder we get along so well," Monica says to me with a grin. "I feel like I've got lost time to make up for, since I couldn't drink a drop last time."

"Well, considering you're staying with us for a week, let's not get carried away," Harrison warns.

"I see you're still no fun, Harrison," she says to him, playfully smacking his arm.

I grab Harrison's hand and give it a squeeze, watching as the duke and duchess walk inside their old house, Bert leading the way, the hunky Scot James trailing after them. I look up at my fiancé. "Don't worry, I think you're fun."

"Only because you've rubbed off on me, love," he says, lifting my hand to his mouth and placing a kiss on the back of it, his eyes boring into mine. "Though it seems I still have a lot to learn."

"Eh," I say with a mock shrug. "You'll get there one day. After all, I'm a good teacher."

He breaks into a grin, making him look devastatingly handsome, before he leans in and kisses me sweetly on the lips. "The best."

Then we walk back inside our house to be with the people we love.

Author's Note

When I sit down to write, I usually have a simple plot or trope figured out, and then I work on character, chiseling away at it like I'm uncovering something that already exists, until the character reveals itself to me.

Sometimes my characters are the furthest thing from my personality, other times it's like some deep, dark part of me is channeling through. And though *The Royals Next Door* is a lighthearted romantic comedy, there was something I revealed in Piper which in turn revealed something about myself.

Bit of a backstory: I have ADHD, something I've written about a few times in the past, and the truth is, I only got diagnosed after I was doing research for my character Magnus in *The Wild Heir*. It was his character that made me realize who I truly was, and that diagnosis was absolutely life-changing for me.

That said, I didn't expect there to be any more surprises for me, and certainly not through Piper. But while doing research, I came to suspect that I too have complex post-traumatic stress disorder (or C-PTSD), brought on by events in my childhood. It was surprising to find a name for it, and it completely explained my thought process at times, and my reaction to certain triggers. It's not as debilitating as PTSD, but it's certainly an affliction, and as Piper navigated her life with this, as well as her anxiety (which I also have . . . really hammering home the neurotic-writer stereotype, aren't I?), it gave me coping skills of my own.

And even though I don't have BPD or DPD, as Piper's mother has, I have been in Piper's position and have a lot of experience when it comes to loved ones being affected. Her relationship with her mother, as complicated as it is, is truthful, and writing it revealed some things about myself when it comes to handling the afflicted.

I know neurodiversity and mental health disorders aren't common subjects in romance novels, but I truly hope they become a more inclusive part of the landscape. It's staggeringly common for people to be affected by a range of disorders, whether it's in themselves or someone they love. The more we talk about mental health and create dialogue without shame or judgment, the more the stigma will fade away.

So I raise my glass to Piper, to myself, and to anyone else who feels alone because they don't fit in or aren't represented by the world at large. Just know that you deserve all the happily-ever-afters to come.

Acknowledgments

Sometimes acknowledgments are the hardest part of the book. There's usually a lot of people to thank, and despite having sixty novels under my belt so far, each book still requires so much support from the people around me. Though writing is a solitary profession (for the most part), no writer is truly alone when it comes to producing a novel. It really does take a village to lift you up, keep you going, and help you make the book the best it can be.

And I needed a village for *The Royals Next Door*. This was the first book I'd written since the pandemic started, so there was definitely some extra friction there when it came to creating something fun, light, and sexy in the midst of so much trauma, sorrow, and chaos. I couldn't have gotten this book done without the people who truly believed in me: my parents; my super-agent, Taylor, who fell in love with the idea within a sentence and told me to run with it; my amazing editors, Sarah Blumenstock and Cindy Hwang (I am in awe of your talent, skills, and tireless patience with me); everyone I've had the pleasure to work with at Berkley; my film agent, Alice Lawson; Nina Grinstead; Colet Abedi; Anna Todd; Kathleen Tucker; Tarryn Fisher; Sandra Cortez; Laura Helseth; all the wonderful bookstagrammers who create such gorgeous art and share my work; every member of my FB group (shout-out to the Anti-Heroes!); all my readers who have stuck with me; Meghan Markle Stan Twitter for providing inspiration; and the locals of Salt Spring Island (my home). And to anyone picking up this book: you're the reason I get to do what I do.

    To Scott (and Bruce): I love you. Thank you for loving me.

DON'T MISS

The Royals Upstairs

COMING FALL 2022
FROM BERKLEY JOVE!

James

IT'S BLOODY COLD, I'LL TELL YOU THAT MUCH.

I'm standing on the side of a runway in what feels like the middle of Norway and have been freezing my bollocks off for a good twenty minutes at least. It's early December, but there's already a fresh layer of snow on the ground, and though it's nearly three in the afternoon, the sun is already setting, suspending the air in this murky kind of twilight. My new employer, Magnus, the Crown Prince of Norway, arranged for a private jet to take me from London to this tiny airstrip, and I'm supposed to meet one of his advisors, who will take me to the nearby Skaugum Estate, where the prince and princess live—my home for the foreseeable future.

I gather my coat collar tighter around me, snowflakes sticking in my hair, wishing I had brought a scarf. When I did my research about Norway, everyone always said that it wasn't as cold as the stereotype and that it rarely snowed in December, but boy were they fucking wrong.

Finally a black SUV screeches to a stop outside the chain-link fence and a man practically falls out of the vehicle, his shoes slipping on the ice. He holds on to the hood, arms splayed, legs slowly sliding apart before he manages to take another step. He straightens up unsteadily, then looks at the ground between us, seeming to have second thoughts.

"Mr. Hunter?" he yells over in a light Norwegian accent.

"That's me," I tell him. "Are you Ottar?"

"*Ja,*" he says. "Would you mind if I stayed here? I don't think my shoes can handle the ice."

I stare at him for a moment. He's on the portly side, though he has a boyish face and black glasses. But the more I stare at him, the more I realize that half his face is banged up. Maybe it's best that he stay where he is.

"Not a problem," I tell him, picking up my suitcase and carefully walking over to the fence and going through the gate. At least my black boots have an ample amount of tread, which is more than he has. I don't know why someone here wouldn't know how to dress for the elements, but I guess I'm about to find out.

"Mr. Hunter," Ottar says, smiling hastily as I approach, sticking out his hand. "It's a pleasure to welcome you to Norway."

I stop and shake his hand. "Please, call me James," I tell him. Now that I'm up close, I can finally get a good look at him. He's got a black eye and a bunch of scratches along his cheeks. "I don't mean to pry, but are you okay? You look bloody mangled."

He laughs and then points at his face. "Oh right, my face. Long story. But I'm fine. Here, let me get your bag."

Ottar takes my suitcase from me and then starts the very long, laborious process of walking alongside the SUV, his hand propped against the car for support as he tries to balance on the ice.

"I can just put it in the back seat," I tell him.

He attempts a dismissive wave, but that movement alone sends one leg flying forward and the other leg flying backward, and it's only by the grace of a Norse god that he doesn't end up doing the splits.

"*Helvete,*" he says, which I'm assuming is a Norwegian swear.

"Are you sure I can't help?" I ask, biting back a smile.

"I'm fine, I'm fine," he says quickly, letting out an awkward laugh. "Just hurt myself the other day, so I'm a bit, uh, overly cautious, as one might say."

One might say that he has a reason to be overly cautious, and that the best course of action is to just abandon the suitcase and make it back to the safety of the driver's seat.

But I'm a man with my own pride, and I'm not about to interfere with the pride of someone else. So I wait, leaning against the SUV, watching as Ottar very carefully makes it to the back of the car and then opens the trunk, throwing my bag in. There are a few more twists and turns and near splits, and then he manages to pull himself back to me.

"Shall we?" he asks, opening my door with a triumphant smile.

And that's when he totally loses ground, holding on to the handle for dear life while the rest of him slides under the door, heels first.

Bloody hell.

I reach over and grab him by the elbows, hauling him up. He's not light as a feather, I'll say that much.

"*Tusen takk,*" he says sheepishly, his cheeks going pink. "That's Norwegian for *thank you.* You know any Norwegian?"

I step inside the car. "Not a word." I'd had a brief affair with a wild Norwegian woman, but the only Norwegian she ever spoke around me was in the bedroom.

"Ah," he says. He shuts the door, almost falling again, then finally pulls himself into the driver's seat, letting out a massive exhale of relief. "I'm sure you'll learn fast. At any rate, everyone speaks English fluently, so it won't be a problem if you don't.

Except for Einar, Magnus's bodyguard. But you probably wouldn't get more than a few words out of him anyway."

He starts the car, and thankfully the tires have more tread than Ottar's shoes.

"Sorry I was late," he says to me, eying me in the rearview mirror. "I run on Magnus's schedule, and that can be off at times. You'll find out soon enough." He pauses. "I really didn't expect them to hire someone this fast."

I give a light shrug, looking out the window at the passing scenery. Farm fields covered in white and orderly forests of pine fly past in the dying light. It's pretty here, I'll give it that much, even if I feel a bit discombobulated about the whole thing.

See, Ottar's not alone in thinking everything had gone so fast. It's literally been a couple of weeks since my former employer, Prince Eddie of England, told me that he and his wife, Duchess Monica, were taking their daughter, Madeline, back to Canada.

Now, I'd gone with them before. Four years ago, they'd moved to a tiny island off the very wet west coast of British Columbia to prepare for Duchess Monica's pregnancy and escape the rubbish media of the UK, and I went along with them as one of their personal protection officers. We did our time there on the island, enjoying the much-needed peace and quiet, then came back to London for baby Madeline's birth.

Now Eddie and Monica have decided that they don't want to raise Madeline in the same environment that Eddie was brought up in, so they're moving back to that tiny island and asked if I would go with them.

I ended up saying no. As much as I loved working for them, the island felt like early retirement. Suffice to say, I opted to stay behind, which then meant I was out of a job. And being a PPO or bodyguard, it's not like you can start perusing the job listings on Craigslist and start handing out applications.

Thankfully Eddie helped out. He nosed around and found out that Prince Magnus and Princess Ella of Norway were looking for a bodyguard specifically for her and their children. I guess one of the kids, despite having his mother and a nanny, is quite the troublemaker and is hard to keep an eye on. One thing led to another, and Eddie arranged for Prince Magnus to hire me without even meeting me. I guess Eddie's word goes a long way in the royal world, enough so that I only found out I had the job just the other day.

"I'm grateful that Prince Eddie was able to put in such a good word with Prince Magnus, especially on such short notice," I tell Ottar. "But from speaking to Prince Magnus on the phone, I got the impression that the role won't be too dissimilar from what I was doing before."

"Yes," Ottar says, rather uneasily. He gives me a crooked smile. "I can see how you would think that."

I frown. "What do you mean?"

"Oh, nothing," he says, adjusting his grip on the steering wheel. "Let's just say that I'm sure that when you worked for the duke and duchess, they ran a pretty tight ship."

"I suppose," I say. "Not as uptight as the rest of his family, though."

"Right. Well, Magnus . . . does not run a tight ship. Ella tries to, but it's hard when she's trying to balance her children and running her environmental group . . . The palace can be chaos on even the calmest days."

"I see," I tell him. This doesn't really surprise me. Prince Magnus is famous for being the wild prince, especially before he settled down and married Ella. Some media outlets even report that their marriage was an arranged one to try and counteract a slew of bad publicity the prince had gotten. Extreme sports, sex tapes, being a drunken idiot—it was hard to go a week without reading something about Magnus in the papers.

Now, since he got married and had children, he seems to have calmed down. He's become a public spokesperson for ADHD, which he has, and runs an organization devoted to eradicating the stigma attached to being neurodiverse, or however they call it. He's actually one of the most-liked royals there are because of how open he is with the public.

"Don't get me wrong," Ottar quickly says, "I think you'll enjoy working here. Everyone is super friendly. Just . . . be prepared for the unexpected."

"Is the unexpected what happened to your face?" I ask.

He nods, looking chagrined. "The other day Magnus wanted to go cross-country skiing. I'm an awful Norwegian, because I'm not the best on skiis."

"You don't say," I comment wryly.

"It's true. It's like I have two left feet. Anyway, Magnus then decided to turn it into a downhill skiing expedition, and wherever he goes, I follow." He gestures to his face. "I had a run-in with a tree. Or two."

"You're not his personal protection officer, though," I point out.

"No, but it's my job to try and keep him in line. When I can. I'd never let him go off and do something like that on his own, even when Einar is with us. I've even been BASE jumping, if you can believe it."

I'm not sure that I can believe it. "Sounds like you have your hands full."

He smirks at me. "I do. But so will you."

"Princess Ella? Every piece of footage I've seen of her, she seems as calm and collected as they come," I tell him.

"She is, thank god. But you're not just protecting her. You're protecting her and her children, Bjorn and Tor, and they are a handful. Bjorn especially. Takes after his father in every single way. Then there's Ella's lady-in-waiting, and the nanny, and they both take the term headstrong to the next level. Now you see? You're not just protecting Ella, but the rest of them too. In some ways, at least there is only one Magnus."

I mull that over. Suddenly everything seems a lot less simple than it did a few days ago. But I'm nothing if not adaptable. I'm sure everything will be just fine, and it's not like I don't know how to handle a few headstrong ladies.

Ottar takes the car off the road and down a long driveway covered by trees.

"Where are we going?" I ask, staring at the frozen fields beyond the trees.

"To Skaugum," Ottar says.

"I thought we were going to the palace?"

"This is the Skaugum Estate," he says. "But you can call it a palace if you'd like. Traditionally it was the summer palace."

I twist around in my seat, looking around me at the bucolic scenery, feeling a bit panicked. "But I thought the palace, the estate, was on the outskirts of Oslo."

"We are on the outskirts of Oslo," he says.

"But there's nothing here!" I exclaim.

"Yes. That's why it's the outskirts. Don't worry, it's only forty-five minutes to the city." His forehead creases as he turns to glance at me over his shoulder. "Did you think you would be living in Oslo? The king and queen live there at the palace, but Magnus and Ella wanted a more private place to raise their kids."

Bloody hell, did I ever get this wrong. The reason I didn't want to go with Eddie and Monica to that tiny island is because I didn't want to work in the middle of nowhere again. The isolation was fine the first time, but it wouldn't be good for my mentality the next time, especially in the winter. I wanted to stay around city lights, and people, and women, and traffic.

And yet as the SUV pulls up to a grand white palace in the middle of nowhere, I realize that I'm about to live in isolation all over again. No more city lights, no more people, no more traffic, and stores, and civilization.

No more women.

Just me and the apparently wacky arm of the Norwegian royal family.

This is not getting off to a great start.

"Well, here we are," Ottar says, parking the car. "Oh, and look, there are the kids. You can meet them already."

I give my head a shake, trying to snap out of it and put my misgivings aside, and slowly get out of the car. Lucky for Ottar we're on packed snow and there's no way for him to fall.

"*Hei*, Bjorn, Tor," Ottar yells over at two kids in snowsuits on the front lawn. "Come say hi to our new friend. He's going to be living with us."

I close the car door and look over at the kids. They're staying put, both immersed in building a snowman. Okay, so a woman is building a snowman for them, but her back is to me, so I can't tell who it is, whether it's the princess, the lady-in-waiting, or the nanny.

One of the kids is pretty young, a toddler, and is sitting in the snow, shoving the white stuff in his mouth; the other is standing by the snowman, staring at me with demon eyes.

Oh. This must be Bjorn.

Ottar hauls the bag out of the back and pauses beside me.

"Sometimes they can be shy," he says. Then he winks. "Appreciate it while it lasts."

Bjorn then rolls up a snowball while keeping his eyes locked on me, and I'm certain he's about to throw it in my face.

Then at the last minute he turns and whips it at the woman's head; it bounces off her down hood, snow flying everywhere.

"*Bjorn*," the woman says to him, exasperated, and a string of sternly worded Norwegian follows.

Suddenly my whole body feels like it's been jerked back into the past. The woman's voice is so acutely familiar that I have to blink a few times to try and ground myself to the present.

This *can't* be.

"Who is that?" I find myself whispering.

"Oh, that's their nanny," Ottar says.

And it's then that she turns around so that I can see her face. I know her name before Ottar can even give it to me.

"Laila," he says.

Laila stares at me, eyes going wide as the moon, her face paling to match the snow.

I feel like I'm in a tractor beam, stuck here in this staring contest that I know at any minute is about to get ugly. I'm glued in place, locked in her gaze, my body swimming in feelings—lust, desire, even a bit of fear.

Holy shit.

It's her.

And she's just as shocked as I am, her unblinking gaze sinking into mine, memories passing through me, making my blood run hot.

"Wait," Ottar says slowly, pointing between us. "Do you two know each other?"

Laila lets out a derisive snort, the first of us to snap out of it.

"I can't believe it," she says, her round eyes going narrow, and that familiar burning sensation of her glare comes back to me. "It's *you*."

"In all the royal palaces, in all the world," I tell her, my voice shaking just a little. "I walk into yours."

"So, how do you know each other?" Ottar asks carefully, probably just realizing that we don't know each other in the best way.

I give Laila a look, raising my brow to say, *Well, do you want to tell him?*

But she learned her lesson from the last time. We both did.

"We used to work together," she says crisply, her posture stiffening, a coldness coming into her eyes—the kind that burns.

Then she turns her attention back to the snowman, like I never existed. I guess she's had a lot of practice.

The two of us had what Lady Gaga would refer to as a *bad romance*.

And that's putting it mildly.

The last person I ever expected to see again was Laila Bruset, my wild Norwegian woman.

"James?" Ottar says to me.

I blink, staring at Laila's back, wondering what the hell I did to deserve this.

Actually, scratch that. I know what I did to deserve this.

My stomach sinks.

I look at Ottar and he gives me a forced smile. "Shall we go inside and meet the rest of the family? I'm sure you'll have plenty of opportunities to connect with Laila."

Out of the corner of my eye I can see her practically bristle.

"Of course," I tell him, raising my chin. I'm going to have to pretend that everything's fine going forward if I want to keep my job. I'm going to have to pretend that the woman I had a very passionate and tumultuous affair with isn't the royal nanny and my future coworker. Thankfully, I've made pretending into an art.

Ottar takes my suitcase and heads down the driveway to the palace, stomping confidently through the snow. The estate is big, though it reminds me more of a rich person's country mansion rather than a royal palace. It's white and sprawling, with pillars, but there's a bit of a rustic quality to it, like it needs a fresh coat of paint. That puts me at ease, just to know that the royal couple isn't as hoity-toity as they could be.

But that ease is short-lived, because I look over my shoulder at the snowman on the lawn and see Laila's cold eyes following my every move as I go up the front steps, so much so that I nearly trip and fall.

"Easy there," Ottar says to me good-naturedly. "It can be slippery. Wouldn't want you to fall."

I give him a tepid look in response, just as the front doors swing open.

"Ahh, you found the new recruit," Prince Magnus says with a flourish as he steps out, arms held as wide as the smile on his face. "James Hunter."

I'm about to bow, as is the courtesy when meeting a royal, but before I can even do that, Prince Magnus throws his arms around me and gives me a rib-cracking embrace. While I'm in top shape, the man is built like an ox on steroids. Must be a Viking thing.

"So nice to finally meet you," he says, slapping me hard on the back.

"Likewise, Your Majesty," I tell him, trying not to wince.

He rolls his eyes. "Please. Call me Magnus. Not Prince Magnus, not Your Royal Highness, and definitely not Your Majesty. You're part of the family now."

"Right," I tell him, feeling a wee bit unsteady, like I'm still standing on ice. His energy is pretty intense.

"It's nice to have a Scotsman joining us," he says with a wink. "You know we're probably related, going way back, since Scotland was the first step for us Vikings."

"Back then with all the plundering?"

"Yes, the plundering and the ravaging of the local ladies and all that unsavory stuff." He grins at me. Not only is he built like a Viking, he looks like one too. Though he's wearing a long gray cable-knit sweater and jeans, I know he's famous for his tattoos. Then he's got the scruffy beard and the dark wavy longish hair. "Like I said, you're family now."

"Speaking of family," Ottar says to Magnus as he walks into the house, "it turns out that Laila and James know each other. Gave him quite the surprise."

Magnus stops in the front hall and gives me a curious look. "You didn't know she was working for us?" He then glances at Ottar. "Laila was the nanny for the duke and duchess, just as James was their PPO. I believe they worked together for about two years?"

I nod, clearing my throat. I hate that this whole thing has caught me off guard. "That sounds about right."

The thing is, if I had given all of this a little more thought, if I'd had a little more time, I'm sure I might have come to this conclusion. When Eddie first told me I had a chance to move to Norway, memories of Laila drifted through my head. She'd left her position as nanny to the Fairfaxes because her beloved grandmother, who lived in a tiny village in northern Norway, had gotten sick, and she wanted to be with her. I know it was a tough decision for Laila to make, but since her grandmother raised her and they were especially close, she didn't have much choice.

At that point, Laila thought I was an outright wanker, so we weren't really on speaking terms anyway. The most I would get out of her was a stiff nod of recognition as we passed each other in the halls. One day I found out that she was gone, and that was that. Never heard from her, or about her, again. Until now.

"Must be a relief to see a familiar face," Magnus says to me. "That's why I put your room right next to hers."

Bloody hell.

About the Author

Karina Halle is a screenwriter, a former music and travel journalist, and the *New York Times*, *Wall Street Journal*, and *USA Today* bestselling author of over sixty novels all across the romance genre.

She lives with her musician husband and their adopted pit bull on an island off the coast of British Columbia, where the trees are tall, the ocean is wild, and the ideas for her future books never stop flowing.

CONNECT ONLINE

AuthorKarinaHalle.com

🐦 MetalBlonde

🅕 AuthorKarinaHalle

📷 AuthorHalle